# Raging Silence

## *A Novel In Five Acts*

By
AMANDA STONE

RAGING SILENCE
PUBLISHED BY SYNERGY BOOKS
2100 Kramer Lane, Suite 300
Austin, Texas 78758

For more information about our books, please write to us, call
512.478.2028, or visit our website at www.bookpros.com.

Publisher's Cataloging-in-Publication available upon request.

Library of Congress Control Number: 2005933141

ISBN-13: 978-0-9764981-1-7
ISBN-10: 0-9764981-1-1

Copyright© 2006 by Amanda Stone

10 9 8 7 6 5 4 3 2 1

*Thank you, Dad and Craig, Shane Hartman,*
*Lynn P$ Vogel, Cynthia and Billy Hall,*
*Luke Buchanan, Susanna Hegner*
*and Nick Halpern.*

Front cover painting, *Raging Silence*
by Luke Miller Buchanan

# Table of Contents

# Dramatis Personae

The Duprees
Bell Alexandra Dupree  *The Matriarch*
Pratt Johnson Dupree  *Husband To Bell*
Pearl Suzette  *Daughter To Bell*
Anna Melena  *Daughter To Bell*
Leopold Winston  *Son To Bell*

The Starlings
Ernest William Starling  *Husband To Melena*
Ernest Blackwell  *Son To Melena*
Luke Bartleby  *Son To Melena*
Elizabeth Anna  *Daughter To Melena*

The Shades
Walker Lux Shade  *Husband To Pearl*
Lucinda May  *Daughter To Pearl*
Bobby Lux  *Son To Pearl*

*"Chilleth the wan bleak cheek of the numbed earth."*

— Antonio's Revenge, *John Marston*

# ACT I

# "Never More Woe in Lesser Plot was Found"

*Antonio's Revenge V,iii,175*

ONE EARLY MORNING IN NOVEMBER of 1964, on the front porch of an old log cabin surrounded by thick evergreens, high atop the Appalachian Mountain range, nineteen-year-old Melena stands holding the screen door open. Inside her pink slippers, her toes curl against the cold.

"Ernest Starling," she calls across the yard as her husband leaves for work, "Are you going to be home in time for dinner?"

Tall and lanky, too youthful for his responsibilities, Ernest walks slump-shouldered, his breath fogging the chilly air. He thinks this is one question too many, but he turns around to face her.

"I've got to go down the mountain and into town after lunch for a Ranger's meeting," he hollers back. "I'm going to pick up some supplies and things so I won't be home until late."

Ernest jumps into his Ford pickup and starts the engine.

"Well, I'm not waiting for you, then," Melena says. "I'm going to take the baby over to Miss Suzy and Miss Laroy's."

Her words are hardly audible to him over the roar of the engine, but he waves at her over the dashboard as he throws the pickup in reverse.

Ernest turns the car toward the road and drives fifteen minutes to the Ranger station where he works monitoring one-minute section of the Appalachian Mountains.

Husband gone, Melena looks at the empty forest surrounding her. Fir trees extend to the top of the horizon, and the crisp mountain air wraps everything in its cold grip.

Ernest Blackwell cries and Melena steps back inside, letting the screen door fall shut. She retrieves Blackwell then bolts the wooden door behind her.

They rent this house, but to Melena, it's hers. She brought the Japanese lamps her mother gave her when they got married, and she's hung pictures of landscapes on the walls. Her New York buying job back home at the Holiday Department Store gave her a worldly flair.

She had planned to go to design college, but Ernest said no. And here now, the baby feels soft and warm to her hands. Holding him, Melena knows that she isn't alone on top of a mountain with no human beings for fifty miles. There are the two withered old spinsters.

The two ancient locals, Miss Suzy and Miss Laroy, live just a five-minute walk down the dirt drive.

"Ernest Blackwell," Melena says to the baby and turns him to face her.

"Son, we will not live in these mountains very long. So you just go ahead and get your fill of the crisp air and the tall trees right now."

Her blond hair pulled back now, she knows that if she were in town, she would have it in a beehive. She and her sister Pearl just love high fashion.

"Your momma is a Dupree," Melena says, "and we are city people, Blackwell, and the Starlings will be too. Your granddaddy, my daddy, owns a very successful cabinet business in Holiday and several warehouses, too."

"Our stay on this mountain is merely a part of our first adventure as a family. So, don't you get attached."

The baby drools, and Melena steps over to the kitchen counter to take a clean towel from the cupboard. She wipes the baby's face, conscious of the breakfast dishes in the sink. A half-empty bag of Redband Self-Rising Flour sits crumpled and open.

"All right then," she says, "Blackwell, you play here on the floor while Mommy does the dishes and I'll put on some music for us to boogie to."

Melena takes a record from a small stack arranged neatly on the third shelf of the bookcase across from the kitchen. She smiles,

Raging Silence

watching it whirl on the player, feels the beat in the song and strikes a pose, her left arm out toward the baby.

"Son," Melena sings rolling her shoulders to the beat, "let me tell you something. This is the King of Rock and Roll."

In spinning steps born of the shag, Melena dances across the floor over to the tiny rectangular kitchen and the baby gurgles. She begins to wash the great stack of dishes sitting on the counter.

"After I finish this stuff, Blackwell, you and I are going to watch a story on the television. Then you're going to take a nap while Mommy does the laundry. When you wake up, you and I are going to take a walk over to Miss Suzy and Miss Laroy's."

She takes a Brillo pad from beneah the sink and continues, "You remember them, old ladies in funny flower print dresses. They dip snuff, something I will never allow you to do. It doesn't become a proper gentleman."

"Anyway, we'll just have them bring us home in their car sometime after dark. Won't that be fun, Blackwell?"

She turns around and regards the baby, wishing he could answer her.

Stopping once to flip the Elvis record, Melena finishes the dishes and joins the baby on the floor to watch her favorite television program, "The Lonely Hearts." The two, resting on a blanket with toys all around, play together in contented bliss.

On the black and white TV, they watch the drama of metropolitan life played out in the agonizing throes of unrequited love in New York City.

An hour into the soap opera, Melena sobs. "That Ricardo," she directs at the baby, "he knows Amy loves him, but he plays with her emotions like she was a doll. She'd do anything for him, but she just isn't good enough, is she?"

Melena wipes her tears on the hem of her skirt. She picks the baby up and twirls him around. "You have a silly momma, don't you Blackwell? All grown and still crying at these TV stories."

Melena takes a bottle of formula from the refrigerator. She feeds the baby, changes his diaper, then paces the floor with him, waiting for him to burp and, inevitably, spit up. Afterward, she lays Blackwell down for a nap. Yawning, Melena turns from the crib, facing her cabin-home and the rest of her "things to do."

Noon finds her outside, hanging her family's wash on the clothesline. The day has grown warmer in modest increments and the sky shines bright blue above the line of trees.

A breeze rolls around the mountain through every thicket and hidden crevice. Melena shivers and pulls her sweater close. The wet clothes drip as she plucks another clothespin out of a cloth bag.

*Just a few more*, she thinks, *then Blackwell and I can go over to the ladies' house and have us a fine time with them.* The leaves rustle in the foliage directly across from her.

"What was that?" Melena asks absently. Her hand freezes on a pair of Ernest's underwear half pinned to the line. Eyes narrowing, she peers into the bushes and watches as the leaves rustle again, this time louder.

"*Ooo*," she quietly screams, darting from the clothesline onto the porch in frightened leaps.

Melena tucks her skirt between her legs and squats low next to the front door. She stares at the tree line directly in front of her. A barren blackberry bush shakes and out darts a fox faster than Melena can imagine.

She gasps as the fox rises on its hind legs and snaps at the hem of her blue nightgown. Yanking the flimsy garment, it pulls the gown from the line and runs across the yard into the opposite clearing, its prize trailing behind.

Still crouched, Melena quivers with nervous laughter.

"Well, I'll be damned," she says and stands. "A little old fox ran me onto my porch to steal my pajamas." Melena goes back to the line. "I can't wait to tell Miss Suzy and Miss Laroy about this one."

In the afternoon, with Blackwell on her hip and a picnic basket filled with egg salad sandwiches dangling from her arm, Melena sets off down the driveway. When the weather is good, these walks to the ladies' house allow her time to muse.

Passing the fir trees, Melena loses the contrast between the branches and leaves. As she walks, they blend and she imagines her future.

*Yes, we will be a mighty family. Maybe I'll have another baby and Ernest and I will keep a home. We'll be together forever, growing old and watching our children grow old.*

*There will be grandchildren, and we will love each other until we die, just like the preacher said. I will be the perfect wife and mother and raise the family that momma and daddy could not without all the political parties and closed door deals.*

Behind her, the wind blows a gust through the trees stirring Melena's dress. She pulls Blackwell close to her and walks toward the ladies' drive.

Approaching the sturdy mountain home, she smiles at the gray-haired women rocking on the porch in two of their collection of white rocking chairs, the rest now rarely used. The shutters, the roof, the wood siding on the house and the women on the porch are pale, creased and sagging underneath the vast mountain sky.

"Fine afternoon, ladies, isn't it?" Melena asks stepping up onto the porch, her ruddy cheeks aglow.

Miss Suzy stands up. "You're a kind soul bringing our little Blackwell to see us." Miss Suzy's aged arms reach for the baby. "How's our dumplin' today?"

"Oh, he's just fine." Melena sinks into one of the chairs. "We had a good morning so I thought I'd bring you ladies a couple of egg salad sandwiches."

"She already knows our favorite, Sister, and she's only been on this mountain two months." Miss Laroy reaches over and coaxes Blackwell out of Miss Suzy's hands.

"Laroy, don't you get snuff on that baby," Miss Suzy says crossly.

Miss Laroy grunts, ignoring her.

Melena rocks quietly for a moment, then impulsively slaps her thigh. "You won't believe what happened to me this afternoon while I was hanging laundry."

"Go on and tell us, girl." Miss Laroy says bouncing Blackwell on her knee. "No sense waiting." Both old women look as if they've been waiting for something forever.

"Well, I was almost done with the basket when I heard something moving in the woods. So, I stopped and listened. Everything was quiet; then I heard it again. Only this time, it was closer. Well, I didn't know what it was, and I wasn't going to get caught unaware, so I ran up onto the porch to hide and watch."

"*Mmm, hmm,*" Miss Suzy says.

"What do you think it was?" Melena asks holding her sides, laughing. "It was a fox! A little old fox and there I was cowering on my porch like a child. You know what that fox did? It tore one of my nightgowns clear off the line, ran across the yard and into the woods just as plain as day with the gown trailing out behind it. Gosh, doggit, I wish y'all had seen it."

She smiles real big. "I suspect I'll lose more clothes that way if I'm not careful."

She turns toward them wondering why they aren't laughing with her, and her smile disappears. The ladies seem to be frowning.

Miss Suzy stands and takes Blackwell out of Miss Laroy's hands. "That's not all you'll lose, girl."

Melena looks at her wonderingly.

"What she means," Miss Laroy says, "is that foxes are not the only thing you have to worry about when you're hanging clothes on that laundry line."

Miss Laroy makes a face at the baby and says, "You live on a living, breathing mountain now, darling, not the city. When you're outside that house, you have to watch for bears."

"Bears!" Melena says feeling foolish.

"That's right," Miss Laroy looks her in the eye. "Bears."

"Three years ago, the last ranger's wife was out hanging her laundry when a hungry mother bear came out of the forest searching for food. I don't believe that poor girl had ever seen a bear. Maybe the bear knew. What a mess."

Miss Laroy shakes her head. "That bear drug her quite a ways before it left that girl for dead. It took the rangers two days to find it, but when they did, they shot that bear dead."

"*Mmm, hmm.* Shot it dead they did," Miss Suzy says.

Melena's face goes white. "Why didn't y'all tell me this before? I need a gun just to do my laundry."

"Dear, we didn't want to scare you," Laroy says. "They shot that bear. It's dead and gone. There's no sense to worry you, but now that you've been up here a while, it's just as good that you know."

She turns to her sister. "Suzy, you give me that baby and go on in the house. Melena needs a cool drink of water. We've done gone and upset her."

Suzy hands over Blackwell and goes in the house while Melena sinks down in her chair contemplating this new complication.

*Bears indeed,* she thinks. *Ernest has put the baby and me in danger. He could come home from work and there we would be, dead in the grass, mother and son.*

*Uh huh,* she rants in her head, *what I told Blackwell this morning was true. The Starlings will not be living in these mountains for very long at all, not if I have anything to do with it. Woman-eating bears, I'll be damned. I'll have to call Daddy first thing and have him send me a shotgun.*

-›-═◉═-‹-

Some years later, in the kitchen of Ernest and Melena's second home together, Melena leans away from the sink and calls out, "Blackwell."

She leans to the side and looks around the corner into the little hallway leading from the kitchen to her son's bedroom. Wood paneling lining the walls gleams with lemon-scented Pledge.

"Blackwell, honey," she says, "it's time for dinner. Now, surely you don't want us to eat alone, do you?"

Melena shakes her wet hands over the sink and grabs the towel off the hook from under the dark green cabinets. Turning her back against the counter, she dries her hands, then rubs them over and down her stomach. Sighing, she pushes her weight off the counter's edge and walks ten steps out of the kitchen into Blackwell's room on the opposite end of the trailer from the bedroom she and Ernest share.

"Blackwell, honey," Melena leans against the doorframe, "didn't you hear me calling you?" Blackwell sits on the floor, a collection of toy cars in front of him.

For hours, Blackwell has meticulously arranged and rearranged each Matchbox auto, lining them against one another by engine strength. "Look, Momma," he says, "they're getting ready to race." His hand rests on a tiny red one. "Which car do you think is going to win?"

Melena looks down over her stomach at him. Her hair curls just above her shoulders.

"I think that pretty red one is going to win. What about you?"

"*Hmm*," Blackwell says and points, "that number 8 Charger right there is going to win 'cause it's my favorite."

"Well," she says straightening, "you won't see now because it's time for dinner. It'll just have to wait."

"But ..."

Melena gives him a hint of "*the look*."

"Okay, Mommy," he stands up, carefully avoiding any contact with the positioned cars, and follows Melena to the kitchen.

In the past five years, the Starlings have moved from town to town with Mancon, Ernest's fledgling business, relocating as the company's new construction sites are begun. In these years, Ernest has established a modest reputation for Mancon, traveling from job to job with his men to oversee the quality of their construction work.

Just recently, an abundance of work allowed them to put down roots in the flourishing city of Larnee, North Carolina.

The trailer they live in, a gift from Pratt Dupree, housed them in each move and has always shone with cleanliness and radiated warmth. The dark wood paneling, foliage-colored cabinets, and couches lend their home a comfortable tree-house feeling. Pictures of ducks in flight grace the walls and a black and white console TV sits on the floor in the center of the far wall.

Linoleum flooring runs through the small kitchen to the edge of the carpet where the round dinner table sits. Blackwell climbs into his chair while Melena dishes butter beans, corn, chicken and potatoes onto his plate.

"Momma?" Blackwell asks.

"Yes, Blackwell?"

"How do you know I'm going to have a baby brother?"

"I know you're going to have a baby brother because he's sitting so high, and he's so big and round. Little girls carry low."

"Oh." Blackwell grips his fork as Melena sets his plate in front of him.

Melena turns to take her own plate then sits, easing down onto her chair. Blackwell takes a small bite of butter beans and Melena taps her index finger on the table toward him. "Blessing," she says and motions for him to put his fork down.

"Okay, I'll say it." He clasps his hands together and closes his eyes. "God is great. God is good. Let us thank him for our food, Amen."

"Very good, Blackwell, darling." Melena picks up her fork and glances at her watch. "Blackwell, sweetheart, turn on the television for Mommy. The news is on and it will make us better people if we stay informed."

Wiping his mouth with his napkin, Blackwell pushes his chair from the table and walks over to the television. He squats down on his knees and raises his arm to the big plastic button at the top of the dial panel. He presses it and an electric popping noise is heard.

A white horizontal line appears on the screen and opens into a black and white picture. Blackwell blinks close to it as the picture comes into focus. Lee Kinard, Larnee's favorite daily weatherman, smiles behind a pair of thick eyeglasses.

Blackwell carefully adjusts the volume dial. "Is that good, Momma?"

"That's just fine," Melena answers. "Come on back to the table now and eat your supper. We can talk about whatever current events there are while I clean up the kitchen."

An hour and forty-five minutes later, Ernest walks through the trailer door. The sound of running water greets him as Melena looks up from her *Good Housekeeping* magazine to the clock on the opposite wall. She hides a small frown.

"Hello there, Ernest," Melena says feeling heavy in the chair. "There's dinner for you in the refrigerator and Blackwell's just brushing his teeth. That boy's been so excited waiting to have a car race with you."

Ernest nods. "We didn't leave the site 'til seven-thirty," he says stripping off his jacket and dusty work clothes. "I got home as fast as I could."

The water shuts off in the bathroom and Blackwell runs out from the hallway. "Dad," he yells, "I've been working on the cars all day gettin'em ready for our race. They're all lined up on the grid ready to go and everything."

Ernest smiles and tosses his son high in the air. He knows that one day Blackwell will be the one to inherit the fruits of his efforts and keep safe his many secrets. Spinning him around high over his head, Ernest, at six-foot-four, swings Blackwell close to the ceiling.

"Now, Ernest," Melena calls, "that's too high. The boy just ate not too long ago and I don't want him to get sick or anything."

"I'm just playing with him, Melena," Ernest says and sets Blackwell on the floor.

"Boy, that was fun," Blackwell says. "Maybe we can do it again later."

"Blackwell, you go on to your room and I'll meet you there in a little while." Ernest motions to the dirt and grime blanketing his body. "I'll have to get this off me before I'm fit to race one of your cars."

Blackwell shuffles his feet under him. "Okay, Dad. See ya later, Mom."

Melena throws a kiss at her son. "I'll be in when you all finish playing cars, dear, to tuck you in."

She turns to Ernest. "How's the church coming along?"

"Well," he sits and she listens to a familiar speech, "the foundation's done, and the frame is finally taking form. I had to stay on with some of the guys to secure that thing, nobody does anything right without me there anyway."

He looks briefly at her out the corner of his eye to gauge her reaction.

"Yep," he sighs leaning back, propping his foot up over his knee, "twelve hours straight today, but that's what I have to do, Melena, if this business is going to thrive. Customers want solid work, fast." He unlaces his steel-toe boots and leaves them by the door.

Her eyebrows furrow slightly. "Seems like you'd be hungry after all that?"

He looks in the refrigerator and shuts the door. "I am, Melena, but I have to take a shower first and then race cars."

"All right then, go on. I'll heat up your food while you're in there with Blackwell." She straightens the pages of her magazine as he moves down the hall and into the bathroom.

Fifteen minutes later, the door opens and Melena pretends to not watch Ernest as he pads through the living room with a towel wrapped around him. She looks down at the article on gingerbread men as the bedroom door shuts behind him. Drawers open and close, and moments later, Ernest emerges heading for Blackwell's room.

"I'll just go ahead and warm that food up," Melena says to an empty room.

She braces her arms on the side of the chair to heave herself upward, steps over to the refrigerator and opens the door as her men race cars down the hall. Fixing Ernest's late dinner, Melena listens to them play and it makes her feel better about Ernest's working so much.

"No, Daddy," Blackwell says. "You can't have the Charger because that's my car."

"Oh, okay then, I'll take the V-8 Ford," Ernest moves toward the other toy.

"Who's going to drive the other cars if we're only driving these two?" Blackwell asks.

"Why, we'll just drag race them till they're all done. Then I'll go eat dinner and your mom'll come in and get you to bed." Ernest grabs his car and shouts, "Gentlemen, start your engines."

Ernest and Blackwell make loud, revving noises. "The light is red," Ernest says, "the light is yellow. The light is green." They race cars around Blackwell's improvised track, constructed of World Book Encyclopedias and small shoes.

They race five times total and Ernest gives up the championship, blaming hunger for his losses. He comes to the kitchen and sits down to the plate of food sitting warm on the table. Melena's leans on the stove.

"There're more butter beans in the refrigerator if you want some," Melena says, "and potatoes, too. I'm going to tuck Blackwell in and get ready for bed."

She goes toward Blackwell's room and Ernest looks up at her. "Thanks, Melena, this looks good."

She nods and goes on. Blackwell's already lying in bed with the covers pulled up to his chin. Melena eases herself down beside him.

22

"I heard you won the races," she says.

"I sure did. Momma!" Blackwell asks. "Why is Daddy gone so much? Why isn't he here more?"

Absently, Melena's hands wander to the top of her stomach. She runs over the list of reasons compiled in her mind and leans forward to kiss Blackwell on the forehead.

"Your daddy is gone," she says "because he's working to build his own business like Granddaddy Pratt built his. One day, all this time he spends working is going to pay off, and then your daddy will build us a fine home somewhere across town where you'll have a big, pretty yard to play in."

She smoothes the covers over him and pushes off the bed to stand up. "You go on to sleep now and you can see your daddy in the morning at breakfast."

"All right, Momma," Blackwell says. "Goodnight. I love you."

Melena smiles, "Goodnight to you, too, you little darling. Pretty soon you'll be saying goodnight to your new brother."

"Goodnight, little brother," Blackwell says yawning.

Melena lays her hand on the light switch. "'Night," she says softly. She turns the light off and pulls the door closed.

-»-=◎◎=-«-

A little over four years later, Melena's sister Pearl and her family have come to Larnee to celebrate the birth of Melena's third child. The cool spring breeze blows and the dogwoods bloom white and pink. The breeze surrounds the two families. From across the yard, it swirls through the woods with a chill, though the sun shines bright atop the high trees.

"Bobby Shade," Pearl says, "you open that door for your aunt this instant. Don't you see her hands are full?"

"No, Momma," Bobby says, "all I see is pink blankets."

"Big Bob!" Luke Bartleby Starling shuffles up the steps in his cumbersome suit.

Just yesterday, Luke had put a large frog in Blackwell's sock drawer. He had hidden in Blackwell's closet, waiting, and Sara, the woman who helps Melena with the housework, went to put the laundered socks in the drawer.

The frog leapt out at her with a *yawlp* and bounced off her stomach. She screamed so loud Blackwell sprinted from the other end of the house and nearly tripped as he came into the room.

"That's my sister!" Luke says now by the door. His bright blond hair reflects the sun.

Bobby pulls the door open with one hand and plants his fist on the opposite hip. He towers, broad-shouldered, over his younger cousin.

"I know that, squirt," he huffs and looks at Melena and Pearl.

"Boys," Melena looks back from the foyer of the house with the newborn baby in her arms.

"Luke," she says, "you come here and help me with Elizabeth. Bobby, go to the car and help your father and your Uncle Ernest bring up the rest of the bags."

"Yes, ma'am." Bobby tosses his dark black hair, shoots out the front door and jumps down the steps two at a time.

"All right, Luke," Melena says, "let's go put Elizabeth in her bed."

Luke is Melena's little angel, who flashes his toothy smile both when he is truly happy and when he is only pretending to be happy. She wants to protect him and it frightens her that his favorite thing to do is pull the brake on his Big Wheel and spin out at the end of their street.

Melena walks up the short, green staircase that leads to the two upper hallways. They stop opposite the landing at the first bedroom door. This room, the baby's new room, is situated within the house like a crossroads between Melena and Ernest's bedroom and the boys' bedrooms.

Luke pushes the door open and holds it wide for Melena. She steps in and lays Elizabeth Anna Starling down gently in her crib.

"Luke," she says, "you're four now, and such a big boy." He looks up at her.

"Four and a half," he says.

"Excuse me, yes, four and a half," she smiles. "Since you are now such a big boy, from this day forward, I am making it your lifelong job to look after your baby sister. She's the youngest, so that makes you her big brother." Melena watches him.

"Is she going to cry a lot?" His plaid polyester jacket wrinkles at the elbow as he peers into the white bassinet.

"Yes," Melena watches the baby's eyes close, "and I'm sure she'll do a number of other things, too." The doctor told Melena the baby would probably be another boy. She never imagined the little girl she wanted would come through their recent arguing.

The baby seems so innocent to Melena. She could never imagine Elizabeth doing any wrong, especially since she is her only daughter. Yet, like Elizabeth's birth, her actions will always surprise the family.

"Her eyes are small," Luke points to Elizabeth. "Is she from China? Did we adopt her?"

"No, silly," Melena says, "Elizabeth needs to go to sleep now, so let's you and me go down to the kitchen and help Pearl put the coffee on. Your aunt and uncle must be tired from their drive."

Melena pats his shoulder. "Hey, you be nice to your cousins as well, okay?"

"Momma, why does she have tape on her head?"

"Oh," Melena leans back over the bassinet, "she didn't have enough hair to tie a bow to so we taped one on instead. She looks really pretty, doesn't she?"

"*Hmmph*," Luke answers. Luke walks away and turns back around. "Do we have to leave the door open for her?" He holds the brass knob loosely, dragging his foot back and forth across the green carpet.

"Leave it open a little bit." She studies him intently. "Luke Starling, do you need to go to the potty?"

"Nope."

"Go on then," she shoos him out, "go to the kitchen. You all can have a snack and then go play."

Thirty minutes later, with Elizabeth asleep upstairs, the Shades and the Starlings sit, cozy in the yellow kitchen. They nibble at carrots and dip and rock with joyous laughter on the tide of conversation. The children sprawl across the floor around the table in various modes of languor while the parents sip their coffee.

Ernest, now older and more accomplished, looks through the glass panes on the kitchen door across the tiled patio and into the backyard. He is glad the baby came home on a Friday and wonders about the Mancon office running without him. *Who will drive the jobs today and supervise the work?*

Thick sideburns, two inches wide, follow the angle of his jaw toward his chin. They make him feel young again, rebellious. His callused hand rests on the door lock, which he slowly turns.

"Why don't you kids run on out back," he says, "and we'll move onto the porch. The sun's out and I think it's pretty warm."

"That's a great idea," Pearl says. "Walker, grab your coffee, honey, and let's go sit on the porch."

Ernest opens the door and the children file past him, relieved to have their freedom. The boys leave their suit jackets slung over a chair in the kitchen, and in their best clothes, they proceed down the stairs and out into the backyard. Melena calls behind them as she slowly gets up from her chair.

"Y'all be careful."

Walker Shade, a sturdy, good-natured man, takes his coffee and pats his wife on the back.

"Come on, Pearl," he says, "don't you worry about the vegetable plate. I think if anyone's still hungry they can come back in and grab a handful."

Melena takes the tray of carrots and cucumbers out of Pearl's hands. "Walker's right, honey. But do carry my coffee for me, please."

The sisters and their husbands, all dressed in cotton and lightweight polyester garments of varying colors, move onto the slate porch that Ernest built with his own two hands. They sit in wrought-iron chairs under a bright yellow umbrella. The flares of their pant legs cover the tops of their shoes; thick blocky heels and shiny wingtips show at their hems.

"Put these on, dear," Pearl says passing a pair of oval, black-to-brown, gradient sunglasses to her sister.

Melena puts the shades on and sits back in her chair. She looks like Jackie O. Facing the porch railing, the two sisters look out into the woods. Their identical Etienne Aigner sunglasses frame their finely-boned faces, and their skin is radiant in the sun.

Raising their cups to their mouths, Melena and Pearl sip their coffee daintily, pinkies extending away from the cups. On the lower wooden-floored level of the porch, Walker and Ernest gaze into the backyard over the railing.

"The house really looks good, Ernest," Walker says impressed with his brother-in-law's accomplishments. Now grown men, they've known each other since Melena and Pearl were teenagers.

"Thank you." Ernest shifts his weight. "It took us a while," he says. "I couldn't afford to pull anyone off my other jobs, so a few of the guys helped me out on the weekends."

These men he refers to are construction workers who have worked with Ernest and Mancon since the company's beginning. They are proud, rugged men who Ernest, as their boss, has had to keep from killing each other on long jobs at the coast and in the countryside.

Ernest watches Blackwell and Luke dash through the woods in front of him. They run with agility and speed, like two foxes, while Bobby and Lucinda follow carefully behind.

The boys' white shirts spatter with dirt as they traipse under the branches and through the piles of leaves. Lucinda, the oldest of the cousins, holds her dainty, peach-hued dress up above the knees.

On the porch, Pearl looks at her sister. "Melena," she says, "Elizabeth is just the most precious thing in the world. How long are you going to let that darlin' nap?"

"I figure I'll check on her after another hour or so." Melena looks at her gold watch. "What time did Momma and Daddy say they were coming?"

"She said they'd be here around noon."

"Oh, good. I can't wait for her to see Elizabeth."

Pearl laughs. "She'll spoil her rotten."

"I think we all will." Melena's hands tap the table. "What do you think we should fix twelve people for lunch?"

"Well, I brought potato salad and my special deviled eggs. We could send Walker and Ernest to Winn-Dixie for some deli meat and bread."

"Yeah, that'll be good," Melena says thinking that Ernest hasn't looked at the baby once since she came home.

"We'll keep it simple, real simple. Pearl, will you go in the kitchen and grab me a notepad so I can make a list?"

Down in the woods below, the wind toys with spring's new leaves. Awed by their surroundings, Lucinda and Bobby trail Blackwell and Luke, who weave in and out of the trees.

"Y'all wait up," Lucinda says.

"Yeah," Bobby hollers, "we don't know where we're going."

"All right, Luke," Blackwell says, "I guess we better slow down."

He turns around, always ready to lead the crowd in what he thinks is a fair and judicious manner. Blackwell walks past Luke toward his two cousins.

"We're going to this secret place," Blackwell explains, "just over on the other side of this hill."

Luke marches up beside him. He puts his hand on his hip and points with the other. "That's where we play cowboys and Indians," he says.

Though Luke follows Blackwell through the woods and around the house now, they do not know that their decisions and ensuing paths will separate them permanently in the future.

Lucinda tugs at her long brown hair. "What time do we have to be back at the house?" she asks. "Momma Bell's coming and I don't want to get my new dress dirty before she gets here."

Blackwell holds a thick branch back so the others can pass. "Yeah, granddaddy and Leopold are coming too," he says, "but we'll be fine. Daddy'll just call out to us when they get here. He knows I'll hear him."

The children reach the top of the hill, and Blackwell runs forward over a grassy plateau toward a cluster of trees. In the middle of the group, an arbor of leaves and branches crisscrosses and interlocks, becoming the two front walls of a makeshift fort.

"Come on," Blackwell calls, "but be careful when you come around the other side. There's a cliff behind it."

Bobby steps to the left of the wall and tiptoes around the enclosure. Luke goes next, Lucinda follows and together they stand in the middle of a small, man-made clearing.

Lucinda peers over the backside. "This isn't a cliff. It's more like a hill."

"How would you know, Miss Know-It-All?" Bobby asks and sits down in the dirt.

"Because, little brother, I saw it in a magazine once."Lucinda pokes at one of the walls. "So, what do you guys do in here?"

"*Ah*, you know," Blackwell says, "we play war and hide out here for surprise attacks."

Luke pushes a stick around in the dirt. "We win every time," he says.

"That's 'cause we're the best." Blackwell pats the top of the wall. "It doesn't hurt that we have the strongest fort."

"Better than who?" Bobby asks.

"There's a ton of kids around here," Blackwell points, "and every single one of them wants to rule our woods."

29

Luke looks up, "but we don't let'em."

"What on earth do you all fight with?" Lucinda asks.

"Mostly walnuts, acorns and sticks," Blackwell says, "but Charlie Hall's getting a BB gun for his birthday."

"Well, you got a gun, don't ya?" Bobby stands up.

"Yeah, Granddaddy Pratt gave it to me." Blackwell shakes his head, "but Momma won't let me use it. She said she'd have Daddy blister my butt if she caught me playing war with it."

Lucinda parades around the inner walls of the fort.

"Blackwell," she says, "you know you have to use your BB gun if that Charlie kid uses his. I mean you can't let them shoot you without shooting back, can you?"

"Yep," Blackwell says looking over the wall and into the woods. "I'll get mine if he has his."

"How come I don't have a gun?" Luke stands up, his hands covered with dirt.

"Cause you're too young," Lucinda says. "Bobby and Blackwell didn't get theirs until they turned eleven." She looks at him more closely.

"Luke, you better keep your hands off that suit. Your momma would be plenty mad if you got it dirty before the grandparents get here."

He wipes his hands against the side of his leg and looks up at her, "*Nah*."

---

"Mom!" Luke yells.

He stands at the top of the kitchen stairs with one hand on his hip and a piece of orange plastic in the other. Another year older he looks slightly taller than before.

"Can we set the tracks up in the living room?"

At the insistence of Ernest, both Blackwell and Luke now attend a Seventh-day Adventist school situated in the countryside near Larnee. The Adventist school is twenty-five minutes from the Starling home; the local public school is less than five minutes away.

"Where do you want to put them?" Melena's been trying to get herself together for over an hour to leave the house and go run errands.

Luke bats the piece of track gently against the wall. "Down the stairs," he says, "across the floor and down the other stairs."

Melena pauses. "Well, I suppose so, but don't lose any of those cars. Do you hear me, Luke?"

"Yes, Mommy, I hear you."

"Good," Melena says, "I don't want to see any of them in Elizabeth's mouth later."

She shakes the water off a red plastic sippy-cup and turns to Elizabeth Anna, who plays on a blanket on the floor tossing tiny painted blocks up and down in her hand. Melena sets the cup on the Winnie-the-Pooh blanket and Elizabeth looks up and gazes at it.

Her eyes light up and she stands to grab it. Melena pats her on the head and leans out to look into the hallway.

She smiles and says, "Hello, Blackwell, have you seen Sara?"

"*Umm*, I think she's in the den," Blackwell says. He sits on one knee with the other propping up his chin.

At almost thirteen, his dark hair and olive skin foretell that he will one day be a handsome man. His looks, combined with his charismatic demeanor, will attract people to him as he grows older. Pearl and Melena swear he inherited these qualities from Pratt Dupree.

Melena steps over the pieces of the orange and yellow tracks past him.

"And your brother," she asks him, "where has he gone off to?"

"I sent him for more supplies," Blackwell says.

"Running him on errands, eh?" Melena points to the kithcen. "Watch Elizabeth for a few minutes, please, while I go talk to Sara."

"Okay," Blackwell answers. He takes a handful of track and sits down on the blanket with Elizabeth, who is busily sipping her juice.

"Save some for later," he says and slides it out of her hand.

Upstairs, Melena walks down the second hallway. "Sara," she calls.

"I'm in Luke's room."

"Oh, hi," Melena says, "I'm going out for groceries and I'm going to leave Elizabeth downstairs with Blackwell and Luke. They're playing with the cars. You're finished down there, right?"

Since leaving the comfort of their cozy trailer, the Starlings now have a part-time housekeeper. Sara, a young Adventist sealed in marriage to a tall man with a mustache, is an important member of their church.

"Oh, yes," Sara replies, "don't you worry about them. We'll be fine." Everything's been so different and new for Sara since she's been living with her husband. Her voice is marked with sadness.

"Do you need anything from the store?" Melena asks.

"No, thank you. I'm just fine. You go and take your time," Sara says, arranging a pile of children's books.

"Oh, I won't be long." Melena turns. She pauses at the hallway that is perpendicular to the one she stands in. It runs from the den on her left all the way down to her bedroom on the right.

Luke labors with a box that showers plastic tracks out of both ends. "More track," he says dragging it in front of her as he passes by.

"I think that's quite enough. Don't let your sister chew on any of that," Melena says, "and you mind Sara."

She slips her purse off the handle of the closet door, and they head downstairs. Luke slides the box off each step banging its contents in a raucous clatter. Melena follows him into the kitchen.

"Blackwell," she says, "you're in charge."

Melena pulls on her tan rain slicker. "I'll see you before long."

Melena fastens the top two buttons of her coat and descends the wooden staircase into the basement. She turns the lights on and off as she goes.

Beyond the kitchen windows, the rain beats down on the slate porch in gray sheets that promise never to let up. Forced to remain indoors, Blackwell and Luke sit on Elizabeth's Winnie-the-Pooh blanket watching Sesame Street and putting pieces of the racetrack together.

Beside them, Elizabeth has a large piece of track in her hand. It flops up and down, and much to her delight; she smacks a group of blocks with it, laughing at the sound.

In the basement, a large multi-colored golf umbrella stands by the door. Melena grabs it as she goes out into the storm. She stops under the porch as she gazes at the downpour with a frown.

The loneliness that she's kept buried suddenly breaks free and the rain amplifies the unhappiness and doubt hidden inside of her. Tears come to her eyes as she lets the umbrella fall from her hands.

On the opposite side of the overhang, a spiral staircase climbs to the deck. Melena shuffles toward it and sits down on the second step overwhelmed by her emotions.

*Thank god, the kids didn't see me cry,* she thinks. *I don't want them to see.* She wrings her hands together.

Marriage, life, they weren't supposed to be like this. Ernest promised that their family was going to be good. He said he would be around, that he would help, but he's never home.

She looks at her ring finger and remembers the day they were married and how Pratt Dupree had offered her a brand new car not to marry Ernest.

Pratt loved his girls and Bell, too. He was always giving Melena whatever she could talk him into. When she turned eleven, Melena wanted a horse, and a horse is exactly what she got.

She did treasure hunts on "Horse" when she was a kid. The palomino had been named when Melena got him, but she renamed him Horse as soon as she saw him.

Melena remembers racing across the fields, Horse jumping fallen trees, back to a time when she wouldn't have put up with a husband who left her to stew in doubt.

In the late fifties, on the west side of Holiday, twelve-year old

Melena sat on her horse, waiting. Horse was a fine steed that her daddy, Pratt, bought from a rich doctor in town.

Leaning over the horse's neck, her blond hair half-covered her green eyes. She twirled the reddish-brown mane under her hands.

"Horse," Melena said, her green eyes looking down the long stretch of highway, "they sure are late today. I wonder if that bus broke down."

Just before lunch, Melena, otherwise known as "Momma's Little Angel," had feigned illness and left school early. The office secretary called Bell Dupree, Melena's mother, and told her that the girl had a stomachache and asked if someone could pick her up from school.

Biting her lip so as not to smile, Melena's insides lit up when she saw Grady and Leopold pulling up to the front door of the school in her momma's powder-blue Cadillac Coupe De Ville. The trick was going to work.

The first thing Momma's Little Angel did when she got home was go and kiss Bell. Laid up in her feather bed with a silk coverlet, Bell felt weak from a party at the house the night before.

After showering her mother with thanks and affection, Melena took off to the warehouses to get a gumball from Pratt. Then she slipped out to the barn to get on her horse, which she rode for the rest of the school day.

Off in the distance, Melena saw the boxy yellow school bus tooling up the road. "Here they come now, Horse," Melena whispered in his ear. "You just be ready when I say, 'ya.'" Melena waved to Leopold on the porch and turned Horse to face the bus head on as it approached. Leopold didn't go to school but waited in his rocking chair everyday for his sisters to get home.

The bus slowed to a stop, churning dust up around the wheels. The black letters painted on its side read "West Holiday Elementary." Melena breathed deeply, watching the windows on the nearest side of the bus fill up with familiar faces. They were all ready.

Motionless and watching, Melena followed Pearl's movement

down the walkway as she stood and slowly approached the door. The bus driver looked at her suspiciously. He tilted his hat and Melena smiled. Everything was quiet until Pearl's foot hit the bottom step. Her long plaid skirt swung out of the bus past her ankles like a signal.

At once, Melena kicked her heels into the horse's flank and shouted, "*Ya!*" The horse jumped and reared up on its hind legs while Melena leaned backward, clutching the reins. "*Yippie kai yai yeah!*" she yelled.

All the kids inside the bus yelled, too.

The horse's front hooves, flush with the bus's roof, pumped in the air and fell back onto the ground. Melena dug her heels into the horse's flank and it sprinted down the highway away from the bus with Melena's laughter echoing behind.

Leopold skipped around the porch and all the kids cheered and screamed while Pearl stepped off the bus looking at the dust trail following her sister. The bus's engine popped into gear and drove on down the road. Pearl called Leopold to her and they stood there waiting for Melena to return. A few minutes later, Melena and the horse trotted up slowly met by a jubilant Leopold.

"Hey," Melena said, dirt on her face.

"Hey, yourself," Pearl smiled.

Throwing one leg over the saddle, Melena hopped down beside her. "Horse wants you to ride him." She offered Pearl the reins causing Leopold to clap and laugh.

Two years older than Melena, fragile Pearl shook her head. "I don't know, Melena. I'm not Calamity Jane, and I don't want him taking off with me again." Pearl preferred to be nice and secure.

"Oh, Horse?" Melena asked cupping her hands to give Pearl a lift. "Horse wouldn't do that. He only goes fast with me. Horse knows you don't like that. He's smart."

Hiking up her skirt, Pearl put one shoe in Melena's hand, heaved herself upward and awkwardly threw the other foot over the horse's back. She sat up and Melena handed her the reins.

"Melena Dupree, you know this horse has a name. You need to stop calling him Horse, and call him by his given name."

"I will not," Melena smiled and said, leading them down the driveway Leopold walking at her side. "I don't like his name."

Pearl giggled. "Dick's a good name for a horse."

"Don't you call him that," Melena said. "I'm changing his name. I'm going to call him Peter, Peter the horse."

"Peter's still funny."

Melena smirked. "Oh, yeah, smarty pants?"

Pearl looked at her wide-eyed and started to protest. Reaching up, Melena slapped Peter's rump and shouted, "*Ya!*"

Peter the Horse took off at a gallop down the driveway with Pearl Dupree screaming wildly on top of him andLeopold running after them hollering, both fist raised. Melena cackled as she watched her sister's arms and legs bounce awkwardly in the air. She picked up Pearl's satchel, then skipped down the driveway toward home.

Now, Melena sits under her porch, still facing the rain. She allows a small grin to cross her face. *I was daring*, she thinks, *so free. I could have been anything I wanted to be.*

The wind lifts her hair. This thought drifts away from her, as she grows stronger thinking about her kids. Her back stiffens and she wipes her eyes. Standing, Melena steps to her umbrella and shoulders her purse. She darts to her Mercedes and decides to get the dry cleaning first.

Underneath those same stormy skies, a yellow neon sign flashes "Gentleman's XXX" into the evening rain. "Girls, girls, girls" is painted in bright red across the front of the small, concrete-block building and its windowless facade hides everyone and everything inside.

Traveling in swooping paths across the musty room, the audience and the stage, blue and red spotlights slice through the billowing smoke of the fog machine. In the center of the runway stage, a lone dancer hangs by her locked ankles that grip a pole at the top.

A booming jazz horn plays a torrid song for her and she wears a hot pink sequined g-string with matching stiletto heels. Her arms extend to the floor, revealing her naked breasts, then move out in waves that she releases from the center of her body.

Upside down, Candy smiles, recognizing the trio of businessmen who sit transfixed at a table directly in front of her.

Clasping the pole between her hands, Candy wraps one leg tightly around the top and kicks the other out in an arc. Placing the bottom of her high-heeled shoes against the pole, she uses her hands and feet to work her body down its length.

The palms of her hands flatten against the floor and Candy balances her backside against the pole, straightening her legs above her to form a perfect handstand.

Suddenly, her legs seem to peel away from the center of her body as they fall to opposite sides in a complete split.

The three men nod and mutter to themselves about her flexibility.

The dancer's legs extend above her again and she allows them to fold gradually to the floor, curling herself into a compact ball. Her great, round ass beams at the men, twitching, and Candy flips her long, bleached-blond hair back over her head toward them.

She turns around on all fours and creeps to their table, one seductive limb at a time, approaching them like a jungle cat stalking its prey.

At the edge of the stage, Candy beckons Ernest forward. He leans in, and she takes hold of his tie.

Twisting its length around in her hands, she jerks him closer and shoves her double-D breasts into his face. Candy wiggles them back and forth slightly, then pushes him away. Ernest's hair is tousled, shooting out in many directions.

Sitting back, Candy bows her posture so that her breasts protrude and flutter kicks her legs toward the men. She turns on her side and positions her hip toward them so they can access her thin strip of g-string.

Ernest waves a dollar bill in front of her and then slides it, folded lengthwise, under the string. Candy winks at him and whispers that she'll come sit with him in just a moment.

He backs away and the two other businessmen lean in to slip her a bill as well.

Aware of the other leering eyes surrounding the stage, Candy slinks across the floor to give each gentleman his "moment" and collect his payment.

Ten minutes later, Candy props herself up on a stool beside Ernest, wearing a strapless red dress that looks like a bracelet. She takes a long-stemmed cherry from her drink and sucks on it while Ernest watches. With a tug of her teeth, she pops the fruit loose from the stem and laughs lightly as she devours it.

"Ernest, baby," Candy says. "Nobody treats me like you do."

"Aww, but you're such a nice girl," he says. "You deserve every bit of it."

Last Tuesday, Ernest had driven a brand-new silver Trans Am straight off the lot to Candy's front door. He gave her the title and the keys.

"I wish everyone could be like you," she pouts, "but they aren't like my Ernest. They can't be, because you're special."

-->==◉◑==<-

"*Oww*, Mommy. It hurts," Elizabeth says face down on an examination table.

The paper covering below her fingernails is torn. She sweats, though she lies shirtless with only her corduroy knickers on.

Melena squeezes her daughter's hand and sighs. She feels paralyzed and helpless, a feeling she encounters more often every day.

Six months ago, she paid a doctor to increase her breasts by two bra sizes. Jealous women stare now wherever she goes, but the outpatient surgery won't fix her marriage.

"I know it does, honey," Melena says, "but the doctor says we have to do it if we want to find out what all you're allergic to. You don't want it to be hard for you to breathe, remember?"

Frowning, Melena looks down at her daughter. She holds the child's hands in her own, while Elizabeth stares at the floor.

The irritated, slightly sadistic nurse says, "Ma'am, we've only done the first ten." She puts her hands on her hips and looks at Melena as if she should try to stop the little girl's crying.

Melena nods slightly and watches the nurse pick up another needle and position it behind the two rows of red welts already forming on Elizabeth's skin.

The nurse, an apparently childless fiftyish woman, pushes the needle in and works it around under the surface of the tender flesh. Elizabeth's face wrinkles in pain.

"Mommy!" Elizabeth cries.

"Okay, Elizabeth," Melena says, "this is what I want you to do. Every time it hurts you, I want you to bite my thumb until you don't think about it anymore."

"Okay, Mommy," Elizabeth says and bites down on Melena's thumb as the nurse sticks the four year old again.

Melena flinches. "You've got a pretty good bite there, girl."

Elizabeth nods, tears sliding across the numerous freckles dotting her cheeks. A strand of her blond hair falls forward, clinging to her damp skin. Melena smiles reassuringly and pushes the hair back behind her daughter's ear.

One hundred and sixteen needles later, Elizabeth sits on the doctor's table. Her legs are crossed and her face pale. The doctor enters the tiny examining room with a clipboard in his hand.

"*Ah*, Mrs. Starling," he says, "and Elizabeth, I hope the test wasn't too troublesome?"

"It hurt a lot," Elizabeth says wide-eyed, "but Mommy let me bite her finger every time it hurt and that helped."

"Yes, that's right," Melena says hiding her thumb. "We two girls managed together like she and I always do." Melena smiles. Elizabeth is the child she never got to be. There were always so many adults coming and going from get-togethers at the Dupree's. Melena had to grow up fast.

She asks, "So, Dr. Evans, how did we come out?"

"Well," he says scratching his large nose, "certain pets are definitely out of the question for you all. The nurse has compiled a list of things you need to keep Elizabeth away from. The most important thing is that you keep down all levels of dust and mold inside your home. This little one is going to show asthmatic symptoms all day and night if you don't."

Dr. Evans turns to the counter and picks up a small notepad.

"Also," he says, "I'm going to write a prescription for some capsules that will help out immensely. Now, she's probably too young to swallow them, so you'll need to open them up. You can mix the granules in some jelly or something and let her eat that." His pen scratches away at the pad.

"Oh," Melena's mind turns over numerous questions, "all right."

Melena tries to cover the possibilities. "Dr. Evans," she asks, "there's nothing that she could severely react to is there? I mean, she's not in any danger, right? And how long do you think she'll have to be on these capsules?"

"No, no," he says, "she'll be just fine as long as she takes her medicine. You just keep checking in with us every six months and we'll monitor her progress as we go." Dr. Evans smiles and pats Melena's shoulder.

"Thank you, Doctor," Melena says and stands. "We'll make sure we stay away from the things on the list and I'll phone you in six months."

Melena picks Elizabeth up off the table and heads for the door. The nurse, annoyed with Elizabeth's continuous crying during the testing procedure, gives her the list of allergens and glares at Melena as she and Elizabeth leave.

Outside the doctor's office, Melena straps Elizabeth into the car, then fastens her own seat belt. Elizabeth looks over at Melena's hands on the steering wheel.

"Mommy, your thumbs are awfully red," Elizabeth says amused by her own power. "Do you think I almost bit them off?"

"No," Melena laughs ignoring the pain in her hands and in her heart. "You did get them pretty good though, and that's because you're so strong. What do you say we go to Mayberry's for lunch? I'll buy you a milkshake for being such a brave girl."

"That's good, Mommy, yeah." Elizabeth pats her hands on her lap and smiles.

⌁⬥⌁

One Saturday morning, Melena wakes from a dream turned nightmare and realizes what she has to do. At first the dream was like she remembered. She was a kid again, racing the Impala, hair blowing in the wind, then everyone and everything disappeared. She was alone on the railroad tracks, out of the car. The train was coming, but straight for her to hit her this time. The threatening blare of the train's horn hurt her ears and she couldn't move her feet.

Lying in bed next to him, Melena retraces the steps of that night wondering if she had beat Ernest, would he have been more attracted to her in some way?

It was a cool fall night back in 1962. The dark southern sky was filled with twinkling stars. Music bebopped through the small speakers attached all around the red and white Sonic Shop on Bragg Boulevard and street lights passed by like lone luminaries in their town.

Teenagers in large, rumbling Fords and Chevys drove around the restaurant in a constant stream that threatened to exceed the parking lot's capacity.

The cars moved slowly while girls in long, wool-blend skirts and tight sweaters darted from one car to another. Ponytails swinging behind them, they stopped and chatted with boys in dark blue jeans and white T-shirts.

On top of the Sonic, three stories high in the DJ tower, Bob the Big Bad Daddy spun LP's. His voice boomed out over the parking lot and could be heard a quarter-mile away.

Rolling down the boulevard, Melena Dupree steered her 1960 Chevy Impala toward the hangout. The cherry-red body of the car matched the scarf tied around her neck.

Mary Bordson sat beside her puckering her lips and primping her hair as they slowed to a stop. In the dark of night, the Holiday streetlights illuminated them, making them look like Hollywood starlets.

"Melena," Mary said, "the wind just makes my hair so much fuller."

Melena glanced at herself in the rear view mirror and smiled. "I told you a little wind in your hair always does the trick."

Inside the glass cockpit of the spaceship-modeled DJ booth, Bob the Big Bad Daddy turned down the dial and pointed at the red Impala as he leaned toward the microphone.

"Hey there, guys and gals, look who's here. It's the girls from 61st High. Go fighting Tigers! Kittens, this one's for you."

Melena and Mary waved as Bob threw on *It's Now or Never*. Elvis crooned sumptuously across the parking lot.

Melena backed the car into an empty spot beside a black and white '59 Plymouth Fury with one big fin on each side.

"I can't believe we got a spot," Mary said.

"I can, but don't get comfortable." Melena turned the engine off. "We've got to meet the girls in half an hour, but let's have a shake."

"Sure thing." Mary leaned out the window and pressed a large red button by the speaker. Melena sat high in the seat and turned the knot in her scarf to the side of her neck.

"Sonic Shop," a girl answered, "what can I get ya?"

"I need two shakes, one chocolate and one vanilla," Mary said. "And, we need that on the go."

"Keep yer skirt on, kid. We'll be out in a few." The speaker clicked off.

"How do you like that?" Mary leaned back and looked around.

To Melena's left, two young men sat calm and cool in the Fury. Windows rolled down, the driver's arm stretched across the back of the white leather seat while the passenger's draped along the window seal. Ernest Starling leaned over the steering wheel, nudged Buddy Roy and called toward the Impala.

"How y'all ladies doing this evening?" He inquired with a nod. "Ms. Dupree, so nice to see you and you, too, Ms. Bordson. Y'all are looking as lovely as ever. Are you girls here to play with the rest of the kids or did y'all come out to see some cars race tonight?"

"Hi to you, too, Starling," Melena said sitting down in her seat and staring forward as if she didn't care. "Little bird told me you're running a lot of heat under that hood."

"Yes, ma'am," Ernest winked. "It's my job to make sure the Fury goes faster than any other car in Holiday."

Melena fluffed her golden blond hair. "You all racing down on Amhurst and Parker Street tonight?"

"Yes, we are," Ernest said, "that's where we were just fixing to head to."

A petite waitress in a red uniform spun around and stopped on Mary's side of the car with a shake in each hand. Mary passed her the money and took the shakes. "Thanks," she said as Melena cranked up the Chevy engine.

"Well," Melena said, "if you're going to the races, see if that car of yours can keep with mine all the way to Parker Street."

Melena pulled out of her parking spot to cut left against traffic; an angry waitress leaped out of her path and glared at the girls in the Impala.

Ernest laughed, cranked the Fury and circled the building. He liked the competition.

The wheels of Melena's car spun on the ground and left a black mark on the pavement as she pulled out of the entrance to the Sonic onto Bragg Boulevard. One hand on the wheel, she slapped Mary on the back with the other.

"Mary, that's Jerry Lee playin' on the radio! Turn it up." Melena's hair blew behind her and the DJ's farewell followed them.

Squeezing the shakes into the space between the door and her seat, Mary leaned forward and laughed. The music pumped out of the speakers, and Mary danced with her hands in the air. Melena yanked on the top of the steering wheel and threw the Impala into a hard right turn. Sliding to the left, Mary landed on top of her, while the Fury's tires screeched behind them.

In the passenger seat beside Ernest, Buddy Roy jumped up and down slapping his hands on the dashboard. Ernest jerked the wheel to the right, turned the corner sharply and fishtailed into the other lane. Jerking the car straight again, he stomped the pedal and laughed. "She can't beat me," he said. "What is that girl thinking?"

Mary bobbed up and down, then turned around and held onto the back of the seat as she looked behind her. "Go, Melena, go!" she said and waved at Ernest and Buddy Roy, her chestnut hair flying.

The Fury's engine roared as Ernest shifted it into high gear. It lurched forward and pulled up to the rear bumper of Melena's car. Slowly, the Plymouth edged up beside the girls and Buddy Roy looked over and smiled.

"How y'all doin'?" He shouted over the roar of the cars.

Mary stuck her tongue out at him and turned back around. Eyes forward, cheeks flushing red, Melena pressed harder on the gas and weaved up the four-lane hill toward the Midtown Railroad. Ernest sped up the incline, holding steady with her front bumper.

As the two cars hit the plateau, Mary Bordson gulped and reached for the windshield. "Holy shit, Melena!" she screamed, "the train! The cross bars are halfway down!"

"I can make it," Melena said. "I just have to pull ahead of him." She pressed harder on the gas, coaxing more power out of the car.

"You can't," Mary pointed. "They're down and only one of y'all is going around them. Melena Dupree, I am not going to die a virgin!"

Ernest held the pedal pressed to the floor. Nosing ahead of Melena's car, the Plymouth Fury loudly took the lead. Pulling the wheel to the left of the street, Ernest approached the train tracks in the wrong lane. Melena let off the gas and eased her foot onto the brake. White lights shone out from the woods where the railroad tracks ran.

The Fury cut diagonally as Ernest broke through the crossbar's open space onto the other side of the crossing. Mary screamed as the Impala screeched to a halt, stopping just short of the red and white cross bars. The red lights, blinking on top of it, ran down the barrier in a line to their right. In an instant, the train thundered past Melena and Mary whipping them suddenly with a big gust of wind.

---

Several months after Elizabeth's torturous visit to the allergy doctor, a large orange moving truck sits parked in the driveway outside the Starling house. Melena watches it blankly.

Insides exposed, the open trailer seems to yawn endlessly. A tweed couch and the recliner from the den sit on the truck along with sealed boxes of various household items: pots, pans, silverware and towels.

At school and unaware that they are moving, Blackwell and Luke go about their days learning while Elizabeth sits on the living room floor playing with her toys.

The movers carry more of the Starlings' possessions down to the truck. Melena, talking on the phone, monitors their progress from the window by the front door.

"No, Pearl," Melena says, "I don't care. I'm not going to call him now and tell him. Not when the movers are almost done. I'm telling you, we'll be out of this house by two o'clock, then I'll pick the boys up and we'll be at Momma's by dinnertime."

Two of the movers walk through the front door and look at her expectantly. "Hold on," Melena says into the phone and turns to the men.

"If you could just get the mattress in the upper hall now." Melena smiles. "Thank you."

She watches them walk up the stairs.

"Melena," Pearl says worried about her sister, "don't you think you're pushing it leaving the house while Ernest is at work? Don't you think you should have told him and sat down to talk this out first?"

"No, I do not," Melena cuts her off. "I don't owe that man anything. If he wants to see his whores, then he can go and come as he pleases. I'm sure as hell not going to be here for him to come home to, cooking his damn dinner and washing his clothes."

Pearl twists the phone cord in her hand. "But you don't have proof he's done anything."

"Don't I? You think I don't know where he goes until nine or nine-thirty every evening? Get your head out of the sand, Pearl," Melena says.

She always thought her sister was a little naive.

"What do you think a man does who comes home four or five hours after his office has closed when he should be at home with his family?"

Melena steps out of the way as the men go out the front door carrying the mattress between them. As they reach the driveway, Melena's jaw drops.

Ernest's pick-up screeches to a halt in front of the moving van. "Holy shit, Pearl!" she says. "He's here. Ernest is here."

"Oh, no," Pearl gasps, "you'll have to stop. He'll make you. You won't be able to leave."

"The hell I won't," Melena says. "I'll call you after we've gone."

She dials another number while below Ernest stands in front of the movers, blocking the ramp to the trailer with his body as they try to load the mattress onto the van.

"Just what the hell do you think you're doing?" Ernest asks.

"Sir," one of the movers says, "we're doing our job."

"And who exactly is paying you to do this?" Ernest asks. "No, let me guess, my wife."

His face colors a deep red.

"You march this mattress right back up there or I'll have you both arrested for theft."

The men look at each other and then back at Ernest. "Sir, we've already been paid for this job, and well, we have to do it. If you have a problem with that, I suggest you take it up with your wife."

Ernest points his index finger at them and his eyes grow wide.

"That's what I intend to do," he says moving up the steps furiously.

Melena hangs up as he comes bursting in. "Ernest," she says, "you're home from work early today."

"That," Ernest says, continuing to point at her, "is because I received a phone call at work from one of our friendly neighbors. They were curious about why we decided to move so suddenly. What in the hell do you think you're doing, Melena?"

"I'm leaving you, Ernest," she says. "I'm leaving you to your whores, and I'm taking what is rightfully mine with me. If you have a problem with that, then I'll see you in court."

Melena escapes into the living room where Elizabeth stares at them blank-faced, doll in hand. She picks Elizabeth up off the floor, seats the child on her left hip and turns around to stare at Ernest.

"You can't do this, Melena," Ernest says. "This is theft. You're stealing my things, too, and you're leaving my house!"

"You made your choice a long time ago, Ernest. Now, I'm making mine. Face it. I'm leaving and there's not a damn thing you can do about it."

Melena runs her hand through Elizabeth's hair. "And, these things are my things and the children's things just as much as they're yours." Melena steps toward the front door.

Elizabeth's Barbie doll falls out of her hands and she protests loudly, reaching for it.

Ernest stands between Melena and the door. "You cannot leave, and you're not taking Elizabeth with you."

"Oh, yes, I am, Ernest," Melena says through clenched teeth, yelling, "Move!"

"I will not move," Ernest yells back at her.

Elizabeth screams and squirms out of Melena's arms toward the floor. She lunges and grasps the Barbie by the legs as Melena snatches her back up in her arms.

"I will not stay married to a lying cheat, Ernest Starling. Now, you move right this minute or I'll get my gun and make you, damn it."

"Mommy!" Elizabeth says. Melena bounces her up and down on her hip.

"Just be quiet, Elizabeth," Melena hushes her and smoothes her ruffled hair. "Remember, we're going to Momma Bell's. You love Momma Bell's, honey. You can play with the dogs."

Ernest screams, "You give me Elizabeth right now!"

Elizabeth shouts, "Stop it, Daddy," flings her Barbie at Ernest and smacks him in the arm.

"Don't you yell at her!" She buries her head in Melena's shoulder and cries.

"Now look what you've done," Melena says.

Ernest shakes his head. "I'm calling the police."

A knock sounds loudly. "Move, Ernest," Melena says, "there's someone at the door."

Ernest flings the door open. "You!" he shouts and the index finger comes up again. "What do you want, Patty Kilyard? Did you put Melena up to this?"

Patty pulls the storm door open confidently. Elizabeth lifts her face off Melena's shoulder and Patty looks at the two of them, confusion in her eyes.

"You're in it together, you conniving bitches. I'm calling the police before this goes any further." Ernest goes to the kitchen and Elizabeth begins to cry again.

"Take her," Melena says to Patty. "Take Elizabeth and go to your house. She'll need a snack soon and I'll be along just as soon as I'm done here."

Patty looks flabbergasted. "What about him?" Patty says jerking her thumb toward the other room.

"Don't even think about it. I'm leaving with my children even if it kills me." Melena stops and listens to Ernest inside the kitchen.

"That's right," he shouts, "theft in progress and I have caught the perpetrators."

Melena looks back at Patty. "Take her now, and I will see you later." She pulls Elizabeth off her shoulder and thrusts her toward Patty.

"No, Mommy!" Elizabeth says reaching toward Melena.

"Elizabeth Anna, you be quiet. Be a good girl now and go with Aunty Patty. I'll pick you up later and then we'll go get your brothers." Melena wipes the tears away from Elizabeth's eyes with the back of her hand.

The phone slams down and Patty steps toward the door. She nods and goes out just as Ernest comes storming back into the foyer.

"The sheriff is on his way, Melena. There's nothing you can do. They won't let you leave."

"Ernest," she laughs, "what year do you think it is? You can't stop me from leaving this house any more than you can control the sun."

"You are my wife, and you can't just walk out and leave me while I'm at work. You're stealing my furniture and my kids."

He looks around. "Where's Elizabeth?"

"She's gone, Ernest." Melena puts her hands on her hips. "It's not like you ever paid that much attention to her anyway. All you care about, if anything, is those boys."

Ernest looks out the long, vertical window. He sees Patty at the foot of the steps just stepping onto the driveway. He beats his fist against the window and dashes outside.

"Patty Kilyard," Ernest shouts from the top of the stairs, "you bring my daughter back here right now!"

Shifting Elizabeth around her body, Patty hurries past the moving truck and down the driveway. Elizabeth watches her father over Patty's shoulder.

"Daddy!" she cries stretching out her arm.

Patty places her hand on top of Elizabeth's head and whispers, "Don't you worry. We're just going to Aunt Patty's house, darling. You'll see your father later."

They get into Patty's Buick as Ernest threatens the movers again. He leaps into the van and picks up one corner of the mattress, dragging it out of the trailer. The men do not stop him, but watch him, frowning.

Suddenly, the bed slams onto the driveway and Ernest begins pulling it back up the steps, one end up while the other sits on the dirty ground. His movements are awkward and ineffectual.

Patty starts the car and Elizabeth, left alone in the back seat while Patty makes the getaway, turns around to look out the rear window.

She watches her father struggle with the mattress and her mother shout from the top of the steps. This will be the first memory from childhood that she will retain as an adult.

Her family grows smaller to Elizabeth's eyes as Patty drives up the street, farther and farther away from her home.

Dressed like Cinderella, Elizabeth runs her hands across the satin ribbon of her baby blue dress and smiles.

"Mommy," she asks, "can I go trick-or-treating with Blackwell and Luke this year?"

In the house that Ernest built, Melena sits across from Elizabeth at their yellow kitchen table. In her flight to Holiday, she found herself in quite a dilemma with all sorts of people roaming about the yard while the furniture just sat everywhere.

Ernest refused to leave the moving truck, shouting and pointing from the men to the house. Then the police came.

Melena felt quite unprepared. She thought she had planned it just right, but someone had tipped him off. Who was it?

She canceled the move and decided to work things out with Ernest for the time being. He's promised her money to redecorate the den and now she sits here, in a world of masks pretending to be happy with the festivities and her home.

"No, ma'am," Melena says smiling at Elizabeth in her frilly dress. She drops a miniature packet of Sweettarts into the last bag. "You cannot go around with your brothers. It's much too dangerous for you."

A pile of candy bags decorated with witches and pumpkins lies between them. Ceramic goblins and Jack O' Lanterns dot the kitchen counters, and a witch on a straw broom dangles from the light fixture above the table.

"But why not?" Elizabeth asks. "They won't let anything happen."

"Elizabeth, you can't go with your brothers because they go too far for a little girl to go. Now, when you're older, you can go with them, but until then, you'll have to be happy going with either your father or me, understand?"

Elizabeth nods, repeatedly smacking her glossed lips together with a pop. Melena takes a pumpkin-shaped tray filled with Halloween bags into the foyer and steps back into the kitchen.

In the middle of the floor, Elizabeth twirls 'round and 'round until the curls in her hair and the ruffles on her dress fly up in the air.

"Look," she stumbles, "I am Cinderella!"

"You'll get dizzy, Elizabeth.,"

Melena recalls Bell and Elizabeth , the two conspirators, at the Holiday Mall. Elizabeth had pushed Bell's portable wheelchair, and Grandmother and Granddaughter snuck off to the dress shop to purchase the very dress Melena had just refused Elizabeth.

Bell understood the way Elizabeth explained it. It was the only dress that would really make her look like Cinderella, and Halloween was only four months away.

"My mother sure loves to spoil you, girl," Melena says. "No matter if I say no, she says yes. Momma made sure you had that blue dress."

Elizabeth stops and falls onto the apple-green linoleum floor.

"The room is spinning and spinning," she says.

A loud thud sounds from behind as Luke lands at the kitchen entrance. He squats low to the floor and looks at Melena and Elizabeth from beneath his mask. Growling, he beats his fists against the wall and jumps up and down like a monkey.

Luke leaps into the room and runs around in a circle. Rattling the cabinet doors, he bumps into Elizabeth, knocking her onto the floor.

She laughs, a pile of blue taffeta.

Luke shakes his mask over her, tickling her until she can barely breathe.

"St-stop it, Luke," she says.

"Luke," Melena calls, "You're going to ruin her makeup."

Wrapped in a black cloak from nose to toe, another dark figure appears as Blackwell leans inside the doorframe. His eyes peer over the top edge.

"Good evening, ladies and gentlemen," he says disguising his voice for effect.

"My name is Count, Count Dracula, *aa aa aa*, and I have come to suck your blood."

Blackwell drops the cape and charges into the kitchen. He bulldozes Elizabeth and Luke into a sprawl across the floor. They wriggle, giggling in their costumes.

"Everyone, that's enough," Melena says. "Blackwell, go make sure the pumpkins are lit out front"

"Okay, Mom," Blackwell says.

Melena follows him. "Samantha and the others will be here soon," she says. "We want the scary tape on when they get here."

A high school sophmore, Blackwell wishes he went to public school instead of the Adventist—a night out with Samantha and the other girls thrills him. They aren't like the devout girls he goes to school with.

Melena turns to Luke with another tray of candy bags.

"Put this by the door, honey," she says. "Your father will be home soon. Elizabeth, where's your tiara?"

"My crown," Elizabeth gasps. "I forgot it."

"Go on then. You know where it is."

"Dad's home," Luke says and sits down at the table.

"Good, go to our room and get the camera off my bathroom counter so he can take some pictures."

"Mommy," Elizabeth says, "I can't get it to stay."

"Don't worry, I'll fix it," Melena thumbs a bobby pin. "Come on over here."

Moments later, Blackwell and Ernest come inside. Ernest sets his briefcase down on the counter and spins around to face Elizabeth.

"Cinderelli, Cinderelli," he claps his hands together.

"Daddy!" Elizabeth laughs. Luke stands in the door.

"And who do we have here?" Ernest asks. "Oh, Cinderelli, that's a terrible monster. You must protect me. I am frightened."

Elizabeth shouts at Luke "Og ogg ogg!" In their private language gleaned from a cartoon about trolls that means *go away mean troll*. Luke lurches toward them in character.

"Dracula!" Ernest calls. "Where is Dracula? Come to our rescue, Mr. Vampire!"

Blackwell waves his cape beside him. "These," he points, "are my victims, wretched monster."

There's one person Blackwell will bite tonight, but he won't see her until later.

Luke gurgles behind his mask and the boys lunge at each other in various postures of aggression. Ernest takes the camera out of Luke's hand and Melena calls them to attention.

"Okay," she says herding the family, "Ernest, where should they go for their pictures?"

"Hold it right there, boys," Ernest says and snaps a shot of Blackwell hissing, fangs aimed at the monster.

"Good," he says. "Now, let's go in the living room."

Ernest takes an entire roll of pictures capturing different images of his children as they twirl, growl and pose. Together, all five of the Starlings walk down the drive to see their home lit in Halloween fashion. An easy fall wind blows behind them lifting Blackwell's cape in ripples.

Enormous old oak trees surround their home, shading the yard and lining the length of the drive. Most of the red-hued leaves have fallen, but the remnants, left high atop the trees, block out the clear evening sky.

"Momma, I can barely see the stars," Elizabeth says skipping along in front.

"That's because I've stolen them," Blackwell says and charges forward to swoop Elizabeth off the ground.

A single leaf, high on a branch above them, shudders and breaks free. It begins a slow descent toward the ground. Elizabeth laughs while Blackwell runs with her in his arms to the end of the drive.

He stops at the grass circle in the middle of their court, holds Elizabeth up to the heavens and points.

"See, Elizabeth, there they are," encircled by the trees, the sky opens wide above them.

At once, neither brother nor sister makes a sound. The vault of heaven is around them. It covers them like a midnight-blue ocean, ruled by a grand luminous crescent hovering in the east, and dappled everywhere with glittering silver stars.

"Wow," Elizabeth says wide-eyed at the moon.

"Yeah," Blackwell sets her down. She still holds his hand.

"That moon sure is pretty," Elizabeth says. "I think it follows me around sometimes."

Standing at the end of the drive, Melena calls, "Elizabeth. Blackwell."

"Come on," Blackwell tugs at the sleeve of her dress. "Let's go start Halloween."

Basking in the moonlight, Elizabeth sighs and follows her big brother over to their mailbox. Ghosts and goblins illuminate the yard while Jack O' Lanterns dot the three staircases.

A tape sounds from the front bushes, beginning with a chilling scream followed by wolf howls and the cackling of witches. The flickering pumpkins shine bright against the darkness. Side by side for a moment, the family stands together admiring the seasonally ghoulish appeal of their home.

--·>===○ ◎===·<·--

Mid-winter, Melena stands in the kitchen, the phone cradled in one hand. With her free hand, she draws continuous vertical lines on a small piece of yellow paper at the top of a note pad.

Like a subtle form of violence, Melena's pen strokes scratch into the next sheets. She always knew it would happen one day and she would be alone. Pearl can't help with the business, she thinks, and Leopold is just a child. Melena and Pearl have always cared for their baby brother.

Ernest comes to the line and Melena looks up. She stares at the blank TV.

"Ernest," Melena says, "it's Daddy. He's had a heart attack."

Ernest leans over an architectural plan and puts one hand down on the design. He takes his glasses off.

He's truly shocked.

"My goodness, Melena," he asks, "is he ...."

"He's at the hospital." She squeezes the pen in her hand. "Pearl said his vital signs are stable, but ..." Melena hesitates, "they don't know how much damage there was."

Closing his eyes, Ernest imagines Pratt sitting in his office with his cronies and tries to figure out what he should do now. He has a three o'clock phone appointment with the commissioner's office.

"I can't leave work right now," Ernest says. "If Pratt's stable, then it'll be all right if I come down this evening."

Melena replaces the pen in a ceramic apple-shaped mug, trying to ignore the fact that she needs his help right now.

"I'm going to throw some things in a bag," she says, "and go get Elizabeth from school. You can bring the boys with you when you come. I'm going to drop Elizabeth off and then I'll be at the hospital. You can meet me there."

"All right," Ernest says and sits down in his chair. "Don't get in that car and drive too fast, Melena. You're upset and you could get in an accident on those back roads."

"I'll be fine," she says. "I know the way. Good-bye, Ernest."

"All right," he says, "good-bye."

Inside her preschool classroom, Elizabeth watches the class's goldfish, swimming in a fishbowl on the window sill. She wrinkles her nose.

"Mommy," she says.

The items in Melena's arms are perched awkwardly as she and Elizabeth stand together in front of a wall of wooden cubbyholes labeled with the children's names. Melena turns around to make sure she has all of Elizabeth's belongings.

"Elizabeth," she says, "do you have everything, sweetheart?"

Elizabeth stands on her tiptoes, peering into the cubbyhole with her name on it.

"Yes, Mommy," she says. "You have my drawing?"

"Yes, I do." Melena pulls Elizabeth's coat tight around her, fastening the wooden buttons.

Elizabeth wrinkles her nose again.

"Mommy?" Am I going to the doctor today? Is that why we're leaving?"

"No, honey, I'm afraid it's not." Melena holds her hand out for Elizabeth and thinks of the doctors she'll have to confront later.

"Are we going to get ice cream?"

"No," Melena says, "but maybe you can have some later at Momma Bell's. Luke and Blackwell will be there tonight and we'll all go out to dinner."

Melena waves to Elizabeth's teacher and leads Elizabeth out the door of her preschool classroom across the lawn of Molls Road Elementary School. They cross to her shiny Porsche, whose paint is the color of a new penny.

The most recent model and a gift from Ernest, it is a symbol of his efforts to improve their marriage . Melena sees that Elizabeth is buckled safely inside and gets behind the wheel.

Elizabeth turns and looks at the tiny bucket seats behind her.

"My blanky," she says reaching for the soft pink quilt.

Melena deposits the blanket in Elizabeth's lap along with her baby pillow. Elizabeth squishes it all in her hands and holds it under her chin. She adapts well wherever Melena takes her.

Melena's hands shake slightly as she hears the high-performance engine come to life. Less than five minutes later, Elizabeth is asleep, lulled by the purr of the motor. Her head presses against the pillow, flattened against the car door as she grips her blanket tightly.

Well over two hours later, Melena pushes open the sliding-glass door of her parents' house, letting out several small dogs. Three poodles, a Maltese and a mutt—Peaches, Honey, Theodore, Suzanne and Nutty—bark in a cacophony of yipping that follows Melena erratically.

"Hello, Alice," she says, trying to dodge the dogs.

"Hi there, Shug," Alice puts out her cigarette and steps over to hug Melena. Her lime-green polyester pants match her striped button-up shirt.

Alice says, "Look at you, Miss Elizabeth, aren't you just all grown up?"

"I'm not grown," Elizabeth says. She yawns and looks at the dogs. Theodore pounces on her, licks her face and runs away. The other dogs scatter and roam throughout the house. None of them really like children.

Melena puts her bags down on the kitchen table. The urgency she feels intensifies.

"Will you watch Elizabeth while I run to the hospital?" she asks.

Alice smiles, "You know I will, child. Your brother's here. I don't know how much he understands of what happened to your daddy, but you go on, I'm doing some stuff around the house."

"You're a lifesaver, Alice."

"It's nothing, baby. You go on now and be with your momma."

She pushes her tinted sunglasses up on her head. Alice has been there for the Dupree family on many dire, hushed-up occasions, some that Melena doesn't even know about.

"I'll send someone back in a couple of hours," Melena says.

She kisses Elizabeth on the forehead and her short blond hair falls forward.

"I'll be back in a little while, Elizabeth. Mind Alice, all right?"

"All right, Mommy," Elizabeth answers. She sits down on a white stool positioned in front of a television.

"Bye, then," Melena says. She speeds in the Porsche, tires squealing, all the way to the hospital.

Alice, dust rag in hand, walks over to Elizabeth who stares at the TV. An Elvis movie set in Hawaii plays on the tiny screen. Hand on her hip, Alice reaches for a pack of menthol cigarettes next to the TV.

Alice and Bell both love to smoke. They take cigarette breaks throughout the day to discuss their favorite soap opera stories. Alice handles a small ashtray.

"Are you thirsty?" she asks.

"Yes, ma'am." Elizabeth turns to her. "Can I please have something to drink?"

"You sure can, baby," Alice exhales a long stream of smoke. "How about one of your grandma's colas?"

"Yeah," Elizabeth smiles.

"I even think there're some candy bars in that refrigerator of hers if you know where to look."

"Can I go get one?"

"Yes, you can, but you come straight back here to Alice, hear me?"

"Yes ma'am, Alice."

Elizabeth walks down the hall toward Bell's room. She passes several doors and turns at the end of the hall. Momma Bell's door stands open. Elizabeth steps inside and shuts it quietly behind her.

Rising on tiptoe, she turns on the light and the room sparkles before her eyes. Glass-encased dolls dressed in satin and velvet stand in several cabinets around the room. Locked away, their porcelain faces smile, forever poised in time.

Under Elizabeth's shoes, the lush carpet contracts and expands as she slowly crosses the floor. Stopping at the large, marble-topped, triple dresser she touches one of the crystal-studded strands that hang from the gold, baroque Italian lamps. It swings, scattering reflected light in shimmering rays.

Elizabeth runs her fingers up the leaf tiers springing from the lamp's center and imagines herself a glorious queen with these shiny trinkets in her crown. Whirling around to face her subjects, Elizabeth stares down the dolls with commanding eyes. She would make them dance for her.

Sighing, she steps to Bell's bed to lean back against the red velvet headboard. *This is where the queen sits*, Elizabeth thinks and lays her cheek against the soft fabric. She sees her velvet throne and herself perched comfortably in her Cinderella dress with many of her adoring subjects laying cookies and cakes at her feet.

Her eyes fall upon the bathroom door, and she relinquishes her throne for the prospect of candy. A small brown refrigerator sits on the bathroom counter, and as Elizabeth opens it, foggy white air pours out the door. A row of glass Coke bottles and piles of Butterfingers wait inside.

Taking one of each, she steps past the blue bathtub, which sits sunken into the floor, and out of Bell's bathroom. Her eyes linger on the glass cases. At the bedroom door, Elizabeth reaches for the switch again and wonders if the dolls will sleep when the lights go out.

In the kitchen, Alice stands over the sink filling a bucket with Pine-Sol and water.

"Elizabeth, you knew just where everything was."

Elizabeth sets the Coke on the counter and opens the candy bar.

"You know," Alice says, "Leopold's been sitting down there in his room all by his self. He just came up a minute ago to get a Popsicle. Poor thing, he never has anybody to play with."

"What's he doing?" Elizabeth asks.

"I think he's watching some of that wrestling on TV."

"Oh," Elizabeth takes a bite out of her candy bar.

"Why don't you go keep him company while I finish the bathroom floors."

Alice waits to make sure Elizabeth is occupied.

Elizabeth grabs her Coke. "Okay," she says and walks to the opposite end of the kitchen out into the dining room.

Here, the walls glimmer with baby-blue satin wallpaper. Shag carpet of the same hue runs the length of the dining room floor and out the right side toward the front of the house.

The carpet extends down four stairs and into a larger room covered in the same satin wallpaper. A long silky couch stretches across the opposite wall and more crystal-adorned lamps stand on the two opposing end tables. In front of the couch, a kidney-shaped gold table sits low to the ground with a bunch of red glass grapes resting in a bunch on one end.

As Elizabeth walks down, she twist her head to the right, turning away from the bright sunshine filtering through the translucent, white curtains. Another TV, this one a little larger, blares from on top of a white desk in the corner.

To the right of the desk, a single mattress bed, stained with food spills, runs vertically into the pretty room like a line that does not belong. Behind the desk sits Leopold, cherry-red Popsicle in hand.

"Cookie!" Leopold cries in his Down's syndrome voice. Thirty now and very overweight, he stays in this room whenever Pratt isn't at home. Red Popsicle syrup drips down his hands.

"Hi, Leopold," Elizabeth says.

He motions for her to come over.

"You're watching wrestling." Elizabeth points to the screen with her Coke bottle, holding the candy bar in her other hand.

Leopold reaches over and picks her up off of the floor, smearing some of the red Popsicle on her shirt. He sets her down on his knee and holds her with one hand.

Melena enters the family room at the intensive care unit of Holiday General frantic for news. A soap opera plays quietly on a TV in the corner, and a small sign near the door bears directions to the hospital chapel.

"How is he?" Melena asks Pearl.

"He's going to have some speech problems," she says throwing her arms over her sister's shoulders for a brief embrace, "and the doctor said Daddy'll have some difficulty walking from now on, but other than that, he's alive."

"Momma," Melena says bending down to hug Bell, "what happened?"

Bell lays her hands down on the armrest of her portable wheelchair thinking she's been cursed. She shakes her head and brushes her tinted, ash-blond hair away from her eyes.

"Paul found him," she says. "He was out in the warehouse walking through the cabinets, looking for Pratt and there he was, lying on the floor, clutching at his heart with one hand. Paul said he ran to the phone as fast as he could, and the men put me in the ambulance so I could ride with him."

Bell's fingers tap on the top of the wide plastic armrest. Her eyes are red. Without Pratt, she wonders how the money will keep coming in.

"Someone's going to have to look in on Paul and the other men," she says. "They can run the cabinet business but not like your daddy. You girls are going to have to keep a check on things until your father is better." Pratt's needed her before. Since the car accident, Bell learned to delegate the work she couldn't see to without her legs.

Pearl and Melena glance at one another, silent. Melena exhales, thinking of her fallen father and his responsibilities now becoming her own.

Bell asks her, "Where's my little lamb chop?"

"Elizabeth is at the house with Alice and Leopold," Melena says.

"Oh good, I can't wait to see my darlin'." Bell pulls her large, white leather purse off the back of her chair. She rummages through it searching for her cigarettes.

Melena runs her hand through her hair and leans against the wall.

"Ernest is coming with the boys this evening," she says.

"You all can stay with me," Bell insists. "We got plenty of room."

She puts a long cigarette in her mouth and starts to flick her lighter.

"Momma," Pearl says, "you can't smoke in here."

"Damn it, shit," Bell says, "stupid hospital. One of y'all take me outside right now so I can smoke."

Dr. Willerby comes from ICU and leans down by his old friend taking Bell by the shoulder.

"He's resting now, Bell," Willerby says. He pulls back his white doctor's jacket revealing clean green surgical scrubs.

"You and the girls can go in and see him, but just remember he's had some impairment."

"Thank you, Dr. Willerby," Melena says.

He nods. "I'm sorry to see you under such circumstances, Melena, but nonetheless, it's good to see you."

Melena manages a smile, steps behind Bell's chair and grips the handles.

"Momma," she says, "you're going to have to wait for that cigarette." Melena pushes Bell forward.

"Come on, Pearl. Let's go see Daddy."

---

Many months pass with Melena and Elizabeth making the two-hour trip between Larnee and Holiday frequently. During this time, the Shades and the Starlings adjust their hectic schedules in order to maintain the Dupree family business.

As the seasons change, Pearl and Melena, feeling the added strain of their new obligations, consider selling the business their father created, but soon enough, Pratt recovers. With help from his associates, he regains control of the warehouses, leaving Pearl and Melena to return to their own families.

Over a year later, Blackwell attends the local high school, Elizabeth is in kindergarten and Luke goes to a Christian school across town.

Relieved at her father's recovery, Melena loads the dirty dishes in the dishwasher with thoughts of Holiday in her head.

"Mom," Luke yells. He's grown now into a gangly adolescent. Most of his time is spent in the woods, riding dirt bikes with the neighborhood boys after school. He's perfected a jump that propels from the back yard through the air to land a good fifteen feet on the driveway. Melena screams in terror whenever she happens to see him do it.

Coming back from her reverie, she asks, "Yes, Luke?"

"Where's my blue toboggan?"

"It should be with your long-johns," she says. Elizabeth comes down the stairs with her new Blue Sapphire Barbie in hand.

"Mommy," she says. "Can I go play flashlight tag with Luke and the other kids?"

"No, honey," Melena says. "You're not old enough to play outside at night."

"What about when summer comes?" Elizabeth turns her Barbie over and over in her hands.

"No, Elizabeth," Melena wipes the counter with a yellow checkered dishtowel. "Luke wasn't allowed to play outside until he was ten. You've got a while yet."

Elizabeth lies down in front of the heating vent beside Melena's feet. Resting on her side, she parades the Barbie back and forth in front of her. Luke jumps down the stairs, flashlight in hand.

Melena smiles at him. "Everyone's coming here, right Luke?"

Melena prefers that the children congregate at her house, believing this will assure their safety.

"*Uh, huh,*" he says.

"And y'all are going to stay in our yard, right?"

"Yes," he says as the doorbell rings.

The Larimore sisters, Kelly, Betsy and Allison, enter the kitchen with Vanessa Jackson and Buck from up the street. Melena addresses them all.

"Now," she says one hand on her hip, "I don't want you kids playing tag down in the woods. It's too dangerous at night and one of you might hurt yourself."

"Yes, Mrs. Starling," the four girls say.

"Buck," Melena looks directly at him, "did you hear me?"

"Yes, ma'am," Buck says.

"All right then, you all go on out. I'm going to call you all back in after a while for some hot chocolate."

"Yes, ma'am," they say.

Luke leads them into the yard and Melena watches as the children fan out amongst the trees. She leaves the front door open to check on them periodically.

The presence of the neighborhood kids fills Melena with a domestic tranquility that eludes her too often. Opening the freezer, she pulls out the ice cream, deciding to give Elizabeth a treat since she cannot play with the older children.

A few nights later, sometime after dinner, Ernest stands beside the dining room table. He calls to Elizabeth.

"Yes, Daddy," she looks up from her Barbies as they ride around in Barbie's yellow Corvette.

"Can you come down to the living room for a second?" he asks.

Elizabeth walks with her dolls in her hands. She has her blue Chinese pajamas on.

"Come on over and sit by me," he says and pats the cushion next to him on the green floral couch.

He doesn't know how to take the next step.

Elizabeth sets her Barbies on the coffee table and climbs up beside her father. Alone in the kitchen, Melena sits at the table looking through a Sears' catalog. She ignores the conversation starting in the living room below.

Fidgeting with his hands, Ernest asks, "You sure like those Barbies, Elizabeth, don't you?"

"Yeah, Daddy. They like to ride around in their Corvette and play in their house."

"That's good," Ernest says. "Elizabeth, there's something I have to talk to you about."

"Okay, Daddy," she folds her hands in front of her and waits.

Ernest looks at her and hates what he's about to say. Melena thought it would be better if he broke the news.

"Your mother and I," he scratches his forehead, "well, sometimes people ... sometimes people who are married, well, they just can't seem to get along together. You know, they have things that make them disagree with one another so they decide not to be married anymore."

He stops to make sure she comprehends what he is saying.

"*Uh, huh*," Elizabeth says thinking about the way her Barbie and Ken fight each other.

"Your mother and I ..." he leans against the couch and starts in again, "well, we have some disagreements, and we've decided not to be married anymore. But this doesn't have to be a bad thing necessarily."

Elizabeth looks up at him. "It doesn't?"

Usually, when her Barbie and Ken fight, the disagreement resolves with one of them running over the other with the yellow corvette. She wonders if that will happen now.

"No, Cinderelli," Ernest says, "it doesn't." He puts his arm around Elizabeth's shoulder.

"You know at Christmas when we go visit Momma Bell and Aunt Pearl and they give you presents?"

"Yes," she says.

"And then my momma and daddy come and they give you presents, too?"

"Yes."

"Well, it'll be just like that," he smiles. "You'll end up having four rounds of presents at Christmas and on your birthday, but they'll all be at different times. Your momma will give you presents, then you'll come see me and I'll give you presents. You'll still have to see your grandparents and they'll give you presents, too."

He pauses, waiting for a reaction from her. Like many men who bring home the money, Ernest associates his emotional contribution to his family with material things.

"Oh," Elizabeth says and looks at the floor, "but where will we live, Daddy?"

His heart sinks; he, never wanted things to go this far again.

"Well, when your kindergarten gets out for break, you and your mother are going to go to Holiday to stay with Momma Bell and Aunt Pearl. After that, I'm not sure. It's going to take some time for us to figure all this out, Elizabeth, but in the meantime you'll get to stay down there and play with all your friends."

"Daddy," Elizabeth says, "I don't want to leave. Do we have to go? Why don't you come with us?"

Ernest frowns. "That's what I'm trying to tell you, Elizabeth. You and your mother have to go. It's what she ... it's the best thing to do for everyone."

Elizabeth looks over at her Barbies lying on the table and starts to cry. Ernest picks her up and throws her over his shoulder, patting her on the back and letting her cry.

"There, there," he says. "It's going to be fine, just you wait and see. You'll get so many Christmas presents you won't know what to do."

⤞═◉═◈⤝

Just before Elizabeth's school lets out for the summer, Melena takes the Porsche to Holiday and swaps it out for Bell's roomy Lincoln, needing something larger for the move. Two weeks later, she steps through Bell's doorway, pushing Elizabeth along in front of her.

"Hey, Momma," she says.

Peaches, looking scraggly and irritable, darts out from under the counter to charge Elizabeth, standing two feet away from her barking endlessly.

"Well, hey there, you two." Bell pushes the knob on her electric wheelchair forward and glides across the room toward Elizabeth. Before she can stop, Elizabeth hops up into her lap.

"Hey, Momma Bell," she says.

"Look at you, Princess Elizabeth. How are you today, darling?" Bell and Elizabeth always pretend to be glamorous movie stars.

Elizabeth bats her eyes. "I'm fine, darling. I brought my Barbies and my toys because we're going to be staying here for a while."

"Yes you are, indeed," Bell says. "And that means you and I are going to spend lots and lots of time together."

Melena arranges their bags in one corner and steps to Bell. She leans down to hug her with one arm.

"Where's Daddy?" she asks already guessing.

Bell taps her polished red nails. "Oh, in the warehouse smoking too many cigarettes," she says. "You need help getting the rest of your things out of the car, don't you?"

"Yeah," she says. "I'll run down there and see who I can find."

Melena closes the sliding-glass door, keeping the dogs inside, and tries to plan the rest of her day as she walks down the brick steps. The early summer heat annoys her and flattens her hair. She crosses the driveway and steps carefully through the woods to the lot where the two warehouses sit—elongated, faded yellow buildings, side by side.

Inside the sprawling Dupree home, Bell turns up the volume on the kitchen TV and pulls out a cigarette.

"Elizabeth, honey," she says.

"Yes, Momma Bell."

"How about being the precious angel I know you are and going to grab us girls a couple of Co-Colas and candy bars."

"Sure," Elizabeth says but stops. "Momma Bell, smoking is bad."

"Aw," Bell exhales, "you'll be fine, sugar. Run along, now."

Over at the warehouse, Melena enters Pratt's office and waves a round hello to the gathered men. The air is thick and gray and smells like an ashtray that hasn't been emptied in ten years. Nutty wanders from behind Pratt's desk while Suzanne sits in Pratt's lap under his hand.

"How y'all doing?" she asks.

"Fine, fine," they say, hardly shifting in their seats. The skin on their faces looks like tanned leather.

"Hey there, Daddy," Melena says. She walks to Pratt who stands up slowly to give her a hug.

"So, you and little Elizabeth made it?" he says tugging the back of his pants upward with one hand and holding Suzanne's little body in the other.

"We sure did." She leans behind Pratt's desk and smiles.

"Hey there, Leopold. Big Sissy's back." She steps over and hugs him, too.

"Listen here," Melena says to the men, "I'm afraid I'm going to have to borrow some of you strong fellas, and that includes you too, Leopold."

Positioned at his father's right hand, Leopold nods, mimicking the other men in the room. He pats his stomach and in his thick voice says, "I'm strong." Since Leopold is an avid fan of wrestling, strength is a concept he understands.

"Y'all come on back to the house then and I'll give y'all a nice glass of sweet tea," she says, frowning at the glass in front of her father.

"It'll be a lot better than that bourbon you all are drinking."

She takes Leopold by the arm and pulls him upward. "Come on, now," Melena says, "time's a-wasting."

Shuffling their limbs and grumbling the way old men do when their peace is disturbed, Pratt and the other men get to their feet. They begrudgingly leave their drinks behind them.

The weathered group follows Melena to Bell's cluttered Lincoln. Under her careful direction, the men carry her belongings into her father and mother's house. By the end of the day, Melena and Elizabeth are settled into a room that they will share on the upper floor. As they rest outside around the patio table, the evening heat of the long Holiday summer envelops them in a cloud of humidity.

"Momma?" Melena asks one morning. "Will you watch Elizabeth? I've got some errands to run."

"Sure," Bell says. "Where you going?"

"The Bordeaux Center to see Pearl at the drugstore, then Patsy's going to do my hair."

"That'll be fine," Bell picks up a cigarette. "Would you pick me up a large jar of Tums?"

"Yes," Melena says, "but I asked you not to take so many."

Bell ignores her, "Alice is here till five, and Elizabeth?"

"Yes." Elizabeth looks up from the Transformers coloring book spread before her on the table. She hasn't played with any Transformers since the last time she saw Luke.

"We'll be fine while Mommy gets her hair done, darling, won't we?"

"Yes, darling."

Sunglasses in her hair, Melena comes to the table and kisses Elizabeth on the forehead.

"All right then," she says, "I'll see you all this afternoon."

Not a half-hour later, Bell drives her chair to the back edge of the kitchen and leans out slightly over the short set of stairs. Her head is in her hand.

"Alice," she yells. "Alice."

Alice cannot hear her. She works in one of the back bedrooms in the basement level of the house. Bell pulls her chair back toward the table and looks at Elizabeth.

"Elizabeth," she says. "Run downstairs for me and find Alice. Tell her to come upstairs, that I need to talk to her."

Elizabeth's eyes widen. "*Uh*, yeah, Momma Bell."

She slowly pushes her chair back under the table and tiptoes out the back of the kitchen, down the stairs to the door that opens to the lower level of the house.

The lower level foyer is a crossroads. On Elizabeth's right is the staircase to the below-ground rooms and on her left, the double doors lead to the road-side of the house where four white columns stand like sentinels on the porch.

In front of her stand two more doors that lead into the great room, the holiday room. It gleams golden and crystal. Behind her are the double doors to Leopold's room. Her hand is just in front of the handle to the basement door.

"I'll *umm*," she says to no one, "I'll just be right back."

Elizabeth reaches for the small brass knob and pulls the door open. Musty air flows over her as she stares down the dimly lit stairwell and into the darkness at the foot of the stairs.

To her right, an electric chair with a fold down, brown leather seat waits, empty and attached to the staircase wall. The metal guiding handle flashes on the armrest.

Elizabeth, though she knows its proper use, thinks it is some horrible device. Reaching toward it, she pushes the handle forward. The loud grinding noise frightens her. She lets go the control and runs down the stairs hesitating at the bottom.

"Alice?" she calls, surveying the dim light emanating from the end of the hallway that runs to her left.

"Alice," she says again, not wanting to go any farther into the room.

"Yes, honey," Alice calls back from down the hall.

Elizabeth relaxes. "Momma Bell says she needs you."

"I'm coming," Alice says. She appears in the doorway of one of the rooms and they go up the staircase together.

Alice follows Elizabeth into the kitchen. "What's wrong, Bell?"

Bell puts her hand to her forehead. "I've a little headache and I just took a BC. Will you watch Elizabeth while I lay down for a while?"

"Sure thing, Bell. Leopold is downstairs and they can play until we have lunch." Alice takes her menthols off the top of the TV. She lights one and blows the smoke over Elizabeth's head.

"You go on now and lie down," she says. "You'll get to feeling better and me and my girl here will get on with our day."

Bell nods and pats Elizabeth on the arm. Followed by Peaches, Honey and Teddy, she drives her wheelchair back to her velvet, satin and gold bedroom, where she lies down on her bed to fall asleep for a few hours.

Alice looks at Elizabeth and leans to the counter to flick her ash into a small silver bowl.

"You hungry, Shug?"

"No ma'am," Elizabeth says.

"Well, I got to finish up downstairs and then get lunch together," Alice says. "You go on and watch TV with Leopold and holler downstairs if you get hungry, okay?"

Elizabeth looks at her feet, "Okay."

Alice returns to the lower level and Elizabeth wonders what Blackwell and Luke are doing. She wishes she could play with them. Standing at the top of the stairs, she looks down into the satin sitting room.

Over the sound of the blaring TV she calls, "Leopold."

"Cookie," he says excited and walks to where she stands.

Leopold takes her by the wrist and leads her over to his desk. He sets her down on top of his bed facing the TV and reaches up to adjust the antennae. The picture shifts, clears and reveals two lovers in bed on "The Young and the Restless."

Elizabeth gazes at the screen wide-eyed.

Fifteen minutes later, Elizabeth stares at the ceiling past the fat hanging down in her face from the back side of Leopold's neck. She gasps for air under his immense weight as he shifts around on top of her. Leopold holds her down and runs his fat, cracked tongue across her firmly shut mouth and cheek. Beneath him she squirms.

"*Ugh,*" Elizabeth gasps, confused, even though this isn't the first time Leopold has done something like this. She tries to breathe. She tries to get out from under him, but his weight crushes her and his strength smothers her useless efforts.

-->==⊙==<--

Before summer ends, Melena returns to Larnee and the Starling home again. Having left Ernest and filed for divorce, Melena thinks now he has seen that she's not afraid to leave him. She believes Ernest will change and tells herself that things will be different this time.

With fall just weeks away, Melena places two brown bag lunches next to the basement door.

"Blackwell," she shouts, "you better come down before your breakfast gets cold."

Melena turns to the kitchen table. "How're the biscuits, you two?"

"Good," Luke says gobbling another one, while Elizabeth nods.

"Ernest," she says, "These kids are going to eat everything."

"I'll be down in a minute," he calls.

Blackwell takes his seat at the table. His rust colored Polo sweater complements his perfectly pressed light khaki pants for the first day of senior year.

Melena taught Blackwell how to dress well and he quickly learned the benefits of making a good first impression. No longer at the Adventist school, all the girls want him at his new highschool, and because of that, all the guys want to be his friend.

Luke sits comfortably in a long-sleeve, red cotton Polo and dark blue Levi jeans. It's the first day of fifth grade at a new private religious school. Elizabeth will be in a building connected to his entering the first. Ernest prefers the children in a strict religious setting though he doesn't like the price, and Melena likes her children in a good school with extensive facilities.

"Mommy," she says, "do you think the Wesleyan school will be fun?"

"Well, sure it will, honey," Melena says. "Luke will be there, and you'll make a bunch of new friends."

Elizabeth asks, "Are you coming, too, Blackwell?"

"No, I go right around the corner." Blackwell winks at his mom practicing his charm.

"I'm done with that kind of school."

"Oh."

"Good morning," Ernest says adjusting his tie.

"Good morning, Daddy," Elizabeth shouts as the boys mumble their hellos. "It's my first day of first grade."

"I know it is," Ernest says. "Don't you look nice in your green alligator turtleneck?" He pinches her on the cheek.

Melena leans against the sink watching her family at the table. "Ernest," she says.

"Yes, Melena?"

"I'm going to need a check for Elizabeth's dance lessons. They begin this afternoon and she has to have ballet slippers and tap shoes, too."

Ernest pinches the bridge of his nose. *All people want from me is money*, he thinks. *That's all I'm good for.*

"How much is all this going to cost, Melena?"

Melena figures the amount in her head and Elizabeth watches waiting for their voices to rise.

"The classes," Melena says, "are fifty a month and the shoes will be twenty dollars each, so ninety will do."

"Melena," Ernest says, voice calm, "next time, please give me a little forewarning before you ask me for ninety dollars at breakfast."

He pulls a large checkbook out of his briefcase while Melena takes a piece of bacon from a plate on the table and nibbles at it.

"Oh, Ernest, I'm sorry, but I know you have the money so I didn't think it would be a problem."

Ernest adjusts the pen in his hand. "I'm not made of money, Melena. Lawyers are very expensive, and we have some very large bills to pay right now."

This fact angers him. Melena whispers toward to his ear.

"Well, maybe if you stayed home at night instead of coming in from work late all the time, you wouldn't have that problem." She looks at his feet and smiles.

"Oh, and Ernest, those are really nice shoes. How much did they cost you, less than three hundred?"

Ernest looks up at her. "You really are something, you know that?"

One time when they were still kids, Ernest saw Melena punch a girl at the drive-in and knock her flat out on the ground. Sometimes he thinks what he sees in his wife is a distorted glimpse of that fiery girl.

Blackwell clears his throat. "So," he says, "it's about time you got going Mom, *huh?*"

"Oh," Melena says looking at the clock. "You're right. Elizabeth, run and get your little green bag, and Luke, get your pack. We've got to leave in five minutes or you'll be late."

Elizabeth and Luke run upstairs to gather their things.

"Now Blackwell," Melena says, "don't speed or be late for school."

"I know, Mom."

Melena straightens the collar of the shirt underneath his sweater. "You look so handsome and preppy."

"Mom," Blackwell says embarrassed.

Luke and Elizabeth hop down the stairs one after the other. "Elizabeth, honey," Melena says, "do not jump down those stairs again. It's bad for your knees."

"Luke did it."

"I know he did, but I have told him a thousand times, and *he* doesn't listen, You can't follow in his footsteps." Melena breathes in. "All right, down to the car you two."

"Good-bye," Elizabeth says waving at Ernest and Blackwell.

"Good-bye, Cinderelli," Ernest says. "You have a great first day."

"I will."

"Come on, Elizabeth." Melena shoos Elizabeth in front of her.

"Ernest, we're having spaghetti for dinner tonight. What time are you going to be home?"

"Melena," Ernest shakes his head, "I don't know. I'd say around six-thirty."

"Fine." she says.

Ernest looks at the television and bites into his second biscuit. He and Blackwell sit silent while both listen to the news. During a commercial Ernest detaches himself from the TV and talks to his son the way he thinks a father should.

"How's football practice going?" he asks, but continues. "I bet you've got some good friends at Brighton by now. No one's giving you a hard time, are they?"

"No, Dad," Blackwell answers, "all the guys are cool."

Sometimes Blackwell wants to tell his father not to complain about the money Melena asks for, but he doesn't because he wants to race and go to college. No one but Ernest has the money to pay for Blackwell's dreams.

"That's good," Ernest says, "and you all have a game Friday?"

"Yep," Blackwell sips his orange juice. "Southeastern. Hey, did that carburetor come in yet?"

"Oh", Ernest says, "it did. We need to finish the engine this weekend. You know, we have to win two more track events if we're going to the championships with a high point standing."

"Yeah," Blackwell says and stands. "I guess we'll be in the garage all weekend. I got to go."

Ernest asks, "How's the Firebird running?"

"It's doing fine."

"Not burning any oil?"

"No," Blackwell says, "runs like a dream."

"Okay then, have a good day."

"Yeah Dad, you, too."

Later on that evening, Melena and the children sit around the table eating dinner. Luke and Blackwell stuff forkfuls of pasta, saturated with Melena's homemade sauce, into their mouths while Elizabeth swirls her buttered pasta around on her plate.

At one end of the table, Melena meticulously eats her dinner one slow bite at a time, watching the clock out of the corner of her eye.

Luke reaches for another piece of garlic bread and smiles at Melena. "This is the best ever, Mom," he says.

Blackwell wipes his chin. "Yeah, I was so hungry after practice I could eat three plates of this."

Melena's sauce, slow cooked all day long, is their favorite and the boys try to please her with their compliments. Blackwell and Luke are both aware of their mother's anger, and they hope to distract her from Ernest's absence.

Elizabeth asks, "Mommy, can I have some more par-may-zian cheese?" She joins their efforts in her own way though none of the children are fully conscious of their wish to act as peacemakers.

"Sure," Melena sprinkles a little onto her plate and resumes her silent watch of the clock.

A door shuts in the basement. Blackwell looks up at Melena as Ernest's footsteps come up the stairs.

Blackwell predicts his mother's every thought. Melena has spoken frankly to him about Ernest since his birth, and his stomach turns at the thought of another dreaded confrontation at the dinner table.

Elizabeth leans across her plate and whispers to Luke, "*Og.*" She's afraid.

"*Og, og,*" he says and shakes his head trying to tell her to just be quiet. Elizabeth tries for a moment.

Melena's shoulders tighten and her manner becomes rigid and formal. Ernest opens the basement door, sets his things down in the hallway and steps into the kitchen.

"Hi, Daddy," Elizabeth shouts. Melena winces at the obvious affection in her daughter's voice.

"Hello," Ernest says, sounding tired.

Melena doesn't look at him, "We waited for you for forty-five minutes, but the kids were starving, and I didn't know when you were coming home."

"That's fine." Ernest walks to the kitchen counter to dole out his dinner. He ignores the tension in the room.

"How was your first day of school, Elizabeth?" he asks.

"It was a lot of fun," she says. "I met lots of other girls and we played outside and some of them dance, too, but not where I do, and we did some Bible study and then we had a snack."

"That's nice," Ernest says sitting down at the head of the table across from Melena who refuses to look up at him.

Elizabeth pushes her fork around her plate. "After that ...."

"Elizabeth," Melena says, eyes fluttering as she represses her rage at Ernest, "sit still and eat your dinner."

"Yes, Mommy," she looks at her pasta. Pulling a couple of strands from the heap she loudly slurps them into her mouth

Blackwell talks about football practice and the pep rally on Friday while Luke interrupts with talk of the Enduro Karts they'll be racing in a couple of weeks.

Melena sits silent, brooding over the serial crimes she feels Ernest has committed against their family. Elizabeth stares at them all, eyes moving intermittently to whomever has control of the conversation.

---

New Year's Eve day, donning denim knickers and a tight, plaid, button-down shirt, Melena adjusts the bright red bandanna folded and tied in a neat triangle across her head. She takes Elizabeth's hand and leads her from the restroom back toward the shop area that sits in the center of the Daytona Speedway.

The infield is packed with campers, trailers and cars scattered all across the grass and in the asphalt parking lot. At each corner of the track, looming high over the protective barrier, is a giant orange ball painted in dark blue with the number '76.

Melena's shoulder-length, blond hair curls around her ears. She waves to another racer's mother as she heads toward the pit area, and smiles. Her natural sophistication and beauty shine beneath the bright Florida sun as she walks hand-in-hand with her daughter toward the garage.

An engine roars behind them and chugs to a slow growl by their side. Melena jumps, pulling Elizabeth up with her. They land and Luke throws his heels out to stop his bike, laughing with his wide toothy smile.

"You shouldn't scare us like that," Melena says.

Engine grease marks his face, and the sleeves of his racing suit sit tied in a knot around his waist. He seems so happy when he's at the track; no one would ever know how unhappy he really is.

"Hey there, little sister," Luke revs the engine on the miniature motorcycle. "Let's go for a spin."

"Yeah," Elizabeth shouts. She lets go of Melena's hand and hops on the Pocket Bike.

"Now, Luke," Melena says, "drive slow with your sister on the back. There's not much room so make sure she holds on."

"Okay, Mom," the children respond dutifully. Luke grins back at Elizabeth. "I'll make sure she falls off."

"Luke," Melena says.

Releasing the clutch, he throttles the engine to full speed. Elizabeth's arms grasp him from behind and she giggles as her perfectly arranged hair now flies in the wind.

Melena shouts after them, but out of her reach, brother and sister terrorize the infield as they weave through groups of people walking from the shops to the track and over by the concession stand. Elizabeth loves to watch the pedestrians jump out of their way and imagines them fleeing from her queenly rule.

Suddenly, Luke stops. Elizabeth peers over his shoulder at the older racer pushing his kart out to the track to race in Blackwell's division. The Pocket Bike's engine chugs as it idles.

The older boy nods and winks at Elizabeth as he leans his chest onto his kart pusher and passes them by. Elizabeth hides behind Luke's back, then beats on it with her fist and yells at him.

"Go," she says, "go faster, go!"

Twenty minutes later Luke and Elizabeth pull into the garage where the Starlings have parked their karts with thirty of the many racers from all over the world. These racers fill all four of the enormous garages, each one lined inside with wooden worktables.

With their tools spread out on the counter around them, Ernest and Blackwell labor over the karts in one corner. Straightening her green corduroy pants, Elizabeth hops off the bike and grins, her hair tousled from the ride.

"That was fun!" she says to Melena who sits in a yellow folding chair. Melena takes Elizabeth's hand and turns her around.

Look at your hair." She pulls a brush from her purse. "You're all a mess."

Melena wants nothing more than for her family to look perfect, and her children to be safe, like they're supposed to be.

Blackwell and Ernest stand over Blackwell's open-wheel Enduro Kart working on the engine. An unspoken excitement lingers between them. The kart rests on a wide scissor-lift and stretches six feet long with two large rectangular gas tanks running down either side of the flat driver's seat. Blackwell's driver number 27 is stuck to the gas tanks.

Small, thick tires fill the garage area in stacked columns, and fresh ones sit on the wheel wells of Blackwell's kart ready to burn up the track at his average speed of 145 miles per hour. The smell of engine oil and grease lingers in the air, permeating their clothes and skin with "racer's perfume."

Ernest wipes his hands on his leather smock and scratches his nose with his pinky finger. Blackwell stands beside him in his black zip-up racing suit, the top part folded over his waist and gloves hanging out of his pockets. His orange T-shirt reads, "CKS, Comet Karts South."

"I believe that'll do it, Blackwell," Ernest steps back, greasy rag in hand. "As long as it holds, no one can beat you."

"'Cept for me," Luke says holding onto the foot pedals. A stronger sense of competition has begun to grow between them.

"Maybe if you were big enough to race in my class," Blackwell says, "but you're not. You're a boy, so you'll be racing with the juniors."

"I could beat you any day," Luke says pulling a pedal down.

Both of them were born with a natural talent for racing, but Blackwell hides his approval of his sibling.

"Dream on, stupid," Blackwell slaps his hand away. "Stop messing with my kart and go screw up your own."

"I want to race, Mommy," Elizabeth says pointing at the kart.

"No, you do not." Melena tries to convince her. "Pretty little girls don't want to race those dirty old karts. What would you do if you wrecked and messed up that beautiful face of yours?"

"*Uh*," Elizabeth says picturing a large scab on her face. "I like the way they smell."

Luke looks at her. "Yeah, Elizabeth, don't you know you're a girl. Girls can't race. If you wrecked, your face would look funnier than it already does."

"My face does not look funny!"

Luke whimpers to make fun, pretending that she's going to cry.

"Yes, it does, Chinese eyes."

"I am not Chinese," Elizabeth shouts. "They're just small."

"Elizabeth's adopted. Elizabeth's adopted."

"I am not," Elizabeth says. She buries her face in Melena's shoulder. "Mommy, tell Luke I'm not adopted."

"Luke," Melena says, "stop teasing your sister. You know good and well she's not adopted. Elizabeth has very beautiful and unique almond-shaped eyes. She's lucky that she has them."

81

"What time is it?" Ernest asks.

Melena looks at her watch, "Almost a quarter to one."

"All right, boys," Ernest says, "let's get this thing off the rack and go weigh in. Luke, you take the front. Blackwell and I will take the back."

Together, they heave the kart up off the scissor lift and onto the floor. They set it down gently and Blackwell turns to the counter behind them to gather his helmet and the stopwatch, which he tosses into the seat.

Luke positions the kart pusher's two forks against the steering wheel. He leans forward and drives the kart out of the busy shop while Ernest places their tools in the red wagon. Melena tucks a couple of foldout chairs under her arm and takes the time board in her other hand.

Elizabeth tugs at Blackwell's sleeve. "Can I sit in it?"

Blackwell smiles, picks her up and sets her down in the horizontal seat. She holds his helmet and the watch while Luke steers the kart from behind.

After weighing Blackwell and the kart together, they arrive at the grid and pull into Blackwell's pole position among the other racers in his class, the highest division. Having qualified into the first heat, he has the lead position. Melena steps over the three-foot guard wall and sets her chairs up behind it while Ernest and the children park the kart on the other side in front of her.

"Elizabeth," she says glaring at the commotion. Melena holds her hand out waiting.

Elizabeth frowns and hops over the wall to sit down in the chair beside Melena. Melena hands her a pair of pink sunglasses and the two sit in the sun watching Ernest with the boys. Luke squats down beside the farthest gas tank and whispers in Blackwell's ear.

"There's one of those Italian brothers," he says, gesturing toward the boy with his head. "I saw him a while ago while we were out riding."

"They're pretty good," Blackwell says, "but not as good as me."

Feeling confident in his engine and relaxed about the race, Blackwell thinks about Giovanni and Angelo's sister Francesca, they met last night behind the concession stand. For Blackwell, there's a girl at every track.

He slips his arms inside the sleeves of his racing suit. Zipped in, he reaches for his custom-painted helmet, air brushed with an Enduro kart on either side. Blackwell smiles at Melena and Elizabeth as he pulls it down over his head.

"You look cool," Elizabeth says.

He flips up the visor. "Thanks. Wish me luck, little sister."

"You're gonna win 'cause you're the fastest," she says.

"Be careful, Blackwell." Melena clutches at her heart. "Oh, Jesus, it would be the end of me if something happened to one of you kids." Though intensely fearful for their safety at times, she feels she keeps a watchful eye over them.

Blackwell lies down inside the Enduro kart. While the rest of his body remains horizontal, his shoulders and head lean against the headrest, which is an arm's length from the steering wheel. Ernest kneels beside the kart on the back left hand side with the electric starter in his hand.

"Gentlemen," the race announcer says, "start your engines."

Luke switches the battery on and Ernest starts the engine. All thirty Open-Wheel Enduros rev their engines, riders pumping the gas pedals to warm up the machines. The boisterous roar of their collective sound overpowers the pit area. Women plug their ears and step away, skirting the burgeoning fumes, while Elizabeth leaps from her seat toward the retaining wall.

Melena clutches the back of Elizabeth's shirt to keep her from jumping over. Iridescent gray and blue smoke flows from the exhausts, and the smell of racing fuel fills the air. The announcer holds the green flag aloft and jerks it down just as Ernest jumps back from the kart. Foot slamming onto the gas, Blackwell takes off in front of the pack and within moments secures a seven-second lead.

As Blackwell rounds the first lap, he signals pit row where Melena and Elizabeth sit. Standing in the grass adjacent to turn one, Ernest holds up his thumb and the time board to let Blackwell know the extent of his lead.

*He looks good*, Ernest thinks. *He really looks good, and that's a hell of an engine.*

Thirty-five laps later, Blackwell completes his victory lap and pulls into the pit past the other racers. The checkered flag flies in his left hand. He has won the International Championship of the World Karting Association for the third year in a row. Two races later, Luke wins the junior division championship and, at eleven years old, it is his first.

This very night the Starling family drives into Orlando to spend the evening and following day at Disney World. They celebrate New Year's Eve under the glittering fireworks display at the Magic Kingdom, and in another few days, they drive home to Larnee.

⤙⊙⤚

In the spring, the children look forward to the end of school and a long summer playing in the woods. The racing season has begun again and, although the boys do not attend every race, they, along with Ernest, leave town once or twice a month to compete. Elizabeth and Melena stay home where Elizabeth spends her afternoons at a dance studio excelling at ballet, tap and jazz.

Arms full of shoe boxes and plastic bags, Melena rings the doorbell of her home and shifts the weight of her packages to keep from dropping them. Elizabeth stands behind her in pink tights and a leotard, clutching her Capezio bag in her hand. The front door swings open.

"Oh, thank goodness you heard me, Sara."

Sara reaches toward her. "Give me those bags, Melena."

"You're a life saver," Melena sighs. "I didn't want to bring it all up through the basement. Come on, Elizabeth." Elizabeth follows her in. "You go change out of those dance clothes."

"Okay, Mommy," Elizabeth says and hops up the stairs to her room.

Melena leans toward her. "Wear the white dress with the strawberries on it hanging on the doorknob of your closet."

She turns into the kitchen thinking that everyone should look special for Grandma Starling's birthday.

She asks Sara, "Are the boys upstairs?"

"They sure are, and I think they're both ready to go. They've got their new ties on."

"I'm going to head on home now that you're here," she says. "Carl and I are going out for our anniversary."

"That's right," Melena says, "you just hold on one second. There's something for you over here."

Melena walks over to the cabinet above the stove and pulls a wine bottle down wrapped in silver paper.

"Oh, you know what this is," Melena says. "I know Adventists aren't supposed to have any alcohol, but I thought maybe you could have a sip when you got home from dinner. Sara, God wouldn't mind a toast to another year."

Sara smiles at her bashfully. "Well, maybe we could just have a sip. We did have a glass of champagne on our honeymoon, but usually Carl doesn't like to." She looks at the bottle. "Thanks, Melena."

They hug lightly and Sara turns to leave. Melena briefly takes her by the arm. "No," she says, "thank you for everything."

"Oh, I enjoy it." Sara waves and walks out the front door as Ernest's steps come up the basement stairs. Moments later he walks into the kitchen.

"Hi, Melena," he says annoyed already from a long day of work and the numerous problems lying in wait for him when he gets to the office tomorrow.

Ernest motions to the table. "What's all of this?"

"Oh, that," she says, "that's nothing, just some stuff Elizabeth needed for her final dance performance and her summer classes. They're going to be bluebirds," she smiles. "You know, I barely beat you home."

"I saw as I was pulling up," Ernest says and walks over to the boxes and bags lying on top of the table. He opens one large garment bag and pulls a blue-feathered, blue-sequined costume out. Looking at it, he shakes his head and lays it back inside the bag. He fishes the receipt out of the bottom and examines the total.

"Melena," he says holding it up, "what is this?"

"Whatever do you mean, Ernest?"

"One hundred forty-two dollars to Nancy Ray Dancing School?"

"Yes." Melena folds her arms in front of her. "It's for her recital costumes, Ernest. She has to have them in order to perform. You remember that your daughter is performing in her very first dance recital next weekend, don't you, Ernest?"

He lays the receipt on the table. "Don't get smart with me, Melena. How can a child's costumes cost this much money?"

"She also needed dancing shoes," she says, "and if you'll recall, our daughter takes three different types of dance."

"I just bought Elizabeth dancing shoes this fall. How could she possibly need them already?"

"Her feet are growing, Ernest. She's a child. They grow rather quickly, so you might want to pay attention."

"I have to work to pay the bills, Melena." This comment is Ernest's answer to every domestic issue he and Melena have. Work controls him and his time. He looks into the other bags.

"What's the rest of this stuff? The Gray Goose?" he asks remembering the expensive dress shop. "Don't tell me you've been back to that store, too."

Melena snaps, "Don't you dare talk to me that way, Ernest Starling. I haven't been there since before Christmas and Elizabeth needs clothes. She can't go around in pants that are too small for her and dresses that don't fit. I don't know why you're complaining. You've got plenty of money."

"Melena," he points at her, "that's the problem. You think I'm made of money. Every damn day it's something else, private school for Luke and Elizabeth, dancing lessons for Elizabeth, new clothes for you and Elizabeth."

"Don't you dare bring my name into this, you son of a bitch," Melena's head jerks to the side. "I haven't bought anything for myself in over a year."

"Yeah?" Ernest throws his arms wide. "Then where do the bills come from for the department store, Melena? How come the balance never goes down on your Belks' charge card?"

Up in her room putting on her shoes, Elizabeth hears her parents. Quietly, she walks over to the staircase, sits on the middle step and leans forward over her knees toward the kitchen. Every time they fight, Elizabeth listens.

"Ernest, how dare you question me about the money I spend on your children. Your sons have to have clothes, too, you know?"

"Did you think your children wouldn't grow or need anything?"

"It seems like a lot of money being spent on just the boys then," he says and picks up the receipts. Ernest looks through his wallet and places them carefully inside.

"Well, it's not," Melena says, "and what the hell do you care anyway? You spend so much money on those damn karts. You never seem to question that, Ernest. All the trips, hotels, all the parts and everything, you know what you are, Ernest?"

"No, Melena, I don't."

"You're a hypocrite and you hate women!" she says. "You spend thousands of dollars on you and your sons and then you have the gall to come in here and accuse me of spending a fortune on your daughter and myself."

"I know you didn't want me to have her Ernest," she says, "but really, you should still treat her the same as you treat your sons."

"Lower your voice, Melena," Ernest whispers. "How dare you say that I don't treat her like I treat the boys? I love Elizabeth, but you lord over her as if she belonged only to you, and don't talk to me about when we found out you were pregnant again."

He points at her. "You kept the appointment."

"And you went out of town and left me here to deal with it on my own," she shouts, secretly wanting Elizabeth to know the truth.

"Oh, but I didn't do it, did I? No, she's my daughter. There I was sitting in the room when I heard her call me. And weren't you pleased when I told you I was going to have the baby? *Hah*! The look on your face was priceless."

"Melena," Ernest says, "I love Elizabeth. Now calm down and be quiet." He scratches his forehead trying to pinpoint one single thought in the chaotic miasma swirling around in his brain.

"The children are upstairs," he says, "and we have to pick Momma up on the way to dinner. What time is it?"

Melena folds her arms in front of her. She feels helpless having no control over her own money. Saying nasty things to Ernest makes her feel better temporarily.

"Are you worried you're going to be late for your mother's birthday dinner, Ernest? Or do you hate her, too?"

"Melena," he says, "buy whatever the hell you want. You're so damn hard to talk to. I can't take it. I'm going to change clothes. We're leaving here in fifteen minutes."

Ernest steps out of the kitchen as Elizabeth scrambles off the stairs and into her room. He stops, seeing her slam her bedroom door.

"Oh, damn." he says.

Ernest walks to Elizabeth's room and starts to turn the door handle, but he stops, thoughts lingering on Melena. *There's nothing I can do*, he thinks. *She wouldn't believe me anyway*. He sighs and steps away to change out of his work clothes.

Inside of Elizabeth's pink and yellow room, she has flung herself into a large pile of stuffed animals gathered on the floor of her walk-in closet. She stares into a pair of large plastic eyes, listening to the conversation she just heard play in repeated fragments that she does not fully understand although she feels the full meaning. The door to her closet stands open beside her, and she clutches a life-sized Ragedy Ann doll tightly in her arms.

---

That summer Melena leans over the stove with a pot lid in one hand. She fans away the steam over a pot of boiling potatoes. Elizabeth sits at the table with a large Wonder Woman picture book in front of her. She looks up as the phone rings.

"Answer that please, Elizabeth," Melena says.

"Okay." Elizabeth hops off her chair and takes the phone. "Hello?"

"Melena?" Pearl stutters, "Elizabeth?"

"Yeah."

"Put your mommy on the phone, honey."

Elizabeth extends the phone toward Melena stretching out the tangled cord. "I think it's Aunt Pearl."

Melena wipes her hands and reaches for the phone.

"Hello?"

"Melena," Pearl says, her distraught voice shaky.

"Pearl, what's wrong?"

"It's Daddy," she says, "he's had another stroke. They said maybe two, and the damage is much worse. He might not make it." Pearl starts to cry. "Oh, dawg 'it, I swore I wasn't going to cry on the phone with you."

Melena grabs the kitchen counter.

"Jesus, Pearl, where are you? Are you at the hospital?"

"Yeah, with Momma and Alice is with Leopold."

"All right, all right," Melena says and surveys the kitchen, "just calm down. I'll stop dinner and put some things in a bag. Elizabeth and I will be down by nightfall."

Chasing down the dusky sky at the end of a hurried two-hour drive, Melena pulls off Raeford Road and onto her parents' driveway. She steps up to the brick porch with Elizabeth holding one hand and a Cabbage Patch Kids overnight bag in the other. Flanked by the dogs, Alice greets her at the door.

"Hey, Melena," Alice takes Elizabeth's bag out of her hand.

"Hey, Alice," Melena says, "thanks for watching her."

"Of course, girl," Alice turns her worried face.

Melena takes Elizabeth's hand and gives it to Alice. She looks to the corner where Leopold sits in a big brown Lazy Boy and wonders if her life would be easier if he could have taken up the slack a brother was supposed to.

"Hi, Leopold," she says half-heartedly and turns away from him.

Melena calls as she goes out the door. "Mind Alice, Elizabeth."

Alice sets Elizabeth's bag on the table.

"Do you have any coloring books, Elizabeth?" she asks.

"I think so," Elizabeth sits in a chair and rests her elbows on the table by her bag.

"Cookie!" Leopold bellows.

"Hi," Elizabeth says, laying her head down on her hands.

Alice sighs, "I imagine you're not feeling good baby from all that driving and rushing around. How about I fix you a grill cheese sandwhich?"

Alice looks around the kitchen for her pack of menthols while Leopold mutters inaudibly and goes to his room.

"I guess he's not feeling good either," Alice says. The TV blares from Leopold's wing of the house echoing into the kitchen. "That's Gunsmoke," she says, "at least his show's on."

⌖

Less than two years later, the Starlings still hold up the image of a perfect family.

At the university, Blackwell maintains a mediocre performance while Luke and Elizabeth continue to bring home pleasing report cards. Luke, now a basketball player, has caught the eye of one special girl and Elizabeth remains a favorite among her third grade schoolmates.

Coping with the chronic damage to her father's health, Melena tries to be firm with the new decisions and roles she undertakes in the name of the Dupree family. She and Elizabeth travel to Bell's every other weekend, and she takes Elizabeth out of school for extended visits when she can. Staying at Bell's leaves time for her and Pearl to look after Pratt and the business, and Alice is always there to help out.

Outside of Wesleyan Christian Academy, the fragrant spring air blows a gust of warmth through the trees and the lush playground grass looks like a great, green carpet stretched across the land.

Under the bright blue sky, a group of privileged little girls, seven to eight years old, sit underneath the bleachers barely noticing the puffy white clouds that float above them. One girl with dark brown hair and cold blue eyes sits at the head of them endlessly talking.

"I told you, I have mountains of candy at my house, way more than anyone else does," Gertrude Eldemaar says. "My daddy owns a candy factory, and I can have candy any time I want. Now if you do what I say, and I like you, then you can have some of my candy, because we're ..."

"I'm tired of talking about candy, Gertrude," Elizabeth yawns. "Can't we play a game?"

Gertrude pulls a lock of hair neatly behind her ear and stares at Elizabeth.

"Yeah, Gerty," Darla Jennings says, "I want to play a game."

Gertrude says, "Do not call me Gerty, Darla. My mother says it isn't proper." She lays her hands in her lap. "If we play a game, it has to be something that won't get my dress dirty."

Elizabeth scratches her head. "*Uh*," she says, "we should play GI Joe!"

"GI Joe is a cartoon," Gertrude says, "and it sounds like I might get dirty."

Darla claps her hands. "It sounds fun."

"And, I know who we can play with," Elizabeth smiles. She motions for them all to lean in closer. "We are the Cobra Commanders and the boys over there are the GI Joes."

"Cobra?" Gertrude sniffs. "Aren't they the bad guys?"

Elizabeth rolls her eyes. "So, they're way more fun and it's better than talking about candy. Now, Courtney, Holly, I want you to go on the other side of the field around the bleachers and sneak up on the boys coming up that side of the hill."

Elizabeth looks at Darla and Gertrude. "You two follow me on this side. When we all get to the bushes, we'll run to the middle and attack them. We have to kidnap their leader."

"Who's their leader?" Holly asks.

"Chad," Elizabeth says, "we must capture him and bring him back to the bleachers. Ready?"

The girls all nod except for Gertrude, who appears apprehensive. Across the field, a group of boys play at the top of the hill near the brick school building.

Halfheartedly kicking a soccer ball between them, Chad Clatter and Aaron Wall throw an occasional glance toward the bleachers. They stop, looking puzzled at the newly emptied area.

"Where do you think they are?" Chad asks.

"I don't know, but I bet they're up to something," Aaron says kicking the ball to Lance.

Slowly and stealthily, Holly and Courtney sneak up the left side of the field while Elizabeth, followed by Darla and Gertrude, creep up the right. The girls dart behind the bushes as they approach the top of the hill.

Suddenly, Elizabeth pops up behind the foliage and waves at Holly and Courtney who watch her from the opposite side. Chad turns around and they drop to the grass immediately. Gertrude's pink dress blows behind her in the wind.

"Did you see something, Aaron?" Chad asks looking out over the field.

"Nope."

Elizabeth motions for Holly and Courtney to go on the count of three. She holds her hand above the bushes and counts it out with her fingers.

"One," she says quietly, "two, three."

Sprinting forward with Darla beside her and Gertrude trailing behind, Elizabeth meets Courtney and Holly in the middle. She shouts, "Cobra!" as they close in on the boys and the other girls shout after her. The boys jump, taken by surprise.

"I knew it," Chad says and kicks the soccer ball out of the way to dart off behind Aaron. The boys flee down the hill, fearful of cooties, and run out across the field with the girls chasing after them.

"You go that way," Elizabeth shouts to Courtney and Holly who run opposite of her to cut the boys off.

Down the field, Chad, Elizabeth and Gertrude collide and tumble to the ground. Aaron and the other boys avoid capture, running back toward the top of the hill. Sitting up in the middle of the throng, Chad stares at the panting, rosy-cheeked girls.

"We," Elizabeth breathes, "have you now, Hawk. There's nothing you can do. We are the Cobra Commanders and you have to do what we say."

"Yeah," Darla says, "Cobra!"

Chad looks at them and spits on the ground. "I'll never tell you anything," he says.

Gertrude stands and looks down at her dress. "*Ah*," she squeals, "you stand up right now, you GI Joe. You made me get my dress dirty and now you're going to pay."

"You heard her," Elizabeth says, "stand up, Hawk, and walk to the bleachers for interrogation."

Elizabeth watches Chad and rises as he does, thinking that she will take him to the tunnel later and make him kiss her. Captive, he walks in between the girls over to the bleachers. From on top of the hill, Aaron and the other boys gaze at the spectacle.

"Look at him," Frederick says. "They're forcing him to go to their hideout."

"We've got to get him back," Aaron says and looks at the boys. "Don't worry. I've got a plan."

Several hours after school that day, Elizabeth sits on the marble floor outside of the gymnasium. Her empty book bag slumps against the wall and her legs, in their grass-stained khaki chinos, stretch out in front of her.

She has her coat on to go outside and she looks very bored and lonely.

Staring at the occasional older student walking through the main hall, she wonders if their parents yell all the time the way hers do. There is no way of knowing, and her only answer is the sound of many tennis shoes squeaking across the floor from inside the gym.

Every few minutes she glances at the giant glass doors that open to the parking lot, although after an hour and a half, she does so less frequently.

Hanging above Elizabeth on the wall, a red banner reads "Onward Trojan Soldiers!" It ripples as the glass door opens to her left and Melena walks in.

"Hey, Mommy," Elizabeth says barely looking up.

"Hello there, Elizabeth," Melena shoulders her purse on her arm. "Stand up and give mommy a hug."

Elizabeth rises slowly and puts her arms around Melena's neck. "The game starts in ten minutes," she says.

"Well, get your things and let's go." Melena's eyes widen. "Oh, Elizabeth! What happened to your pants?"

Elizabeth looks at the floor. "I was playing and I fell."

Melena frowns. "Well, next time try to play something that doesn't make you fall, honey. Come on."

Elizabeth quietly puts her things back in her bag one at a time.

"Elizabeth," Melena says tired of that frown, "I'm sorry I'm late, but I just couldn't help it."

She bends down. "Let mommy help you." Melena rises with Elizabeth's book bag and offers her daughter her free hand. "Come on now. Your brother must be wondering where we are."

They enter the gymnasium together and the crowd's swelling voices envelop them. Walking along in front of the bleachers, they pass the visiting school's cheerleaders and then Wesleyan's own. At a break on the far side, Melena steps up into the stands.

"Hi, Melena," Loren Clatter says with a slow wave of her manicured hand. "Hello there, Elizabeth."

Loren thinks Melena always dresses Elizabeth so well.

"Hello, Loren," Melena says ushering Elizabeth down the bench in front of her.

"Hi, Mrs. Clatter," Elizabeth says scooting past her. She looks at Chad who sits beside his mom, ducking behind her.

"Chad said you all had a nice time at recess today," Loren straightens her long skirt over her knee. "Something about GI Joe?"

Elizabeth looks at her, shrugs and says, "Recess is fun."

Melena situates herself and Elizabeth beside the Clatters while Chad and Elizabeth begin to play. Out in front of the bleachers, the Wesleyan Academy Middle School basketball team warms up before the game.

Luke trots around the court looking handsome in the Trojans' gold and red uniforms, while Chad's cousin, Kristie Cason, waves to Melena from the bench in front of them where she and the other cheerleaders sit.

"That Kristie," Melena says, "she's such a pretty girl." Melena imagines the day when Elizabeth will be a cheerleader.

"I know," Loren laughs, "my brother sure got lucky when

she took after me."

Passing under the goal to the back of the lay-up line, Luke steals a glance at Kristie and halfway waves at her without his teammates noticing.

Kristie waves back behind her pompoms, and she and the other cheerleaders giggle. Luke nods at Melena, but does not wave for risk of being seen, while Loren looks down at Chad and Elizabeth playing on the bleachers.

Everyone looks so perfect on the outside.

Loren coos. "These two just always have so much fun."

"I know," Melena says, "and they've been friends for so long now. I still remember that summer when we were all at the beach."

Loren leans back away from the children and a look of concern crosses her face.

She asks, "So, how are things, Melena? Is your father doing better now?"

"Well," Melena thinks of her marriage and everything else and sighs, "His speech will never be the same. Sometimes we can barely understand him, but the hardest thing is that he just isn't who he used to be."

Loren nods. "Randolph and I are so lucky that we both still have our parents in good health."

"I just ..." Melena shakes her head, "I always thought Daddy would be there." She's felt exasperated and has wanted to say that aloud for so long.

"Growing up, anything we needed or anything that needed taking care of, he would figure out, but I guess that's gone now. There's no point dwelling on it. It is what it is."

Melena looks for Luke.

"So, how about this game?" she asks. "Do you think the children will win?"

"Oh, I hope so," Loren says. "I know Kristie was thrilled the team made it this far. If they win this game, they'll get to go on to the state finals."

"Wouldn't that be something?" Melena says and smiles as she watches her son run in for his lay-up.

"It sure would."

"Oh, look," Melena nods, "there's Blackwell."

Blackwell steps into the gym and stands in front of the door, scanning the crowd. Melena waves at him and he crosses the floor in front of the bleachers toward his sister and his mom.

Melena beams, "He's home from school for the weekend."

All the girls in the crowd, and some of the mothers, stop talking to gaze at Blackwell as he passes by. He wears a red Polo shirt with khakis and a belt.

His dark black hair and dazzling smile cause women everywhere to swoon and sigh when they see him. They always think he looks like some movie star or another, and Melena is so proud of him.

"Hi, Mom!" Blackwell says and leans down to give her a hug.

"How was traffic?" Melena asks.

"Not too bad," he says. "Hi, Mrs. Clatter." Blackwell reaches forward and tousles Elizabeth's hair. "Hey, you."

She looks up and smiles at him, "Hi."

"Don't you have a hug for your big brother?" he asks.

"Yeah," Elizabeth stands up and hugs him.

Very often, Ernest cannot make it to many of these after school events due to his hectic work schedule. Whenever Blackwell happens to be home from school, he steps in.

"Well, Blackwell," Loren says, "I'm sure you have lots of girls calling you up there at State."

"Oh," he blushes, "I don't know about that." At school, Blackwell spends a lot of time drinking at football games and dodging persistent girls.

The game commences with the gawky boys running down the court after one another. For over an hour Melena, Blackwell and

Elizabeth watch Luke and the Trojans beat Southwest Day School. Luke scores ten points, and Kristie winks at him several times while she cheers.

After the game, the four Starlings stop by Pizza Hut for dinner and then head home. Melena boxes the leftovers for Ernest and leaves them in the refrigerator. He comes home late from a meeting with the city superintendent.

---

"Stop pushing me!" Elizabeth yells from the back seat of the Suburban. She elbows Luke and throws a pillow in between them. The early summer heat has them packed tight, windows up, and the air conditioner blasting.

Luke smiles. His two front teeth gleam, and she wants to knock them out.

*I got her,* he thinks. He takes the pillow from between them and fans the air around him over to her side of the seat..

"Mom," Elizabeth shouts, "Luke farted and now he's blowing it on me."

"Don't say that word, Elizabeth," Melena says. "Say 'passed gas,' and you, mister, open the window right now. You are to leave your sister alone for the rest of the trip."

They're going to Talladega on a family trip to one of Luke's races. He looks out the window.

"I didn't do anything to her. She's back here elbowing me and scattering her crayons all over the seat. I'm just sitting here very quiet."

"Ernest," Melena looks across the seat at him, "tell your son to behave."

"Luke," Ernest calls from behind the steering wheel, "if you don't leave your sister alone, then I'll have to let her drive in the race instead of you."

"Yeah," Elizabeth sticks out her tongue. "Be mean to me, Luke, go ahead."

He rolls his eyes at her while Melena leans over toward Ernest. She whispers, "Do not encourage her about those karts, Ernest. You know how I feel about that." A picture of Elizabeth crashing against a wall appears in her head.

"Fine, Melena," Ernest says, "but you asked me to step in and I did. If you don't like it, then next time, don't ask."

"Ernest, all I was saying is that I don't want you to encourage Elizabeth's interest in karts."

"I wasn't encouraging her, Melena; I was threatening Luke."

"Fine," Melena says and looks at her magazine.

"How much longer before we're there?" Elizabeth asks trying to interrupt them.

"Oh, I'd say about three hours, Elizabeth," Ernest says, his knuckles white on the steering wheel. "And, when we get there, you'll see all your old friends, and then we'll watch Luke win another race."

Luke asks, "You think so, Dad?"

"Well," Ernest says proudly, "with the hours we've put in, and your driving, I'd say it's as close to a sure thing as you could get."

Luke sits back and daydreams of the day he will drive a championship Indy car and then of his quick progression into Formula 1 competition. Fueled by the thrill of his many victories, he visualizes his hands cradling the wheel of the imaginary race car as it hugs the deadly curves of a European racetrack.

Elizabeth looks at him admiringly and peacefully begins to color a racecar. None of the other girls in school have a brother who can drive like hers can. She says to him without looking, "*Og*."

He looks at her and tilts his head to one side. "*Og, og, og.*" The magic of their language is in the pronunciation and inflection of og.

"*Og, og. Og, og, og*," she says laughing.

He nods, "*Og, og,*" and they continue in this manner, escaping into their own nonsense where no one else can discern their meaning.

Two and a half months later, Melena went to Holiday in search of a private school in a good neighborhood for Elizabeth. To Melena it was time to leave again, moving back into Bell and Pratt's home was an unbearable thought but a small apartment close by her parents suited her well. This time she swore she would enroll at the community college and take some flower design courses. Without an education, she had no way to pay to live on her own.

Melena packed what she and Elizabeth needed with the speed of practiced motion. The movers came, though Ernest didn't want to enter into divorce proceedings again. When she left, Luke stayed behind and Melena refused to beg him.

Jolted by the move, Elizabeth has since been moody with Melena. Their things have been unpacked, though they've only been in the new place for two weeks, and Elizabeth sits on the floor playing with disinterested idleness. Melena stands by the kitchen table folding bath towels.

"Mommy," Elizabeth says, prone on the carpet, "I don't like the Catholic school that much."

"What's not to like, Elizabeth? They have a big playground, monkey bars and I'm sure there are plenty of nice children there."

Melena doesn't want to hear any more discouraging news. She feels like she already has so much to deal with and now is the time to try to get out.

Elizabeth whines, "But I have to wear a uniform and I miss my old school."

"Well, Elizabeth," Melena says, "you know why we had to leave. If your father were a better man, none of this ever would have happened. You know he goes with those other women and how he treats the boys better than he treats you. I couldn't stay with him any longer and let him do that to us."

Elizabeth starts hitting her Barbies together, smashing their faces like cymbals.

"I miss Luke, Mommy," she says. "When are we going to see him? Why didn't Luke come with us? Why does he get to stay at Wesleyan and I had to leave?"

"Elizabeth," Melena says, "Luke prefers to stay with your father. What can I give him when his father has money to buy him anything he wants. You stay with me because I am your mother and you belong away from that kind of corruption. Besides you will get to see Luke next weekend" She reaches into the basket for another towel.

"Don't act like you don't have friends down here, Elizabeth. You make friends wherever you go. You're just like I was when I was your age, a people person. Luke and Blackwell are the same way. You all inherited it from me, you know. Your father doesn't even like to have people over."

Elizabeth grinds her teeth as she continues to bash the Barbies' heads together, ramming the tops of the skulls.

"Elizabeth, honey, stop that," Melena says. "You're going to break the Barbies if you keep hitting them against one another."

She sets a stack of towels to her right and says, "You know Katrina has been asking Pearl when she's going to get to see you."

Elizabeth looks up, "She has?"

Melena nods.

"She was mean to me last time," Elizabeth says. "She called me a little kid and said I couldn't play with her Magic Sand because I would spill it on the floor."

"Oh, I think you're exaggerating," Melena says. "Besides, we're going to Momma Bell's, and Aunt Pearl will be there and Leopold. You can see the dogs."

Elizabeth rolls over and lies back on the floor with her Barbies on her stomach. "Mommy, I don't feel good."

Melena steps into the living room and looks down at her. "What's wrong, Elizabeth?"

"My tummy hurts," she says.

"Again?" Melena shakes her head. "We're going to have to see Dr. Willerby about that. I'll make an appointment first thing tomorrow. Here, chew on these." Melena hands her some chewable Pepto Bismol.

Elizabeth lies on her side, chewing on the chalky pink tablets and hitting the Barbies against the floor. She eats the Pepto Bismol like candy now. Melena pats her on the head and walks into her bedroom reemerging with her purse on her shoulder.

"Elizabeth, go and get your jacket," she says. "I have to meet Pearl at Momma Bell's in twenty minutes."

Elizabeth rolls over and crawls in slow motion into her bedroom. She walks back out with her jacket in her hands, a Barbie wrapped up inside it.

The drive to Bell's takes them out of their shady neighborhood and down Bragg Boulevard past the neon lights of the abundant pawnshops and bars. Holiday has always been an army town, but its face grows ever seedier and dirtier with time. Hookers and topless bars abound, but just outside town sit homes with wide lawns surrounded by acres of land.

They pull onto Highway 62, and the natural sounds of the countryside replace the glare of city lights. At the Dupree's driveway, Melena stops for a second and looks at the light illuminating the office of the main warehouse.

"*Hmm*," she says wondering who's inside. No one should be in there this late and Melena likes to think she's maintaining a watchful eye over her father's business.

When Melena and Elizabeth walk up the porch they see everyone sitting around the patio table talking and carrying on.

"Hi, y'all!" Melena says.

"Cookie!" Leopold shouts and picks Elizabeth up in the air.

"Hi, Leopold," she says quietly.

"Leopold," Melena says to her brother, "put her down, please. She's not feeling well."

Leopold looks at Melena and curses at her in his garbled speech that only she and the family understand. When Leopold was young there weren't any schools in Holiday for Bell and Pratt to take him to. The public schools couldn't cater to his needs so they tried their best to keep him happy. Neither Bell nor Pratt had the education to teach him and Leopold learned to manage his speech in his own way taking what he wanted from TV and his family. Melena looks at him sternly, and he puts Elizabeth down.

"Pearl," Melena says, "who's in the office?"

"Walker's over there looking at the accounts," Pearl says, tired all at once.

Melena sighs, "Getting a head start, *huh?*"

Pearl sips her tall glass of iced tea. "Well," she says, "they had somebody quit at the station this week and he's picking up the slack. He's been getting up at five every morning, and he just wants to get to bed as soon as possible."

Walker wears the uniform of a United States postal carrier. Unlike Ernest, he never desired the stress of running a company, but instead, preferred the comfort of family life.

"I guess," Melena says, "we should go on then and get this out of the way."

The girls are finally ready to undertake the sale of their father's business and the surrounding property. Melena thinks the books will balance in their favor and eventually provide them with a lucrative transaction. She wants to use this money to build her parents a home farther out in the country with lots of land for them to entertain themselves on riding around in brand new golf carts. Pearl takes her tea and follows her down the staircase.

"Momma," Melena calls from the drive, "remember her stomach's been bothering her, so don't give her any candy."

"Okay," Bell says and rolls her eyes. She always thought Melena was too careful with her kids.

"Elizabeth, Leopold, it's getting chilly out here. Let's go inside."

"Okay, Momma Bell," Elizabeth says.

In the kitchen with its once white walls now heavily stained with cigarette tar, Bell holds a bottle of Coca-Cola out to Elizabeth.

She says, "Take this, honey. It'll settle your stomach."

"Thank you."

A little later, Bell bathes in her blue bathtub at the back of the house and Elizabeth stares at the satin wall paper ensnared in large arms.

Over the doorway to Elizabeth's right, a plastic clown face, bright red, seems to glare at her. A long cord with a plastic hook hangs from beneath its moveable chin, and several times a day, Leopold pulls this cord.

Every time someone pulls the cord, the clown's jaw detaches and emits a series of wild cackles that echo throughout the house. Guests find it amusing, Pratt has one just like it in the warehouse that the county Sheriff sits under every time he drops by. Elizabeth hates the clown so intensely she wants to break it into many small pieces, but she doesn't know how.

⸱⤐⊙⫯⸱

Over a month ago, Melena's savings ran out and she didn't want to resort to selling her family rings. The night school courses were too expensive and after one class she became afraid of the long lonely walk in the dark to her car. She didn't want her family to support her and Elizabeth forever and Pearl encouraged her to return to Ernest for the children, to make sure Elizabeth could afford college.

*Her daughter,* Melena often thought, *the first girl in the family with a bachelor degree, maybe even a doctor of some sort.* Under her own necessity for a certain kind of life, Melena conceived of a new strategy for the time being, return and survive, restock the cavalry to come to battle later, better prepared.

Now on a cool fall Larnee day, Elizabeth sits on the floor watching the Macy's Thanksgiving Day parade while building a Lego throne for her Barbie. Melena stands over the sink with a knife in her hand preparing a turkey. Her concentration shows in little lines around her lips that, with age, will become permanent. The tension in her face releases abruptly like a fallen mask, and she calls over her shoulder toward the kitchen table.

"Come here, Luke, and help me with the turkey." She has giblets all over her hands.

Now as tall as his mother, with dark brown hair like his father, Luke grimaces at the mess she holds.

"Where's that going?" he asks.

"This," she says, "is for the gravy. You pick up Tom and put him in the pan over there. Have you washed your hands?"

Luke shakes his head and goes to the sink. Afterward, he picks the turkey up with confidence and transports it to a deep, black pan.

Because Luke chose to stay with his father, Melena mothers him from a guarded distance. The kitchen is the only space where they feel at ease with one another. Yet, Luke would never admit to a need for, or an attempt at, reconciliation with her, and Melena would never acknowledge the obvious gap.

"Luke," Melena says, "you're such a good helper. Now, stir the beans for me while I finish with the turkey."

"Who's coming to eat?" Luke asks.

"Oh, it's real small, just us," she says and smiles. "Is your brother up yet?"

"He's sleeping," Elizabeth yawns. "I looked at him a few minutes ago and he's snoring very loud."

Elizabeth has a habit of watching people sleep, but she mostly does it in the middle of the night. After waking from one of her frequent nightmares, she runs down the hall to go stand at the foot of Melena's bed until she opens her eyes. Elizabeth's unexpected presence gives Melena quite a fright at times.

Melena steps back from the turkey happy her children will go to college and wishes someone had thought she needed the benefit of an education.

"I suppose studying wears you out," she says.

"I bet it's not studying," Luke smiles. "I bet it's Sareena."

"I like that name, Sareena." Elizabeth's eyes widen. She brushes her Barbie's hair imagining a terrible sorceress with long black locks and wings.

"*Ahem*," Melena shakes her head at Luke and asks him, "Where's your father?"

"He's in the basement," Elizabeth says.

"He's working on the karts for next weekend." Luke looks in another pot and pretends to do something to keep him in the kitchen.

"I guess I should be helping him."

Melena pinches his cheek and says, "But you like being around all this food."

She's happy her son has chosen to spend time with her rather than his father. Often, Melena feels there is competition between her and Ernest for the children's affection. She cannot understand why Luke would choose to stay with him rather than leave with her.

"Elizabeth," she says, "go ask Daddy when he's going to done with his project so we know what time were having Thanksgiving Dinner."

Elizabeth runs to the basement door, which opens with a loud creak. She creeps down the first few steps, running her hands across the wood paneling as she goes and pauses before the curve in the staircase. She stares at a little door high in the wall to her right.

Over the years, this door has grown to represent a gateway to her fears. In her dreams trolls and monsters rule stairwells and bridges ready to hinder all passers by. Asleep, she's seen creatures exit this door beneath the stairs and walk to wait in the basement below. Never asking, the mystery of this door's use plagues her overactive imagination.

Other spots in the house scare her with her own fears, easily pictured from her dreams, when, in reality, she's always alone.

*Bats in there*, she thinks, *like Dracula or monsters*. Elizabeth holds her breath and runs down the steps beneath the door to jump down the last couple and hit the landing with a thud. She stands and turns to the lower staircase, descending it calmly.

"Hi, Daddy," she says, "what'cha doing?"

"Penelope Pit Stop," Ernest shouts looking at Elizabeth from behind a large pair of welding goggles.

He turns the flame down on his propane torch and sets it on the counter. Pulling the goggles off, he leans down toward the kart, which sits high on the platform, and examines the work he just completed. Elizabeth climbs onto the tall swivel chair beside him and looks at the kart, too. For a few moments, they contemplate together one section. Elizabeth pretends to examine the area closely.

"You see that band on the tail pipe there?" he asks wanting to impart some knowledge to her, to anyone who will listen since the boys don't seem to.

"Yes."

"I just welded those two pipes together to make one continuous piece." He takes his work gloves off.

She points at him. "Daddy, you have black stuff all over your face."

"I know," Ernest says, "that happens when you mess around with this stuff. Where's that no-good brother of yours? What's he up to?"

"He's upstairs because he likes food," Elizabeth says. "Mommy wants to know when you'll be done so we can eat Thanksgiving Dinner."

Ernest's shoulders slump; he wonders, *why does the whole damn dinner have to be dependent upon me? I'm the one fixing Luke's kart by myself so the boy can race and not be idyll to get in trouble.*

Ernest thinks Melena tries to make these jabs at him like he's holding the family up when he's trying to do good. He told Melena hours ago that he would be ready whenever she wanted him to. It depresses him that everyone always has to make him the leader. No one in his life, neither at work nor at home, can make a decision without him. He wishes he didn't have to be responsible for everything and everyone's happiness.

"Well," he says, "I'll be ready when dinner is ready, of course. If I'm not mistaken, that'll be awhile. Has your mom put the bird in the oven, yet?"

"She just took his insides out," Elizabeth says, "but he's in the pan now and the oven's hot."

"See, I have plenty of time. It'll be tonight before we eat. You go on and tell your mother I'll be ready before dinner is." He picks up a grease-stained rag and looks at Elizabeth wondering what type of person she will grow up to be.

"Okay, Daddy," Elizabeth says. She runs back up the stairs two at a time and doesn't give the small door on the wall a glance.

⊙━◈━⊙

The following February, on a lonely Friday night, Melena shouts from the bedroom doorway.

"Ernest!"

Her stricken face glares across the green-carpeted distance that lies between them.

Outside, the chilly night darkens the landscape of empty woods and leafless trees around their home. Elizabeth wanders from the kitchen to stand at the foot of the stairs, looking anxiously up into the hall.

Ernest turns toward Melena from the opposite end of the house. "Damn it, Melena, what?"

She leans against the doorframe, arms crossed in front of her. "Where were you tonight? Visiting another one of your whores?"

One large vein in his forehead pulsates. "You have no right to say that to me, Melena."

"Oh, I don't. You lying son of a bitch," Melena takes a step toward him.

"I know all about the Trans-Am you bought for your redneck slut. A silver car, Ernest? Really, that's so tacky."

Ernest shakes his head. "What nonsense are you on now, Melena? I don't know which one of your gossiping friends lied to you this time, but you're talking crazy."

As their voices grow louder, Elizabeth steps up the stairs hugging the wall.

"Really, Ernest?" Melena sneers. "I found the goddamn tax record of it down at city hall. How the hell are you going to explain that, you damn liar?"

Having just learned how to do research at her school's library, Elizabeth gasps silently. She thinks, *I found that today on the microfiche with Mommy. Is that what she was so happy about?*

"You really are a treat to live with, Melena. You know that? You are just the kindest, most tender wife, really."

He steps into the den and turns around. "You just go on believing all that beauty-salon gossip from your bitchy friends all you want to."

"You're pathetic. You can't even sleep in your own bed," she shouts and turns away from him.

"That's because you made it so fucking unwelcome."

Halfway into the room, Melena spins around. She takes a small brass alarm clock from their dresser.

"You son of a bitch," she says hurling it at Ernest's head.

Elizabeth's jaw drops as she watches the clock soar through the air. Ernest ducks as it slams into the wall..

"You tried to hit me!" he says.

"Too bad I missed."

"You're crazy, you ..."

"Daddy," Elizabeth says stepping into the hallway between them.

"You stop yelling at Mommy! Stop it right now! Stop fighting and yelling!" She stomps her foot and screams.

"Stop it! Stop it! Stop it!"

"That's just perfect, Melena." He watches Elizabeth's tantrum. "Are you going to throw something else now?"

"Come here, Elizabeth," Melena says.

Elizabeteh crosses the room and takes Melena's hand.

Ernest looks at them, dreading every word Melena will say about him when he's gone. "Fine, Melena, I know your game."

He picks up his briefcase and goes toward the kitchen stairs.

"Where the hell are you going?" Melena asks.

"I'm leaving. I'm going somewhere where I can find some peace and quiet." Ernest opens the basement door and starts down the stairs, door slamming behind him. Melena releases Elizabeth's hand and storms after him. She flings the door open and shouts down the stairwell.

"You coward!" she screams. "You're nothing but a cheating liar!" She slams the door shut again and marches back up the stairs. Elizabeth still stands in front of Melena and Ernest's bedroom door.

"Go watch TV, Elizabeth," Melena says sliding past her daughter and shutting the bedroom door between them.

Elizabeth stares at the white door and turns to walk back down the carpeted stairs and into the kitchen. A chair from the table sits in front of the TV. She looks around the room vacantly and resumes her seat. Returning to an earlier station, she watches *M\*A\*S\*H\** re-runs. Later on, she fixes a cheese sandwich and sits in front of the small TV with her dinner.

⤙═◉═⤚

The young blond nurse leans out into the waiting room from behind the admittance door. "Starling," she says, "Elizabeth Starling."

Melena tugs at Elizabeth's sleeve. "Come on, honey," she says, "that's us."

Elizabeth gets up from her chair reluctantly and shuffles in front of her mother over to the nurse who waits by the door. The nurse smiles down at her and motions them through.

The nurse asks, "How was your lunch, Elizabeth? I know you had to be plenty hungry after skipping breakfast for those tests."

"It was good," Elizabeth answers. "I got to have bubblegum ice cream from Swenson's. It's my favorite."

"Wasn't that nice," the nurse says. She motions with her hand. "You two go into number 6 and Dr. Evers will be with you in just a moment."

The room reflects cold white sterility. Melena follows Elizabeth in and Elizabeth steps onto the footstool in front of the examination table. She sits down on the edge of it dangling her feet. Leaning over her, Melena pulls a few stray hairs behind Elizabeth's ear and pats her on the shoulder.

"How are you feeling, Elizabeth?" she asks.

"I'm fine," Elizabeth says. "Can I see that *Highlights* magazine, Mommy?"

"Sure." Melena hands the magazine to her. She takes a *People* magazine from the pile on the counter, sits in a chair against the wall and indifferently flips through it. A few minutes later, Dr. Evers walks in.

"How's my star patient doing?" the middle aged doctor asks. "I bet Mom treated you to a pretty good lunch after all those tests. I don't like drinking that pink stuff anymore than you do and they make us doctors drink it every day before work."

"They do?" Elizabeth asks.

"Only on Fridays," he says and winks at her like a vaudevillian. "So, Melena, I think we've found out what's going on with our girl's stomach here."

Melena sits up hiding her nervousness. "What is it Dr. Evers?"

"Believe it or not, this little girl has a stomach ulcer," he scratches his forehead. "I don't have to tell you that it's pretty rare for a nine-year-old to have a stomach ulcer. Ulcers are usually an adult stress disorder and Elizabeth has no sign of infection. I have to ask myself, how can a healthy kid get an ulcer?"

"Well I don't know." Melena looks at Elizabeth and asks, "What on earth could you be worried about?"

Elizabeth shrugs her shoulders and looks at Dr. Evers. She says nothing, but in her mind a series of images passes, fanged, demon-eyed monsters of all kinds and snakes everywhere like she can't get away from them. Lately, she's decided to tell the monsters, if they come for her, that she'll become one of them so they don't kill her.

Frightened she refuses to acknowledge her fears to anyone and wonders what on earth she could really be worried about. Nothing but her made up monsters comes to her and Melena doesn't like talk about scary monsters. She always tells her not to talk about negative things like monsters or the fighting in their home, so much so, that now the thought would never occur to her. Silence is all that remains.

Dr. Evers smiles at her and asks, "Are you playing a lot of sports, Elizabeth?"

"No."

"Do you get along with the other children at school?"

Politely, "Yes."

"Dr. Evers," Melena says, "Elizabeth gets along with everyone at school. Her classmates adore her. Maybe she just has a sensitive stomach?"

"Maybe," he says and picks up his prescription tablet.

"Until we see some improvement in the stomach lining, I want you to give her this medication. In the meantime, I want you to keep an eye on Elizabeth and make sure there's nothing that could be making her uneasy. She needs to stay away from spicy food, and you can give her a little antacid to help coat the stomach."

"I certainly will, Dr. Evers," Melena says somewhat in shock at Elizabeth's diagnosis.

"Elizabeth, you promise me that you'll come back to see me in three weeks," says Dr. Evers.

"I promise," Elizabeth swings her feet up hopping off the end of the table.

Dr. Evers follows Melena and Elizabeth out the door. "You two take care now," he says as they walk down the hall and back into the waiting room to schedule Elizabeth's next appointment.

In Melena's mind, the child simply has a nervous stomach.

--->--==♦==--<---

After a summer of continued arguing about Ernest's after work schedule, Melena hired a detective and soon felt she had something she had been looking for. Detective Folton's case seemed worthy of conviction in court, presented to her with pictures of Ernest frequenting a residence not too far from their home as well as several "inappropriate" entertainment establishments. She called her lawyer from Folton's office and demanded child support, alimony and money to move as soon as possible.

Last time, when Melena tried to leave, she was stranded, alone with no money in the small apartment. She got scared because the only job she could get was minimum wage, but now, Ernest had sunk himself.

Melena's well known lawyer, Sandra McNair, convinced her client the judge would rule in her favor and that the award to Melena would be plenty of money for her and Elizabeth to live on. Besides Folton's case against Ernest, Melena had seen Mancon's books and she knew there was no way he could deny paying her once his worth was proven in court.

In the fall Melena was awarded a temporary settlement of alimony. With this money she paid the security deposit on a brand new two bedroom apartment. The only rental housing in the vicinity of the Dupree's new rural home, she and Elizabeth live ten minutes away in the township of Stayerville. With the settlement money banked from the sale of the warehouses, the girls built Bell, Pratt and Leopold a large two-story home on the outskirts of Holiday that looms like a castle in the middle of fifteen acres covered with pinetrees.

The dirt is sandy loam, and the evergreen trees litter the ground seasonally with their needles. Both Bell and Leopold have their own golf carts. They drive across the land checking the peppers and tomatoes in the garden and the fish and turtles in their little pond.

Pratt wanders from his bedroom to the sunroom to watch TV all day long in his pajamas. Once in a while on a pretty day, he walks to the end of the driveway and sits in a wooden chair watching the occasional car go by. Still a tall man, he is slightly stooped in his old age, and his face holds a wise expression.

With more freedom in the new house, Leopold explores the entirety of the piney woods pretending to be a Wild West Cowboy. He traverses the dusty trails winding through their acreage in his golf cart while heading for the same spot every day to set up a line of soda cans that he shoots down with his BB gun. When they were little, Pratt spent time almost every weekend shooting cans with the kids behind the warehouse, just like he and Walker taught Bobby when he was eleven. With each soda can Leopold hits, he slaps the toy badge the old sheriff gave him and nods his head.

Melena and Elizabeth live in what they call *their* small town, not even a mile from end to end. Stayerville has a post office, an ice cream shop, a general store and four brand new two bedroom apartments. The town council recently annexed the land for those residents of Stayerville who couldn't afford homes. The four, one-story apartments link together in a lonesome row sitting on a large dirt lot.

Mason's Apartments are the first in the township but the land is annexed for another building. A small creek runs close to dry through Carolina Clay near one end of the complex. A fifth grader now, Elizabeth plays near the creek with some of the kids from school.

"Go down there, Elizabeth," Susan says. A year older, and a little taller, Susan stares at Elizabeth imposingly.

Elizabeth points to the red clay thinking about what that mud would do to her new Keds. "Susan," she says, "I'm telling you that ground down there is not dry."

Susan crosses her arms. "We're not going to get any crawfish from the creek if you won't cross the bank at the bottom."

"Why don't you get your brother to go?" Elizabeth asks.

"I'm not tall enough," Gregory says with a defensive whine.

Elizabeth puts her hand on her hip. "You mean you two brought me out here just to climb down this plank and fetch a bunch of crawdads for you?" Thus far, Susan and Gregory are her only friends in Stayerville.

"Yes," Susan says, "you're always talking about your creek back home and how you all did this, and you all did that. Well, I don't believe you. I want to see it."

"Fine," Elizabeth says, "but you're a big fat chicken."

A wide plank tilts inward from the ten-foot bank down into the creek at a forty-five degree angle. Elizabeth places the toe of her white shoes on the edge of it and turns around. A crow flies out of the bushes across from her with a loud caw. Startled, she stares at it as it flies across the sky.

"You two have to come hold this board," she says. Gregory and Susan kneel beside her and Susan holds out a plastic cup.

"Take this," she says.

With the two other children holding onto the plank, Elizabeth inches her way down and carefully holds her balance. She remembers walking across the fallen tree that covered a twelve-foot drop over their creek back in Larnee. Gracefully, she reaches the bottom while the crawfish squirm in the muddy water below.

"Okay," Elizabeth calls to them. "Hold the board tight. I'm going to step off now." Elizabeth extends her foot and stands in the mud nervously.

"See," Susan says, "I told you it was fine."

"Yeah, yeah." Elizabeth steps forward toward the wiggling crustaceans.

Her foot quickly submerges into the mud and keeps sinking. She tries to hop out unsuccessfully as her other foot follows the first. Elizabeth screams.

"Susan," she says, "my momma's going to kill me." Elizabeth stands with her feet and her jeans sunk into the red creek mud all the way to her knees. She looks down.

"How am I going to get out?"

"Get back over to the plank," Gregory calls, trying to be helpful. "We'll hold it for you."

"Yeah," Elizabeth says, "you better hold it or I'm gonna kick both your butts."

Slowly, Elizabeth pulls her leg out of the mud. The mud around her feet makes a loud sucking sound and one of her shoes slips off to remain encased in the red earth. She winces at the site of her once white Keds and carefully picks the shoe up trying not to sink any further.

After sloshing over to the plank, she climbs back up the board using her hands to help pull her upward. On the bank, Elizabeth faces Susan and Gregory

"I have a good mind to throw both of you in there," she says. "Do you know how much trouble I am going to be in? My mom just bought these shoes yesterday and we don't have a lot of money right now. Dad didn't send the check, and now my mom has to sell her jewelry just so we can have food. So what do you think she's going to say about these shoes?"

"*Ugh,*" Gregory says and looks at his big sister.

"We'll come with you when you tell her," Susan says, "and we'll tell her it was all our fault. That we were playing and Gregory pushed you in." Her bouncy blond hair blows in the wind.

"Right," Elizabeth sits down and shakes her head. "I really do not think she'll buy that one. You don't know my mom very well."

Elizabeth's finger flicks a large glob of mud onto the ground, and she frowns. Stepping on one shoe and holding the other, she gets to her feet and the three children slowly walk back toward the apartments. They cross the dirt lot and stop in front of Elizabeth's door. Elizabeth knocks quickly and scurries behind Susan to avert Melena's attention.

Melena opens the door with the phone in her hand and motions for the children to wait. Her cross look fixes on Elizabeth. The rural land looks empty around them. It offers no refuge, and Elizabeth wishes they had never come here. In another second Melena says something hurriedly, then puts the phone down.

"Elizabeth," Melena says angrily, "I just got off the phone with your teacher, Mrs. Wiffle and we had a ...."

Melena stops. "What is that?" She points to the bright red mud on Elizabeth's legs and covering one of her shoes.

"*Uh*, I fell," Elizabeth says.

"You fell?" Melena asks. "Elizabeth, where is your other shoe?"

"She," Susan hesitates, "*uh*, we were playing near the edge of the creek and Gregory accidentally pushed her in!"

Melena eyes her daughter harder. "You fell right in on your feet?"

"Yeah," Elizabeth nods.

"Susan, Gregory," Melena says to each one, "I'm going to have to ask you two to go home to your mom now. Elizabeth can't play anymore this afternoon, neither will she be able to play for the rest of this week or the next. In fact, the next time you want to play with her you need to ask me first. I don't know when she will be allowed play."

"Yes, ma'am," the children say. Gregory pulls at Susan's arm, and they turn to walk home.

After the children leave, Melena turns angrily to Elizabeth.

"How could you do this, Elizabeth? You know those are brand new shoes. I can't afford to replace them, and now you're just going to have to wear them stained. You know we don't have any money right now."

Melena grits her teeth. "Your father isn't helping me pay for you like he's supposed to. He doesn't even send the damn checks, but what do you do? Not only do you get in major trouble at school, you also ruin the clothes and shoes that I buy you."

Melena points at Elizabeth's feet. "Take those pants off right now and come in the house. You better have your other shoe, young lady. I know all about the little notes you've been sending."

Elizabeth's face flushes and her body grows hot with guilt and fear.

"But Mommy," she says, "I can't take my pants off outside. I won't have any clothes on."

"Oh, yes you can," Melena says. "You're not going to track all that mud on the carpet."

Elizabeth slides her jeans off . She sets her things in a pile and looks back up to Melena. Melena bends down and picks the pile up carefully, frowning harder with each stained item, and shoos Elizabeth in through the door.

"I want to know who Jason Scott is," Melena says closing the door behind her with a thud.

Elizabeth sits on the floor recalls the pen scrawling across the paper full of angry energy. It made her feel so good.

"Why did you write him a note with curse words in it, Elizabeth?"

"Because."

"Because why, Elizabeth?" Melena asks a little louder. "Mrs. Wiffle told me every single dirty word you called him in your note. She even said you called him these things over and over again filling up the entire page with obscenities."

"She did?" Elizabeth blinks.

"Yes, she did." Melena paces across the floor in front of Elizabeth.

"How could you? How could you do that to us Elizabeth? How could you let people think that I brought you up to talk that way? We're new in this town. What will they think of us? You're a lady and you will act like one."

Melena crosses her arms and stares down at Elizabeth. "My mother would have popped me," she says, "but not yours. No. I'm too easy on you. I can see that now. Tell me, Elizabeth, why did you say all those things to this boy?"

"He makes fun of me," she says aware of her own anger. "He's made fun of me since the first day I came here."

"How has he made fun of you?"

"We had to say the multiplication tables out loud and Mrs. Wiffle was calling on everyone to answer them and when she called on me, I didn't know it. I just sat there because I didn't know what to say. I don't know the multiplications. I don't know any of them."

She shouts, "I'm dumb and he made fun of me right there in class. He laughed at me and said I was stupid and everyone else laughed, too. So, I wrote him that note and told him I was going to kick his butt if he laughed at me again."

Eyes welling up with tears, Elizabeth breathes in and lets out a long wail.

"Well," Melena says, softening, "that's still no reason for any daughter of mine to be using this kind of language. You should have come home and told me at once that he was making fun of you. We can, and we will, get you some help with the multiplication tables."

"It's ..." Elizabeth wheezes, "it's not just math. I don't know anything they know. They're all way ahead of me, and I didn't want to tell you."

"But you always did so well at Wesleyan," Melena says and sits on the couch. "Why on earth would you be far behind here of all places? Elizabeth, honey, you are smart, smart enough to be a doctor someday. And why wouldn't you want to tell me that a boy was picking on you? I'm your mother."

"You always say everyone likes me," Elizabeth cries. "They don't."

"Oh, Elizabeth," Melena says and stoops down in front of her. She pulls her gently by the chin and smiles.

"You're exaggerating. Everyone likes you. You're just having some problems adjusting. Now, I want you to go to your room and stay there 'til dinner. All of these things are still no excuse for this letter you've written."

"You're grounded for the next couple of weeks, but in the meantime, you need to go lie down and stop crying. We're going to Momma Bell's tonight, and you can't go to dinner all upset. What do you think Aunt Pearl and Momma Bell would say?"

"I don't know," Elizabeth sniffles.

"Well, I do," Melena says and stands. She hands her a couple of tissues. "Now, go to your room and I'll call you before we leave."

"Okay," Elizabeth says and shuffles off to her room still in tears.

A couple of hours later, Melena opens Elizabeth's door and finds her sleeping on the carpet surrounded by her stuffed animals. She wakes her and tells her to wash her face and comb her hair. Then together, they go to Momma Bell's for a family dinner.

When they arrive, Pearl and Walker stand in the kitchen preparing steaks and Momma Bell sits near the television smoking a cigarette. Reminiscent of the movie stars of her youth, Bell puffs two times and draws in a lungful of smoke through a long, black cigarette holder.

"Hey there, sugar," Bell says to Elizabeth as they walk through the door. "You come over here and give me some love."

Elizabeth runs to Momma Bell and throws her arms around her. "Hey, Momma Bell," she says burying her head in her grandmother's shoulder. Bell would never yell at her.

"Now, Elizabeth," Pearl calls washing her hands, "you better come over here and give me a hug, too."

"Okay," Elizabeth hops up and dashes over to Pearl.

"Well, look at that," Walker says, "I think there's a turkey running loose in the house. Somebody better get it."

"I'm not a turkey," Elizabeth giggles inside Pearl's arms.

"Let me see you," Pearl steps back. "Why are your eyes swollen? Are your allergies bothering you?"

"No," Elizabeth says to the floor. "I got in trouble today."

"Elizabeth has had a small problem at school," Melena says, "but she's fine." In her mind, this setback has her determined she'll encourage Elizabeth to study more and go into a profession like medicine. She thinks about this idea as she sits at the long Formica bar on the left side of the kitchen.

Bell drives her chair toward them. "What happened?" she asks. "You better tell me right now."

Elizabeth looks over at Melena for permission and Melena nods.

"This boy was making fun of me in class because I didn't know the multiplication tables," Elizabeth says. "He called me stupid, and everyone laughed at me, so I wrote him a bad note."

Pearl's eyebrows rise with her natural innocence. "What did the note say, Elizabeth?"

"*Hmm*," Elizabeth waits and decides to leave out the more intense profanity, "I called him a butt hole, a jerk and every other really, really bad word I could think of, and then I wrote it lots and lots of times until it filled up the whole page."

"What else?" Bell asks with an encouraging tone.

"I told him I'd punch his lights out if he ever made fun of me again." Elizabeth stares at them waiting to be told that good little girls don't say things like that.

Bell smiles, "Good for you," she says and pats Elizabeth on the head. "You don't take shit from nobody."

"Mother!" Pearl and Melena say.

"Mother," Melena sighs, "please do not encourage her to use foul language. No daughter of mine is allowed to speak that way."

"Melena's right, Momma. You can't tell a child that they can do things like that." Pearl says, "You would've popped us black and blue if we'd been caught passing dirty notes."

Elizabeth's eyes dart from Melena to Pearl and then back to Bell who smiles.

"*Aw*, damn," Bell says and drives back to her cigarette, "I would've told him to go to hell."

"Mother!" they say again.

"That's a fine thing to tell Elizabeth to do." Melena shakes her head.

"Elizabeth, you are my daughter and you are not allowed to use language like that ever again. If you do, you will be more than just grounded for three weeks, trust me. You've been warned."

Elizabeth skips over to Bell and stands beside her. She plays with her grandmother's ash-blond hair. Pearl and Melena shake their heads and focus on dinner while Elizabeth leans over and whispers in Bell's ear.

"I love you, Momma Bell."

"I love you, too, honey," Bell says hugging Elizabeth to her and blowing the last puff from her cigarette over Elizabeth's head.

At the other end of the house, a door creaks open. Leopold pulls up the top of his pants and tugs the polyester fabric over his belly. He walks out of his new room, wandering toward the voices in the kitchen. He comes in and shakes Elizabeth by the back of her shoulders playfully.

"Cookie!" he says.

Elizabeth whips around jerking her shoulders out of his grasp. She stares at him with hellfire and hate in her eyes.

Leopold calls her by the nickname again.

Elizabeth's lips pinch together in disgust and her whole face gets tight.

She snarls, "I don't want to play with you, Leopold."

In his brain, Leopold comprehends some level of animosity directed at him. He throws his hands on his hips and becomes very angry with her, calling Elizabeth by the name he uses for her when she does something he doesn't like.

"Meety Ma," he hollers and shakes his finger at her.

"Leopold," Bell says, "lower your voice."

"No, Leopold," Elizabeth says and sticks her tongue out at him. She walks over to the bar where Melena and Pearl are cleaning corn and tugs on the lapel of Melena's shirt.

"Leopold's scaring me, Mommy," she says wanting to get him in trouble.

"What?" Melena asks. "Well, just go help Uncle Walker with the grill."

"Okay," Elizabeth says and smiles. She looks back at Leopold and laughs maliciously as she skips to the porch where Walker is toying with the grill.

# The Passing of Four Years

FIVE MONTHS AFTER ELIZABETH'S profane note, she and Melena returned, as usual, to Larnee, heads held high. With this final return, Melena enrolled Luke and Elizabeth in the public schools close to their home. Much to Melena's dismay, the testing system quickly labeled both children academically deficient for their grade levels.

After careful thought, Melena reluctantly concluded that the private school's poor academic curriculum caused her children to fall behind. This conclusion prompted her to seek help for the children, and with tutors and much effort, Elizabeth and Luke gradually caught up to their classmates.

In middle school, Elizabeth made friends with children she recognized from kindergarten while Luke Bartleby grew into a man tall in stature with a handsome face. Brighton High School has treated him well since his older brother Blackwell paved the way for him. In his freshman year Luke played football and basketball, but as those things interfered with his one true love, racing, he left them behind.

Race after race, he excelled and won while many marveled at his natural skill. In his sixteenth year, he took another national championship; this time winning thousands of dollars against more experienced drivers.

The girls of Brighton High adored him though he feigned shyness at first. Unlike Blackwell, Luke neglected the junior and senior proms since they conflicted with the biggest race of the season. With Melena imploring, Luke did escort a homecoming attendant, just to give his mother the photo opportunity she wanted.

Ernest Blackwell Starling completed his university courses and applied his new business degree to a management position as

Ernest's top man at Mancon. Financially secure and confident about his future, he proposed to his college love.

In an elegant ceremony in a historic church in downtown Hollow Town, Ernest and Melena saw Blackwell marry, Katherine Evelyn Blake. After years of dating and living together Blackwell knew they could make it work despite the troubled marriage witnessed his whole life. So proud of the couple, Melena and Ernest threw the kids a giant pool side party for the rehearsal dinner and with the Blakes sent them to Italy for their honeymoon.

Settling into life together, Blackwell and Katherine reside with their dog Zappa in the house that Ernest bought for them. They are young, good looking, and their life seems charmed. In college, Katherine and Blackwell secured powerful and success-bound friends, and from those relationships, they will prosper.

For these last four years, Ernest William Starling and Melena Anna Starling have eked out an emotional existence together. Their relationship has been like a horrific carnival ride soaring up and down, and at its most intense moments, crashing headlong into disaster.

While Luke and Elizabeth spent more time at after school functions, Melena opened a retail store and pursued a design business. Her repressed talents flourished as she began to lite a fire in the interior-decorating world. Many nights she has enjoyed working late on her creation. Many nights Ernest has worked late and, sometimes, Ernest slept in the den and Melena slept in the master bedroom, all alone.

Melena has developed a recurring and mysterious illness, which no doctor in Larnee or specialist in the country has been able to diagnose. Every battery of tests result in more questions and no answers. She suffers bouts of weakness and pain, attributed to an inflamed pancrease, with symptoms teetering on the human threshold.

Melena's even been to the Mayo Clinic where they found traces of arsenic in her blood, but no one could figure out where it came from. No doctor or detective could explain the mystery so Melena came up with her own explanation, either her fake breasts had leaked some vile chemical into her system or Ernest had been trying to poison her.

This illness, as it comes and goes, has kept Melena from her business for weeks at a time. It has confined her to her bed where she lay in a sickened stupor digesting only the medicine prescribed to ease her pain and the nutritional supplements meant to sustain her.

As Melena's bouts of sickness come more frequently, Elizabeth has cried herself to sleep at night, worried that she will lose her mother. The unexplainable aspect of Melena's sickness has enveloped the family in a cloud of suspicion and confusion.

Since Luke left Larnee for college, he rarely comes home. He will never really want to again. Elizabeth has begun high school at Brighton and remains in the house with Ernest and Melena. They focus on their careers. Melena tries to stay healthy and all three struggle to survive in their unhappy home.

## Act II

# Everyone Belongs in
# The Cornucopia of Anger

IT IS THE MIDDLE OF FALL. Elizabeth jumps down the stairs and throws her book bag by the basement door. Tall and thin as a reed, she saunters into the kitchen, spins around in front of her mother and sits at the table.

Melena finds herself struggling daily to keep Elizabeth looking the way she wants her to. Neither of the boys ever objected to the clothes she bought for them, but now, she just can't seem to connect with her daughter.

"Elizabeth," Melena says, "what are you wearing on your feet, and why do you have my skirt on?"

"I'm a gothic princess, Mother," she pulls her long brown hair back. It has darkened closer to Ernest's color as she's gotten older. "Don't I look pretty?"

"You look morbid. Why don't you put on that pretty dress I bought you yesterday?"

Elizabeth's dark-painted lips and pale face make her look like an evil china doll. She loves it.

"I don't want to wear that dress, Mother," she says. "I want to dress differently now and I think it's cool to wear all black."

"Well, I don't," Melena says and lays a giant pancake down on the plate in front of Elizabeth. "Don't you want to look happy and nice? Everyone likes that."

"Not everyone is always happy, or nice," Elizabeth says reaching for the butter. "I am not *everyone* anyway, and I am not going to let other people dictate what I wear."

"Well, your lipstick is too dark. It almost looks black."

"I know," Elizabeth says excitedly. "It was really hard to get it that way, but I lined my lips with eyeliner and that made it a lot better."

"Elizabeth Starling," Melena says, "what are your friends going to think of you? You look so strange. You used to look preppy and cute."

"Mom," Elizabeth slams down the syrup bottle. Her temper has become increasingly violent.

"I don't care what my friends think, okay? They're so mean to people sometimes, and who knows if they're really my friends anyway. I want to dress this way and I don't care who likes it and who doesn't."

"Don't you raise your voice to me, Elizabeth," Melena says edgily. She sits down at the table.

Every time she looks at Elizabeth, Melena sees Ernest in her daughter's eyes and it's hard to be patient.

"I'm not raising my voice," Elizabeth says and takes a slow breath to remain calm. She's so tired of trying to be what everyone else wants her to be.

She asks, "Are you coming to my volleyball game today?"

"Yes," Melena says pleased with her ability to delegate work. "I'm leaving Ferdinand at the store and Katherine is coming, too."

"Cool," Elizabeth says. "When's Luke coming home again?"

"Your father said he'd be home this weekend to get ready for their next race, but I think it's just for the day. You know he's doing that fraternity pledging and they've got him worn out from it."

"Hey, Dad," Elizabeth says as Ernest comes into the kitchen, "are you coming to my game today?"

Elizabeth wants her family to get along and do things together but she's losing faith that they could ever live in harmony. Alone at night, she cries over this lost dream.

Ernest loops one end of his tie over the other and says, "I'm going to try, Elizabeth."

He would like to do more things with his daughter, but that means Melena will be there too and her presence can be so very hard for him to deal with, especially after a long day at work.

"Do you have a busy day, Ernest?" Melena asks.

"Yes, Melena," Ernest says. "You know I'm always busy."

Melena pretends to bore a hole into his mind with her eyes. She never believes a word he says, and when she does talk to him, there's acid in her voice.

"Do you want something to eat, Ernest?" Melena asks.

"No," he says, "I'm running late already and I'm not very hungry."

"Mom," Elizabeth interrupts, wanting to circumvent their fighting, "we have to go or I'm going to be late for school."

"All right then, Elizabeth." Melena pats the yellow Formica table top.

"Ernest," she says, "doesn't your daughter look pretty today?"

Ernest looks at Elizabeth as she gets up from the table. He stares at her white powdered face and combat boots as she traipses out of the kitchen. His eyebrows rise.

"Are those combat boots, Elizabeth?" he asks.

"They sure are," Elizabeth says and puts on her black coat. "This girl at school gave them to me."

Ernest shakes his head and takes his briefcase in hand. "Why are you wearing combat boots?"

"Because I like them. Come on, Mom. We have to go now."

Melena frowns. "I said all right, Elizabeth."

"Bye, Dad," Elizabeth says as she goes. Melena puts her coat on and reaches for her purse and keys.

"Melena," Ernest asks, "are you encouraging her to dress this way?"

"Of course I am, Ernest," she snaps, "that's why I spent fourteen years fighting to dress her in nice clothes."

"I simply asked you a question."

"Please," she says. "You're an ass," and walks through the basement door.

Ernest turns back into the kitchen and steps over to the TV. He turns it off and walks back toward the basement door where he switches off the kitchen, living room and hallway lights before going to work. On the way, he thinks about the electric bill and how no one gives a damn how high it is as long as he pays it.

After homeroom, Elizabeth walks down the hall toward English class. She steps through the crowded hallway with Melena's long flowing black skirt billowing behind her.

This is her class's first year out of middle school and most of them think they are very adult now. Eva, Nicole and Jenny, together for the most part since kindergarten, stand in a circle with a few of the boys they have all grown up with.

Shocked by this odd-looking Elizabeth moving toward them, Jenny elbows Nicole in the arm as she sees Elizabeth all in black, looking like a specter.

They all turn and stare at her, then snicker behind their hands in disbelief.

Nicole whispers a little plan in Eva's ear. Eva smiles, breaks the circle and walks toward Elizabeth. She steps in front of her and stops, pulling her white-blond hair out of her face.

"Hi, Elizabeth," she says maliciously.

"Hi."

"So," Eva looks back at Jenny and giggles, "nice outfit. What? Are you going to a funeral today?"

"Yeah," Elizabeth sighs and looks at her prettily, "yours." She walks past Eva toward the doorway to her own classroom.

As she passes by, John Douglas calls out from the middle of the girls, "Great clothes, Morticia." They all start laughing.

Elizabeth turns and looks back at him.

"Go fuck yourself, John Douglas."

He yells incredulously, "Nice mouth!"

The bell rings in the Brighton hallways and the separate crowds disperse into particular rooms. The Brighton students cover a wide socioeconomic range, which determines what classes the guidance counselors put them in. The children sit in their separate classrooms and gradually adjust. English class, Elizabeth's favorite subject, is the best hour of her day though her grammar skills still lag behind. For the next two weeks, Mrs. Harken's class, including John Douglas, Eva, Elizabeth and those other students Elizabeth has not yet had a chance to meet, will read *Romeo and Juliet* out loud. While Mrs. Harken assigns temporary parts, Elizabeth happily reads the list of characters and contemplates performing one of Juliet's monologues in drama class that afternoon.

"I'm home," Elizabeth shouts as she opens the basement door and slams it behind her. She races up the stairs, down one hall and then another as she looks for Luke.

It's Friday afternoon and she's been waiting all week for her brother to come home. She thinks Ernest and Melena don't argue as much when he's there. Elizabeth stops, bursting into his room.

"When did you get here?" she asks. He sits on the floor staring blankly at his television. She wants to run toward him and give him a hug, thankful for his presence.

"A little while ago." He doesn't look at her. He hates coming home. To him, the house seems to seethe with years of screaming and yelling. Luke thinks he can feel the anger, like walking through a wall of tension, as soon as he steps through the door even if his parents aren't home.

"Don't barge into my room like that again," he says. "You should ask first."

"You look tired," Elizabeth says. "How's school?"

"It's good. Move out of the way. You're blocking the TV."

"Sorry," Elizabeth says and sits down beside him. "What are you watching?"

"MTV, can't you see it, too?"

"Yes, but I didn't know if it was a show or something."

Elizabeth wants nothing more than to hang out with Luke. With him at college, the empty house closes in around her, so much so that she even misses their fighting. Sometimes she wanders up and down the halls through everyone's rooms just looking at their belongings.

"Hey," Luke says, "you need to be ready to go eat in thirty-minutes." He yawns. "We're going to Osaka's for dinner and we're meeting mom and dad there."

"Great," Elizabeth says.

Finally he looks at her and asks, "What the fuck are you wearing?"

"Whatever do you mean?"

"All right, smart ass," he says. "I'll just tell Mom and Dad you're on drugs."

"But I'm not." Elizabeth smiles at her brother. She doesn't care if he picks on her right now. She just hopes that with him home tonight maybe Ernest and Melena won't fight.

Osaka's hums with the Friday night crowds. Steam rises from the hibachi tables as chefs shout and swing wooden shakers with a practiced flair.

Leaning over her unused, empty plate, Melena comes closer to Luke and examines him. She squints as she observes the puffiness under his eyes.

"Luke," Melena worries, "I just don't think it's a good idea. It can't be. Look at you, you're absolutely worn out. Those circles are horrifying, and God only knows what that fraternity has made you do."

She sits back a little angry, wanting more information. Melena will always want more information from Luke and from everyone.

"I wish you would tell me what they're making you do," she says.

"No way, Mom." Luke nudges his plate forward for the chef to place a heap of vegetables on. "If I told you, I'd have to kill you."

"Luke," Melena says, "do not even joke about a thing like that."

138

Elizabeth asks, "Do you guys have a secret initiation? I heard they make you do weird things with farm animals."

Melena coughs, "Elizabeth, please."

Luke picks up his chopsticks. "Yes, we do have an initiation and I can't tell any of you anything. I'll carry this information with me forever and never tell anyone."

Ernest looks at his son proudly. He's happy that Luke has had a semi-carefree youth since he spent most of his own working.

"I bet you all have some kind of parties up there," he says and imagines the group of boys, most of whom he has met, drunk, swaying and surrounded by lots of girls.

"Are you kidding me?" Luke asks. "All the athletes pledge our fraternity, and all the girls want to come to our parties. We only mix with the best looking sororities."

Although Melena is proud of her handsome son and his ability to win the hearts of his friends at school, she still tries to keep a motherly hold on him.

"I hope you're doing more at school than pledging and going to mixers," she says. "You're there to get an education."

"I'm making A's and B's," Luke says. "That's all that matters, right? Anyway, I'm not the one you need to worry about. Vampire girl is the one you should be watching."

"Cool," Elizabeth says. Her black-rimmed eyes sparkle. *Vampire girl*, she thinks and says, "I like that."

Melena shakes her head and sits back. "She won't be dressing like this for long. Elizabeth is trying out a new fashion," she says, "that's all."

"No, I'm not," Elizabeth says. "I like dressing this way much better than how I use to dress. It's more me."

"It is not more you," Melena huffs trying to set her foot down without becoming angry. "You are a nice girl, Elizabeth. And nice girls do not wear all black and parade about as if the world were a dark place."

"But ..."

"Luke," Ernest changes the subject, "you know we've got about fifteen hours to put in on that engine if we're going for it at the end of the month."

Ernest has of late developed a frustration with Luke since he seems to be the one doing all the labor for the races. He asks Luke, "Are you coming home to put the work in?"

"Does a bear shit in the woods?"

"Luke Bartleby," Melena says, "you do not use that language in front of your parents or your sister. Save the dirty words for your fraternity."

The chef interrupts their conversation, serving their second course while entertaining them with his skill.

The Starlings begin to eat, conversation slowly dying as they consume the food before them. Melena and Elizabeth cannot finish theirs, but nothing goes uneaten.

The following Tuesday evening, Luke is pledging back at school, safely withstanding Greek life, and Melena, Ernest and Elizabeth spend a quiet evening at home.

Dinner over and put away sometime ago, the inhabitants of the Starling house move in and out of their separate and isolated corners occasionally conversing with one another, though not always by choice.

"Ernest," Melena says from the hallway. She leans into the den to make sure that he listens.

"Yes, Melena."

"I really think it's time we did something about the carpet in this house. It's very old and worn, plus the color, well, this green is just too much these days."

Envisioning several of the homes she has decorated since she opened her store, Melena imagines her own sparkling with the same elegance she bestows on her customers. She wants to live in a beautiful place, too.

"Melena," Ernest says barely turning from the TV, "I just spent money on a new bedroom suite for Elizabeth last week. Now you want me to recarpet the entire house?"

"It's not like you don't have the money, Ernest."

*I'm the one cosigning your massive company loans,* she thinks. The figures stick out in her mind and she pushes for more, the way she has always pushed for more for her family.

"You certainly have enough money to buy all your expensive clothes and go on costly racing trips. You would think that you'd have some left over to change the carpet in your own house."

"Don't throw that in my face again, Melena." He pushes the land proposal in front of him for a seventy-two unit apartment complex funded by the federal government to the side. "I work my ass off to support all of you," he says. "Can't your business afford to replace the carpet in the house?"

"Why, heavens no," she says leaning against the door. "I don't have a design degree, Ernest, so I can't charge my customers as much as people who went to school. My business is still so new, and it has too many bills to pay."

He looks at the carpet underneath his feet. "It isn't even worn yet," he says.

All Ernest wants is for people to stop asking him for things, all sorts of things, solutions, advice, his time and money.

He shakes his head. "You think I'm here to make everything happen for everyone, Melena, but I'm not. I was not put on this earth to be a damn slave."

"Ernest," she says in a calm voice, "the carpet is seventeen years old. And you are a selfish son of a bitch. Did you know that?"

"Melena," his voice rises, "you always have to come in here and attack me. I think it's your favorite thing to do."

The hallway stretches behind Melena a battlefield between enemy lines, and Elizabeth's room is at the end of the adjoining hall.

"Don't you raise your voice to me," Melena shouts. "Maybe if you didn't sleep in the damn den every night then I wouldn't have come in here."

Down the hall to the right of the den, Elizabeth opens her bedroom door. She listens from inside then slowly creeps down the hall clutching the wallpapered walls.

Always she listens, policing them as if they were children in case anything were to ever cross a physical line again. The whole in the wall from the clock Melena flung was a glaring reminder left for months before fixing.

Ernest takes his glasses off and rubs the bridge of his nose. "I sleep in here, Melena, because you make it impossible for me to sleep in the bedroom."

"Oh, I do, do I?"

"Yes, you do," he says. "You keep the TV on very loud all night, and I work so I have to go to bed."

Melena says, blood boiling, "So, then it's my fault you can't sleep in your own bedroom?"

"You say it however you want to say it, Melena." Ernest throws his hands in the air. He stopped sleeping in there so long ago. Their marriage is such a sham.

"I don't care," he says. "You never listen to a word I say anyway, neither you nor Elizabeth."

Melena remains there in the doorway. "You sure are one smug son of a bitch," she says.

Ernest gets off the couch and steps toward her pointing. "You are a hard, hard woman, Melena, and one day ..."

"Stop it," Elizabeth screams lunging from the hallway. They both look at her. Ernest breaks away and shakes his head.

"Stop it right now," Elizabeth says again. "You stop yelling at her."

"Elizabeth," Ernest says, "do not speak to me that way. You have no idea what's going on."

"I don't care," Elizabeth says halfway hysterical, "just stop yelling. Stop it! Stop it! Stop it!"

Elizabeth leans down and grips the door handle. Ernest turns from the threshold and sits down on the couch while Elizabeth slides the door shut and turns around to stare at Melena.

"Go to your room, Mom."

"Your father is such a son of a bitch," Melena says standing there. She frowns at the closed door and turns to stalk down the hall toward her bedroom.

Elizabeth sighs as she watches her walk away. She goes back down the hall to her own room, which was originally Blackwell's, and shuts the door behind her.

Elizabeth increases the volume on her stereo and blasts heavy Industrial Metal music out of her speakers to drown her emotions in the sound. She turns around and kicks the wall with her boot.

Hopping up, she lays on her new princess bed with a large, blank-paged spiral notebook in front of her and a stick of charcoal in her hand.

Across the page, a few horizontal streaks run recklessly sketched in thick lines at the top of Elizabeth's notebook.

She looks at the drawing's lack of form and puts her face into her comforter, crying into its softness, angry, silent tears that make her want to scream.

Lifting her reddened face, she holds the notebook tight in her hand and bears down hard with the charcoal.

*I am in hell*, she writes in large black letters at the top, *and no one can save me.*

Writing this makes Elizabeth feel better, almost as if she were not alone, but she quickly flips the page. Not wanting to face the fact that is so obvious before her, she begins to draw a pointy-eared monster with long sharpened teeth and eyes shaped for the color of red death.

Lying flat on her stomach, her legs bend upward at the knee and swing aimlessly above her. She sporadically bangs the heels of her combat boots together as hard as she can and sings.

Looking closely at her drawing of the monster, Elizabeth cringes and scratches through it until it can be seen no more. She turns the page and runs her hands down a fresh blank sheet. Her voice echoes the Industrial music pumping from the stereo.

"Destroy us or make us saints."

No one can hear her. Destruction fascinates her, and she continues to sing along, scribble, and sketch in her notebook. Then something starts to take form on one page and Elizabeth doesn't let go of it.

The words she writes begin to mesh together into coherent lines, angry free-form poetry. They arise like petroglyphs on a cave wall, one line after another, revealing what her subconscious has hidden for so long.

Absorbed, Elizabeth vents, unaware of the tale framing itself in the poem. Lost, she doesn't care to sort out the differing emotions and reasons for her present state. Her mind dwells on shouting voices and the perpetual state of her broken home.

Elizabeth stops to look at the tiny world she has created on the page. The first line startles her and opens a tiny door kept quiet and locked away from the outside.

*Pretty rooms contaminate ....*

The next line grabs her imagination and tugs her backward so that she remembers being six.

*Persephone ....*

Shaking herself out of the vision, Elizabeth stares at the marks on the paper and they blur in front of her. She's shocked. These memories were gone.

Elizabeth, suddenly violent inside, releases an uncontrollable fury from her body. Satin ribbons run in vertical lines down the newly wallpapered walls of her room. She flings her notebook at them feeling alien to their beauty, and it falls onto the floor with a crash.

Rolling onto her back, she looks at her Misfits poster and beats her fist into her plush bed. Furious, and needing something to demolish, she rips the new blankets and sheets from on top of her bed and throws them into a pile on the floor.

Leaping off behind them, Elizabeth, in her boots, stomps up and down on the mass until she slips and falls into them. Unwilling to really destroy any of her new things, she pulls off the tags and sinks down into the soft heap to fall asleep and dream of a better world.

The third period bell rings just as Elizabeth walks through the door to Algebra class. Almost through with her fall semester of high school, she has secured her new identity. Other students shuffle in, sliding into their seats unnoticed, while two of Elizabeth's older classmates sing the Adam's Family theme to announce her entrance.

"*Da na na nuh,*" they say, "*da na na nuh,*" snapping their fingers, "*da na na nuh, da na na nuh ....*"

"Matthew, Jonathan!" Mrs. Carlson turns on the overhead projector, "that is quite enough, boys."

Mrs. Carlson favors these two candy-coated delinquents. They are older than the freshman in her class, popular and considered handsome by most girls at Brighton, including the teacher's own daughter.

Fully aware of Matthew and Jonathan's combined efforts to ruin the reputations of as many girls as possible, Elizabeth hisses at them as she walks back to her seat.

"Elizabeth," Mrs. Carlson harps, "don't you start, too."

Rolling her eyes, Elizabeth sits down and throws open her notebook. She continues the sketch of a dragon she began at the end of her last class.

The classroom is bright and dull, adorned with silly pinups that are supposed to inspire students to love math. Mrs. Carlson methodically calls the roll, checking names off her list with a red Sharpie pen.

Matthew leans toward Elizabeth, eyebrows raised.

"Hey, Morticia," he whispers, "what'cha doin'?"

"None of your business." Elizabeth stares at her paper wishing she could make the dragon spit fire at him.

"You gonna put a spell on me, Morticia?" Matthew says, hopeful. "I heard freaky girls like to fuck."

"In your dreams, asshole."

"What was that, Elizabeth?" Mrs. Carlson calls from the front of the room.

"I was just giving Matthew back his pencil," Elizabeth says. "He dropped it."

"*Uh huh*," Mrs. Carlson says, "well, let's not have any more pencil dropping and picking up for the rest of the period. Okay, young lady?"

"Certainly," Elizabeth says and returns to her drawing.

Matthew hides behind the girl sitting in front of him and laughs. He makes obscene gestures with his fist and his mouth, but Elizabeth doesn't look at him. Instead, she focuses on her own creation growing in front of her.

"I want everyone to turn in their homework first thing today," Mrs. Carlson says. "If you have not done it completely, then you will get a zero for today. Those of you with two or more zeros so far, I want you to be forewarned that I will be meeting with your parents."

Elizabeth turns in her somewhat completed homework and blocks out the sounds of math that disturb her thinking. Unable to focus at home, she no longer cares how well she does in school as long as she passes.

Under her fast-moving pen, a full army of trolls streams down the side of the mountain and a fire-breathing dragon flies overhead.

Later that day, with the nearly black lipstick washed off and her long hair bound up in pigtails, Elizabeth bends down and pulls her kneepad up over her right foot.

After today, the volleyball team has two season games left in the year and they have to win all three to make it to the playoffs. Elizabeth loves to play and the net keeps her from fighting with the opposing players.

When Elizabeth played soccer and basketball, her opposition always seemed to throw elbows. Elbows always led to Elizabeth's getting a penalty.

Smiling, she lets her kneepad hang down over her ankle mirroring the one on her left leg, and closes her locker to walk out toward the sinks where her teammates stand. She really is a normal girl just like them.

They pose in front of the mirrors, some fixing their hair and others adjusting their shiny blue uniforms.

Elizabeth squats low behind a shorter girl and ties big blue ribbons in each of her ponytails. Having them in her hair makes her feel like a Barbie.

"Cool ribbons, Elizabeth," Jennifer Shawl says.

"Thanks," Elizabeth fills out the bows with her fingers. "I got another one if you want it. I figure with us playing Jackson, I had to break out the biggest ones I had."

"Yeah, you don't mind?"

"No way." Elizabeth hurries back to her locker and retrieves the wide blue ribbon. She comes back to the mirror and hands it to Jennifer.

Jennifer asks, "Hey, will you put it in for me?" Her waist-length, red ponytail swings behind her.

"Sure," Elizabeth says and pulls the ribbon through the rubber band. She wraps the ribbon around once, ties it and stretches out the fabric until the bow is full. "How's that?"

"Awesome," Jennifer smiles. "I think we're going to win today. With you and Mary on the front line, we're a powerhouse."

"Oh, stop," Elizabeth says and turns around in the mirror to make sure her uniform is straight.

The locker room door opens and a petite Korean girl leans into the bathroom. Lynn Haley holds the wall and scolds, "Coach wants us upstairs *now*!"

Lynn and Elizabeth used to be friends. She stares at Elizabeth. "You better not be late," Lynn says and turns around. Her jet-black hair swings in a semi-circle with her.

"*Ugh*," Elizabeth says. She looks at everyone else still lagging in the bathroom. "Like I'm the only one here." She walks out and jogs up the stairs to the gymnasium.

Katherine, Elizabeth's sister-in-law, waves from the stands as Elizabeth walks through the door. She waves back and looks around for her mom. Katherine taps her watch. Melena is running late. Elizabeth gives her a thumbs-up and walks to the ball rack to take a ball.

Lynn, the only other player in the gym, has her own ball and smacks it against the wall warming up by herself. Normally the girls would play pepper together. But Lynn has disowned Elizabeth for her wardrobe and social choices, and she would never stoop as low as Elizabeth again.

Elizabeth smiles as Katie, the new girl, walks in. "Hey, Katie," Elizabeth shouts, "want to pepper with me?"

"Sure," Katie says and walks over to Elizabeth.

Lynn stares at them out the corner of her eye, decides to get Katie before Elizabeth can next time, and in retaliation, grabs the next player to walk in.

Melena makes it to the match after Elizabeth's team has won the first game. She smiles and waves to her daughter from the bleachers.

When Elizabeth has the ball, she shouts and screams clutching onto Katherine frantically always afraid that Elizabeth will be responsible for losing a point. Her nervousness is contagious and serves to increase Elizabeth's tension on the court.

Toward the end of her freshman year, inside one of the two all-ages clubs in Larnee, Elizabeth leans against a black wall with scores of heavily painted faces, Mohawks and shaved heads surrounding her. Hopeful, she sighs through her darkened lips as she continues to watch the door.

This volatile environment has become her favorite place, and she holds the anarchistic crowd high on a pedestal. Her head leans back and her breath stops as she catches sight of the rowdy group walking into Nowhere Else Tavern. She pinches her friend Casey on the arm.

"They're here." Elizabeth tilts her head toward the door.

"*Oww,*" Casey whispers.

"I told you they'd come to this show." Elizabeth tries to look calm. "They're not gonna miss War Hero."

"Yeah," Casey says, "but who all came?"

Casey's eyes are lined with heavy black eyeliner and her T-shirt bears a hollowed-eyed skull on its front. A year older, she met Elizabeth in chemistry class and soon found they had a number of things in common.

Along with punk rock music, both preferred hanging out downtown and going to shows instead of partying with the kids they grew up with.

"Oh, shit," Elizabeth turns away, "don't stare." She looks back toward the stage area where the band will be playing. "*She's* here, and she just saw us looking at them again."

"Man," Casey says, "they never go anywhere without her. Last time we were here I tried to go near that big guy with the eagle on his head and she made sure she got between us. She shoved me toward the wall like I was going to infect her or her friends."

"Well, I'm not having it." Elizabeth leans forward. "I'm not afraid of her. I mean, I guess if she wanted to, she could have them all beat me to death, but some of those guys are nice."

Elizabeth sighs, "A few of them smile and say hello now. She's the only one who acts so mean."

"Shut up." Casey leans against the wall and turns to the side. "They're headed this way."

From across the room, a motley crowd traverses the floor. While this group seeks the same aesthetic life that Casey and Elizabeth pursue, their individual backgrounds are different and on a less fortunate scale than the two, well-to-do girls.

Invading the hall, they fill the area in front and to the sides of the stage. Blue-collar boys and girls dressed in plaid, with shiny black flight jackets and heavy boots revel in their strength and play-fight with one another.

One of the boys is shoved into Elizabeth. She stumbles back on her feet and catches him in her arms. Slowly, she stands upright against his back and he turns around, still so close, to look at her.

"Sorry," he says embarrassed. The youngest of the crew, his face looks angelic and strong. Leaning against her, his blood warms.

"Why did you push me into this nice girl, Darren?" he says and jumps across the room to leap on Darren who, at six foot four, is built like an ox.

Darren shouts, "You think she's pretty!" Big, bald and proud, he swats his large hands at the younger boy. "Jack likes the punk rock girl," he says loudly. "He wants to marry her and kiss her. *Ha. Ha. Ha.*"

Elizabeth's cheeks, which her gothic fashion demands she whiten, turn a bright red. Her eyes cut to Casey who shakes her head against any visible reaction.

Elizabeth stares at Darren and Jack jumps on Darren hitting him with his elbows. The girl who shoved Casey steps forward having heard Darren's teasing. She grabs Jack by the back of his shirt and pulls him off Darren.

"What's he talking about, Jack?" asks Laura.

Jack shakes her hand off him. "Nothing. He's just being stupid."

Darren laughs behind his cigarette. "Jack likes the punk rock girl."

"What punk rock girl?" Laura asks turning around and staring hatefully at everyone in the room. "I don't see any punk rock girls here."

"That girl right there," Darren says and nods at Elizabeth. "The one who always wears the black and white, striped tights."

Jack punches Darren in the gut. "Shut up, man."

"Her? Whatever," Laura says eyeing Elizabeth. "That girl ain't nothin' but a new jack. She doesn't know the first thing about punk rock. The only punk rock girl in this town is my sister, Sally, and Sally hates new jacks. She'd beat the shit out of any punk rock poser."

Darren smokes his cigarette and Jack looks from Elizabeth to Laura. Casey fidgets nervously while Elizabeth returns Laura's cold stare. Neither girl blinks. Then Jack steps in.

"*Ah*, leave her alone, Laura," he says. "Everyone knows Sally's the biggest punk in town." He takes Laura by the shoulder and marches her off toward the bar.

Elizabeth's eyes follow them and she smiles as Jack briefly looks back at her.

About fifteen minutes later, the first band, a local hardcore group, begins the violent, mad, Dionysian revelry this crowd feeds on. Casey stands on top of a chair to the right of the stage while Elizabeth stands on the floor at the edge of the swirling pit.

Bodies, mostly boys, but not all, go flying past her in a circular motion. Their muscular arms punch and stretch forward as they move through and against the crowd, heads bobbing.

Laura darts in and out of the human vortex, shoving and hitting anyone in her path. Her plaid miniskirt swings in the air and her boots stomp a vicious trail on the dance floor.

From her blind side, a tall skinhead with red Nazi laces in his boots, pushes her back with all his force and sends her across the room. She flies into Elizabeth who keeps her from falling on the floor.

"Get off me!" Laura growls shrugging Elizabeth's hand away from her.

Laura leaps away and charges back across the room, driving her way through the melee. She marches up to the skinhead who pushed her and rises on tiptoe to get in his face.

His laces and his attitude don't belong in her skinhead group.

"You got a problem, mother fucker?" Laura shouts at him. "Why the hell did you push me?"

"I thought you were a skinhead girl," he says looking Laura up and down. "Or maybe you're just a big baby dressed up like one?"

"Look, you fucking Nazi," Laura breathes one inch from his face, "don't touch me again!"

Elizabeth and Casey stare at the scuffle in disbelief and the band keeps playing as the pit thrashes around. Their eyes dart from Laura to the Nazi and then back again.

Laura turns her back on him, quickly looking for Darren and Jack, but the Nazi steps forward and runs his hand across the top of her shaved head. He pulls on the fringe at the nape of her neck.

A wave of revulsion and shock passes through Laura and she wheels around to her left to punch the guy in the mouth with a hard right. He grabs his lip and spits blood on the floor.

Elizabeth smiles while Darren, Jack and the rest of the crew stop dancing and look at the Nazi. Others, unaware and uninvolved, continue to dance bumping off the crew and into others.

The Nazi grins with red teeth and punches Laura in the gut, toppling her over onto the dance floor.

As she falls, Darren, Jack and the rest of the crew leap on top of the Nazi and begin pounding him with their fists.

The lone Nazi is quickly joined by his friends who have been drinking at the bar and a minor riot ensues, two bands earlier than normal. Blue-collar skinheads beat Nazi skinheads while punk rockers fight Nazis in between.

Laura gets to her feet and jumps on the Nazi who hit her. She bites his ear and scratches his face, attacking him from behind while the front of the club deteriorates into a fighting arena of chaotic bodies and broken glass.

Jack flies to the right out the middle of the fracas entangled with a much bigger guy. Fearful, Casey clings to the wall, but Elizabeth steps near the two as they wrestle toward her. The guy throws Jack onto the ground and pulls his leg back to kick him in the face with his boots.

Springing toward them, Elizabeth punches him in the jaw as hard as she can while Jack rolls over and gains his feet. The Nazi staggers backward, then forward and punches Elizabeth in the face. Jack watches as she flies away from him back onto the floor.

His angelic countenance suddenly darkens as a new rage sweeps over him. He runs, leaps on the Nazi who hit Elizabeth and tackles him to the ground. Jack pins him there with his knees then hits him in the face repeatedly; all he sees is red.

The Nazi and all his helpless friends roll around on the floor with their hands over their faces trying to protect themselves, but Darren and the rest of their crew kick them over and over again with their steel-toed boots.

Laura screams at her aggressor, "You don't know what a skinhead girl is, Nazi loser!"

Jack leans back away from the guy beneath him and wipes his hand across his face. It smears a streak of blood down his innocent cheek. Elizabeth looks in his upturned eyes and smiles. She offers him her hand and pulls him to his feet.

Over the crowd, Darren shouts from the door. "Sirens! Get out of here, now!"

The skinheads and punk rockers that still can move scatter and fly toward the exit, yet Jack stays there holding onto Elizabeth's hand, unaware of the world around him. She smiles again, but Laura yanks at his shirt from behind.

"Come on, Jack," she says and runs toward the entrance. Jack stares at Elizabeth.

"I have to go," he says.

Elizabeth nods, "You should before you get in trouble."

"I'll find you next weekend," he says and runs toward the door.

She watches him leave and looks down at the guy moaning on the floor at her feet. Blood runs out of his nose and mouth. His face looks like mush.

*Jack beat the crap out of him because he hit me*, she thinks.

Casey yells, "Come on, Elizabeth or I'm leaving you."

Elizabeth shakes her head, grins and spits on the man writhing on the floor. Like the other kids at the show, anger fills her tormented thoughts and to see Jack avenge her eases part of the pain. Happy that someone made a stand for her, Elizabeth runs to the exit kicking her boot heels up behind her.

Casey grabs her by the arm and they dart outside to hop in Casey's car as the sirens grow louder. They pull out of the parking lot seconds before the parade of black-and-whites arrives.

"That was close," Casey says speeding away in her little green sports car. She's much more cautious than Elizabeth.

"I can't believe that guy messed with Laura," she says. "You shouldn't have jumped in like that, Elizabeth. That was stupid."

"Who cares?" Elizabeth says. "Did you see what Jack did?" She looks at the blood on her hand from where she held his. "He went insane because that guy hit me."

Casey shakes her head and Elizabeth sits back in her seat to watch the stars out the window. She dreams of Jack as a vengeful knight, the two of them united in a mythical battle.

--➤➔◉◎➔◄--

Summer brought intense heartache and longing to Elizabeth's world. After the bust at the War Hero show, Jack vanished from the crew and Elizabeth spent the summer watching the rest of them, forlorn, desperate to ask his whereabouts. Uninvited into their social circle, she remained silent, pining the hot Larnee days away in a fantasy world of love and violence.

The painkillers, infinitely prescribed to Melena, have not fixed the mysterious problem that ails her; instead, they have kept her semiconscious floating in a dreamlike state where she is helpless against the pain and sadness that hover on the edge of her reality.

Her life never was supposed to be this way, and yet the cycle of sickness has continued.

Many days, lonely in their house and helpless to find a solution to her mother's ailments, Elizabeth has stood in the darkened bedroom at the foot of Melena's bed to watch her breathe.

Sometimes, Elizabeth has sat on the floor beside her, even talked to her, revealing many tempting thoughts that she has concerning such things as pills and razors, but Melena has never heard her words. After a two-week confinement to her bed, Melena has gone into the hospital again.

Sophomore year, the first week of school, Elizabeth finds herself home with Ernest though she spends most of her time at volleyball practice and hanging out with her friends who have cars. Her behavior has grown increasingly loud.

Now in the hospital, Elizabeth takes the elevator to the floor where Melena stays. Neither having anything to say, she stands with Ernest in the elevator staring at the metal walls. These hospital trips, repeated many times over the last five years, have become mechanical for all the Starlings.

Melena's sickness offers no diagnosis or cure, only an inflamed pancreas; yet it provides the family with some consistency. Melena has been sick, will always be sick, and in a lot of pain until they discover what torments her body.

Elizabeth looks over at Ernest as he incessantly picks his teeth with a toothpick taken from a jar in his glove compartment after their brief fast food dinner. He had to eat and work on the phone the entire twenty-minute ride over.

The elevator chimes and settles as it reaches Melena's floor. The doors open slowly and Elizabeth follows Ernest out and down the interconnecting halls toward the wing where Melena stays.

Nurses pass by them walking the opposite way, some pushing carts filled with plastic vials and tubes, and others wearing the blank look of another workday come to an end. Elizabeth wonders about the injuries they've seen and catches up with Ernest.

"Do you think they let her eat solid food today?"

"I don't know, Elizabeth, maybe," Ernest says. "The whole point of her being in the hospital is for her to regain her strength. That's why they feed her through the IV's. Her body doesn't seem to do very well with food right now."

"I know," Elizabeth says, unsatisfied with the pat explanation. They turn left down the corridor toward Melena's room.

"I wish you had taken that ridiculous lock off your neck before we came up here," Ernest says to her, approaching Melena's room. "Your mother is in the hospital and seeing you with that padlock around your neck isn't going to help. You know, your dressing like that could kill her."

Elizabeth chews the inside of her cheek to keep from cursing at Ernest. He pushes the door open to Melena's room and Elizabeth takes a breath, bowing her head as she steps in behind him.

This darkened room faintly glows with the light of the silent television attached high on the wall opposite Melena's bed and one fluorescent light bulb shining over the sink by the door. In her medicated sleep, Melena stirs as they lay their coats down. Her eyes open and flutter as she focuses on Elizabeth.

"Hey, Mom," Elizabeth says.

"H-hey," Melena's voice is thickened by the painkillers. "Elizabeth, honey, is that you? I was just dreaming away."

Elizabeth walks over to her and holds the bed's metal rail beside Melena's head. She looks at her mother, wishing she could wave her hand and make it all better.

"I'm thirsty," Melena says separating her dry lips. She tries to reach toward the food tray, but Elizabeth cuts her off.

"I got it, Mom," she says. "You just lie still.."

Elizabeth hands her a cup of water with a flexible straw. The straw escapes Melena for a moment until she lifts her IV-laden arm up to still it. She takes a long sip and hands the cup to Elizabeth who sets it on the tray again. Melena sighs and her eyes look around the room.

"Hello, Ernest," she says. "I guess you and Elizabeth got some dinner."

"We did," he says pulling air through his teeth as he continues to clean them.

"You know, if you have something to do, then Elizabeth and I will be fine here."

"I do have a few errands to run for tomorrow," he says and stands. Ernest stopped feeling comfortable around his wife a long time ago.

"Elizabeth," he says, "you stay here with your mom and I'll pick you up in a couple of hours."

"Okay," Elizabeth says.

She pulls a chair over beside her mother's bed, thankful to have some company in her own isolated world. The door shuts softly behind Ernest, and Elizabeth looks at Melena whose eyes open and close as she drifts into a state of semi-consciousness.

"We have a game tomorrow, Mom," Elizabeth says trying to keep her awake. She hasn't been able to hold a decent conversation with her for a week and a half.

"*Mmm*," Melena mutters.

"You know," Elizabeth says, "the new coach might be really good for the team. I hope she is. We could be so good. Jackson has an ex-pro coaching them, and we get a PE teacher. She's been making us run sprints, and sometimes my asthma bothers me. I start feeling like I'm going to have a horrible attack and ..."

"*Mm*," Melena barely moans.

"Mom?" Elizabeth asks, frustrated to have lost her so soon.

Melena doesn't answer and Elizabeth leans up in her seat to look over at her mother. Melena's eyes are closed and she has begun her familiar, soft snoring.

Elizabeth's shoulders slump as she stares at her mother lying connected to IVs in the hospital bed. Melena's face is white and drawn and a film has collected in the corners of her mouth.

*She looks frail*, Elizabeth thinks, *like she could break at any moment.*

The faint light of the room shows Melena's surroundings and Elizabeth leans back in her chair to absorb them. The white room is bare except for an arrangement of flowers left by Katherine and Blackwell.

Something flashes on the TV, capturing Elizabeth's attention.

Reaching over Melena, she pulls the remote over to the chair with her. Pressing the "up" button, she scans the TV channels to stop at a rerun of *Cheers*.

Turning the volume down slightly, she stops when the voices come out of the tiny speaker box in slight whispers and pulls the device close to her head.

For almost two hours, Elizabeth sits by Melena's side staring at the TV and listening to the quiet voices. Every so often, she glances over at Melena who snores and occasionally murmurs an inaudible jumble of words.

Around seven, Melena's door slowly opens and Luke walks in with his new girlfriend, Emily. They beam with a pleasant happiness, foreign to Elizabeth's world as Emily smiles brightly with a benevolent attitude.

"Hey, kid," Luke says softly to Elizabeth.

"Luke," she says "hey, Emily."

"Hey, Elizabeth," Emily says, sweeping her luxuriant brown hair behind her shoulder. Her brow is confident and her flawless skin glows warm on her perfect face.

Luke walks to Melena's side of the bed and peers down at his mother. A wave of fear washes over him as he observes her weakened state.

"She's been sleeping for a long time now," Elizabeth yawns. "Dad dropped me off a while ago, but he should be back soon."

"Mom," Luke says gently.

Melena's eyes flutter and stay open. Her eyes go from Elizabeth to Luke and then Emily behind him.

"Oh, Luke," Melena says with less thickness in her voice than before, "I'm an absolute mess. I can't believe you brought Emily up here to see me like this."

"Hi, Mrs. Starling," Emily says in a soothing voice. "I just had to come see you. Here, let me help you with that."

Emily crosses to the bed and steps past Elizabeth. Leaning down, she raises Melena's bed. From her seat, Elizabeth stares at Emily's back with hard, jealous eyes.

"Oh, thank you, Emily," Melena says, "that's so much better."

"Good, good," Emily says and walks back around to the front of the bed to stand beside Luke.

"Luke," Melena motions, "get me a warm washcloth will you, honey, and a cup of water?"

Emily steps in. "Oh, I'll get it," she says and turns to the sink taking a wash cloth out of a basket on the counter. Elizabeth rolls her eyes.

"Thank you, dear," Melena smiles and takes the cloth out of Emily's hand.

"Y'all sit down," she says as she takes a sip of water and wipes her forehead. After that she wipes her cheeks, then her mouth.

One other chair sits in the corner of the room in addition to the one Elizabeth sits in.

"*Ah*," Melena sighs as she washes her face. Elizabeth jumps up from her chair and starts to move around to the other side of the bed.

"Here, Emily," she says. "You can sit in my chair and Luke can sit in that one. I'll sit with Mom on her bed."

"Don't you dare," Emily coos. "I wouldn't dream of it. You just stay right where you are and I'll sit on the edge of your mom's bed."

"Oh," Elizabeth says as her eyebrows cross together. She feels like she wants to hit Emily.

Elizabeth looks at her mother as Melena hands the cloth back to Emily, and Emily folds it and lays it back in the sink. Melena scoots her legs over underneath the blanket and Emily sits down on the edge of her bed next to her. Elizabeth glares at her in disbelief.

*Bitch,* she thinks. *You're just showing off so everyone will like you. Meanwhile, I've been sitting here for two hours.* Elizabeth slumps back down into her chair and stares at the TV again.

"Elizabeth," Emily turns to her, "that's such an interesting shade of lipstick you have on. Where did you find it?"

"I got it at Eckerd," Elizabeth perks up. "It's called Midnight. Revlon makes it."

"Oh, it looks good on you," Emily laughs, "but I don't think my sorority sisters would like it very much."

"Oh, right," Elizabeth says and thinks, *I'm not like you.*

Luke leans forward. He's so proud of Emily. She is the woman he wants to marry one day.

"Elizabeth," he says, "Emily's not into all that scary stuff you're into."

"Luke," Emily bats at him, "stop teasing your sister," she says. "We're here to see your mom."

Elizabeth looks at the both of them and wants to throw up. Instead, she turns away to imagine herself a television star with thousands of fans. She wears a stole, a black silk gown and flashy red jewels.

Beside her, Emily and Luke hold an active conversation with Melena. She has become quite loquacious after her long nap, and Elizabeth, quiet and alone, tunes them all out.

"The medication must be wearing off some now," Melena says. "I'm feeling much more awake."

Forty-five minutes later, Ernest comes to pick Elizabeth up. He says hello to all and confirms that Melena has all she needs until morning. Actions are how Ernest expresses himself with his family since he feels he cannot communicate with them otherwise.

Ernest and Elizabeth leave shortly after his arrival. After all, she does have homework and school in the morning.

Luke and Emily, with the evening still young for them, stay behind. This is the first girl Luke has truly fallen in love with and he dotes on her constantly while she takes this opportunity to play the dutiful girlfriend for Melena.

They decide to wait to leave until after she receives her next dose of painkillers. Melena will be awake until then and Luke likes to stay with his mother when he can. It allows him to step across that quiet void that stands between them, relieving the anxiety he feels for staying with his father. Before it's too late, Luke and Emily will say goodbye to Melena and she will drift into another long nap.

Two weeks into the school year, Jack resurfaces and finds Elizabeth at a huge punk rock show downtown. He stands in the middle of the crowd and Elizabeth stops to turn as she feels his presence like a soft electric sensation.

Jack faces sideways away from the band and stares at Elizabeth. Hypnotized by his cold blue eyes, she looks back at him waiting for the earth to crack in two.

Quite suddenly, in a *Clockwork Orange* manner, Darren bumbles out from the people behind Elizabeth and shouts, "Hey, O."

He shoves Elizabeth on the back and she soars into the people dancing in front of her. Picking his way through the crowd, Darren catches up to Elizabeth and pushes her again. She flies forward into the middle of the pit and spins through the dancers with her fists balled tightly.

A large black boot happens to move upward and kicks sideways into Elizabeth's stomach. She gulps and tilts back on the way down, but Jack catches her arm and pulls her away. His hand feels like it burns her skin and his eyes light up with the same sensation that courses through her veins.

Nervous and filled with a long-awaited excitement, Jack and Elizabeth stay near each other through the next performance, talking in abbreviated sentences whispered close to each other's ears.

Before the last band goes on, Darren and Todd, their crew's funny guy, wrangle the bunch into leaving and they all go riding in three or four different cars. For the first time, Casey and Elizabeth are invited to go drink forties with the crew at the end of a dead end street.

On their way home for the night, in the green sports car, Casey drives toward the neighborhood Jack lives in. She and Todd listen to Slapshot as loud as the speakers will play without blowing them out. They shout the lyrics and beat their hands on the dashboard.

In the small back seat, Elizabeth precariously puts her hand on the console between herself and Jack. He eyes it like prey from the other side of the car and takes it in his own, almost leaping for it.

Fingers clamping firmly around his, Elizabeth sighs but nervous, still faces the window. Her touch shoots through him, and he tugs her hand pulling Elizabeth closer to face him.

Their eyes ignite in one another with a pent-up fire that burns up the space between them. Jack takes her by the shoulders and kisses her with a fierce passion.

A moment later, Casey's car stops as Todd shouts for her to pull over. He turns to the back and starts laughing.

"Omigod, you two," he says with a pretend Long Island accent, "stop mauling each other."

After this night, Elizabeth and Casey hang with the crew permanently and some members still give them a good verbal hazing. Those same ones will never really stop. They don't think kids like

Elizabeth and Casey, with their pampered backgrounds, belong with them. But Elizabeth still feels understood by her new friends even though none of them know any of her secrets. They all have secrets. Everyone has secrets.

"Elizabeth," Ernest yells in a loud voice. He stands in the doorway of Luke's old bedroom trying to compete with the music coming from her room. Ernest hears nothing but the continual noise and clamor from Elizabeth's stereo.

Her health having improved, Melena works late at her store, The Green Gallery, going over the Christmas order with her floral designer, Ferdinand, who Elizabeth adores.

"Elizabeth," Ernest shouts louder this time but again to no avail.

From her princess-perfect room, heavy Industrial music blares out of the speakers at a deafening level. Finally, Ernest steps across the hall and knocks on her bedroom door.

The music abruptly stops and Elizabeth appears in the doorway. Eyes lined in thick black, she stares at him expectantly.

"Yes," she says. "You knocked?"

"That music is way too loud," he frowns. "I can't even hear the TV in Luke's room because you have it so loud."

"Fine," Elizabeth says. "I'm just getting ready to leave anyway."

She starts to shut the door but Ernest says, "Where are you going dressed like that?"

Elizabeth's skull T-shirt is mismatched next to her floral-print, Ralph Lauren blankets and cherry canopy bed. But her contrast here is nothing new; she's worn the same style of striped stockings and miniskirts almost every weekend since she's been going to see bands play downtown.

Elizabeth stares at Ernest wondering why this is an issue now.

"Where are you going dressed like that?"

"Out."

"Out where?" he says, arms crossed.

"Out with Casey and some other people." She grabs a black sweatshirt not wanting to go too far into detail. She's been having such a good time lately.

"I think we're going to see a band play."

"You know," Ernest says, "I really don't approve of you dressing that way. You look cheap and morbid, and that horrible music you're listening to isn't doing you any good at all."

"You know, Dad," she says thinking no one has a right to say a damn thing to her, "this really wasn't a problem before you started staying in Luke's room instead of the den."

"Don't get smart with me," he points at her. "You're on the fast track to a bad life, young lady. Just you wait and see."

Usually, Ernest doesn't say anything to Elizabeth about curfews or the way she dresses. She and Melena spend so much time together, and both husband and wife avoid one another almost completely, except when they clash.

"Well, that's just great, Dad. I'm sure I'll enjoy the journey."

"You know," he says turning around, "I can't say anything to you at all. You're just like your mother. You won't listen to a damn word I say."

"Whatever," Elizabeth says and slams the door. She turns the music back up and throws her things in a bag.

Ernest opens the door. "Do not slam the door on me in my own house, Elizabeth. I pay for this house and everything in it. You will not disrespect me this way."

"Right." Elizabeth ignores him and grabs a handful of cassette tapes.

"You know, Elizabeth," he shouts, "If your mother allowed me to be a bigger part of your life, you would not be acting this way. Do you hear me?"

She ignores him.

"Wipe that smug look off your face."

"You," Elizabeth shouts back at him, "don't tell me what to do!"

"That's because your mother lets you do anything you want. You run around with all that weird makeup and strange clothes on. Do you think God wants you too look that way?"

"Who cares about God?" Elizabeth screams at him. "Get out of my room!"

Ernest's face flushes red and he puts his hand on the doorknob. "Mark my words, Elizabeth, with the path you're on, you are headed for disaster."

He shuts the door behind him with a slight bang.

Elizabeth runs to it and screams, "Great! It wouldn't be any different from what life has been so far!"

She kicks the door and looks around furiously for her bag. Grabbing it, she turns off her stereo to stalk out of her bedroom and down the hall without looking back at Luke's closed bedroom door.

⋅→▬●◎═⊱⋅←

Early that spring, the Starling family crowds around a rectangular hibachi table at Osaka's, each having been called that morning by either Blackwell or Katherine, requesting their presence.

Luke has driven in from college, Elizabeth has agreed to meet up with her friends later, and Melena and Ernest have arrived on time in separate cars.

"Scoot over, Luke," Elizabeth says trying to settle down in her seat.

"Hey, easy there," he says. "Let Mom and everyone else get a chair before you start throwing a fit."

"I'm not throwing a fit." Elizabeth struggles to move her chair closer to the rest of the family. "Your chair is pushing mine off the edge of the table, I'm all the way out in the walkway."

The two of them don't get along all the time. Luke spends most of his days cold and aloof to his family since being at home makes him feel trapped in Melena and Ernest's battlefield again.

"Oh, okay, Miss Princess," Luke slides his chair slightly to the right. "Sometime you should think about others instead of yourself."

"Shut up," Elizabeth says and rolls her eyes.

Melena walks out of the ladies' room to sit down beside Luke and share the corner of the table with him. Then the door to the restaurant opens and Ernest walks in behind a family of four. He looks around expectantly.

Elizabeth waves and he brushes his hand through his slowly thinning hair as he crosses the dining room to sit at the table beside Melena.

"I'm starving," Elizabeth says ready to make an attempt at family conversation. "What are you going to do when class gets out, Luke? Are you coming home again?"

"No way," he says.

Elizabeth frowns. Now she knows she will be stuck alone with Ernest and Melena until she moves out.

"I have that apartment and some of the other guys are going to stay for summer school. Only time I'm leaving there is to drive a racecar."

"Luke," Ernest says scratching his nose, "the new issue of *WKA* listed the top ten drivers in each division and you're in the number one seat."

"Of course, he is," Elizabeth says. "He's Racer X."

"Don't call me that."

"Well, I'm glad you'll be getting a break from that fraternity," Melena says. "All that drinking isn't good for you or your liver."

She reaches toward his face to brush away a low hanging strand of hair. "You just always look so tired."

Luke squirms from her hand.

"Hey," Elizabeth nods. "There they are."

Katherine, chestnut hair and warm, understanding smile, waves from the door as she and Blackwell head to the table.

Many nights she listens to Elizabeth's desperation and her wish to flee the volatile home she lives in. Katherine reminds her she doesn't have much longer to live there.

Elizabeth hops up from the table and runs to her, hugging Katherine as Blackwell hugs Melena. Then Melena and Elizabeth switch and all the rest receive a pat on the shoulder. The family sits down and a tall young man comes over to wait on them.

"What can I get you all to drink tonight?" he asks.

The Starlings order green tea, Japanese beer, water and soda then relax in the familiar atmosphere of the restaurant. They eat here so often the whole staff knows them.

Blackwell leans back in his seat with a proud look on his face. He puts one arm around Katherine and smiles at them all.

"Well," he says beaming, "we didn't want you guys to have dinner with us just for the heck of it. I mean, Luke I'm glad you're home from school and all, but we have something we wanted to tell you as a group."

"What?" Melena cries. "What?"

"Katherine's pregnant," Blackwell says satisfied. "We're having a baby."

"Oh, my goodness," Melena shouts.

"I wasn't positive until yesterday when I went to the doctor," Katherine says, "but it's official."

"You stand up and give me a great big hug," Melena says scooting out of her chair. She throws her arms around Katherine and holds her tight.

"Well, Son," Ernest says, "congratulations. Call me granddaddy from now on."

"And me an aunt," Elizabeth says. She points to Luke, "you're an uncle."

His smile is as big as his brother's.

"That's right," Katherine says from over Melena's shoulder. "Aunty Elizabeth."

Elizabeth stands and runs back to her sister-in-law and hugs her again.

"Yep," Blackwell sighs, "you know, when you got it, you got it."

"Blackwell," Melena says and leans down to hug him.

"What can I say," he hugs Melena back, "I'm potent."

Melena, Katherine and Elizabeth sit back down in their seats as the waiter comes back with their drinks. Melena looks up at him and smiles as he sets a green tea in front of her.

"We're celebrating tonight," Melena tells him.

"Oh, yeah?" he says. "What are you celebrating?"

"Our first grandchild," Melena smiles. "My daughter-in-law is pregnant."

"Terrific," the waiter says. "Congratulations."

"Thank you," Katherine smiles.

"I'll give you all a few more minutes," he disappears discreetly.

A thought crosses Melena's mind and she reaches past Ernest for Katherine's hand. It's probably the closest the two of them have been in months.

"This doesn't mean you all will move closer to your parents, Katherine, does it?" she asks.

"Oh, no," Katherine says though she likes the idea.

Blackwell picks up his beer. "I couldn't do that anyway, working with Dad. But it does mean we need a bigger house."

"Well," Ernest says ready to step in, "I'll help you look into that."

A middle-aged couple sits down in the two empty seats at the end of their table. Melena smiles at them and says hello as they unfold their napkins and place them in their laps. They smile back at her curiously and nod.

"We're pregnant," Melena says to them. "I mean, she's pregnant with our very first grandbaby."

"Oh, congratulations," the couple says.

"Thank you," Katherine nods.

The waiter returns and they share a delightful dinner filled with many questions about the baby, names and the future. Melena quickly lays down the law that she is not to be called Grandma, but instead, Nanna. Everyone seems delighted and filled with good will.

·-·=◎◎=·-·

Two years and three months creep by at a painfully slow pace for those still living in, and somewhat chained to, the Starling family home.

Between her bouts with her mysterious illness, Melena occupies herself with The Green Gallery and her outside design work, which with her careful attention and aggressive energy, has blossomed into a rewarding career.

Equally tied to his work, Ernest continues to cover the land with offices and homes, maintaining the weight of the Starling empire on his shoulders.

Ruled completely by their respective careers, the two have allowed these jobs to become the perfect excuse for total avoidance of one another while keeping the family together, at least as far as appearances go.

Melena works late at her store and Ernest works late at his office, while Elizabeth finds various ways to spend her time.

Luke and his picture-perfect girlfriend Emily have spent a wonderful few years together at school, and soon he will graduate. The fraternity life, private college and love have done wonders for his personal growth.

Emily seems to take the chill from him when she is around and makes him more tolerant of his family. Now, Luke thinks he has the experience he will need to wheel and deal the Starling family's fortunes.

Across town, Blackwell and Katherine raise a daughter named Isabelle, doted on by all the Starlings. Blackwell has worked with Ernest for some time, but the prospects of the family business do not reach the height of his aspirations.

An income capped in the lower six figures won't be the financial limit of his future. Already he has had three ventures on the side that have not taken him yet where he wants to be. Blackwell, gifted, has inherited that salesman's charm Pratt carried all his life, up until the strokes.

After a long battle with heart disease, Pratt Dupree took his last breath and the girls buried him beside his mother in a historic Holiday cemetery. The funeral brought out the remaining town elders of Pratt's time as well as their children who remembered the man their fathers spoke of.

Deciding it best to move Bell and Leopold to Larnee for a change, Melena asked and Ernest helped her purchase a house for them. Relieved to be able to look after her family, Melena sees her mother on the way home and the way to work nearly every day.

Each family member lives and breathes inside his or her own microcosm, while Elizabeth remains a prisoner in the family house. Kept miserable by Melena and Ernest, Elizabeth finishes her remaining days of high school longing for an escape.

Though she's president of the drama club and captain of the volleyball team, this strange girl is an outsider to the people she grew up with who still delight in making fun of her black boots, black clothes, powdered face and nearly black lipstick. But they are not the end of her.

Elizabeth's fostered a second home downtown with her crew of wild friends. Having them fortifies her emotional walls, and allows her to all but dare her childhood peers, with her obstinate will, to make her conform to their ways.

Inviting their ridicule yesterday with a short, black wig, she informed them after their pointless questions that she'd cut off her long red hair.

Though it's changed colors over the years, they of course knew she hadn't. She didn't expect them to believe her, and now she sits with them in the brightly lit lunchroom.

"Oh, god, Elizabeth," Harry Brighton, the spoiled and rich namesake of their school says to her. "What happened to your black hair?"

"I ate it," Elizabeth says and pours the contents of her brown lunch bag onto the table. For the last twelve years, her lunch has been subject to very slight variations by Melena. The consistency makes Elizabeth feel safe.

"My, my, Elizabeth," snippy, blond Evelyn says. She looks around the table and laughs.

"How did you get your hair to grow back so fast?"

"Miracle Grow plant food," Elizabeth says and takes a bite out of her peanut butter and jelly sandwich.

"Elizabeth," Harry says, "I heard you scalped a bunch of Asian kids and sewed all their hair together."

The kids who've participated on either side of this sort of rivalry, stop eating to listen.

"Morticia," Harry shakes his head and plays his voice up for his audience, "you just had to go and kill someone, didn't you?"

Evelyn and Nicole toss their hair and laugh loudly.

"Harry," Elizabeth sighs. "Evy and Nic here have an excuse. They're just stupid, but you, you should be quiet. Do you really want everyone to know?"

Nicole smirks. "To know what, bitch?"

"Oh," Elizabeth says, "that the reason Harry's doing this is because I wouldn't hook up with him at Susanna's last weekend."

Evelyn and Nicole stop and stare at Harry in disbelief. Once Elizabeth crossed over and changed her looks, they considered her beneath them. Harry's eyebrows rise. He was so angry that she wouldn't have him.

"Like I would ever want to hook up with you, you dirty whore." He high-fives Patrick who sits next to him.

Elizabeth smiles, "Don't call me a whore you fucking mamma's boy. I bet it really sucks having your parents buy your friends."

Harry's always bragging about his family's money. Evelyn and

Nicole, along with others of like mind, thrive on that sort of snobbery. These high school kids love to lie about and ruin their classmates for the entertainment of it.

"Oh," Harry shouts, "this little Satanist has such a pretty vocabulary, doesn't she?"

He turns around. "You know what I heard?" he asks. "I heard you like to sacrifice children before you have sex with the hordes of low-lifes you hang out with downtown."

"Sometimes," Elizabeth says teeth gnashing, no longer bothering to dispute him, "it gets messy."

"Face it, Elizabeth," Harry pronounces, "you're nothing but a low-life gutter whore, just like all your gutter friends. You're just a dirty little slut waiting for the next guy."

Elizabeth picks up her sweet tea and throws the full cup into Harry's face. She stands up, looking down on him as his face and Polo shirt drip with brown liquid and bits of ice.

"You're a liar," she says.

Harry's eyes flicker. He picks Patrick's enormous taco salad plate up and hurls it at Elizabeth.

She swats it down back toward Harry before it can hit her. The contents of the taco, salad lettuce, ground beef, tomatoes and sour cream, fly all over Evelyn and Nicole who sit horrified.

"You low-life bitch," Harry shouts.

In one move, Elizabeth leaps across the table, reaching to tear his face off, but Assistant Principal Bowman dashes from his watch to grab her by the back of her shirt and pull her back down.

"Young lady," Bowman says in his deep booming voice.

Reginald K. Bowman wrestles with Elizabeth as she tries to attack Harry. He played football at a lower-division college back in the '70s, but now, he's overweight and the kids don't respect him.

"Young lady," Bowman says struggling to hold her, "what's going on here? You stop that this instant."

Elizabeth relaxes and jerks away from him.

"Harry started it," she growls. "I just sat down to have lunch and he started calling me a whore and saying all these horrible things."

"I did not, Dr. Bowman," Harry says. "You know me. I would never say anything like that. She's hysterical."

"Yeah, I got your number, too, Mister Brighton." Bowman shifts his weight, now holding Elizabeth by her arm. He's the only faculty monitor on this lunch shift and when he leaves, the lunchroom will get wild.

"Both of you," he says, "are coming to my office right now so get your things."

Elizabeth leans down and picks up her book bag, leaving her brown lunch bag and her sandwich behind. She smiles at Evelyn and Nicole, both of whom sit in absolute shock at the grotesque mess covering their cardigan sweaters.

Assistant Principal Bowman walks Harry and Elizabeth out of the lunchroom, one on each side, while everyone else watches, most amused. News of their food fight sweeps across the school like wildfire for the remainder of the day.

Back in Dr. Reginald K. Bowman's wood paneled office, the afternoon light streams through the slanted blinds in soft beams. It falls on several pictures of Bowman from his younger, much thinner days before the accident, when he still had all five fingers on his left hand.

There isn't a day when he doesn't think, damn that mower. It makes him mad sometimes, especially when he has to deal with the kids he thinks are from good, stable homes.

Harry and Elizabeth enter the office and Reginald follows them, closing the door and taking a seat at his desk. He does not open the blinds. Harry turns, sits and blurts out a torrent of words in his defense.

"You know," he says, "she wasn't always this way. Elizabeth used to be like the rest of us. She used to be normal, but now she wears those damn boots every day and she dresses like a freak."

Before freshman year, ever since that eighth grade Halloween party where she came dressed like a hooker, Harry imagined having sex with Elizabeth. But she never thought twice about him.

"So, what you're telling me then, Harry," Bowman says and pauses. He leans forward and adjusts his wide glasses thinking it makes him seem more credible.

"Harry, you think Elizabeth has somehow dissociated herself from you and the rest of your classmates and that this dissociation has hurt your feelings?"

"Exactly," Harry points at him and sits back in his chair. He feels comfortable manipulating people to get what he wants.

"See, Elizabeth," Bowman says now turning to her, "Harry wants to be your friend. He admits to having a problem though because he feels that you no longer want to be his or the other kids' friend."

"That's a bunch of crap and you know it Dr. Bowman." Elizabeth shakes her head. "You see the stuff that happens in this school, but you don't care. Girls get harassed like prostitutes and boys get tormented in all sorts of ways. Why don't you ask Harry about it yourself? He started doing it to me years ago."

"Now calm down, Elizabeth," Bowman points and jabs his hand at Elizabeth, emphasizing his words.

"Maybe you offended them with your choice," he says. "I mean, after all, how many of Brighton's students dress the way you do?"

Reginald remembers the weird kids even when he was back in school,and, as a football player, he did his share to harass them.

"I travel these halls," he says, "every day among you kids and I'll tell you, Elizabeth, those of you who do dress this way all have problems with the other kids. The other faculty and I have discussed it before. It appears to us like you just don't want to be a part of the group."

"I can't believe you're saying this to me." Elizabeth laughs. "This isn't my fault, and you have no right to tell me what to wear. It has nothing to do with my clothes."

Her voice gets louder. "Harry called me a dirty, low-life whore," she says. "What should I have done, Dr. Bowman? I asked him to be quiet, but he just kept going on and on lashing out at me all because I wore some stupid wig yesterday."

Bowman leans forward. "Young lady, if your clothes are causing a disruption with your classmates, maybe you should ..."

"Maybe I should nothing," Elizabeth interrupts. "My clothes are not the problem. The problem is that you let these jerks do whatever they want just because they look the part you want them to play as 'the good little students.'"

Harry smiles and Elizabeth says, "You think just because he wears neatly pressed, expensive clothes that he doesn't go out every weekend and do drugs while trying to have sex with everyone in town?"

"Miss Starling, you need to calm down," Bowman warns.

"You know what, Dr. Bowman?" she says, "I am calm and rational, but you aren't. You're sitting here siding with this weasel trying to blame me for everything he's done. Well, I don't have to take it." She stands up to walk out.

"Miss Starling," he says, "where do you think you're going? This meeting isn't over."

"Oh, yes, it is," Elizabeth says. "I'm going to call my mother. You can speak to her about this if you want. She knows what's been going on with Harry and the others for the last three years."

Elizabeth steps into the main part of the office and asks the receptionist if she can use the phone. The disgruntled office aide asks her what the number is and dials it while Elizabeth waits with the receiver in her hand. Melena's voice comes over the phone, and Elizabeth tells her what happened in an even but hurried voice. A few minutes later Melena asks to speak with Dr. Bowman.

Elizabeth hands him the phone and the two of them converse for the better part of five minutes. Melena does most of the talking and when she has finished, Dr. Bowman hands the phone back to

Elizabeth. Melena tells her to go on and get her things, then just come to the store for the rest of the day.

Elizabeth thanks her and hands the phone back to the receptionist. Dr. Bowman tells her to leave in a very polite voice, and that he'll take care of everything in the office for her. Reginald seems flustered and Harry watches Elizabeth as she walks out the office door.

Dr. Bowman steps back to his desk and sits down across from Harry. He yanks one polyester clad leg up so he can relax his knee.

"Seems like you and I have a few things to talk about, Harry," he says.

Later that day, after wandering aimlessly around the mall with her friend Amy, Elizabeth comes home to a house that stretches out in darkness around her. The hum of the appliances is the only sound.

Quickly, she turns the kitchen and hall lights on, walks to the refrigerator, opens the door, looks inside and shuts it again. Elizabeth tosses her book bag on the table and takes a glass from inside the cabinet above the kitchen sink.

These movements are an integral part of her everyday latchkey kid routine as she goes back to the refrigerator to pour a glass of Mr. Pibb. Pulling a chair from the table, Elizabeth scoots it over in front of the TV where she sits down to watch reruns of old sitcoms for the remainder of the afternoon.

Now that she has a car, Elizabeth moves independently for the most part. With volleyball season winding down, she's had to find other things to keep her from being at home. Usually, neither Melena nor Ernest arrives until hours after the sun has departed and night has taken over, which leaves Elizabeth in the big house all by herself.

Here in Melena's yellow-wallpapered kitchen, Elizabeth stares at the small TV. The walls surround her like a protective cell barricading her with scores of corn baskets encircled in yellow halos that run down the white background toward the floor. This scenery hasn't changed once since Ernest built the house and the yellow looks old and worn.

Elizabeth tries to ignore her loneliness and the mounting fear she feels inside her home, but she cannot. *I'm just paranoid*, she thinks saying it over and over again in her mind. *There's nothing here, nothing that can hurt me. Maybe I'm crazy, and they'll take me away, but I hate the trees outside.*

She looks out the window and thinks, *It'll be dark soon. I just wish someone else were here.*

An hour or so later, Elizabeth steps over to the table and sits down to look over, but not complete, her homework assignments.

Every time she tries to concentrate, bad thoughts and loud voices fill her mind to distraction. Reading remains her only salvation, and she takes out her English homework to finish *The Good Earth*.

Later she kneels in front of the lower cupboard where the snacks are kept, mostly in Tupperware containers, and opens the door. She sits down in front of it and pulls out a box of vanilla wafers. Eating a few, she lies on the floor with her head resting inside the cupboard door.

Outside her home, the sun has gone down and the bare windows of the kitchen fill Elizabeth with unease. They loom above, eye level with the back porch, black and empty. She envisions all the creatures that could ascend the back stairs and tap on those very windows.

Placing the vanilla wafers back in the cupboard, Elizabeth takes her bag to go upstairs but leaves all the lights on behind her. She walks up the stairs and down the hall toward her own room.

At the edge of the hallway leading toward her end of the house, Elizabeth hesitates. The light switch is halfway down its length, waiting in the dark.

*No one is hiding in the shadows*, she thinks, *or around the corner by the sliding glass door.* She sets her bag down, darts to the switch and exhales as the light comes on.

Obsessed by the possibility of a threat, she leaves her things on her rose-colored, carpeted bedroom floor. Going from switch to switch, Elizabeth turns on all the lights in her bedroom, Luke's room and the connecting bathroom. She then wanders through the house, turning on every other light she can find. The house has too many shadows for her comfort, too many bad memories cluttering up its corners.

"I just need a little light in here," Elizabeth says to herself as she walks back through the halls. But even this total illumination fails to make her feel safe. Her issue with fear cannot be resolved without escaping the confines of Melena's and Ernest's walls. It is what she dreams of daily. She will never feel safe here.

Stopping in the den, Elizabeth picks up the phone and dials Melena first.

"Hi, Mom."

"Hi, honey," Melena says, "are you feeling better?"

"Yeah," she says, "I went to the mall and walked around."

"That's good," Melena says. "I told that principal how Harry treats you and that I wasn't going to tolerate it anymore. I think he got the message."

"Yeah, I think so." Elizabeth asks, "What time are you coming home tonight?"

"Probably not until eight o'clock," Melena says looking at the design catalogues strewn across her desk. "Maybe a little later." She has to have her spring order in by mid-morning.

"Oh," Elizabeth mutters. She turns away from the enormous windows in the den, trying not to look out. They, too, open to the back patio and the woods beyond.

Melena says, "Go ahead and have a snack and I'll fix us something when I get home."

"I'm so hungry," Elizabeth lies. She wants attention so badly she becomes childish in an attempt to lure Melena home.

"Well, Elizabeth, that's why I told you to fix a snack. I'll come home as soon as I'm done at the store, but you know how busy we get here."

Most nights Melena and Elizabeth go out to dinner together, meeting wherever they decide. Lately, Melena's customers have been so greedy for her time that she's had to stay later than she expects. Often, Elizabeth sits by herself at some restaurant telling the waiter her mother is on her way.

Familiar with this, Elizabeth says. "Well, I guess I'll see you when you get home then."

"All right, Elizabeth. 'Bye."

"'Bye."

Elizabeth hangs up the phone and calls Ernest next.

"Hey, Dad."

"Hello, Elizabeth," Ernest says. "How are you today?"

"I'm fine." She twists the phone cord in her hand and turns around on the brown tweed couch.

"I was just wondering," she says, "what time you were coming home tonight."

"Oh, let's see." Ernest rocks back in his chair on the other end of the phone, eyeing the work in front of him.

"I'd say about nine thirty."

"Oh," Elizabeth says. "Okay, well I'll see you then."

"Yeah, *uh*, is everything all right, Elizabeth?" he asks.

*No*, she thinks, *damn it. Everything is not all right. I'm afraid there are monsters lurking around every corner of this house waiting to kill me. I feel like I've lost my mind, looking under beds and behind closed doors, but I am really scared. I just wish one of you were here even if you were fighting.*

The house brims with years of the family's negative emotions, and they seem to float around her like phantoms. Elizabeth is miserable in their company and her mind locks in this irrational torment almost every afternoon.

"Elizabeth?" Ernest asks.

"Yeah, oh, yeah," she says. "I'll see you when you get home."

"Well," he says, "okay then, bye."

Hanging up the phone, Elizabeth stares at the fireplace in front of her.

*Maybe I want to die*, she thinks. *Then I won't have to be afraid anymore because then the monsters can have me and I'll be one of them. No one would care anyway. They didn't even want me in the first place.*

It's funny how the things a child hears always stays with them never to be forgotten.

She stands up and walks into the hallway bathroom where the floor's soft pink throws feel nice under her feet. This bathroom, hers as a child, has always had pink throws as Melena has replaced the old ones with different styles and shades.

Elizabeth pulls out one of the drawers and picks up an old comb left there years ago. Running it through her hair for distraction, she turns around and gazes at the blue bathtub. Spying a silver blade, she reaches over and takes the razor from the ledge.

*I wonder what they would do with themselves if they came home and found me dead*, she thinks. *Here I would lie on the bathroom floor, blood spilled in giant pools that stream from my wrists in tiny ribbons.*

*That would be something pretty for them to see. They would have to deal with it together, and I would be gone forever into silence. They would have no idea why and then they would realize they had been too busy to know.*

Elizabeth lays the razor down on her wrist and imagines slicing open her veins for the blood to pour out and onto Melena's pink throws. Her eyes blink in disgust as she hurls the razor away from her as hard as she can. It bounces off the blue bathtub and lands in pieces on the floor.

Elizabeth walks back down the hall toward her end of the house feeling like a ghost already. She steps into Luke's room to turn on the television and sits down on the floor to pick up the phone.

"Jack," she says as the other line picks up.

"Elizabeth," he says, "I was wondering when you'd call."

"I got in a fight today in the lunchroom."

"Oh, yeah?" he asks. "Nobody hit you, did they?"

"No," she says. "It was more like a food fight, but I jumped across the table and would have beaten his ass if the principal hadn't grabbed me."

"His?" Jack asks. "You're telling me you got in a fight with a guy today?" Now, he wants revenge.

"Yeah," she says, "I wore my wig to school yesterday and the whole lot of preppy losers made fun of me, which normally I don't give a crap about. But today, Harry said all this really bad stuff in front of everyone. He just kept going," she says, "and I had to do something. That bastard called me a low-life whore and said all my friends were gutter trash."

"Maybe," Jack says, "this joker needs to *meet* some of your friends." He props one foot up on his bed and thinks about the entire crew storming her school like hooligans.

"You know, baby, you don't have to take that shit from those jerks even if you did grow up with them. Just let us come to one of their parties and we'll shut them up for good."

"No," she shakes her head, "they're not worth it. Besides, you do fine at your school."

"That's because I'm invisible," he says. "I'm so stealthy they don't even know I'm there."

Jack prides himself on going unnoticed in and out of most places. He would be the perfect thief and Elizabeth loves this quality about him. She wants to disappear with him inside a fantasy novel.

"They're fools," she says. "You're too wonderful to ignore."

Jack smiles. "You're not too bad yourself, my dear. So, when can you hang out? I'm dying to see you."

They talk for over an hour, the same way they've talked on the phone for the last couple of years discussing books, bands and their immense love for one another.

Finally, they hang up after Jack's mom calls him to dinner for the third time. Left staring at the TV set in her brother's room, Elizabeth sits alone once again.

A horror movie plays on the television, and Elizabeth, aware of what her mind will do, knows she shouldn't be watching it when she's home by herself. She cannot make her hands change the station though. In her inner world, she identifies with the monster and sits entranced with the self-reflection.

The wind roars outside Luke's windows bashing tree branches against them, and the tips scrape against the glass. The thrashing emits several high-pitched sounds and Elizabeth leaps up to look around. She thinks of claws made of knives as the darkness outside encroaches on her.

With Ernest working at the office during the week and in the new garage on the weekends, the house has grown more unkempt with each passing year. The bushes and trees overrun parts of the yard while household projects go undone. No one wants to invest any time in the forsaken home, nor be there any longer than they have to be.

All the lights throughout the house are lit, but still, Elizabeth feels disaster in the air. She slinks down the hall away from her room and turns right at the end.

*A murderer could be hiding in Mom's room or my old one*, she thinks. *I'll just have to get something to protect myself with. That way if anything happens, I'm ready.*

With soft, hushed steps, as if someone would hear her movements and spring upon her, Elizabeth goes to the microwave and stops. She pulls out the largest knife from the chopping block and holds it up in front of her feeling defended. The blade is two inches wide at its base and shines in her hand.

"See out there," she says to the windows, "if you come in here, I'll cut you."

Armed, she walks back up to Luke's room. Setting the knife down on the carpet, she thinks of its inadequacy if she were to fight with it alone.

Fed by the fantasy novels and horror movies she watches, Elizabeth's imagination loves to dwell on battles. Even when she's in school, she thinks about that movie where the Communist invade America and plots her escape.

Inside her own room, she reaches under the bed and pulls out a hockey stick and a baseball bat. Carrying one in each hand, Elizabeth goes back to Luke's room and sits down on the floor with the knife in front of her, the hockey stick on her left and the baseball bat on her right.

*I swore I wasn't going to do this again,* she thinks, *but if something were in here, at least I could kill it before it kills me, survival of the fittest.*

Relaxing against the back of Luke's bed, Elizabeth tries to ignore the constant beating against the windows. It's way past eight o'clock and she sits counting the minutes away, and waits for Ernest and Melena to come home. Out of spite, she has not eaten.

A little before nine o'clock, the basement door opens and closes. The sound echoes up to her and she stands to take the weapons back into her room. *Don't want anyone to see how crazy I am,* she thinks.

Sliding the bat and stick underneath her bed, Elizabeth carefully places the knife in the top drawer of her nightstand. She turns the lights off in every room on her way to the kitchen and hurries down the stairs. Relieved, she steps inside and sits at the table.

"Hi," she says to Melena.

"Hello, Elizabeth," Melena says. "I stopped by Subway and got us some sandwiches."

"I'm so hungry I feel like I'm going to pass out," Elizabeth says.

"I told you to have a snack, Elizabeth."

Melena, largely unappreciated her whole life, spent so many years, so much of her time, providing for her family. Now that she's finally doing something for herself, it annoys her when one of them makes her feel guilty for following her dreams.

"You knew I was going to be home late," she says.

In a low voice, Elizabeth says to the table, "You always get home late."

"What did you just say?" Melena asks turning around, hands on her hips.

"Nothing."

"You know, Elizabeth, I cooked for this family every night for over twenty years, and now that I have this business, I just can't do it anymore. I work very hard, and I would expect you to be aware of that, but you aren't. The only thing you, or any of you, care about is yourself."

Elizabeth backtracks and tries to prevent a fight. "I don't care about the food, really."

"You know," Melena huffs, "your father could come home early, too, and you could have dinner with him every night. He could look after you the way I do, instead of coming home so late."

"Mom," Elizabeth says voice rising, "I said I didn't care about the food. I don't need Dad to take care of me. I'm fine."

After years of defending Melena who has convinced Elizabeth of her father's gross injustices against the family, Elizabeth's stomach turns to think of giving him more attention than her mother.

"Don't you raise your voice to me, young lady," Melena says. "I don't need you to yell at me, too."

"I'm not yelling!" Elizabeth shouts losing her temper. "You know what, just forget it."

She stands and opens the refrigerator door to take another soda and whisk the sandwich off the table. She pounds up the stairs and she storms, warped by pain and confusion, toward her room. Setting her dinner on the floor, Elizabeth turns on her television and watches the old black and white TV shows while she eats.

After dinner, she brushes her teeth and gets into bed. Next to her lamp on her bedside table is a paperback Tolkien novel Jack gave her, worn with use. She picks it up and reads it until the early hours of the morning trying to forget her life.

--»=◉◉=«--

Daytona Beach, Florida, late January, a gusty ocean wind whips around the Daytona Motor Speedway chilling the spectators and drivers who watch the night race run. Tough men with grease-stained hands and racing jackets of every imaginable hue pull their collars closed against the stiff wind.

The same wind ruffles a paper stack of numbers Elizabeth holds down with her slender wrist. Beside her, Melena stands with two identical NFL sleeping bags that have been in the family since before Elizabeth was born.

She unfolds one, throws it around Elizabeth's shoulders and wraps one side over the other at her neck. Melena hates to think of her children catching a cold, and Elizabeth and Luke have always been sensitive to it.

Elizabeth slides the eighteen-by-twenty inch time board lying in her lap out from under the blanket. The wind picks the numbers up and they make a ripping sound as the thick pages flap on the spiral binder.

In a yellow fold-out chair, Melena sits next to Elizabeth and carefully wraps the other blanket around her own shoulders. It's a little past midnight and Luke is in his third leg at the multi-class, twenty-four hour race at Daytona.

The infamous track has a lap length of 3.56 miles, curving like a snake in the road course, and allowing for sprints in the straightaways. In front of Melena and Elizabeth stands a heavy metal guardrail. Two feet beyond that the three different classes of cars race by at speeds averaging 190 miles per hour.

Melena feels she needs to be in this particular spot, one of the course's most treacherous elbows, so she knows Luke hasn't crashed into the guardrail while she sits somewhere safe. They've given him extra hours to drive and she's worried that he'll tire.

"Here he comes," Elizabeth says. "I'll time him this time."

Pulling a small red stopwatch out of her pocket, Elizabeth holds her thumb over the start button. Comfortable with the continuous resonant thrum of the engines, she listens as the cars race by at varying levels of loudness and intensity.

These auditory variations reveal the abilities of the three different classes of cars: Unlimited, Grand Touring and Showroom. At this race, rank is determined by the suspension and transmission modifications each car has, or has not, received.

While Luke rides tight with two cars from a higher class, Melena leans forward anxiously. She wants him to let the other cars pass, but he drives the silver G.T. Trans Am nailed to the bend as the trio heads straight toward Melena and Elizabeth.

Behind Luke, the rear right tire on the number 43 car edges out into the grass, destabilizing the rear end and causing it to slingshot slightly to the left. Oblivious, Luke keeps the wheel and holds his lead in front of the other cars. Engines roaring, they fly by the guardrail within inches of his family.

Elizabeth snaps her finger down on the button.

"Got him," she says watching them speed away. "I don't see why he can't race against those other cars. I mean he's obviously a better driver."

"We don't want him to do that, Elizabeth," Melena says. "It's dangerous what he's doing. He should let the faster cars go past him and only race the ones in his class."

"Well," Elizabeth huffs watching the numbers on the digital clock whiz by, "he should be in that class. Everyone else sucks compared to him."

"Elizabeth," Melena sighs, "please don't say 'suck.' I've asked you not to before. You know it sounds like a bad word. Say something else."

"Okay, well, they stink."

Completing the far bend, a tight pack of five cars barrels toward them. Their hot wheels bump against one another, and two of the cars bounce around like pinballs. Three cars drive in the lowest class, Showroom, and two are from the fastest unlimited division.

Tires screech loudly and the black rubber smokes. As they drive out of the turn, one of the cars fishtails and Melena cringes at the inherent danger.

Elizabeth smiles at the smell.

"That doesn't look good," Melena says.

Elizabeth yawns. Above them a new crescent moon creeps across the sky. Only a few of the brightest stars shine over the city and, on the opposite side of the track, Ernest stands with one foot propped up on the rail. He grips another stopwatch tightly.

In the Trans Am G.T., Luke holds the wheel steady as he makes for the straightaway. His arms relax in complete synch with the car. Fastened in by several harnesses, Luke feels himself moving with the machine like one great, raging beast.

The drone of the engine drowns out all the other sounds and thoughts that normally clutter Luke's mind. The overwhelming noise comforts him like a lullaby, and his consciousness clears, leaving him to master the road course alone and free.

Aware of the other class of racers gaining on him, Luke veers to the right, allowing the unlimiteds to pass him. He frowns for a split second wishing he were driving in the higher class of cars.

With four drivers splitting their twenty-four hour time period, the Russo brothers, who own the Trans Am Luke drives, have opted out on two shares of their time. Each driver normally takes a break after two hours, but since Luke has pulled the fastest times, they've given him nine hours of the race to drive.

"He's coming," Melena says leaning forward again. Luke passes by with the other two cars in front of him.

"God, he's quick," Elizabeth says. "Hold the clock while I fix the numbers."

Melena takes the clock and says, "I'm glad he let those other two go on." She bundles back up again feeling a little more at ease.

A few minutes later, the pack of five pulls around the far turn and, having driven another lap pinned in, the faster drivers have grown impatient. In their own cars, the thunder of the engine shapes their desire to go faster.

Suddenly, number 9 nudges the rear of the showroom number 62 that blocks the road in front of him. They run bumper to bumper and flip each other off as they go around the corner.

"Did you see that?" Elizabeth shouts. "Holy crap, they're getting pissed. That guy rammed him on purpose."

"My God," Melena shakes her head. "I'm just glad they're behind Luke, and Elizabeth, don't say pissed either."

Elizabeth ignores her mother and stands up to get a better view of the rest of the track.

As the pack leaves the infield a few turns past Melena and Elizabeth, number 9 slams his front right bumper against the left side, rear tire well of number 62. They hit a little too hard and together they skid out toward the wall coming out onto the straightaway.

The showroom car spins clockwise and, on its second time around, clips the front end of the number 9. This car, traveling over 190 miles per hour, tips on its side, flips up and over the slower car rolling over and over until it slams into the wall. The other car hits the wall farther ahead and veers down to slow at the grassy infield.

The echo of the crash reverberates around the track and Melena screams. Red lights flash and sirens blare through the speedway as the ambulance heads toward the wreck. Up high on the flagstone, the flagman waves the yellow caution flag and every driver slows his car.

"Don't worry," Elizabeth says, "Luke's probably on his way back around all ready." She bites her lip, moves to stand on the second rung of the guardrail and looks for Luke's car.

Ernest, on the edge of the infield and having just seen Luke pass by, runs toward the sound of the crash to see how bad it is and who was involved.

One car lies upside down; its dark blue frame crushed into a box-like shape. A gloved hand thrusts out the window and the driver pulls himself from the wreckage to fall on the ground outside the heavily damaged machine.

People standing and watching when the accident happened, and now running toward it, cheer to see the driver emerge seemingly unharmed. They look to the other cars on the track that slow as they approach the incident.

All the cars downshift and rev their engines, as they test their motors. Luke, driving at a crawl, keeps his tires warm by sweeping the steering wheel from side to side.

Elizabeth waves at him and he gives her and Melena a thumbs-up as he passes by. In another two hours, Luke will bring the car in for one of the Russo brothers to drive. A short while after that, the ignition box will fail, leaving them to repair it in the middle of the night as the race continues on the track.

Within an hour, the crew will have the Trans Am back in the race, but it won't regain its second place ranking among the grand touring cars. The Russo team comes in twelfth, surviving the mechanical delay, and Luke loves every moment of it.

--→--●◀--●--→--

In the spring, Elizabeth stands by The Green Gallery's white delivery van, arms extended as she waits for Melena to fill them. The sun blinds her though the day is mildly cool, and she squints trying to be patient.

With three and a half weeks of school left, Elizabeth counts the days till the end of summer when she will finally be able to leave Larnee. Planning to major in Fine Art , she dreams of creating enormous sculptures out of metal and glass while leading a different life away from all that she has known.

"Elizabeth, honey," Melena says holding out a bag full of Styrofoam containers, "go on and run this stuff in the house. Then come back and help me with the rest."

"Okay," Elizabeth says taking the fried flounder, hush puppies and coleslaw up to Momma Bell's front door. This house may be smaller than her last two but Bell loves being close to Melena and Elizabeth.

"Hey, Momma Bell," Elizabeth says walking through the front door.

"Hey there, darling." Bell moves her wheelchair toward her. "Don't you look pretty," she says. "That dress just flows right with you."

"Thanks," Elizabeth says. She leans down to give Bell a kiss on the cheek. The long black dress, one of her favorites, curves in dark waves when she moves.

Entertained by Elizabeth's wild thoughts, Bell favors her drawings of storms and gloom. She always supported her flamboyant choices. The same eccentric genes that teach Elizabeth to draw and dress flourished in her.

Elizabeth turns from Bell and walks into the kitchen. She jumps as Leopold, now gray haired, disheveled, and his weight unhealthy, bursts from his room.

"Meety Ma," he says loudly. He began calling Elizabeth this after she got in trouble about that dirty, angry note at school. She seemed to be upset about a lot of things then and began to exude a pure, invisible wrath toward him.

She catches herself and thinks, *Nobody knows.*

Leopold opens his arms coming toward her for a hug.

With practiced moves, Elizabeth skirts him turning to the side and moving around the counter. She sets the bag down, hiding from Bell her disgust for him behind it, and darts quickly toward the front door.

"I have to help Mom with the rest," she calls back to them when she's safely across the threshold.

A few minutes later, she and a pleased Melena come back into the kitchen to set the remainder of the food, and a few shopping bags from the mall, on the table.

"Momma," Melena says, "I got you some of those silk night-gowns from Belks that you like so much. They were on sale today marked down twice so I really got a deal."

Melena hands Bell a shopping bag full of pastel shades of silk. She always held a pang of guilt in her heart for not staying in Holiday where she could have looked in on her parents every day and bought them things.

Bell peers inside the bag.

"Oh, they're so lovely," she says holding one up to her and batting her eyelashes. "I just look gorgeous in baby blue, don't I, Elizabeth?"

The last twenty years Bell's perspective has become increasingly negative. She wakes with it daily having lived with a decrepit Pratt until his death and taking care of her feeble son while being confined to a wheelchair for the majority of her adult life.

She was such a wild thing before the car accident crushed her legs, only thirty-three and people called her the most beautiful woman in all of Holiday. It has made her bitter.

Most often, Melena and Pearl take the brunt of her unhappiness. Elizabeth is the only person who really eases her mood and makes her laugh. To Bell, she seems so intelligent and free.

Elizabeth looks at Bell and imagines her dolled up like the picture taken of her when she was sixteen that is hanging in the hall.

"Gorgeous," she says, "yes, you certainly do, darling, just like a movie star."

"Well," Melena says noting Bell's smile, "let's eat." She opens the bag and checks each Styrofoam box before giving it to the proper recipient.

"Y'all have to be starved," she says. "Leopold, honey, come on over and sit down at the table."

Melena props open a heaping container of fried fish and sets it on the table for him with utensils, a Coca-Cola and a giant bottle of ketchup. She positions it all neatly around his plate.

Heaving his weight into the chair, Leopold smacks his lips and his fingers clutch at the air as he looks over the food. His tongue, moves erratically and he picks up the Hunt's ketchup bottle and squirts the dense red liquid across the mountain of fish and hush puppies.

Elizabeth, watching, winces and snarls. His eating habits repulse her.

Melena opens Bell's container and arranges it in front of her, then sits down across from her mother. Elizabeth stares at the one seat left for her opposite Leopold at the table.

Begrudgingly, she sets her dinner across from him and turns her chair sideways so she faces Melena. Elizabeth picks up her fork and pokes at her piece of flounder flaking off little bites one at a time, but the sounds of Leopold eating distract her.

"Mom," she says attempting to block out the noise, "I really think I'm going to get into State. My Thoreau essay will be a hit."

"Of course, you are." Melena sips her tea. "They'll be thrilled to have someone as brilliant as you."

"My grades didn't help."

Bell puts her fork down. "Elizabeth," she says, "you were always the smartest of my grandbabies. Did you know that?"

"No."

"Well, you are," Bell says. "When you were just a little thing, I could tell you were smart 'cause I could see it in your eyes."

Melena frowns and motions with her fork. "Elizabeth," she says, "that is not how we sit at the table."

"But ..."

"But we do not sit at the table that way," Melena says. "Swing your feet under and face forward like a lady. Keep your shoulders

192

back, too. You don't want to start slouching when you go to school."

"Fine."

Elizabeth turns forward and looks at Leopold. She pretends she's a dragon spitting a long gush of fire to burn him alive. His tongue, covered with specks of coleslaw and ketchup, darts in and out of his mouth as he chews his food. Elizabeth looks down at her plate and lays her fork down.

She tries to focus on Bell and Melena's voices, but they have fallen into heavy conversation about bills and the sale of the Duprees' former home. To Elizabeth, the room seems to move around her to the rhythm of Leopold's eating.

The food in his mouth obstructs his voice as he attempts to say something to her. Though she understands his garbled speech, Elizabeth ignores him. Leopold speaks again and an item flies from his mouth and lands across the table.

Elizabeth stares at the tiny fleck of slaw and screams loudly inside her head. Her eyes grow wide and she stares at him. Finally, Leopold shakes his fist at her and stands.

"Leopold," Melena says, "sit down and finish eating."

His angry voice booms through the house.

"Meety Ma," he says followed by a long slur of jumbled words as he points from Elizabeth to himself and then back again at the table. Leopold holds his fist out at her and stomps cursing in his own way back to his room.

"Elizabeth," Melena asks, "did you say something to him?"

"No," she says, "I don't know what's wrong with him."

Elizabeth picks her fork up again and smiles.

The following Saturday night, Elizabeth and her friends overrun a small, all-ages nightclub right off the main thoroughfare in downtown Larnee. The Turtle, relatively new and still exciting to Larnee's scores of untamed youth, hosts punk rock and hardcore bands.

Flat and square across from downtown, the club shares its city block with all the worst neighborhoods. Larnee once was a factory town, but now, most of the factories have closed.

Outside of the Turtle, Elizabeth sits in the back of a seatless, seventies-style, blacked-out van. Her leather jacket, painted with skulls and laden with chains, jingles as she takes a neatly rolled joint in her hand and puts it to her mouth.

Pulling on it hard, she holds her breath in and passes the joint to Jack. He stares at her intensely over the quavering fog that now fills the van. Starting to cough, Elizabeth blows her smoke out into the existing cloud.

"Drink this," Darren says and hands her a gallon of bourbon. He likes to make sure everyone is drunk.

Elizabeth smiles, eyes squinting, and turns the bottle up with both hands to swill the liquor down. She pulls it away from her and gasps loudly as she passes the gallon to Jack.

"That shit burns," she says. "What is it?"

Darren giggles. "Wild Turkey," he says. His smile and his friendship are generous. Pleased, he sits back to light a cigarette.

Laura fans her hand through the air and says, "Open that window, Darren."

Propped against the side of the van, she sits between her latest boyfriend, Charlie, the drummer for Curb Job, and Todd, otherwise known as Fathole. Curb Job, an Oi band from Hollow Town, is made up of skinheads from the brother crew to this Larnee one.

The punk rock and skinhead gangs in Larnee, Hollow Town, Holiday and Williamson think of themselves as a rambunctious extended family that makes frequent trips to stay with their relatives. Most of their parties, doused in beer and featuring loud music, end when the cops show up or when they attack a group of belligerent racists or Nazis.

Calling for the joint in a Brando-like voice, Todd says, "Pass that over here."

Jack leans forward with it in his hand, "Such a comedian, you." He falls back, throws his arm around Elizabeth and she leans into him to grab him by the back of his neck. They start to kiss.

Darren watches Todd as he pulls on the joint. "Hey, Fathole," he says, "puff, puff give."

"All right, all right." Todd tries to keep the smoke down in his lungs and passes the joint back to Darren.

"Charlie," Laura says, "you better go ahead and light that other one 'cause these assholes are going to smoke it all before it makes it around again."

"Sure thing, sugar." Charlie would do anything for Laura. She's the prettiest skinhead girl in the state. He pulls another joint from the inside pocket of his flight jacket and hands it to her.

"We," Darren coughs, "have to finish half of this gallon before we go in there and beat the shit out of everyone."

He laughs and kicks Elizabeth and Jack's entwined boots. "Stop it, you two," Darren says, "and drink some of this fucking liquor."

Looking into each other's eyes, Elizabeth smiles at Jack. She bites his lip and pushes him back off her. Sitting up, she sticks her hand out for the bottle. She feels bad inside and she wants to run with the toughest crowd.

Darren points at her and says, "You have to take at least a three-second pull."

"*Ah*, she can't do it," Laura says. "She's still a new jack."

"I am not." Elizabeth lifts the bottle to her lips.

Darren counts for her. "One Mississippi, two Mississippi, three Mississippi," he says and she lets the bottle fall away from her mouth. Bourbon drips down her chin and her face contorts against the burn.

"All right, Jacky Boy," Darren says, "now it's your turn."

Jack takes the bottle and drinks the liquor calmly. It doesn't take them long to drink to their goal and smoke all the pot. When they finish, they walk intoxicated into the Turtle as the second band begins to play.

Immediately, they take over the area in front of the stage where Laura looks around, sly and threatening. Anger and derision are traits in her family. Seeing an old acquaintance, she laughs out loud and steps over to Darren, blatantly pointing the guy out.

"See him over there?" Laura slurs. "That guy tried to start a fight with Gretchen and me when we were hanging out on Tate Street last week."

She stands up straighter and says, "He had the nerve to call us a couple of skinhead whores."

"Oh, yeah?" Darren asks.

"Yep," Laura says. Her face turns serious as somewhere in her mind, she hears her father yelling and yelling, "*You're no good, Laura.*" She deeply needs to seek revenge.

"Nobody's gonna say that shit about me," she says. "I'm going to kick his fucking punk ass."

Darren puts his hand on her shoulder and pulls her back. "Just wait a few minutes, Laura," he says. "Let the band play a few more songs and then we'll take care of him. You and Elizabeth can come in afterward for a boot party."

A white fog blows out of a smoke machine to the right of the stage covering them. Everything in their lives ... their homes, their futures ... remains clouded, and they don't want to see the truth.

"I can do it myself," Laura shouts.

Darren pets the top of her shaved head. "I know you can," he says. "You're a mean girl, but why don't you let the boys have a little fun, *huh*?"

"Well," she says, "since you put it that way. Have at it, kid." She slaps him on the back and turns around to find Charlie.

The songs grow more vehement and the six of them dance throwing each other around. They fly into everyone as everyone flies into them, and together all become tiny, tumultuous sparks of life performing their fleeting dance.

Elizabeth gets up on stage and looks out into the crowd for Darren. Her hair, dyed a purplish-red, hangs in two long pony-tails on each side of her head. Darren nods at her, and she smiles as she runs toward him, finally launching herself off the front of the stage.

Bracing himself against the crowd, Darren catches Elizabeth and sets her on the ground. He's big enough to catch all his friends when they need him to. A few songs later he starts to swing his large, powerful arms toward the guy Laura pointed out. Then their violent fun really begins.

---

A week before her high school graduation, Elizabeth sits on the third floor of the mall in the middle of the food court sipping a large cherry Icee. Lounging in a white chair across from Katie, she pulls the wide red straw away from her lips and sets the cup down.

"Katie," she says, "you're the only person I've ever told."

Elizabeth looks at a mother dragging her child along on a leash and frowns. The scene seems familiar to her as if Melena had been dragging her along her whole life.

"You know, I blocked it out for a long time," Elizabeth says. "I guess my brain thought I couldn't handle it or something."

Katie looks at her thoughtfully, her soft features formed into a permanent look of understanding.

"I'm so glad you felt like you could talk to me about this," she says, "but you know you've got to talk to some adult. You should tell your mom."

"No. There's no way in hell I'm telling her," Elizabeth says. "It's her baby brother, and they all love him more because of what he is. He's like their little prince and I'm not going to be the one to ruin that image."

"Who cares what they think about him?" Katie asks. "You need to tell them so he can't do it again."

*Monster*, Elizabeth thinks. *He's is one, I am one and it is my secret not theirs.*

She sighs. "Well, I just can't tell them. My mom would totally freak out and besides, I just can't do it."

"You know who you should talk to?" Katie asks.

"Who?"

"My mom," Katie says. "All my friends in Florida used to talk to her about everything. She just has that thing about her that makes you want to talk."

Elizabeth shakes her head. "I think telling you was enough for now."

Before today, the words to her dark tale had gotten stuck in her mouth like a piece of dry bread that is impossible to swallow. Speaking once does not make it any easier to speak again.

Elizabeth says, "I mean, I just can't take it with him living in the same town. I have to eat dinner with him all the time. I hate it."

"I bet, man," Katie sits back, "I don't know how you haven't snapped. I would've gone crazy and flipped by now."

Katie's ex-hippie parents have brought her up to be a laid back adult, but that doesn't mean she doesn't have her own problems, too.

"Yeah," Elizabeth says picking at the black fingernail polish flaking off her fingertips. "I think I have flipped a little bit already." The drugs in her high school have given her temporary illusions that please and frighten her, mostly the latter.

Katie draws on her cherry Icee. "Well, everyone's been eating that acid like candy."

"Not me. Not anymore," Elizabeth says. "Acid isn't fun when all you do on it is freak out and cry. Maybe after doing it for two or three years, you just stop having fun trips. I still can't believe that about Jeb and Michael, and all because they ate so much of that bad batch."

Katie's eyes grow wide. "I know," she says, "dropping out of school two weeks before graduation. I feel so bad for them. Every one of our dumb asses ate some of that Orange Sunshine, but they ate too many. Now, they're fucking crazy, and they probably will be for the rest of their lives."

"It's scary," Elizabeth says, thankful the bad batch only affected her with minor, unwanted flashbacks.

"So, what are you going to do?" Katie asks. "I mean about what you told me?"

"Nothing," Elizabeth says. Her mind teeters on the edge of fantasy and reality preferring created images over what surrounds her daily. "I just needed to get it off my chest that's all. I won't be here that much longer anyway."

"Well," Katie says, "I still think you need to talk about it. You have to work it all out in your head. Girl, until you do, it's going to eat you away inside."

Elizabeth says, "I've done enough for now." The finality in her voice brings the subject to a close and she looks ahead of her thinking about the future.

"Hey," Elizabeth smiles and says, "let's go look at bathing suits. I just have to have a new one for summer."

"Okay," Katie says as she slurps the rest of her drink.

They get up from their chairs and walk through the mall happy to be young and almost free.

Elizabeth's hair glows fire red under the florescent lights and her shoulders are strong from the many volleyball games she plays. The facts of her life that have weighed so heavily upon her now seem manageable.

-->--●◖◗--<--

Graduation at Luke's private college falls on a mildly warm, sunny day. Rows upon rows of white folding chairs stretch back across a wide grassy lawn while family and friends of the graduating class mill about the area. They smile, wave and take pictures.

Ernest, Melena and Elizabeth walk with Blackwell and Katherine, who holds their baby, Isabelle, on her hip. The ladies' spring dresses blow backward in the gentle wind.

Across the lawn, Emily, tall and lovely with her golden complexion and brown hair, waves at the Starlings, a straw hat in her hand. Melena waves back at her, and they all meet in the middle exchanging hugs and other pleasantries.

"Luke's back there in line with the rest of his class," Emily says. "They're supposed to file in when it starts and they'll be sitting in front of us. I've saved a whole row of seats for everyone behind the graduates. You guys follow me."

They all sit down together as a family. Katherine bounces Isabelle up and down on her knee making her laugh and coo. Melena reaches for her and the baby lights up with a smile.

"That's my precious girl," Melena says squeezing Isabelle in her arms. "She knows her Nanna." Isabelle is an immediate and pure source of joy for Melena.

Setting his cameras and camera accessories down by his chair, Ernest leans over and makes a silly face at Isabelle. She giggles, swats her arms toward him and he does it again adding a string of nonsensical words.

Melena doesn't want Ernest to intrude on what she sees as her and the baby's perfect world. She bites her lip at the exchange and pulls Isabelle closer toward her. Holding her free hand over her eyes, she pretends to look off over the crowd while Ernest plays with the baby.

"Look," Elizabeth says, "here they come."

Luke Bartleby Starling stands in a mass of the dark burgundy robes of his university. Katherine takes Isabelle away from Melena, and Ernest pulls out his video camera.

"Do you see him?" Ernest asks. "Elizabeth, point out your brother."

"Okay, Dad." Elizabeth turns around in her chair and searches the throng. "You'd think he'd be easy to spot as tall as he is especially with that, oh, there he is, Dad.

He's standing over to the right about the tenth one before the end."

"Got him," Ernest zooms in on Luke capturing his face and gestures as Luke waits for his graduation. "Wave at him, Elizabeth, and see if you can get him to notice us."

Since high school, Luke has withdrawn, trying to keep out the pain that dwells in his subconscious for fear of continual rejection from his mother. Though they both wear jovial masks with one another, the rift between them remains.

Elizabeth raises her right arm and waves in a wide, sweeping arc. Luke nods and waves as he sees her. She is the only member of the family able to reach his true self. Emily smiles watching them and settles back in her chair.

"Elizabeth," Melena says, "sit straight or you're going to wrinkle your dress."

"*Ugh,*" Elizabeth says and sits forward. She would like to rip her dress off and crumple it in her hands until it looks like a wad of trash to be laid at Melena's feet.

As the graduating class files in, Ernest follows the procession with his camera. With such a long line, and Luke toward the back, he turns the lens on Elizabeth.

"So, Elizabeth," Ernest asks, "With your graduation in a few days, how do you feel sitting here in the big leagues?"

"I feel," she says, "like I'm ready to go. I plan on having a fabulous time in college." *Since I won't be living with any of you*, she thinks.

"Just remember you're there for school," Ernest says. "Now, smile pretty at the camera."

Elizabeth smiles radiantly beaming with thoughts of her flight from Larnee and pulls a long lock of her bright red hair behind her shoulder. Ernest draws the camera away from her and focuses on Melena.

He asks her, "And you, mother of the graduate, how do you feel now that your son is leaving school?"

"I am very, very proud of Luke," Melena says. She smiles and holds her chin high to reduce the appearance of wrinkles. "He's destined for great things. All my children are."

Ernest pans the camera down the aisle toward Blackwell and Katherine, who bounces Isabelle in her lap, while Emily plays with her.

"And, you two," Ernest asks, "brother and sister-in-law of the graduate, do you have any words of wisdom to bestow on our viewers?"

Over the years, Blackwell's relationship with Ernest has deteriorated.

Blackwell gives the camera a thumbs-up. He says, "You finally made it, and here I was getting worried."

Katherine says, "Congratulations!" and looks toward the baby. "Isabelle says congratulations, too."

Isabelle blows clear bubbles that escape from her mouth and roll down onto her dress.

"And you, Miss?" Ernest asks Emily. He, like Luke as a child, is a joker at heart. "What have you to say to this son of ours?"

"I say to him," she smiles, "that I know his future will be brilliant, and that I only wish I could graduate with him and not next year."

She waves to the camera, and then Ernest turns it upward to film the last of the students filing in. Luke nods, proud of his family for a fleeting moment, and flashes his wide, toothy smile.

# ACT III

# Take Flight and Forever Flee

IN HER THIRD-FLOOR DORM ROOM, Elizabeth rests on her stomach, draped across the couch with two of her new friends from college. Held up by a thin belt, baggy pants sag off her backside while a black skateboarding T-shirt hangs down to her knees. Her long, bright-red hair bounces behind her in two pigtails that fall on top of her Sesame Street, Elmo doll backpack.

The room, covered in ghoulish posters of punk rock bands she could never put on her walls at home, has become her personal refuge.

"I told you it was going to be *phat*," Elizabeth says to her friend Tatiana. "They said Lady Miss Kier was going to spin, but I just want to hear her sing."

In the beginning of summer, Casey came home to Larnee to live with her parents until the fall semester. She and Elizabeth started driving to Hollow Town on the weekends to hang out with the people Casey met her freshman year of school. These kids were real party people equipped with drug candies, and they introduced Elizabeth to a whole other style of dancing.

Elizabeth shakes her ponytails toward the ground and watches them swing.

"Casey and I saw them in Baltimore a few months ago," she says. "It was so obvious she was on something exotic, if you know what I mean. She was so droopy, swaying and saying, 'I love the trees. Everything's wonderful.'"

Elizabeth frowns. "People get so slimy."

Tatiana looks up from the large, red cushion she sits on and begins to wrap her waist length, dark brown hair in a knot on top of her head.

She says, "There's no way any of those guys would quit, man.

They're those international jet-setter types fully stocked with access and means."

"Well, none of that will matter anyway," Elizabeth says. "Casey said Tom picked up those half moons, so we'll all be rolling hard from what I heard."

Elizabeth slides her backpack off, falls down across the couch and looks at the ceiling. "I hope they're a lot better than the pills we had last weekend."

"I know," Angie says. With both hands she strangles a Cookie Monster doll lying in the middle of her lap. "Those things sucked. I kept trying and trying to get off, but it never happened all night. Everyone else was out of their skulls, and there I was with nothing. I wasted fifty bucks."

"You guys just need to make sure you buy your pills from the right people," Tatiana says. "You should always know your drugs before you get them."

Recently arrived from the American school in Tokyo and having taken a graduation trip through Europe, Tatiana has a certain superior knowledge about this topic.

Elizabeth sighs, "Well, we thought we knew these and we weren't the only ones that got screwed. You're right though. I'll start getting my drugs from your hippie friends. Hippies always get good drugs."

Tatiana winks at her. "Hey," she says, "did you finish your Japanese homework?"

"Of course," Elizabeth says, "I wouldn't want to disappoint Ms. Kashimira. She's too darn cute."

"She is," Tatiana says. "She's like a Japanese doll or something that you just want to take home."

Elizabeth's phone rings.

"Hello," she says.

On the other end of the line, Jack props his foot against his bedroom wall. "Hey, you," he says.

"Hey, Jack," Elizabeth exclaims, "how was your day?"

"Decent, but infuriating," he says. "I miss you. When are you coming home again?"

"Soon," Elizabeth leans back, "maybe next weekend. We're going to see Dee-Lite tonight. Can you believe it?"

"Not another fucking rave," he teases. "No, I can't believe it. Pretty soon you're going to be a full-fledged raver."

"Shut up," she says. "I am not."

"Yes you are," he says. "How many of those damn things have you gone to this year?"

Jack's never done ecstasy. He thinks the whole scene is no good and so does the rest of their crew.

"Raver Princess," he says. "You've been to one every weekend for the last three months. You're eating rolls all the time, wearing those baggy ass clothes and if you're not careful, everyone at home is going to disown you."

Elizabeth rolls her eyes ignoring the truth. "I have not been to one every weekend," she says. "I mean, I almost have, but I was home for Halloween. Besides, it's fun. I never did this stuff before and I'm such a good dancer now."

"Whatever," he says, "I still say you're brainwashed. Next thing you know, you'll be going up to people telling them how much you love them and how beautiful the world is. You'll turn into a damn hippie."

Elizabeth pouts. "I am not going to turn into a hippie," she says. "I promise. I'm always the darkest looking creature ready to beat the shit out of plenty of people, and I still hate everyone, too." She looks aside.

"No offense, Tatiana."

Tatiana nods and bats her hand downward.

"Who are you talking to?" he asks.

"Tatiana and Angie," she says. "We just went to the park and got high, but I think I'm being rude. Are you going to be home for a while?"

"Yeah," he says, "till about seven-thirty, then Fathole's coming to pick me up."

"Let me call you back then."

Jack taps his boot against the wall. "All right, Rave girl," he says. "I'll talk to you later."

"Shut up," she says. "Now, I have to kick you the next time I see you."

He smiles. Jack adores her aggression. "I love you, too," he says.

"Fiercely," she says, makes a loud kissing noise and hangs up.

Angie throws the Cookie Monster away from her. "Skinhead boyfriend?" she asks. That's what the girls like to call him. They've all seen Jack and Elizabeth's pictures of him.

"Yeah," Elizabeth says.

She remembers their mid-summer talk outside of Dunkin Donuts. It was a hot, humid night. The starry sky sat above them, but everything Elizabeth saw looked so empty.

They were sitting on the ground leaning against the back of the building, the smell of the dumpster wafting toward them. Driven over the edge, Elizabeth was finally infuriated with Leopold's proximity to her home. She was tormented trying to decide what to do, who to tell or if she was to speak at all.

At that moment, she couldn't stomach the thought of a boyfriend, even one she had loved for so long. Convinced of some poisonous guilt naturally bestowed upon her at birth, her monster identity consumed her to a point where she could not let go.

"You know," she says to Angie, "we aren't officially boyfriend and girlfriend anymore. For Christ's sake, I'm in college now and there are way too many members of the male species here to have a boyfriend."

"But you're still a virgin," Tatiana says, "so, it's not like you utilize them anyway."

"No, but I have my eye on someone."

"You've been talking to that blond skateboarder again," Angie asks. "Haven't you?"

"Kind of," Elizabeth says, "he asked me to hang out the other night. It was okay, but this girl we were with had to puke when we were in the car. We pulled over at the Tower Mart so she could throw up a bunch of Kool-Aid and Vodka. I held her hair 'cause I'm a saint."

"Hey," Tatiana says. "It's getting late. We should go to the dinning hall if we're going to get our groove on tonight."

"Right," Angie says, "don't want to eat late and then take a pill. I'd be spending all night in the bathroom then, and no one wants to vomit when they're wearing silver."

Elizabeth hops off the couch and grabs her campus ID. She holds the door for Tatiana and Angie as they go out. Locking it behind them, she says, "Don't let me forget to call Jack."

"Don't worry," Tatiana smiles. "I'm sure you won't forget your skinhead boyfriend."

Elizabeth says, "Right."

That night around one o'clock in the morning, Elizabeth and ten of her friends from State weave their way in and out and through the techno-pop crowd at the Dee-Lite show. They all suck on Blow-Pops, pacifiers or snort Vick's Vapor tubes incessantly. A party favorite, the menthol sends them further into orbit with every whiff running through them like a cool spasm.

The ecstatic eyes of girls and boys alike roll backwards peering over the top of inhalant respirators. They breathe the gooey vapor rub spread over the backs of paper masks and swoon.

Dancing with imaginary boxes, they expand, throw around, contract and put in their pockets, the mask-wearers look like megalomaniac doctors come to steal and operate on all your childhood toys.

At this underground fanfare of mixed-up youth, fashion, dancing skills and overall attitude determine just how cool you are. The brandname Jnco and Buggirl pants the partygoers wear flare wildly to the point of exaggeration.

Most of the glitter-dusted girls are thin from using crystal meth or youth. They sport tiny halter-tops, and some of the boys do, too. Various Sesame Street character backpacks stretch their fuzzy arms across the backs of many while Hello Kitty packs are strapped on others. Under the flashing lights, the party kids glow like rock stars.

Her Elmo pack filled with candy and vapor tubes, Elizabeth wears a pair of blue silky Adidas pants and a black mesh tank top. She dances in the center of the floor in a group of seven random people who all seem to flow with each other.

Having procured two pink glow sticks from a boy with his hat on backwards, Elizabeth manipulates the sticks furiously while he watches the light trails in amazement. Elizabeth shoots her arms out in a horizontal spinning circle, sticks gripped tight in her hands, making pink figure eights in the air.

*Got ya*, she thinks, *now I got you, and you, and you.*

Heavy into her roll, she sees the pink glow sticks moving like little comets under her control. They seem to spring out from her hands like laser lights, an infinite supply coming from her palms.

In her mind, the little pink comets smash and destroy the people she aims at.

Body moving as fast as possible, Elizabeth thinks she floats in the air, her feet barely touching the ground. Angie comes up to her from behind and grabs her by the shoulder.

"Hey," Angie says pulling her pacifier halfway out of her mouth. "These things are awesome!" Her hand squeezes Elizabeth's shoulder and her eyes roll back in her head as she tries to control them enough to focus on Elizabeth.

"No shit," Elizabeth shouts as she stops dancing, out of breath. "I'm higher than god! Did you see all the people I shot with my lasers? The Power Rangers ain't got shit on me."

She hands the glow sticks back to their owner. He snaps out of his gaze and touches Elizabeth's hand. "You're the best dancer I've ever seen," he says.

"Thanks," Elizabeth smiles. "I might need them again later." She turns to Angie whose teeth chatter and grind.

"I love you," Angie says grabbing Elizabeth by the face. "You're so beautiful, man. Do you know how beautiful you are? You're a goddess!"

"So are you," Elizabeth says. "You're super beautiful. Hey, let's go find Tom and everyone and see what they're up to."

"Yeah," Angie says teetering. "I'm rolling so hard."

"Here," Elizabeth says, "hold on to me." They walk through the crowd hand in hand until Elizabeth leads them to a group of people, half of whom lie on the floor in a moving arrangement of entangled bodies.

"Hey, girl," Tom says and takes Elizabeth by the other hand. He rubs down her forearms applying pressure to her muscles.

"Oh," Elizabeth says as the erotic sensation multiplies exponentially. "That feels so good."

She clenches Angie's hand inside her fist and they both stand in front of Tom like two mesmerized zombies.

Tom says, "These rolls are fantastic girls, aren't they?"

"You said it," Elizabeth swaggers. She lets go of Angie's hand, and Tom spins her around as Angie is absorbed by the orgy-like throng on the floor. His hands rub up and down Elizabeth's back as if his life depended on it.

"Oh, oh, you're such a wonderful person, Tom," Elizabeth says. "Did I ever tell you that?"

"Maybe at the last party," he says.

"Well, you are," she says stretching her arms out above her.

Elizabeth grabs Tom by the face and kisses him. After a few seconds, he turns her around again and continues to work on her back needing to release all the extra energy.

--›-‹--⊙-⊙==‹--›--

Early in December, Elizabeth's depleted bank account and failing grades glare back at her with negative numbers and reflect the mess she has become. Before she can attempt to examine her mounting problems and find a solution, Momma Bell becomes ill, and the doctors confine her to the hospital.

For weeks, Melena, Pearl, Walker and Ernest keep watch over her relieving each other in shifts. Mostly, the two sisters camp out in their mother's room while their husbands maintain the economic structure of their lives. Walker travels between Holiday and Larnee continuing his postal route, while Ernest stops by The Green Gallery every afternoon to make sure Ferdinand has all he needs to handle things in Melena's absence.

Now that they both live in Larnee, Blackwell and Luke stop by the hospital almost every day. Elizabeth, stuck in Hollow Town at school, struggles through her exams. She tries desperately to absorb three month's worth of mathematics and psychology, the two subjects she neglected most, in an effort to pass her final exams. Between studying sessions, she comes home whenever she can.

Bell's impending death becomes a long, painful vigil for the family. At some point, she slips away from them to drift in a semi-comatose state where her only action is to gasp for air as her weakening heart beats.

One Wednesday, hearing desperation in Pearl's voice, Elizabeth races home though Melena assures her it isn't necessary.

Her combat boots stomping down the hall, she enters Bell's room and sits close to her on the hospital bed. Elizabeth ignores the web of IV lines running out of her grandmother's hand and takes it in her own to squeeze it.

Bell's eyes flitter open to fix on Elizabeth.

"Elizabeth," she says, cognizant for one fleeting moment.

Melena and Pearl sit straight in their chairs. This is the first time they've heard Bell's voice since she succumbed to the coma and the last time the family will hear from her.

"Momma," Melena says.

Nothing, nothing can be heard but Bell's raspy breathing as she drifts away.

"I love you, Momma Bell," Elizabeth says. She leans down to kiss her on the forehead and whispers good-bye.

Brought home again to Holiday in a long black hearse, Bell is buried alongside Pratt in the old southern graveyard where their mothers lie. Her funeral procession runs through town accompanied by 12 police cars, a tribute left over from the days when she and Pratt hosted the entire department at their parties.

Like most funeral services, almost everyone cries while the loved ones hug people they barely know and haven't seen in years. Sitting in a country church, those in attendance nod while listening to a preacher talk about righteousness and the precious life that has now escaped its earthly bonds.

Elizabeth, privy to her grandmother's indulgences and having inherited Bell's flare for vulgarity, laughs inside and wonders if Bell actually ever went to church.

*The preacher seems to have known her,* she thinks, *what with the stories he's telling. Everyone in Holiday knew who she was at some point or another and every person needs someone to watch over them, especially gun-toting, liquor drinking grandmothers.*

Elizabeth smiles, but catches herself, not wanting anyone to see her. On either side, the Starling men look appropriately serious in their black suits. Directly in front of her, Melena leans over Pearl in this, her time of need. Together, the sisters sit and look after their baby brother who looks neat and tidy in the suit they bought for him.

For reasons unknown to Elizabeth, Melena has grown angry with her daughter for some transgression Elizabeth committed against her. Maybe it was her stubbornness in wearing "those damn boots" to her grandmother's funeral or maybe it's because she looks so much like Ernest in the eyes that Melena can hardly stand it.

Now shut out, Elizabeth stares at the back of her mother's head wondering what she's done. Silent in their grief, mother and aunt sit in the pew in front of her like two untouchable matriarchs carved in stone.

The day after the funeral, all the distant relatives have gone home to their respective towns. The Starlings and the Shades remain in Holiday together spinning old stories, visiting with one another and wrapping up all the details that need to be taken care of when someone dies.

Before everyone heads out on their own, the two families come together at the local Marriot for a giant, all-you-can-eat Sunday brunch. They sit down at a long table to talk of things to come. Pearl takes a sip of sweet iced tea and looks up at her sister.

"Melena," she says, "why don't you keep Leopold with you for the first few months? All his stuff is in Larnee anyway and then I'll take him come the end of March."

Elizabeth gags on her scrambled eggs and asks, "What?"

"Leopold is going to stay with us at the house," Melena subtly snaps, still chilly toward Elizabeth.

"He'll be with us for a while staying in your old room and then he'll go to Pearl's for a few months. That way neither of us will get too worn down from the extra work."

Pearl looks above her as if she were calling on God to help and sighs. A self-styled martyr, she's felt the burden of caring for others all her life.

"I'm telling you, Melena," she says, "sometimes it's just not that easy to look after him. When Momma and him were living here in Holiday, I'd break my back trying to get those two settled. You've got to do the bathing, the washing and the cooking."

"They've been in Larnee for a while," Melena interrupts disregarding her sister's complaint. "Taking care of Leopold is nothing new to me."

Elizabeth puts her fork down. This new fact disturbs her immensely since she hoped Leopold would now return to Holiday.

"So," she says, "you mean that he's going to be staying with us over Christmas?"

"Yes," Melena brightens, "with you home and everyone in town, we're going to have one full house this year."

"Oh," Elizabeth stares at her food. Suddenly, she feels like she has worms crawling around in her stomach and eating away at the insides.

Ernest returns from the buffet line, sits down at the table and puts his napkin in his lap. He has a large pile of fruit on his plate.

"Dad," Elizabeth says, "did you know that Leopold is going to be staying with us?"

"Yep," Ernest says and forks a strawberry. "He's going to be staying in your old room."

"My old room?"

"Not your room *now*," Ernest says, "the little one, before you moved into Blackwell's."

"Oh, right."

*What a freaking outrage*, Elizabeth thinks. *How dare they give Leopold my room! My stuffed animals are still in that closet.*

"Mom," Luke says from a few chairs down, "will you pass me the pepper?" He sits between his cousins Bobby and Lucinda, whom he rarely sees.

Melena sends the pepper down and looks at Katherine who sits across the table with Isabelle on her lap. Katherine feeds Isabelle small green grapes while taking bites of her own food in between. On her right, Blackwell constantly monitors the feeding situation and occasionally brings a spoonful of yogurt up to Isabelle's mouth.

Months ago, with Ernest's blessing, Blackwell left Mancon to enter a multi-level business that he feels has unlimited potential. Creating his future as he goes, Blackwell's network marketing company specializes in preventive healthcare. His ability to charm others and his tireless efforts, have already made him a leader in the organization.

Luke, forlorn over his troubles with Emily and longing to race again, has taken over his brother's old office. The reins to Mancon, cultivated by Ernest for so many years with the hope of passing them on, have now been placed in front of him. Warily he skirts the responsibility as he dreams of doing other things.

"That Isabelle," Melena says, "really likes those sour grapes. She's like her Nanna and her aunty. Katherine, why don't you let me hold her? That way you can finish eating."

"Really, I'm fine," Katherine says, "but you can hold her if you'd like." She passes Isabelle over the table and her light blue dress puffs about her as she kicks her feet in the air.

"What are you kicking for?" Melena says and sets Isabelle down in her lap. "You're just the best little grandbaby in the world, you are." Isabelle giggles and smiles back at her.

"So," Elizabeth says still stunned by the news about Leopold, "I'm going to have to go back to school once we get done here. I've got a couple finals this week that I have to study for."

"Oh, baby," Pearl says, "I wish you could stay. Walker and I would love to have you at the house for a few days."

Bobby looks up at his younger cousin and says, "Elizabeth, which way do you drive back to school?"

Bobby Shade is a highly decorated officer of the Holiday Sheriff's department. Having saved two men from drowning during Holiday's most devastating flood in the early nineties, he's the type of man to give Elizabeth Blockbuster coupons for Christmas to keep her out of trouble. He figures if Elizabeth is at home, then she won't be at the mercy of the crime filled world he has to deal with.

"I just cut up 92 and take 36 into town," she says. "It only took me an hour to get here."

"That sounds about right," Bobby says. "Just make sure you don't speed. We wouldn't want you to get a ticket going up 92."

Macy, Bobby's wife, smiles at her husband's concern.

"Trust me," Elizabeth lies, "I don't speed."

"When do you come home for Christmas break?" Melena asks.

"I think I have this week, next and then that's it." She's already contriving ways to get out of staying home.

"Well, good," Melena says rocking Isabelle back and forth in her lap.

"Hey, squirt," Lucinda says, "you got a birthday coming up soon, don't you?"

"Yeah," she answers, "nineteen."

"Well," Bobby leans in. He, like Pratt Dupree, loves the moments when the family gets together.

"Leopold's birthday is just before yours. Maybe we could have a big birthday party for the both of you in Larnee. We could drive up and that way we'd all be getting together again real soon. What do you say?"

"We can have it at our house," Blackwell says. "It's not 'til April so the weather will be nice enough to have it in the back yard."

"Sounds like a plan to me," Bobby says. He thinks, *I'll bring the cooker for the pig and we'll have a pig pickin'*. "That'll be real nice for Leopold, too. You know I wonder how he's going to take Momma Bell being gone?"

Elizabeth looks at her plate longing for a portal to another dimension. Bell was one of her favorite people in the whole world. *Ha, ha,* she thinks, *I'm the only one she woke up for. Momma Bell is dead, and Leopold is alive. I hate Leopold. He disgusts me, and now he's going to live with us.*

Growing dizzy, Elizabeth listens to the conversation around her. She wants to throw up with all this worry over Leopold.

"You're right, Melena," Pearl nods at her sister. "I think he'll be fine. He seemed to understand when Daddy died, but you know, I can't figure how much of the loss he really comprehends."

"*Um*, I really don't feel so good," Elizabeth blurts out. She clutches at her stomach.

"What's wrong?" Melena asks.

"I don't know," she says. "My stomach hurts and I'm not hungry anymore. I think I need to go lay down upstairs before I drive back to school."

"Well, okay, honey," Pearl says. "Come on and give us all a hug before you go."

Elizabeth makes the rounds at the table hugging each of the Shades and telling them how good it was to see them and that she hopes she sees them soon. Then she goes to Melena and gives her a hug.

"I'll come up to check on you before you leave," Melena says. "So, don't go until I see you."

Elizabeth nods and starts to walk away. "See y'all upstairs," she says to the rest of the Starlings. She makes her way out of the dining room and back to her and Luke's hotel room to writhe in distress upon the bed.

-->==◉ ⊂==--

A few days before Christmas, Leopold lounges in his new room fiddling with a remote control. His old television and radio sit on top of a white, five-drawer dresser and desk set. The dresser is to the left of the bed and the TV in front of it, just the way it was at home throughout the years.

His Popsicles are downstairs chilling in the freezer and already he has begun to feel like he has a position of importance here. He gets up to walk around the house whenever anyone comes home.

At the other end of the house, Elizabeth sits in her room with the door closed. Until last night, she hadn't stayed in it since she left for school, and now she dreads the nearly month long Christmas vacation.

As she puts her makeup on, she hums along to the loud music. She used to play this same demented CD when she lived here, and she plays it now because it always seemed to be the perfect music for her pretty room.

From the connecting doorway into Luke's old room, Melena opens the bathroom door. She wears a lovely red sweater that accents her voluptuous breasts. It blends well with the holiday design sale she has going on at The Green Gallery.

"Hey," Melena says. She leans back against the wall and puts her hand on the counter.

"Will you turn that music down, please?"

"Oh, sure," Elizabeth steps into her room and comes back a moment later to resume applying her black eyeliner, ringing her eyes.

"Where are you going today?" Melena asks checking her own hair in the mirror. She pretends that Elizabeth prefers her makeup lighter and her clothes more cheery.

"I'm going to pick up Jack and we're going to the mall to act like we're Christmas shopping. We'll probably have a fake snow fight."

Melena frowns. "I thought your father said he would give you money to buy presents with."

"He did," Elizabeth says.

She already decided to keep the money. The zeros in her empty bank account loom over her since she spent everything she had on three month's worth of designer drugs, but she's not telling anyone else that. Elizabeth must handle her current dilemma on her own.

"Well, can you please come back home and check on Leopold when you're done?" Melena asks. "Then you can just bring him over to the store and I'll have him until dinner."

If Melena only knew, she would never ask Elizabeth such a thing, and with the story unspoken, all becomes a horror show. It is a created world Elizabeth could destroy if she only had the strength to break the secrecy.

She steps back from the mirror, pulling the pencil away from her eye and holds her upper lid open to prevent an errant tear from ruining the thick black line she just created.

"Mom," she says trying to remain calm, "I'm going to have Jack with me. Plus we're supposed to meet up with Darren and everyone across town later. Those guys don't have cars and I'm going to be gone all day."

"Well," Melena says, "Jack can sit in the back and you can come home long enough to bring your uncle over to my store." Melena looks her daughter up and down.

"Elizabeth." Melena stops and grabs her arm. "Did you eat any breakfast? You look really thin, too thin."

"I told you," Elizabeth says, "I've been having trouble keeping any food down lately. I don't know what's going on. I get these really harsh pains in my back and then I puke."

"Elizabeth," Melena says alarmed, "I didn't know it was that bad. You have got to go to the doctor immediately."

Melena's face adopts her most influential and imposing guise. It is the 'you must be careful' face she dons whenever her children do something dangerous.

"Don't worry, Mother," Elizabeth says, "I went to the doctor at school and they said it was something that would pass soon."

She lies.

"I'm sure I'll be fine in a few days." Escaping into her bedroom, Elizabeth evades the conversation.

She hasn't gone to the doctor because she's afraid her problem with regurgitation could be coming from all the Ecstasy she's eaten in the last few months, though the Dee-Lite show was where she took her last pill. Now, she's trying to be a good girl.

"Elizabeth," Melena says and follows her, "you need to see a specialist."

"Maybe if I have time later in the week."

Melena looks at her and shakes her head wanting to force her to go, but she hasn't been able to get her to do what she wants in so long.

"You are so stubborn sometimes," she says temporarily losing her composure. "I'll see you with Leopold sometime after lunch?"

"Fine," Elizabeth scans the room for her black velvet coat.

"You know," Melena says, "you should be nice to him. He just lost his mother and he is your uncle."

"Mother," Elizabeth says through gritted teeth, "I am nice to him. I have to go. I'm late."

Elizabeth grabs her bag and walks down the hall toward the front door. Melena watches her walk away wondering why she has so many different things to look after and care for.

"Bye," she calls to her daughter.

"Bye," Elizabeth says. She turns the corner as Leopold comes out of his room. He stands in the hall like an observer at a parade.

Elizabeth scoots past him and he says something to her, which she ignores. She slams the basement door shut behind her and flees down the staircase as fast as she can, but really, she's only taken one tiny step.

⤙⫶◉⫶⤚

Back at school, into the first week of her second semester, Elizabeth stares at the ceiling above her. She remembers little from her first semester classes and her grades were mediocre at best.

She passed gym, got an A in English and Japanese, but nearly failed Math and Psychology pulling off a D and a C somehow in the end. Casting a dreamy veil over her problems for nearly four months straight, the Ecstasy she took left her wondering where all her money went.

Now that she's stopped taking pills, her issues loom in front of her, and her body is mysteriously breaking down. Since the end of

November when Bell first got sick, Elizabeth hasn't been able to eat much of anything except Saltine crackers.

Elizabeth loves to eat. Neither anorexia nor bulimia explains her inability to digest. Her body tortures her from the inside and she can't figure out why.

Now, lying in her upper bunk, she's been gazing at the ceiling for hours stalled by an excruciating pain that sweeps over her in waves. Around three o'clock in the morning, she crawls out of her loft and onto the floor. The shooting pains in her back and stomach blind her. Lying on the floor in tears, she doesn't know what to do.

"Jesus Christ," Elizabeth says angrily, "what the hell is wrong with me?"

She squirms in a little ball on the floor and pulls up her shirt to let her stomach lie on the cool marble. Temporarily, it relieves her. She tries to be very still and relax in this brief moment of comfort, but then the spasms start again.

"*Ugh*," she breathes heavily through her tears faced only by the ugly pattern running through the marble below her.

*I'm going to die*, Elizabeth thinks, *and I'm going to die alone. Christie will come home from Paul's to find me on the damn floor lying in a pool of vomit.*

Raising herself up on her knees, Elizabeth crawls over to the door. Between spasms, she reaches up for the handle and pulls it open. She falls out and onto the carpet in the hall to lie there for several minutes before she tries to move again.

The bright hallway lights hurt her eyes, which she covers with her sweaty hair. Gathering her strength, she raises herself up again and crawls slowly down the hall to Angie's door just a few rooms down on the opposite side.

"Angie," she whispers as she gets closer, "Angie, wake up. It's Elizabeth, Angie."

She reaches Angie's door, extends her arm out to knock and collapses on the ground in front of it. Propping herself up on her elbow, she throws her hand up this time against the door as hard as she can. Elizabeth bangs on it three times.

"Angie, wake up," she says desperately. "I'm sick, Angie. Help me." Her arm falls down beside her face and she writhes against the doorframe in pain.

A large crashing noise sounds from within and a few seconds later, Angie opens the door.

"Holy shit, Elizabeth!" she says. "What the hell is wrong with you?" She squats down and smoothes Elizabeth's hair away from her forehead.

"Sick," Elizabeth moans and rolls over.

"Yeah, but what the hell is it?"

"Stomach, and my back," Elizabeth says. "Feel like I'm going to die."

"You're not going to die, at least not tonight. Has this ever happened before?"

"Yes," Elizabeth shakes her head, "for a while, but this ... bad." Her face contorts and she draws her knees to her chest and rocks in a ball.

"What should I do?"

"Stay with me," Elizabeth says.

"Of course, I'll stay with you," Angie says. "Do you want to go to the bathroom?"

"Can't make it there."

"Oh, yes, you can," Angie stands up. "I'll help you." She takes one of Elizabeth's arms and tries to help her to her feet.

"No, no, no," Elizabeth tries to shout, "can't walk."

"Should I call a doctor or the RA?"

Elizabeth shakes her head *no* violently.

"Okay, then crawl. I'll help you."

"Need to throw up," Elizabeth says.

"Then come on. We've got to get you to the bathroom."

"Okay."

A girl throwing up in a college dormitory really isn't that odd of a thing. Young girls get sick for many different reasons.

Slowly, Elizabeth crawls to the bathroom with Angie encouraging her the whole way. She stops a few times doubling over from the pain, but Angie pushes her along until they make it there.

"Come on, Elizabeth," Angie waves, "I've got this stall all ready for you, and I'll even hold your hair."

Elizabeth crawls across the blue tile to the front of the toilet and pushes herself up on her knees. Leaning over, Angie takes Elizabeth's long black hair in her hands and looks the other way while Elizabeth rams her finger down her throat as far as she can. She gags loudly.

"That's good, Elizabeth," Angie says. "Do it again. I promise it'll all come up and then you'll feel better."

Elizabeth rams her finger down her throat over and over until she finds that magic spot. She vomits. She vomits again, and then she dry heaves for a few minutes. Gasping for air, she leans backward away from the toilet.

"I think you got it all," Angie says.

Elizabeth lies back on the bathroom floor, her head coming out of the stall, heedless of the dingy locale.

"What's wrong with me?" she says. "I can't keep anything down. I feel fine for a while and then I start feeling really bad. Then this happens. Do you know how many times I've puked in the last couple of weeks?"

Angie frowns, "I didn't even know you were sick. I mean you said your stomach hurt a few times, and everybody pukes at parties, but ..."

"I think I'm all right now," Elizabeth breathes. "Thanks so much, Angie. I promise I'll make it up to you somehow. You can go back to your room. I'm sure I'll be fine."

Angie folds her hands in front of her and sits down in front of a sink. "I'm not leaving here until I see you safe in your own bed," she says. "We'll just take our time and get there when we can."

Angie and Elizabeth sit on the floor inside the dormitory bathroom for another thirty minutes while Angie recounts stories of growing up on her father's tobacco farm. Elizabeth listens trying to imagine herself there instead of wallowing on the bathroom tile.

Refusing to leave her, Angie guides Elizabeth back to her room and sleeps on Christie's bed. They make it through the night without any more interruptions.

⤞⊙⊙⤝

On Valentine's Day, Elizabeth lies in a hospital bed in Larnee weakened by her inability to keep anything down and frustrated that she's still there. Melena forced her to go, and now the medical community has examined her and her strange condition for the last twenty-four hours.

Poked and prodded early this morning, Elizabeth had an unfortunate incident with an elderly nurse, a catheter, the woman's failing sight and shaky hands. As if the embarrassment of her private parts being scrutinized by the woman, and eventually another nurse, wasn't enough, the acute pain of the procedure was finally too much for her to bear.

Above Melena's protestations, Elizabeth cried mutiny, stood up in her open back nightgown, took her IV stand in hand and tried to flee the hospital. She cursed loudly all the way down the hall until, in the end, Melena coerced her into turning around just as she reached the main elevators.

Seeing Elizabeth back into bed, Melena rushed down the hall and found someone to help make her daughter's stay a little bit easier. After a shot of Demerol, Elizabeth grew to like the hospital very much.

Elizabeth's doctor, Dr. Lockhaus, who works in the same clinic as Melena's doctor, comes in and lays his notebook down on the windowsill. Exchanging pleasantries, he checks her vitals and then addresses Elizabeth and Melena in a more serious tone.

"Ladies," he says, "this is a very strange case indeed. All of our test results are negative, which on one hand is a good thing. But the problem is, we can't figure out what's wrong with you."

Elizabeth stays silent though she has her own ideas about what's wrong.

"You've run everything imaginable?" Melena asks.

"We sure have. The only evidence we have is of her weakened system and malnourishment."

"Oh, Elizabeth," Melena says thinking of her chronically ill state, "I sure hope you don't have what I have, whatever that is."

Elizabeth fears Melena's ailment because she knows her own derives from the same problem her mother has. She suspects the emotional stress of their lives, a lurking disease ready to destroy them all; and, she's watched her mother deteriorate from it over the years.

"Mrs. Starling," Dr. Lockhaus says. "I think we're dealing with two entirely different things here." He taps his pen against the chart in his hand and looks at Melena.

"Would you mind if I spoke to Elizabeth alone for a few seconds?"

"Why, not at all," Melena says, her curiosity rising. "Elizabeth, honey, I'm going to go downstairs for a few minutes. I'll pick you up some magazines."

"Okay," Elizabeth says, smiling from the drugs.

Melena leaves the room and the doctor looks after her.

"Your mother's a terrific lady," he says, "but I thought we could have a more frank discussion with her gone."

"Right," Elizabeth says and sits up a little bit.

"So, Elizabeth, how long has this been going on?"

"A few months," she says. "It all started when my grandmother got sick. After she died, it got worse, much worse."

Dr. Lockhaus relaxes and sits down in a chair next to the window remaining close enough that the space between them seems private. Having spent some time in the Far East, he fosters beliefs blending Western and Eastern medicine.

"I've seen things like this before," he says, "and I want you to tell me the truth. Was there anything else that happened, maybe not now, but sometime that would trigger your body to act with such an extreme physical response?"

Elizabeth looks hard at him and thinks for a second. Would he actually believe the connection she's made between her memories and her sickness? The Demerol makes it easy for her to talk and she only wants to get out of here and stop getting sick.

"You," she points, "have to promise me that you won't tell anybody, and if you do tell, then that'll be really bad karma for you."

"I promise," he says. "Part of my job as a doctor is confidentiality, and I've heard most everything you can hear."

"You know," Elizabeth says sounding a little drunk, "I never ever was supposed to tell anything to anyone, and so I haven't. I wouldn't want to embarrass anyone, you know?" She takes a deep breath and continues.

Thinking the confession a way out, she tells him all about her years at Bell's house and how no one ever knew. Then she tells him about Leopold moving in with them since her grandmother's death and Dr. Lockhaus listens quietly.

In his work with adolescents and young adults, he's heard lots of similar stories before. She tells hers frankly and calmly. He nods his head at the appropriate moments and when she is done, she looks at him.

Elizabeth says, "So, that's that."

"I think we've got the problem," the doctor says. "I've found over the years, that sometimes when people experience unusual amounts of stress or emotional pain, their bodies seize upon the source. If the mental anguish isn't dealt with externally, then the body struggles with it internally."

"So, basically, I'm going to puke when I eat for the rest of my life?"

"Certainly not, I would hope, but that all depends on you."

"What do you mean?"

"Elizabeth," Lockhaus says, "You're going to have to tell your family. First of all, they need to know so that you don't have to see him anymore. Secondly, there's the risk of him doing it to someone else."

"Right," she says in her *whatever* Generation-X voice.

"The most important thing though is that you have to get better. The only way I see that happening is with some therapy."

"You mean a psychiatrist?" she asks.

"Exactly," Lockhaus says. "You may not be ready to tell your family, but you're obviously okay with telling a third party. I know someone in Hollow Town who will be perfect for you to talk to. I'm going to give you her card and I want you to promise me that when you get out of here and back on campus, you'll give her a call."

Elizabeth takes the card from him. "I'll do it," she says truthfully. "I don't want to be sick like this anymore."

"Good," the doctor says, "This is between us Elizabeth, but I'm going to verify with my colleague that you schedule and appointment."

Elizabeth smiles and yawns.

"I'm going to get out of here so you can get some rest. I'll check on you later before I leave the hospital for the night, and maybe we can talk about when you'll be getting out."

"Okay," Elizabeth says. She leans back in the bed. Her eyes close quickly and she falls fast asleep.

⚮

The following April, the Starlings and the Shades gather in Larnee for the double birthday party. It's so rare when the Shades make the drive to Larnee, and everyone present seems hopeful in their spring attire. Isabelle, the brightest star in this show, shines as the various family members seek to hold and twirl her above them in their arms.

Ever since Blackwell fell in with his network marketing business of preventive health care, they've been researching Asian medicines as a family. Isabelle hasn't had a cold yet, and now, Blackwell speaks on the topic to crowds all over the east coast convincing them with his charm.

Katherine's decor throughout the house welcomes visitors with scented candles and cultured sophistication. The hosts have prepared a wonderful array of dishes ranging from corn on the cob, grilled chicken and steak, salad, bread and platters of hors d'oeuvres.

Melena really loves Katherine and approves of the style with which she decorates her home, most of its designs coming from The Green Gallery.

Mingling with her family, Katherine makes sure that everyone is satisfied and Isabelle is looked after. For a moment, the den clears out and Leopold sits on the couch next to the fireplace staring at Pearl who has Isabelle in her arms.

"Leopold, honey," Pearl says hurrying off. "I have to go tinkle. Watch Isabelle for a minute."

She'll only be a second.

Leopold, ready on the couch, shakes his head *yes*, though how much he understands no one really knows.

Just to reassure herself, Pearl gesticulates moving her hands back and forth slowly, pointing between her eyes and Isabelle's.

Leopold tells her yes and slaps his hand on his knee while Pearl disappears around the corner.

Remember, it's only for a second.

Right away, he picks Isabelle up, sets her on his lap and begins to bounce her on his knee.

Upstairs, Elizabeth comes out of the bathroom just as Pearl comes up to use it. She smiles at her aunt and Pearl pinches her on the cheek as they pass by each other. Elizabeth hops down the stairs while holding onto the rails.

Jumping onto the landing, she turns the corner into the living room and the previous moment is gone. Elizabeth's face drops from a smile to a cold stare, but she doesn't stop walking through the room. Immediately she stands beside Leopold prying the baby out of his arms.

"I don't think so," she says.

Leopold utters a series of comments in his own language. The summation of this speech communicates a rage directed toward Elizabeth for robbing him of his baby-monitoring duties.

Elizabeth hoists Isabelle on her hip and quietly exits the room before Leopold's tirade can upset the tranquility of the toddler. Everyone else, except for Pearl, has wandered outside, where they mill about on the back lawn. Elizabeth moves toward them passing through the kitchen.

"You should never play with him, ever," Elizabeth says to Isabelle who gurgles unintelligible sounds as they walk outside.

Elizabeth smiles at everyone to cover her anxiety of the previous moment and makes a beeline for Melena.

"Hey, Mom," she says, "look who I just found. I think someone needs her Nanna."

"Oh, you give me that precious angel right now," Melena says and sweeps Isabelle up in her arms. Quickly, Lucinda, Bobby, and Betsy his wife, form another cluster around Isabelle and Melena.

Elizabeth backs out of it, relieved, and turns around to survey the crowd. Her eyes stop as she spots Katherine and, casually, Elizabeth crosses over to her.

"Hey, Katherine," she says and hugs her, "thanks a lot for throwing this party. It's really nice."

"Hey," she smiles, "what's family for?"

"Yeah," Elizabeth says. "Hey, *uh*, do you maybe have a minute to spare? There's something really important I need to talk to you about."

"Sure," Katherine says, "what is it?"

Katherine never knows what to expect with this family. When she and Blackwell were in college, he went through a horrible time during one of Melena and Ernest's separations. She saw them at their worst then and nothing now would stun her.

"*Um*, do you mind if we go upstairs?" Elizabeth asks. "I don't want everyone to hear us."

"Oh," her eyes flutter with a slight curiosity. "Well, come on. We can go up to Isabelle's room."

Together they disappear inside the house. Elizabeth leads Katherine through the kitchen into the hall so they avoid the living room where Leopold can be heard ranting loudly to Pearl.

Balling his large fist, he shakes it in the air at his imagined foe. Yelling again, he punches it into his hand.

Katherine stops at the foot of the stairs and asks, "Wonder what Leopold is upset about?"

Elizabeth smiles as she steps on the first step.

"He's mad," she says, "because I took Isabelle away from him."

"Oh," Katherine nods at an odd angle as her curiosity grows and she follows Elizabeth up.

They walk into Isabelle's room and Elizabeth shuts the door behind them. She walks over to the window on the far side of the wall and motions for Katherine to follow her.

This secrecy is familiar to Katherine. Someone in the Starling family always seems to be pulling someone else to the side to whisper secrets in their ear.

They peer out the window down into the backyard.

"Look," Elizabeth says, "I brought you up here because I didn't want anyone to hear me at all, and I mean that. I'm only telling you this because it could affect Isabelle and I want you to swear to me that you won't tell Blackwell, or Mom, or anyone."

Elizabeth's eyes narrow, "Swear it."

"I swear," Katherine says.

Elizabeth looks at her waiting and says, "Leopold isn't the cherubic innocent everyone thinks he is."

For the next few minutes, Elizabeth talks, explaining without much emotion. Katherine's face grows pale as she leans out the window to make sure Isabelle's there with Melena.

"I had to tell you," Elizabeth says. It was much easier for her to say it this time.

"No one else knows and that's how I want it to stay. You promised me you wouldn't say anything so you better not."

Katherine asks, "Don't you think keeping this inside is what's been making you sick? You know, if they knew then, you wouldn't have to be around him."

"Yes," Elizabeth says matter-of-factly, "but I'm seeing a psychiatrist, and she's helping me a lot. Besides, I'm feeling much better, really I am."

Christmas was a bad time for Elizabeth. Bell died, Leopold moved in and her body just couldn't take the overwhelming strain.

Katherine's hand rests over her mouth.

"What are you going to do?"

"Keep going to the doctor for now," Elizabeth says. "I'm not moving home when the semester is out. I know what Mom's going to do soon, and I don't want to be around for it. I'm getting an apartment here for the summer, somewhere downtown."

She fidgets with the window sill. "Then I'll be headed out of the country off to the Netherlands, and it won't matter anymore."

"That's right," Katherine says, "but what will your parents think of you getting an apartment on your own?"

"That really doesn't matter at this point."

She thinks about all the fighting that house still holds insides its walls.

"I can't go back there," she says. "I have a job lined up already, and I refuse to live in the same house with him, or them."

"I don't blame you," Katherine says. Her frown grows deeper.

She knew Elizabeth couldn't live there much longer anyway.

"Hey," Elizabeth says and moves toward the door, "we shouldn't be gone for too long. Everyone will start to wonder and that's the last thing I need."

"All right, Elizabeth," Katherine says, "I won't tell, but you have to tell them yourself at some point. He'll still be around if you don't."

"That's why I'm going to the doctor," Elizabeth says. "I need more time first."

Katherine follows her down the stairs.

At the bottom of the staircase, they go in different directions. Elizabeth smiles as she walks into the living room where Leopold still argues with Pearl.

"Elizabeth," Pearl says, "did you say something to Leopold to make him mad?"

"I came through and took Isabelle outside to Mom," she says. "She was crying so I thought it would be better."

"Oh," Pearl puts her hand on her hip, "well, I wonder what he's so upset about?" She's been trying to calm him down for the last ten minutes.

"I don't know," Elizabeth says and feigns curiosity, "maybe he's losing his mind. He is getting very old."

---

The early weeks of summer have been tense. The tension, initiated by Ernest and Melena, has reached a new, highly secretive level where phone taps and private detectives spy on certain members of the family.

Refusing to live with her parents, Elizabeth has moved into a one-bedroom apartment in downtown Larnee. Ernest, disapproving of this choice, has employed someone to follow her on her drunken, vandalistic meanderings.

No one, except for Katherine, understands why she would move into an apartment for only three months. Yet, Elizabeth, with two and a half months of weekly therapy behind her, is almost able to eat normally again.

The atmosphere of the house she escaped has boiled quietly for as many years as Elizabeth's been around.

For the last five years, Melena has gathered resources like a squirrel in preparation for winter, waiting for the time when she must hibernate and feed off her own ammunition. Ernest, the patriarchal laborer, has worked and continued to do other things that no one will ever be sure of.

In their separate, adult lives, Blackwell and Luke have somewhat evaded their parents' turmoil. Away from Ernest, Blackwell collects the data and people he needs to build his business while Katherine maintains their very important social calendar.

Daydreaming of racecars, Luke enjoys the self-sustaining quality Mancon provides for him. In him, Ernest sees the future. Nepotism relieves Luke of any real pressure to perform at work, and that allows him plenty of time to think about speed and acquire new opportunities for racing.

After her first year of college, Elizabeth continues on her path of self-destruction. Her downtown apartment has become a drinking hub for all her friends, before she takes flight to Holland at the end of summer.

Early one night, Blackwell phones Luke from his downstairs office where Post-it notes cover the walls and motivational books line the floor. The phone rings and he closes the door for privacy.

"Luke," Blackwell says, "hey, what's going on at your house tonight?"

Though not often, the two brothers occasionally meet at different bars around town to have drinks. Blackwell will sit at the bar with Luke and his friends, but the rift between Melena and Luke has begun to drive a wedge between the brothers.

"Not too much goin' on here," Luke replies. "Just thinking about whether or not I'm going to make it to this race in Virginia."

"Yeah," Blackwell says, "you've been doing pretty good on the circuit this year, haven't you?"

Blackwell hasn't raced a kart since he started dating Katherine in college.

"Won four, lost one and that's just because the engine broke."

"Man," Blackwell says thinking about driving again, "I'd like to hop in a car and drive myself, but I can't really do that anymore. I mean not with the baby and all. It'd be too much if I got in a wreck. You know?"

"Guess so," Luke says wondering why his brother really called.

"So," Blackwell says, "have ya been seeing anyone lately?"

"No," Luke says not liking to be reminded of it, "I haven't really wanted to since Emily and I stopped dating."

"You know," Blackwell says trying to motivate him the way he does the countless members of his down-line with Live Well, "at some point, you got to get back out there and try again."

"Yeah, well, I will when someone interests me enough."

"Fair enough, fair enough."

"Hey," Blackwell says with a sigh, "I have to tell you something."

"Okay, tell me." Luke waits, thinking he will hear something about their father that Melena seems to really want him to know.

"There's no other way for me to say it but to say it," he says. "Something happened to Elizabeth and I don't know when or what exactly, but it had to do with Leopold. She told Katherine, and I'm not supposed to say anything about it, but I'm pretty sure it's going to come out soon anyway. I just thought it would be better for me to tell you so that no one else would have to."

"Damn," Luke says not really understanding or wanting to understand what Blackwell has just told him.

"I don't really know ... *uh* ... damn."

The two of them, grown men faced with an terrible secret, speak in monosyllables for a few seconds the way men do when they hear something they cannot comprehend emotionally. Neither do they dwell, nor ask for details that with their life experiences they cannot handle.

Having communicated the barest details, they hang up and wish only to forget. Blackwell opens his office door and steps into the living room. He smiles at Katherine as she walks in with Isabelle and a bag of toys. He turns on the television and the three of them watch the evening news.

A few blocks away, Luke tries to wipe his mind blank and goes into the kitchen to take a beer out of the refrigerator. He sits down on the couch with two of his roommates and watches *Sports Center*, escaping into an argument between two commentators about next year's pro football season.

The next day, Melena and Elizabeth sit in Melena's plain white work van outside of Osaka's. Melena hates this van and the fact that she does not have another car to drive besides this. She wants a luxury sedan just like her husband has. Melena looks at Elizabeth and smiles.

"I'm leaving the bastard in a week," she says. "I have everything ready now, and I'll be filing on him first thing next Monday. You know, I have him on videotape with that woman outside of a Red Roof Inn."

Triumphant, Melena shakes her fist over the steering wheel. She's been seeking to validate her accusations since the failure of their marriage began.

"I finally have proof, so now I can leave him forever. You better believe I'm going to sue her too. I'll get her for alienation of affection. See, Elizabeth ..."

Melena looks out the window, mildly hopeful. "This is exactly why you have to get an education. If I had gone to school and could support myself, I never would have stayed this long."

"Good, Mom," Elizabeth says trying to be supportive. "That's really good. I'm happy for you. I know that it has been really hard for you to stay this long."

"I only did it for you," Melena says. "I wanted to make sure that you got to college and that it was paid for. The way your father is, it wouldn't surprise me for him to pay for the boys to go to school and then not pay for you. I really do think he hates women."

"Yeah," Elizabeth says. She decides to speak.

"Mom, I have to tell you something and you aren't going to like it. I want you to just stay calm though and listen to me. It's about Leopold."

Elizabeth takes a deep breath and tells the fragments of a story that she's been putting back together for the last couple of years. Sparing many details, she says only what she can handle with her mother.

Melena's shoulders fall and she slumps over the steering wheel in aching pain and disbelief. She cannot fathom this happening to her daughter who she thought she protected more than any other thing in the world.

"But, I was there," Melena says. "I watched you with everyone. I always made sure you weren't around strangers. I would never let anything happen to you."

"I know that, Mom," Elizabeth says, "but it did. It's not your fault or anyone else's. It just happened."

Melena freezes up and her face contorts with rage and pain. She looks to Elizabeth for answers.

"How can I ever look at him again?" she cries.

Melena shakes her head *no* and slams her hand against the dashboard.

"He's at our house right now," she says, "and I am the one who has to deal with him, me. For god's sake, I have to take care of him."

She lets out a brief wail. "I cannot go in there and eat dinner with you, Elizabeth. We're going to have to leave right now."

"That's fine, Mom," Elizabeth says, relieved the experience is almost over. "You can just drop me off at my apartment. "But, Mom ..."

"Yes."

"You cannot tell Dad. I know that you're going to leave him and all hell will break loose, but I am going to tell him. I have to. It's part of my therapy, and I'm going to tell him tomorrow."

"Oh, god." Melena starts the car, suddenly frightened thinking of every possible way Ernest can use this against her in court.

After dropping off Elizabeth, she gets on her cell phone to make arrangements for Leopold's departure back to Holiday. In the unconscious recesses of Melena's mind, a safety mechanism already erodes Elizabeth's statement and turns it into something less than what was said.

This minimizing of the facts is the only way that Melena can handle the situation. Otherwise, she would break down, maybe permanently, in the face of the truth.

The following Sunday, Melena and Ernest stand in the front yard of their house doing what they do best together, fighting. On a gorgeous summer day, the sun filters through the canopy of leaves, and the blue sky is filled with scattered puffy clouds that drift by slowly in the wind.

"You son of a bitch!" Melena screams holding on to the storm door. "Get back here!"

Ernest turns around and shouts at her, "I will not, Melena."

He has a small duffel bag with his toiletries in one hand and a pair of pajamas in the other.

"You want a divorce and that's fine with me," he says. "I'm not going to rot with you in unhappiness until it happens. Just look at the fine mess we've made. You know, it has really been wonderful until now."

Melena stands on the porch with her hands on her hips and yells, "What the hell is that supposed to mean?"

"It means that our lives are shit!"

"Your life may be shit, but mine isn't." Melena points at him. "You have a guilty conscience and that's why you're miserable."

"Not that again," he says. "When are you going to give it up, Melena? I am a decent man, and I have done nothing but give my blood, sweat and tears to this family."

She laughs and sneers, "Along with every woman out there you can find."

Ernest shakes his head. "Well, I can certainly say you've done a great job with our daughter. What am I supposed to do with her now? She's on drugs, spray-painting office buildings, God knows what else, and now this. I can't comprehend it."

"She's your daughter, too, Ernest," Melena exclaims, "but you probably hate her like you hate other women."

With finality, Ernest says "Good-bye, Melena." He steps down the wooden stairs to the bottom.

"If you leave me," she threatens, "I will destroy you. I will take every goddamn thing you own. Do you hear me Ernest William Starling? I will destroy you if you walk down those stairs!" Melena wants him to suffer in the house with her until the divorce is final or she knows he will drag it on for as long as possible.

Ernest looks back at her, his face calm and composed. His competitive spirit flares, unable to accept any defeat.

"You just try it," he says. Ernest's words hang on a threat as he walks down the drive to get in his car.

Melena watches him and storms into the house in a wild fury. The first thing she does is pick up the phone, pressing buttons hastily. Her lawyer's secretary cheerfully answers and puts the call through.

Days later, Elizabeth comes over to the house. She and Melena wait inside the master bedroom. They've been having a visit.

Elizabeth sits on the corner of the bed staring at the blur on the TV above her and Melena washes her hands. As she finishes, the tape that was rewinding clicks to a stop.

Some things people can't get away from.

They'll chase you.

"The tape is done," Elizabeth says.

Melena told her she thinks Ernest has been poisoning her slowly. It's an afternoon of revelation, and Elizabeth has decided to watch this tape. It's not like there had ever been a choice about watching it. Blackwell's seen it and she knew she would, too.

Melena steps inside her room and presses play. She sits on the little brass bench at the foot of her bed. They both stare upward.

"Here it is," she says. "You see the date and the time moves in the corner there."

"*Mmm, hmm*," Elizabeth just looks. She doesn't care anymore anyway, but she looks because Melena wants her to. There's a hotel, a woman and ....

--->==◉▭◉==<---

After a weary summer, fall descends and brings new life to some members in the family leaving others to seek emotional closure on their own. In a small café near The Green Gallery, Katherine, Isabelle and Melena sit around a table topped with multicolor tiles.

Local attempts at modern art hang above them as they sip hot decaffeinated tea out of chic black mugs. Their shared lunch, soup and half a sandwich each, will hold them until an early dinner, which Melena eats by herself almost every night.

The stress of Melena's pending divorce weighs on her mind. Every evening after work, she sorts through a paper trail of her marriage to find the financial evidence she needs to secure her future. These brief lunches with Isabelle and Katherine ease her grief temporarily especially since a second grandchild is on its way.

"Melena," Katherine says wanting Melena to relax, "you don't have to hold her. She'll be fine on her own."

"No, no," Melena says. "I'm having my Nanna time right now. You go on and finish your tea."

"Juice," Isabelle says, "juice."

"Yes, Isabelle," Katherine says, "here's some juice."

She hands her a red sipping cup.

Katherine sighs, "You know even when you've already had one baby, everyone still makes a fuss. Five months left, I'm barely showing and I haven't been sick in weeks."

"I wasn't as sick with Luke as I was with Blackwell," Melena says. "That's for sure. My second delivery was a lot easier, but Luke was so heavy. He definitely was my biggest baby, and sick, too, when he was little. That boy had a cold or an earache every time I turned around."

Melena can talk about Luke being a baby and not grow angry. For her, Luke as a child has been partitioned into a separate identity from Luke as an adult. Now, he never does what she wants him to and she thinks it's all Ernest's fault.

"You don't seem to have those problems so far," Melena says. "Our girl here is too gorgeous to be sick."

"I hope she'll adjust well to her little brother," Katherine says. "Isabelle's been the focus for so long. She'll have to notice the difference in some way."

"She's going to be a wonderful big sister," Melena says. "Won't you Isabelle?"

Melena bounces the toddler up and down in her lap and makes faces at her.

"Nanna," Isabelle says..

"Hey," Katherine says, "did you say that painting was coming in soon or did they think it would take another couple of weeks?"

"Oh, no, honey," Melena says, "that piece came in yesterday and I've got it sitting in the back of the store wrapped up and waiting for you. I told the gallery that my daughter-in-law had to have it this weekend."

Melena makes sure that Katherine and Blackwell get preferential treatment.

"Melena, you didn't have to do that."

"I know I didn't," Melena says. She's thrilled to decorate Blackwell's home since he has always stuck by her. "I refuse to let the wall above your fireplace go bare when all your friends are in town."

"You're so good to us," Katherine says. "We really appreciate it. Hey, have you heard from Elizabeth lately? Did she get our care package?"

"She did and she said thank you," Melena smiles.

Elizabeth wouldn't have made it to Europe if it weren't for her. Ernest cut off all money toward her college expenses for two reasons: Melena wanted him to pay, and he thought Elizabeth's going to Europe would only end in disaster.

"Apparently," she continues, "the cereal selection is horrible over there and you know how that girl loves her cereal. She told me she had to hide the Captain Crunch so that no one else could eat it."

"Yeah," Katherine remembers her own summer exchange adventures. "The Paris markets were small to me, and they didn't have anything I was used to. In Europe, I think if you don't have any money for eating out and you don't cook for yourself, you'll starve. Elizabeth will have to learn a lot."

"I hope she tries some new foods," Melena says and wonders if her daughter will take care of herself. She's still reeling from Elizabeth shaving her beautiful red hair into that horrible Mohawk.

"She was such a picky eater growing up, and now she's got to take what she can get."

Katherine sips her tea. "Did she say how the weather was in The Netherlands?"

"Oh, gosh," Melena shivers thinking about it. "Rainy and she says it's going to get very cold."

"Northern Europe does have harsh winters." Katherine replies. "Have you talked to Luke in the last week or so? Blackwell left him a message about watching the football game, but he didn't hear from Luke."

"No," she says, "and I don't want to talk about Luke. He's

brainwashed by his father and he refuses to see the truth. You know he wouldn't even watch that tape?" She shakes her head.

"I'm so glad that Blackwell stopped working for *him* when he did. Luke has always been closer to his father, and I think he always will as long as *he* has all the money."

Katherine shuffles her feet under the table. "I'm sorry to upset you, but I know what you mean. I'm so happy Blackwell left there when he did, too. I really think that getting away from *him* was the best thing he could have done."

"Do you know that Elizabeth wouldn't have been able to go to Europe if it wasn't for me?" Melena asks. "He didn't pay a damn dime to send her there, not one cent. He hates women."

"I just hope he acts like a man," Katherine says, "and the divorce ends quickly."

Isabelle starts to make a fuss.

"You are an angel," Melena says to the child. "My perfect angel, and you make everything so much better. Who cares about all the horrible people in the world when I have a precious angel like you?"

Katherine is filled with pride as she watches her child's effect on her mother in law. She contemplates the beauty of the life inside her and all the joy this child will bring when it finally comes.

The ladies stray to an easier topic of conversation, and then another, before they gather their things and leave the café. Afterward, they go straight to Melena's store to move the painting into the car.

The Venetian café scene will be the newest object d'art in Blackwell and Katherine's home. All their wealthy friends will adore it, and they will be the envy of the neighborhood.

---

The house that Ernest built sits unoccupied except for Melena, who keeps the master bedroom alone.

Almost every night, that familiar Larnee wind blows the

overgrown tree limbs against the long, vertical windows in Melena's room. The startling noise sounds like nails on a chalkboard, and now three heavy locks fasten her bedroom door against anything that might try to enter from the other side. Every night Melena locks herself in behind them.

Tricky little incidents, unexplainable repeated noises, and things like the cellar door being found wide open, convince Melena that Ernest is using scare tactics against her. Their upcoming divorce is the talk of most of Larnee's society.

Oblivious to the costs of their aggressions in this war, both parties will fight to the death.

The king size bed fills nearly all the space in her room, and Melena lies, watching TV with her white comforter tucked up under her chin. Suddenly, she pauses and grows very still as a light dusting of something falls down on her like snow. Her eyes turn toward the ceiling directly above her.

*Damn it*, she thinks. *There it is again.* Melena cuts off the television and stares at the ceiling in wonder.

Someone could be on the roof; no, I would've heard them walking up there before now if they were. She turns on the lamp beside her bed and looks at her comforter.

"Damn," she says.

Wood dust from the ceiling is sprinkled on top of her blankets. She swipes it away onto the floor and looks at the ceiling again. Taking a flashlight from underneath the bed, she climbs onto the bed and stands with the flashlight pointed at the ceiling.

Scanning the length of the beams, Melena stops as a small movement catches her eye. A large black ant crawls out of a tiny hole and clings to the wood of the ceiling.

Furious, she watches it move forward and then fall.

Melena quickly steps off the bed and leans across it. Her hands rummage through the comforter as she locates the ant and promptly disposes of it with a tissue. Her balled-up fists rest on her hip as she walks out of the bathroom.

Behind her, the sound of the toilet echoes. It doesn't seem to be flushing properly and continues to run on and on quite loudly. Looking from the hole in the ceiling to the warm spot where she was just lying down, Melena sits on the edge of the mattress and shakes her head.

*The floor is going to fall through in the bathroom,* she thinks. *That son of a bitch knew it was rotting out, and now I have ants dropping on me in my sleep. This nightmare house is falling to pieces around me, and somewhere Ernest is laughing.*

*I bet he's sending people over here when I'm at the Gallery to sabotage the house so that I'll be afraid. That bastard wants to torment me, but I'm not going to let him.*

*I will not let him win,* she reassures herself. *I will destroy him first.*

Melena crosses over to the other side of the bed where Ernest once slept. She tugs on the large mahogany nightstand that sits adjacent to what was long ago his side of the bed. The heavy piece will not budge.

Melena tries to move it again, but fails. She stands looking down at the bed and realizes that for tonight she cannot move it away from the ants.

She grabs her pillows from the other side and bangs them together to remove the dust and anything else that might be on them. With a frown Melena lays her pillows where Ernest used to lay and sits down on the bed to rest against them.

Remote in hand, she turns the television on and contemplates her inability to exact full revenge on Ernest at this time. The ants become a physical symbol of Melena's new mantra.

*One day he will pay,* she thinks, *one day he will pay.*

She settles down, whispering the words over and over again in her mind, as the effects of her sleeping pills begin to kick in.

Somewhere in the Netherlands, Elizabeth slums it with her new crew of friends riding on trains and going to shows. She's the only girl in their small, conservative Dutch city with a Mohawk.

Traveling by himself all across the United States, Blackwell speaks to wide audiences about the benefits of various products and lifestyle choices concerning personal consumption of food. People trust and love him. They flock to him for advice and support.

Melena can't afford to hire extra counsel like Ernest can so Blackwell clears his schedule to support her when she needs him. Since he was born when she was young, it is as if they grew up together and Blackwell feels responsible for Melena's welfare.

Striving for extreme neutrality, Luke fails to convince Melena of his refusal to be involved in either side. In her view, he's the prime candidate for spying on Mancon, and Melena refuses to believe him when he says he cannot help her. Everyday he works on his plan to get into a stock car, calling people and scheduling meetings.

Early in the morning, on a nine-to-five workday, Melena's lawyer, Sandra McNair, has her secretary phone Ernest's lawyer, Roger Thornsby.

The young secretary's long red nails tap at the edge of the phone.

"Thornsby and Horton," a female voice says, "this is Peggy how can I help you?"

"Yes, this is Danielle calling for Sandra McNair. Mrs. McNair would like to speak with Mr. Thornsby if he is available."

"One moment please." Peggy presses the red hold button and buzzes Roger in his office.

"Mr. Thornsby, Mrs. McNair's office is on the phone for you."

"*Ahh*," Roger says, "the Starling case. Yes, Peggy, put her through." Roger and Sandra go way back.

"Thornsby on one," Danielle says listening for both parties to pick up.

"This is Roger Thornsby," Roger says in his courtroom voice.

"Hi, Roger, this is Sandra." She sits back in her chair and toys with the phone cord. Her angular face looks cold.

"We missed you this weekend at the club. I thought you and Virginia would surely make it to the city for the Homeless Fundraiser."

"Sandra," Roger says, "you know we wouldn't miss it for the world, but we just didn't feel like flying up this weekend. I let the kids go instead with some friends of theirs from school."

He stares at his golf clubs leaning in the corner. "Now that they're getting older," he says, "I trust them with the apartment. It's exciting to have another home outside of Larnee."

Sandra taps her pen. "I know. My girl has been pressing me to let her move there, but I told her, Manhattan is my weekend getaway. She's old enough to find her own."

"Anyway, Roger," she says, glancing at the file lying open on her desk. "I was calling you about the Starlings. By now, you must have received the subpoena for all of the Mancon and Westerland documents."

"I did, Sandra," he pauses, "I did, but you'll have to go to court for the Westerland documents. It's a separate entity from Mancon, and you know it's going to take me quite some time to gather all of that extremely detailed information from my client. We'll have to make a copy and review it all before we pass it along."

"Oh, Roger," Sandra says, "the Westerland Company was established eight years ago while our clients were married and living together and with your client's direct funding. You take your time though," she says, "Court can wait. We're going to Aspen for a few weeks, and I'm not going to touch anything in this case until I get back."

Sandra thinks about their private cottage on the mountain.

"Oh, and Roger," she says, "If I were you, I'd make sure I did a damn good job with this one. We're prepared to see our case all the way to a jury and, by the way, you'll be getting a bill from me for my client. Since Mr. Starling is now paying Mrs. Starling's legal fees, I thought I would send you the first bill."

"Well, Sandra, we haven't had an official ruling on that yet, but give me a figure for now."

"Let's see," she says, "two hundred fifty an hour, plus a retainer. I'd ballpark it around ten thousand."

"All right then." Roger puts his foot against the brass kickplate running across the bottom of his desk.

"You don't think we could settle this one without a trial, do you?"

"I seriously doubt it," says Sandra. "Your client owes mine quite a bit of money, and until he is willing to pay his dues, we will hold out for the trial."

"Don't plan on a cave-in on this side. My client will not concede to the exorbitant amount of money your client is seeking. I'm afraid I see many hours in this case before we're done." He jokes, "Let's just hope the better lawyer wins."

Sandra chuckles without really laughing. "Don't worry, I will win, you old joker, you."

"We'll see about that." He stands up. "Tell Frank I said hi, maybe we'll see you all in the city this weekend."

"Sounds great, Roger, and tell Virginia I said hello."

"I will," he says, "good-bye."

"Good-bye."

Sandra hangs up her phone and buzzes Danielle who sits in the reception area just beyond her own office door.

"Danielle," Sandra says, "I would like a Perrier, please. Oh, and make sure you start a new billing file for the Starling case. It's going to be thick."

"Yes, Mrs. McNair," Danielle says, "anything else?"

"That'll be all for now," Sandra says, "but don't forget my lemon, please."

"Coming right up," Danielle says. She goes to the refrigerator where she prepares Sandra's Perrier with a freshly cut lemon wedge.

‹—◦◉◦—›

The week before Thanksgiving, a community phone rings on the second floor hallway of the International Student flat for the Catholic University Brabant in a town called Tilburg. Outside the cozy, white-brick apartment building, a light, continuous rain drizzles and it's cold.

As the phone rings again, a young Englishman with curly blond hair emerges from his kitchen to pick it up. His build is lean from biking through the Dutch countryside.

"Hello," Oliver says wiping a bit of Nutella from his mouth, "this is Oliver speaking."

His voice booms with resonance while hers is slow and deliberate. Melena never knows who she's going to get on the phone since all eight of Elizabeth's roommates are from different countries.

"Hello," Melena says, "I am Elizabeth Starling's mother. Is she at home?"

"I believe so, Mrs. Starling," Oliver says. "Could you hold on one moment, please, and I'll just knock on her door to check for you?"

"Oh," Melena says, "thank you."

Oliver steps to Elizabeth's door and taps on it a few times. Inside, he hears two voices chatting away over the music.

"Elizabeth," he calls rapping on the door with his knuckle. "Elizabeth, it's your mum phoning from the States."

Elizabeth's door swooshes open. A Bjork CD plays quietly in the background. A long, apple green Mohawk runs down the middle of her head, which has been shaved weekly these last few months on both sides.

The front part of the Mohawk stands in two spikes angled by the shape of her head and held together with egg whites. The rest hangs behind her in a knotty green mess.

Excited, but apprehensive as to the nature of the call, Elizabeth looks over her shoulder back into her room as she picks up the phone.

"I'll probably be a few minutes, Maria," she says to one of her two Swedish flatmates. Petra and Maria are the only ones from the same country.

"Okay, I'll just wait for you in the living room," Maria says.

Elizabeth smiles at Maria, puts the phone to her ear and starts, "Mom."

"Hey, girl," Melena says, "how are you?"

"I'm fine. My roommate Maria was putting my Mohawk up for me." Elizabeth touches one of the crusty spikes. "You should see it, Mom. It's so tall."

Melena asks worried, "Does Maria have a Mohawk, too?"

"No," Elizabeth says. "She's a normal Swedish girl with the mind of an analytical genius, one who sees symbols and patterns."

Both Swedes have shown Elizabeth museum books filled with pictures of Europe's fine art. Having nearly memorized them, Elizabeth has planned a trip to Madrid to visit the Prado.

She's learning so much in her new environment.

"I'm the only weirdo running around here with a Mohawk," she says. "The people at the university aren't like the kids at State."

"You know, Elizabeth, you're just as smart as that girl. Don't you remember your IQ tests?"

"Yes, Mom," she says, "I remember."

"You're a genius, too," Melena sits down at the table.

Elizabeth loves to hear this story. It gives her hope for her one talent, drawing. All her recent sketches have been attempts to mimic the classics in their grandiose form and she's got her eye on one specific Ruben's painting, *Via Lactea*.

"That's what the tests said," Melena insists, "so don't you forget that when you start getting enamored of people there. Your second semester grades were excellent. With you being that smart and all, I don't see why you don't get rid of that ugly Mohawk." Melena shakes her head. "Your hair was so pretty and long before."

"Mom," Elizabeth grits her teeth. She doesn't want to argue about it again.

"It's cool," she says, "and I like it. I am a punk rock goddess over here and after three months, I've finally made all these Dutch friends in town. They love me and look after me. None of the other exchange students know as many locals as I do."

"All right, Ms. Punk Rock Goddess," Melena changes the subject. "Have you been getting your care packages?"

"Yes, I have." Elizabeth sits down on the floor.

She can't figure out what half the things are in the grocery store and bread and cheese only go so far.

"Thank you," she says, "and tell Katherine thank you, too. I'd probably starve if you guys weren't sending me any cereal."

"You have to eat more than cereal, Elizabeth. You probably aren't getting nearly enough vitamins. I want you to go to the grocery store and buy some green beans and some chicken, but make absolutely sure you cook the chicken all the way through. It can't have any pink at all or you'll get Salmonella. You know, people die from that all the time. I saw it on *Dateline*.

Late at night, in bed and sometimes in the kitchen, Melena watches news programs. They feature consumer advisories and health risk warnings that Melena, compelled by her maternal instinct, then imparts to everyone she knows.

"Right," Elizabeth says, "I'll try that."

"How's your money holding out?" Melena asks. "You know you have got to be absolutely thrifty and not put anything on those credit cards until I can get the balance down some."

Elizabeth's entire trip thus far has been funded by credit cards given to her by Melena. Melena thinks Ernest will have to pay for them eventually, one way or another.

"I'm fine," Elizabeth says in all honesty, "I haven't been touching them."

"Elizabeth," Melena says her tone shifting to one of serious inquiry, "I need you to tell me the truth. Has your father called you since you've been over there?"

Melena feels the outdated, yellow kitchen surrounding her as if its walls could close in.

"*Uh*, no," Elizabeth says wishing they didn't have to talk about him every time Melena called. These conversations defeat the purpose of Elizabeth's leaving home.

"Well, I must know if he has or if he ever does." Melena taps her pen on the corn-colored Formica in front of her.

"You know what he said in court?" she asks. "He said he wouldn't pay a damn dime of your trip to Europe or for you to go to college anymore. Don't you worry though, my lawyer will take care of that lousy son of a bitch. She says he has to pay."

"Yeah," Elizabeth says and stares at the floor. She lets the words wash over her so she can forget them later.

"He paid for your brothers and he's going to pay for you," Melena says. "It's because you're a woman. It's women. You know, he hates all women."

"Right."

"If he ever contacts you," Melena says, "you have to tell me immediately. Would you even talk to him after all the things he's done? I mean, what kind of father has he really been to you? You wouldn't talk to him, would you?"

"*Uh*, no," Elizabeth leans back against the wall, but one of her spikes hits it first and she leans forward again so not to damage it. She deplores having to keep secrets.

"But I do talk to Luke a lot. He came to visit me a couple of weeks ago."

"Do not mention your brother's name to me ever again," Melena fumes. "I only have one son as far as I'm concerned. Luke is completely in league with your father."

"Oh, right," Elizabeth says. Over the years, Luke and Blackwell have been disowned by Melena at one time or another, and more than once. Luke has been disowned far more than Blackwell, and Elizabeth has watched, afraid of the day it will happen to her.

"So," Elizabeth says, "how's Katherine doing? Isn't she due in February?"

"She is," Melena says brightening. "We think it's going to be a boy. Isabelle's doing so well now, and I think they are just going to be perfect little friends." Melena smiles and puts a pot of water on the stove for tea.

"There is no way your father will be allowed at the hospital when he's born either. Until he can make right his wrongs, he's not going to have a damn thing to do with those kids. He had a family, and he gave it up. Now, it's lost to him forever."

Melena's anger keeps her warm at night.

"Right," Elizabeth says. Things go smoother if she just agrees.

"Well, listen, honey," Melena says. "I have to go. These phone calls are pretty expensive and with the money I'm spending on you, we really have to be careful with the finances."

Melena quickly tries to think of any warning she might tell her daughter to keep her safe.

"Stay warm over there," she says. "Don't you go anywhere by yourself. Use your best manners and behave. Okay?"

"Oh," Elizabeth says, "I always behave myself, Mom."

"Good girl," Melena says. "I love you, be sweet."

"I will," Elizabeth says. "You be sweet, too, and I love you."

They say good-bye and Elizabeth hangs up the phone. She rubs her forehead trying to push back the swarming angst behind it. Elizabeth walks around the corner into the tiny community kitchen and lounge area where the rest of her seven flatmates sit, watching Dutch TV.

"Hey," she says to Maria, "I'm off the phone. Do you mind finishing these last three spikes for me so I can go to the show?"

"Not at all," Maria says closing her book. "We can't have you going out halfway done. I do hope we have enough egg left."

"*Ah*, if we don't," Elizabeth says, "we can just steal some of Mario's. Right, Mario?" She winks and jabs her Italian roommate in the arm.

His plaid sleeves rolled up, Mario leans away from the stove and pushes his glasses up his nose. "Do what did you say, Elizabeth?" He always says his English isn't so good.

"Oh, nothing Mario," Elizabeth smiles, "I was just going to steal some of your food."

"Okay, Elizabeth," Mario says continuing to cook his dinner. "You should eat more."

Elizabeth and Maria disappear back into Elizabeth's room where Misfits and David Lynch posters illustrate the walls with American subculture images. Across the large window at the back, an enormous Dutch flag stolen by Elizabeth and an older Dutch student her first weekend in The Netherlands covers the entire wall.

A small wooden chair sits in the middle of the room adjacent to the wardrobe holding Elizabeth's clothes.

Elizabeth sits down in the chair and Maria stands behind her. She reaches into the wardrobe to pull the bowl of egg whites Elizabeth prepared off the shelf.

"I think that last spike we did is dry now," Maria says. "What do you say we go on to the next one?"

Elizabeth gropes the hardened base of the last spike. "I think you're right. Please proceed."

"How was your mom?" Maria asks astonished by the things that go on in Elizabeth's home life. "Did everything go okay this time with her on the phone?"

Elizabeth doesn't need to respond.

"I remember the first time I left Sweden to study abroad," Maria says. "I was so apprehensive something would go wrong, but my excitement overran all my fears and, well, ..."

Maria steps to the side and looks at Elizabeth whose face has turned ashen.

"Elizabeth," Maria asks, "what's wrong? I can tell you're quite disturbed."

"My mom asked me if I had talked to my dad." Elizabeth turns toward her.

"See, when they split up she showed me this tape with him and this woman outside of a hotel. I was insanely mad about the whole thing and he dragged me into this family counselor's office in the middle of summer."

Elizabeth remembers screaming and storming out of the woman's office in a fury. She felt confused but powerful in her rage.

"I cussed at him really bad in front of this lady and told him I would never talk to him again unless he admitted to having an affair."

"I see," Maria says.

"I hadn't talked to him at all since that day, and that's exactly the way my mom would have it. She hates him, and she wants me to hate him, too, but it's hard, really hard. My whole life I've been taught to hate him and I'm tired now. I don't think I can do it anymore."

Maria frowns and sits on Elizabeth's bed across from her.

"You shouldn't feel like you have to hate your father," she says. "People always make mistakes, Elizabeth, but your family is your family. You need to have them in your life whether or not the other people in your life like it."

Elizabeth looks at the floor. "Dad sent me a card through Luke when he came to visit. It had four hundred dollars in it. I kept the money and then I called him. It was really good to talk. I hadn't spoken to him in so long and I missed him."

"As you should," Maria says, "he is your father. I think it's really wrong of your mother to try and make you hate your father. It's their business, not yours. I just don't understand why she would want you to be involved with it at all."

"Because that's not what she thinks," Elizabeth says.

Melena isn't the only member of the family who thinks everyone should be involved in the divorce. Luke and Elizabeth are the only two with an ounce of sanity as they desperately try not to get involved.

"She asked me if I had heard from my dad," Elizabeth says, "and I told her I hadn't. I lied. Do you know what she would do to me if she found out I had talked to him?"

Elizabeth quakes with fear at the thought.

"She would yell at me, disown me, then ignore me forever, and I would become a villain too."

"Elizabeth," Maria says standing back up again, "Elizabeth, you are nineteen years old, you are an adult. You've got to start letting your family realize this. You cannot continue to let them manipulate you in this way."

Maria is a very calm and mature twenty-five year old.

"That's easy for you to say," Elizabeth says. "When my mom gets mad at me, I can't handle it. It's like I have this switch inside of me and I just drown in depression and guilt until I feel like I could die."

Maria coats the next spike. "Then you must definitely stop this pattern of behavior. No matter what has happened between your parents, it is not your burden to judge their actions. You must simply try to maintain a relationship with both of them."

"That sounds nice and all, but it'll never happen." Elizabeth looks forward as Maria dries the spike with the hair dryer on low.

"If my mom finds out that I've spoken to my dad, all hell will break loose and she'll never talk to me again. They'll probably end up killing each other before it's all over anyway."

"Stop that," Maria says and turns off the dryer, "don't say such things. Your parents wouldn't really do anything like that, would they?"

"Maria, our home phone was bugged for years while they were spying on each other. They've hired half a dozen different detectives to trail one other around. Then they found unusual levels of arsenic in my mom's blood and no explanation for how it got there."

Elizabeth thinks about Melena and the ants. "Plus," she says, "there's been all this creepy stuff going on at the house since it's just been my mom there. She told me she passed my dad on the street a few weeks ago and swerved her car, tempted to hit him. At this point, nothing would surprise me."

✦

One lonely day just after Christmas, Larnee looks barren in the wasteland of a sharply cold winter. A new year arrives in three days, but there's no promise of anything new for Luke and Melena.

Mother and son meet at one of the new Chinese restaurants in Larnee. They didn't see each other on Christmas, and this hastily arranged lunch is their half-hearted attempt at communicating.

Like Nancy Drew, Melena has to find things out. Everyday she thinks, *They are my children and they should help me. I raised them.*

Luke Bartleby, hopeful they could make it through one lunch in peace, mutters the best speech he can come up with while trying to remain uninvolved in his parent's divorce.

Melena is frustrated by Luke's continuous refusal to help her with the facts and numbers she needs.

It's all about facts, papers, numbers, deeds of ownership and all the other pieces that come to play in divorce battles.

Inside the Red Dragon restaurant, large, gold fish swim in a tank built into the wall. The lovely Asian waitress smiles as she takes the menus from Melena and Luke.

Sitting back in the booth, Luke pushes a strand of hair off his face. Melena opens up a packet of Sweet'N Low and pours it into her tea. She stirs it with a long spoon until all the sweetener dissolves.

Luke leans forward and tries to find a safe topic to engage in. "So, how's the store going?"

He doesn't ask about the Christmas sales. Neither of them would mention the word "Christmas" since this is the first year they didn't celebrate it together.

"Oh," Melena says, "the store is doing just fine. I'm so busy all of the time though. I get really worn out. Standing on my feet all day on that horrible concrete floor really isn't good for my knees."

"You're out a lot doing work in people's houses though aren't you?"

The best interior designer in town, Melena puts all the Larnee designers to shame. Luke, who even as a child saved his money to buy expensive things, has always been proud of his mother's refined taste.

"Sure I am," Melena says, "but Paul and Diane really don't help me with the physical things. His weight slows him down."

She hates to say it, but she thinks maybe if Luke understood how hard it is on her then he'd help.

"Sometimes," she says, "when we're trying to carry something inside a home, he can't even make it up the stairs."

Melena feels the pain in her knee and it makes her mad. "I end up lifting all the heavy pictures and things," she says. "My body pays for it every day. I really don't know how much longer I can do this."

"But everyone in town loves you so much," Luke says. "All around, wherever I go, people rave about you."

"I've been very lucky, but I've also earned it. If I had gone to school ...." she says shifting her leg to ease the permanent ache.

"Luck has nothing to do with it," Luke says. "You're extremely talented."

"Luke," Melena huffs, "I can't afford to hire someone to hang the pictures or carry the statues. I have to do it all myself, me!"

"Perry Sheldon said he's been trying to get you for weeks, but you're booked up."

"I am," Melena says.

"The Sheldons would be a big job, Mom, lots of money."

"I spoke to Perry," Melena says, "but there's too much going on.

I can't work them in."

She stares out the window absorbed, and all her tasks seem to float in front of her eyes. Melena is tired. She needs something to alleviate her internal suffering, but she does not know what that is.

"I think I'm supposed to call when I'm available," she says, "but it's really hard for me to keep up with everything. I don't have the money for big time, expensive lawyers to do all my footwork. I sort through thousands of files myself, so many files."

Whoever holds the money has dominion. Luke sets his water down and looks out the window. Melena stares at him.

"You know, Luke," she says, "I know you still don't believe that your father had an affair. You think he's some kind of saint, but I have physical proof."

In her mind, she will never be able to understand why he doesn't believe her or why he won't just look at the damn tape. She can't decide which one it is.

"I really wish you would look at it once," Melena says, "so you can know just what kind of a son of a bitch he is."

"Son of a bitch" and "bastard" are almost the full extent of Melena's vulgar vocabulary. She says it with a firm southern accent every time.

"Mom," Luke says calmly, "I'm not going to look at any video-tape. I don't want to."

"No," she says, "you aren't, are you? You don't want to believe that he had an affair because then you wouldn't be able to live with yourself anymore for taking his side."

"I'm not taking anyone's side, Mom." Luke pleads. "I'm neutral and I'm trying to stay that way."

"Do you honestly think that working for your father and taking his money is neutral?" Melena asks. "He's buying you off just like he buys everybody else off."

"Mom," Luke says, "I have a job where I go to work every week, five days a week."

"You work for *him*," she says heatedly, "and he's probably putting everything in your name so that he doesn't have to divide it with me."

"Mom ..."

"I realize how your father works," Melena says. "I sure lived with him long enough to know. I just hope you're happy with the wicked life you're creating for yourself."

The waitress comes back to the table with two steaming plates full of Chinese food. She sets them down and smiles.

"Do you need something else?" she asks.

"No, thank you," Luke says.

The waitress nods her head and tries to smile at both of them as she leaves. Melena looks down at the table and back up at Luke after she's gone.

"You know what?" She says, "All of a sudden, I'm not very hungry. Why don't you take this back to the office with you. I'm not going to stay here."

"Mom, don't," Luke says. "Why are you leaving?"

"Because," she grits her teeth, "I am too angry to sit here with you knowing the choices that you've made. If you really loved me you would help me."

Melena picks up her purse and steps out of the booth without another word to Luke. She glances at the waitress's confused look as she walks out the door.

Luke sits in the booth with two plates of food in front of him. After watching for a few moments, the waitress comes back and asks if he's doing all right.

"Oh, oh yes," Luke says and flashes that smile, "it's wonderful. She just had an emergency and had to go. Could you box hers up for me, please?"

She takes the plate away and boxes it up while Luke tries to eat. He stares forward as he sits at the table, hurt and dejected.

⊱─◉═◉─⊰

Early in February of that same year, Ernest wakes up one

Saturday morning and steps outside to pick up the paper. He smiles faintly at the cloudless sky and brings the paper into the kitchen where he turns on the television to watch the morning news.

The paper lies on his blue-tiled counter. Ernest goes straight to the refrigerator to pull out a small Tupperware container filled with pecans, then a small carton of fat-free yogurt and a bottle of Perrier.

This house he now lives in was once occupied by his mother in the years just before her death. Ernest will continue to stay here because his finances will be impacted until his divorce comes to an end.

Settling down at the kitchen table, Ernest unfolds the paper in front of him and sets a bowl down filled with a mix of pecans and yogurt. He eats his breakfast, glancing at the front page of the paper between bites. The phone rings and he steps over to his desk to answer it.

"Hello," Ernest says.

"Ernest," his assistant Priscilla says in a jubilant voice.

"Good morning, Priscilla."

"Ernest, I can't believe you! Why didn't you tell me?"

"I don't know," he wonders, "why didn't I tell you what?"

"Why didn't you tell me Blackwell was having another baby?"

"Excuse me?"

Ernest and Blackwell haven't spoken in almost a year.

When Blackwell left Mancon, he left behind a large credit card debt and his relationship with his father. Ernest forgot about the money, but he never forgot his son.

He always thought his first-born would help him look after things one day, run the company, but that hasn't happened for him. That dream has died. Since the divorce began, Blackwell became Melena's champion and all communications between father and son have ceased.

Ernest decided that Blackwell no longer had a need for him since his business had taken off, but he never would have foreseen this.

"How ..." Ernest says stumbling over his tormented thoughts, "how did you find this out?"

Priscilla, silent for a moment, regrets the call. She hates giving him bad news.

"I'm so sorry, Ernest," Priscilla says. "It was in the paper this morning in the Announcements section."

"You're kidding me?" He looks at the paper, front page unfolded.

"No, Ernest," Priscilla says, "I'm not. I guess Blackwell didn't call."

"No, he didn't."

Ernest sits down in his chair. "Look, Priscilla, I'm going to have to call you later."

"Okay, Ernest."

Distracted, he hangs up the phone, picks up the paper and turns it to the Announcements section. Creasing the pages in half, Ernest scans the columns until he sees the Starling name.

He reads, "Ernest Blackwell Starling and Katherine Evelyn Starling became the proud parents of a son, Joshua Blackwell Starling at four o'clock in the afternoon on Friday the ninth of February. He was born at Myerly Hospital and weighed seven pounds four ounces."

Ernest stares at the paper in disbelief. He feels betrayed as if every good thing he had ever done in life meant nothing to anyone. Ernest didn't even know they were expecting.

Rising from his chair, Ernest struggles to make it to the couch. He clutches at his chest as his heart rate soars uncontrollably. These spells with his heart have come more frequently in the last few months.

Stricken with grief and the physical pain inside, Ernest grabs the arm of the couch and slides down onto the floor. He lets his head fall back against the piece of furniture as he tries to breathe long, slow breaths.

Thoughts of his long, work-filled life flood over him and he wonders how he became the villain. His eyes flutter and close. Ernest's life has been one long race, with competitors in every corner, and few wanting him to win.

*Even when I was a boy,* he thinks, *and now, this race. What has it become? Where was the track and how did it lead me here?*

His subconscious begins to answer these questions. Ernest allows his mind to take him back to a morning when every part of the world held some form of hope for him. This race, his race, in one form of life or another, is all he'll ever know.

Sweltering in the heat of a southeastern summer, a young Ernest, scruffy but clean, pulled his Soap Box Derby Racer on a piece of borrowed rope behind him. The Carolina country road he walked wound around the outskirts of Holiday. The year was 1952.

The bright car rolled behind him, ball-bearing wheels creaking in loud intervals as the rope slackened and tightened in time with his step. Under the relentless sun, the day-old paint job gleamed red and the number 2 stood out in black on either side of the racer.

With weeks' worth of wages from his job at the dairy, Ernest painted the deuce and purchased a new set of wheels.

At the foot of a tall hill, Ernest stood looking up. He grinned at the pack of kids running around the summit. Shouldering the rope over his white T-shirt, Ernest tugged on the knee of his Levis and lunged with each step to bring the car up the hill faster.

Halfway up, a little boy shouted, "Look! It's Ernest. He's brought the Deuce."

A few boys ran down to meet him. "Hey Ernest," Timmy Parkson said, "swell paint job."

"Thanks," Ernest said and moved past them. The boys walked with him up the incline trailing him like adoring fans.

"Hey, Ernest," a redheaded kid told him, "Buddy Roy's here, and he's got a racer that won three times over on Blanchard Hill."

"That's nice," Ernest halted at the top and looked across at the competition. Aligning his car on the starting mark with the rest, he smiled over at the other racers.

"How y'all doin'?" Inside he knew he would leave them all in the dust.

Buddy Roy stepped out of the line. "You think just 'cause that car of yours has a fancy new paint job, you can beat my Mean Green?"

The other kids, silent, watched the two taller boys.

"I ain't sayin' nothin' to no one." Ernest leaned over and patted his boxcar racer. "Unlike some cars, Old Deuce here doesn't need no boasting."

The kids gasped then looked back toward Buddy Roy.

"We'll see about that, Starling." Buddy Roy signaled his hold man and stepped in his car.

Walking through the line and out in front of the cars, Timmy Parkson called out to the racers. "Y'all listen up." He spat. "Go on and get in your cars. When I say 'go' and my hands drop, you hold men let go."

Timmy scanned their eager faces. "You fellas ready?"

They all nodded their heads gravely. The redheaded boy stood behind Ernest's car holding on to the rear.

"You get one push-off," Timmy said, "so race fair."

Timmy raised his hands. "First one to the bottom wins," he said. "On yer marks, get set, go!" Timmy's hand dropped. The hold men pushed off and fewer than a dozen racers sped down the hill.

One boy's wheels fell off and rolled down the incline before his car could even get going. Stopped, he slapped the top of his car. It sat flat on the pavement. The other racers traveled in crooked lines as the boys tried to control their cars.

Neck-and-neck, Mean Green and Old Deuce raced out in front. Buddy Roy looked sideways, nervous, holding the wheel tight. The Deuce's nose edged out ahead of Mean Green. Buddy leaned down and picked up a rock from inside his seat. Holding the car steady with one hand, Buddy threw the rock at the Deuce's wheel.

Pulling on his right hand steering wire, Ernest bounced in the seat and dodged the rock without losing focus. Buddy cursed as his steering wheel locked to one side. The finish line was in sight, and Ernest crouched low in his seat to gain more speed.

The car rattled loudly around him. Ernest tucked his elbows inside and the Deuce took the lead. Buddy Roy and the Mean Green skidded to the side of the road where his out-of-control racer slammed into a mass of Holly bushes.

In seconds, Ernest crossed the finish line. All the boys streamed down the hill after him, whooping Ernest's name.

"Ernest! Ernest! Ernest!"

He rode out along the flat stretch until the Deuce slowed. The noisy boys surrounded Ernest and patted his back as he stepped out of the car. On that day, he was victorious and all the people liked him except for Buddy Roy.

# Act IV

## People Strangled by
## The Ties That Bind

IN A SEGMENT OF SOUTHERN society limited by fortune and leisure, concentric circles have formed around both Melena and Ernest as the upper echelon gossip and delve into the torrid history of the Starling family.

Melena plays the victim, wronged to the worst degree, and against her, there's Ernest, the licentious patriarch who hates women.

Listen in on another circle though, and hear the story of Melena the vengeful, enraged like Juno. Wrapped in the wrath of the furies, she attacks Ernest the defender, the moneymaking slave, the provider.

With her soon to be ex-husband running around town, Melena finds it hard to escape her bounty of bad feelings and now she thinks Larnee is a hateful place. Her joy, so absolute and precious, is found only in her grandkids, Isabelle and Joshua, as they grow in front of her eyes.

The children relieve the continual torment that plagues her. Neither work nor her home can do that for her.

On this hot spring day, Melena works in the home of two of her most treasured friends, a very wealthy couple living in one of the finer golf communities of Larnee. Their grand house sits on top of a hill overlooking several acres of rolling lawn, laid out like plush carpet.

The Lotfields, especially Claire Lotfield, adore Melena. She always longed for a friend with such excellent taste and sophistication and took to Melena quickly at their first meeting.

Since then, the Lotfields have invited Melena to several outings with them. On several occasions, they've flown Melena on their private jet to their other home in Albuquerque.

Seated in Claire's parlor, Melena sips an iced sweet tea and discusses some new changes they'll be making together throughout the house.

"Claire," Melena says setting her drink down carefully on a linen coaster. "You really should think about getting rid of those beach paintings in the sunroom. They just don't capture the look you've been going for in the rest of the house."

"You don't have to tell me twice." Claire brushes her platinum-blond hair away from her late forty-something face. "Monty brought those back from the coast and absolutely insisted on hanging them somewhere in this house. I tried to tuck them away in the best possible place, but what do you do with sailboats? I said to him, 'Darling, we live on a golf course, not the coast.' I mean really, inland homes shouldn't have aquatic pieces. Right?"

Melena thinks of the condo Ernest had used when he was building a seaside property. The kids were so young.

"You're right about that," she says. "Most oceanic pieces should be limited to coastal homes only. But I was thinking you should change the entire color scheme of the room."

Claire nods and Melena continues. "The way it is now, it feels washed out and blank. I think you need much richer colors to give the room some life, maybe some deep burgundies and a hunter green. Monty said you all were going to paint and replace the couch in there, right?"

"Oh, yes," Claire says, "and you must help me decide which couch to go with. I'm at a loss without your influence, and you know Monty thinks everything you do is wonderful. He told me just this morning, 'You tell Melena I said do whatever she wants.'"

Melena smiles, "Your Monty is a good man, Claire."

"Melena," Claire says haltingly placing her hand on Melena's shoulder, "how are things going with the divorce?"

Melena's face flushes and her positive thoughts disappear.

"That man is pure evil," she says. "I believe he'll do everything in his power to get out of dealing with me fairly. He wants to run me into the ground forever."

"*Mm, mm, mm,*" Claire utters and shakes her head, "I just wish it were over so you could go on with your life. You are a beautiful woman. There are so many good men out there who are just dying to meet you."

"No, no," Melena says, "that's the last thing, another man. I would never do anything until the divorce is completely over. Besides, what do I want with another man? They're all full of lies."

"I have two beautiful grandbabies," she says, "who love their Nanna. They are all I could want in the world right now."

"Has *he* seen them?" Claire asks.

"Thank heavens, no, and no, again. I hope he never sees either of them."

"Good," Claire says, "he doesn't deserve to."

"What do you say we talk about better things?" Melena suggests.

"I most certainly agree," Claire stands up. "Why don't we move into the sunroom and come up with a plan to rid this house of that dreary eyesore of a room."

"Wonderful," Melena says.

The ladies pick up their glasses and walk gracefully through the first floor of the house toward the sunroom.

Melena steps into the sunlit room, and Claire spreads her arms out to encompass the space they will change together.

"What to do?" she asks Melena.

"Oh, don't you worry," Melena says. "When you and I are finished, it'll be lovely."

❦

The first week of June, Elizabeth leaves her Dutch boyfriend's small second floor apartment, which sits over a flower shop adjacent to the main bike path leading to town.

In the side streets of this agrarian lake village, Elizabeth hides from the world an hour and a half train ride southeast of Amsterdam. With a list of errands in her pocket, she pulls her bike out of the downstairs hall onto the cobblestone path outside and rides into town.

Above her, the sun shines on a bright, expansive afternoon sky. In the Netherlands, the skies aren't often so sunny. Elizabeth thinks it unfair they should have such beautiful weather just before she leaves.

The wheels on her Mary Poppins-style bike squeak alternately as she rides across the narrow stone path that leads to the main thoroughfare. Having shaved off her Mohawk some months ago, Elizabeth's hair now lies flat, short on her head and dyed black.

The breeze tousles it as she moves toward the train station. Pulling up to the newly constructed glass and metallic building, she hops off her bike and drags it along with her to a line of blue phone booths. Leaning the bike against the booth, she opens one of the glass doors and steps inside.

A yellow and orange plastic card flashes in her hand. Elizabeth picks up the receiver and slides the card into a horizontal slot at the bottom of the telephone.

The face of the phone is lettered in the same bright blue as the metal of the booth. Dutch words appear in yellow against the background.

A dial tone, unlike the pitch from the one at home, sounds like a droning computer tone as Elizabeth punches in a series of numbers that connect her to the United States. The familiar hum of her own long distance carrier sounds and she enters her telephone card number.

A few seconds later, a phone in Larnee begins to ring.

"Hello," Ernest says as he picks up on the other line.

"Hey, Dad," Elizabeth says. She still feels confused about talking to him, and she still hasn't told Melena.

"Penelope Pit Stop. How are you today?"

"I'm fine, Dad. How are you?"

"Oh, I'm making it," Ernest says with a big sigh. "One day at a time. I've been having some trouble with my back, but you don't want to hear about that. Aren't you coming home soon?"

"Yes, I am," she says. "I leave the day after tomorrow."

"Well, how about that?" Ernest says and tilts back in his chair. "It seems like you've been gone forever. I sure will be glad when you're safe and sound back on our side of the ocean."

He says, "You know, I didn't think that you would do very well over there at all, but you proved me wrong. I never would have been able to stay away from home that long. Everybody speaking different languages, I'd have gotten fed up and come home."

"No, you wouldn't, Dad."

Elizabeth looks at a bus pulling into the station and watches the people as they get off to rush away in different directions. Some of the passengers go to bikes that are chained on various stretches of the ongoing rows that hold thousands of other bikes waiting for their commuting owners to claim them. Some walk away down the street, some go to the trains and some stop in the station for a coffee or pizza.

*I'll never see this at home*, Elizabeth thinks, *and this is the last time I'll see it for a while.*

She says, "You'd do well in The Netherlands, Dad. The people are really nice here and the public transportation is wonderful."

"Where have you been staying lately?" he asks. "I tried to call your old number, but couldn't get an answer there."

"Well, I've been staying with a friend of mine who lives in Enschede. I had to come here when they rented my room to someone else. I've been here on and off for the last month or so."

Elizabeth feels so different away from home. She remembers Berlin and Marburg. Thrilled by her travels, Elizabeth is fine with them coming to a quiet end here, especially after spending this last weekend in Bruge.

"I didn't really have anywhere else to go," she says. "I wasn't ready to come home, so I've been here finishing up a last bit of traveling around The Netherlands and Belgium."

"I hope you've been safe," Ernest says imagining the worst.

"I have, Dad, don't worry. I have plenty of friends who look after me over here." Elizabeth thinks of her crew in Tilburg.

"We just went to a three-day metal festival on the airport grounds," she says, "and camped the whole time in tents. Everything was really dirty and we were pretty covered with mud from the rain."

"My goodness," Ernest shakes his head. "Metal!" he says.

"Now, Elizabeth," he says, "I'd love to be at the airport when you arrive, but I'm sure your mother will want to be there and it wouldn't be appropriate for me to come."

He pictures who else will be there, the grandchildren he's never seen.

"I would like it," Ernest says, "if you'd call me when you get in so I know you made it. Then maybe when you have some time, you can get away and come see me and your brother."

Elizabeth twists the phone cord in her hand. She knows she's going to see Luke at the airport.

Two high school boys come by in large puffy jackets. Their heads are shaved because they're Gabbers, subculture youth who listen to heart-pounding techno.

"You're probably right about the airport," she says, "but I still wish you could be there. I arrive pretty early in the morning so I'll give you a call sometime that afternoon. I have some presents for you."

"Elizabeth," Ernest says, "don't you spend your money on me. Do you have enough to get home?"

"I do," she says. "Thanks for helping me out with this last month. It was getting a little tough with the trains."

The clock outside the station tells her she must be getting along. She doesn't have very much time left, and there is a pair of boots she must have.

"Well, look, Dad, this phone card is going to shut me off in a minute. I just wanted to call and say hello, and let you know what time I'd be getting back."

"Okay," he says, "I do appreciate your calling and I am looking forward to your coming home." Ernest looks down at his feet, quiet for a moment.

"Oh, Elizabeth?"

"Yeah, Dad?"

"Did you know that your brother had a baby boy?"

Her face grows more serious and she makes a fist out of her hand.

"*Uh*, yeah, they sent me a picture of him."

"Good," Ernest says choking back the tears. "I haven't spoken to your brother in a long time, but we won't talk about that either. You just get home safely. You hear me?"

Luke and Blackwell aren't getting along since the birth of Blackwell's new baby, and nothing seems like it will ever be right again, if it ever was. Elizabeth uncurls her hand.

"Yeah," she says, "I hear you. I love you, Dad."

"Well, Elizabeth," Ernest says, "I love you, too."

"See you soon."

"Okay, bye-bye," he says and hangs up the phone.

Elizabeth hangs up her phone and the card spits back out accompanied by a harsh beeping noise. She takes it and opens the door to the phone booth staring at her surroundings as she steps outside. It's an unbelievably nice day. Elizabeth's thoughts take her back to Larnee and the mess she will be confronted with when she gets home.

Taking her bike by the handlebars, Elizabeth breathes deeply and throws her leg over the seat. Her headphones will keep her company as she rides to the lake to watch the country people and enjoy the sun.

Busy people move about around her, mothers carrying children and their groceries on their bikes while day-trippers go from bus to train to bike all over town.

Their lives seem so much simpler and better than what she has known, though she knows they probably aren't. Flexing her hands on the grip, Elizabeth taps into the well of resolve that she has recently discovered inside herself.

She pedals onto the bike path, enters traffic and decides to banish all thoughts of home.

⤙━◉◉━⤚

Oh, the summertime in Larnee, the sky looks clear and the wind blows a bit cooler against the heat than it does in Holiday. Holiday's summer-long spell of suffocating humidity stifles the population every year.

In Larnee, the mountains are a few hours away. Mountains filled with woods, the same kind as around Larnee, and all the trees have secrets.

With four futures to look after, Blackwell and Katherine continue to build their wealth. After implanting himself in a profitable healthcare marketing company, Blackwell's masterful performances afford him the opportunity to build a new house in Hollow Town.

Live Well's leaders bestow award after award on Blackwell and ask him to fly all over the country to speak at their biggest conferences. The multi-level company's credo states, "Preventive supplements for the healthy family."

Katherine stays home managing the house, the finances and the kids. She recycles and avidly reads style magazines and books while Blackwell pours his energy into his business.

Blackwell and Luke live three blocks from one another yet seldom talk. They seriously disagree with each other's choices.

One afternoon, just after lunch, Blackwell phones Luke at Mancon. Blackwell asks Luke to meet him at the tavern between their homes for a beer after dinner that night. It's been over three months since they've spoken, and even then, it was only a brief hello.

Around seven o'clock, Luke walks in and joins his estranged brother at the bar. He sits down with a sigh.

Deep down neither of them would really want to have a shouting match in public. The Spring Street bartender smiles at Luke whose familiar face is well known in this trendy Larnee neighborhood.

"Hey, Luke," Blackwell says slapping him on the back. "You look tired. What've they got you up to at your house these days?"

Luke bought a house, and now he's anchored in Larnee working at Mancon. He fills in with the family business and operates in the lower ranks. Finding his way into cars and races, a new team sent him to test at a school in California. Luke thinks of nothing but racing all day long. To think of other things would disturb him too much.

Luke dates lots of girls, all attracted by the magnetism that hides his inner world. He rents out the other rooms in his house to a couple of guys he knew in college.

"Been working all day," Luke says. "I'm trying to put a deal together for a team."

The bartender nods and asks, "Luke, draft?"

"Yeah, Mike. Thanks."

Blackwell sips his own beer and looks for a doorway in to their conversation. He sticks to what they both know, but it's painfully obvious how unfamiliar they are with one another now.

"So, are you going for the point challenge this year?"

"No," Luke sits back, "this deal is for a stock car. I'm trying to get a ride."

"Well, good for you," Blackwell says and imagines speeding down a track.

"That ought to be a lot of fun."

Ever since he had the kids, Blackwell knew racing was a part of his life that was over for good.

"Yeah." Luke takes a sip of beer and sets it down.

"How are your kids?" he asks.

"They're doing fine," Blackwell says checking himself. "Isabelle is talking up a storm and Joshua is growing every day. I tell you, having children really changes your life. It puts so many things in perspective."

The natural verbal rhythm that comes from Blackwell when he's conducting business now flows in every facet of his life.

"I bet it does." Luke looks into his beer thinking that his father still hasn't seen his only grandson.

"So, Elizabeth's back."

"Yeah," Blackwell says, "we had her and Mom over for dinner a few nights ago. I think I prefer her without the Mohawk. I must say I was surprised to see her with hair, and a normal color at that."

"Yeah, well, when I saw her in Europe," Luke says, "she met me at the train station with a hat on. She pulled it off and there was green hair all dreaded in knots." He shakes his head. "She's braver than I am."

"Yeah, me, too," Blackwell laughs. "I don't think I'd have the guts to go out with green hair, probably wouldn't look that good."

"Right," Luke says and wonders why his brother asked him here.

"Look, Luke," Blackwell says in his business voice, "I know we haven't talked that much lately. You know, the divorce really makes things so much harder. Mom doesn't really know what's going to happen to her life, and everyone seems to be frozen in this hellish limbo because of it. I'm just trying to hold things together as best I can."

Compelled by responsibility, Blackwell protects the mother who seemed to grow up with him. He wants to see to Melena's welfare and help her carry this burden.

"Okay," Luke says waiting and knowing that some plan must be coming.

"I think that you and I need to try to bring Mom and Dad together to settle this stuff with a mediator."

Luke's eyebrow crooks with suspicion and Blackwell lets the idea sink in for a second.

"After all," he finally says, "you and I are their sons. If I'm able to bring Mom to the table, and you're able to bring Dad, then maybe we can help them divide everything and it'll all be over with."

Luke's face is expressionless. "That's a nice thought, isn't it," he says.

Blackwell shrugs his shoulders. "I don't think it's impossible, but I don't think it would be the easiest thing either."

"You know," Luke says calmly, "Mom already has it in for me because I haven't chosen a side like you have."

"She seems to think that because I haven't chosen her side that I have chosen Dad's. I am neutral," Luke states for what feels like the hundredth attempt.

"I am not going to choose a side. If I show up in a lawyer's office with Dad, don't you think that will convince her that I've chosen to support Dad?"

"I guess you've got a point there," Blackwell says, "but I still think that it's our job to do everything we can to put an end to this."

"Our *job*?" Luke asks. "Blackwell, this isn't my divorce. My mother won't even talk to me because I work for my father. She can't even sit through an entire lunch with me, and I'm her son. How do you think that makes me feel?"

Blackwell sighs and sips his beer. "Fair enough," he says, "fair enough. You don't have to come then, but maybe you could talk to Dad and get him to come?"

"I'll mention it," Luke says, "but who's going to mediate it?"

"Well, I'll be there," Blackwell says, "and together we can all choose a fair, qualified mediator."

"Yeah," Luke says and looks at him, "don't you think it will seem a little stacked in Mom's favor with you there?"

"I'm all she has, Luke. She can't afford a team of lawyers like Dad can. If I don't help her, no one will. Katherine and the kids

279

and I are her entire life now. It's like we keep her going, give her something to live for. You know her health isn't good."

"Well," Luke says wanting to leave, "you keep doing whatever you have to do then, and I'll try to talk to Dad."

He takes a last swig of his beer. Amidst his inner confusion, he's glad that his mom has help.

"I'll give you a call tomorrow afternoon and let you know how it goes."

Blackwell nods. "Okay, I'm working out of the house right now, so you can reach me there."

"I will," Luke stands. "I have to go now." He doesn't like getting this close to all the details.

"Yeah, me, too."

They both throw money on the counter. "It was good to see you," Blackwell says.

"Yeah," Luke nods, "good to see you, too."

He walks out of the bar while Blackwell goes back to the bathroom so that they both don't have to go to the parking lot at the same time.

--⊷⊚═⊷--

Inside a conference room with slate walls, Melena sits on one side of a long mahogany table and Blackwell sits beside her.

She stares, hatred pouring out of her eyes, at Ernest who sits across from her, poised in thought. Everyone in the room is waiting for an answer from him.

Ernest looks at the man sitting to his left, then glances at the financial reports and other documents scattered across the table and lifts his glasses off his nose. He rubs the indentions left by the glasses.

His chest heaves once as he begins to speak.

"I respect your attempt to fairly distribute our assets, Mark," Ernest says, "but you do not seem to understand that I do not own these two properties that you have marked here for sale."

Across the table, Melena rolls her eyes.

"Both communities," he says, "were funded by partnerships that involve tax credits sold to other entities. I'm in no position to sell them, even if I wanted to."

Melena slaps her hand down on the table.

"You could sell those properties," she shoots back. "You created the agreements that built them and you can take them apart as well."

"Blackwell," Ernest says still unnerved by his son's presence, "would you please explain to your mother that I cannot make this sale. They do not belong to me."

It is the first time Ernest has seen him since the divorce began. Ernest wonders if Blackwell has any remorse for not letting him see his grandson.

Silent and refusing to comment, Blackwell looks to Mark, the mediator. Mark looks at Ernest and lays his hands on the documents in front of him. He's gone over the Starlings' information three times.

It would be difficult, and probably would destroy numerous financial relationships, but in Mark's opinion, he doesn't really know if it can be done. He can't think of any other feasible arrangement.

"All right then Ernest," Mark says, struggling with the obvious, "what you're saying to us is that this agreement doesn't work for you. Is that correct?"

"The agreement does not work for me," Ernest says, "because it is impossible. How do you expect me to take the capital for something I don't own?"

"I'm sick of this," Melena shouts turning to Blackwell. "He's never going to answer anything honestly or give me what I deserve."

Melena eyes Ernest like she could cut him in two. "Half, Ernest," she says.

The words hang in the air.

"Half," she repeats. "I raised your children and took care of your home so you could work and not worry about those things. This money belongs to me as much as it belongs to you."

"I understand that, Melena," Ernest says calmly.

Everyone's money must come from him.

"I am willing to give you half of our assets at the time of our divorce. That however, isn't enough for you. You want more."

It's true that when Ernest left that day and took his walk down the stairs, their combined worth was dismal compared to his future possibilities. On paper, and in reality, the Starlings' finances endured the financial poundings of three attempts at divorce prior to this one.

"Don't give me your sorry-ass excuses." Melena grips the table. "I'm not married to you anymore and I don't have to listen to them."

"Mark," she says, "this meeting is over. We've been sitting here for three hours and this greedy, pathetic excuse for a human being is going to keep lying for the rest of his life."

Ernest shakes his head and looks at Blackwell as he stands to accompany his mother out the door. Blackwell refuses to look up at him.

"I'll see you in court," Melena says uttering the words like a curse. "Then we'll see what the judge has to say."

She takes hold of the door and slowly pulls it open, then turns back to face Ernest again.

"I hope you rot in hell," she sneers and walks out the door with her son following behind.

Ernest looks at Mark and sighs. Leaning back in his chair, Ernest appears much older than when he walked in this morning. The mediator starts to gather his things arranging them inside his briefcase.

"Mr. Starling," he says, "I really am sorry that today didn't work for you and Mrs. Starling. Both of you seem to have certain, fixed ideas about things."

Ernest leans forward resting his elbows on the table.

"I just don't have the money that she thinks I have," he says.

"Even if we liquidated everything, I still wouldn't have that much money. Those values she contrived are tied up and do not even belong to me."

"Well," Mark says hating it when he cannot make people come to an agreement. "I wish you the best of luck, sir, and please, feel free to call me if you ever need my services again."

"Yes," Ernest says troubled, "thank you."

Mark picks up his briefcase and departs, while Ernest sits at the table staring at the wall in front of him. The sounds of children's laughter echo in his ears as he remembers the first time he and Blackwell raced Hot Wheel toy cars all those years ago.

⤗▬◉◖▬⤙

Outside Melena's bedroom door, a tiny knock sounds. It travels through the room to her ear to wake her out of a dream. She hasn't been feeling well lately, and this dream is thick and full of shadows. Her eyes flutter open.

"Come in," she says and wipes the sleep away from her eyes. It's around five thirty in the afternoon and Melena has been asleep for at least three hours.

Drawn out soft and sweet, Elizabeth says, "Hey."

Back from the Netherlands, Elizabeth stays with Melena in their family home. The family home minus half the family. She loves her mother and she wants her to feel good. Even when she was a kid she wanted Melena to be happy.

But she's a hypocrite though, too, still hiding secrets. How long can this reprieve of hers really last?

Moving to the windows, Elizabeth pulls the long, white curtains back allowing some light into the darkened room. She turns around smiling, full of an energy Melena doesn't remember seeing in a long time.

"Are you feeling better now?" she asks as she sits down, "or is the pain still really bad?"

Melena looks around her across the white quilted comforter pulled up under her chin. The sleeping pills make her feel drugged, but everything in the room stayed just where she left it when she fell asleep. "I'm feeling somewhat better," she says and sits up slowly. "Thank God that pill finally kicked in, now the pain isn't so bad."

*The pain,* Elizabeth thinks. *I've found my path to salvation; maybe you'll find yours.*

Life-long repression has a negative effect on the body and Elizabeth won't be sick because of her formerly hidden memory again. The Shades will keep him away.

Elizabeth's own life will envelop her, but she fears for her family. Will they let go?

"That's good, Mom," Elizabeth says. She comes around the bed to prop a pillow up behind her. "Do you want some water or anything?"

"No." Melena shakes her head. She looks at the glass on the table beside her.

"I'll be fine, honey." She takes a sip of the water. "I just need to rest and get my strength back up. That's all."

Elizabeth steps around the other side of the king size bed and turns on the lamp. All day long in the kitchen she's been sitting in her old spot before the TV.

"You need some more light in here, Mom," she says. "How about we watch a little TV?"

"Sure, that'll be fine."

Elizabeth sits on the bed beside Melena and turns on the television. She takes her shoes off and swings her feet around to lounge beside her mother and keep her company.

Elizabeth flips through dozens of cable channels looking for a movie. Every film running looks tired and old.

"There's never anything good on in the afternoon," she says and continues to flip stations while she ponders her problem.

Elizabeth still has her secret. She would cringe and die if Melena found out she had visited Ernest. Nonetheless, her nervous energy and her wish to bring Melena back to some better life cause her to chatter.

"You know, Mom," she says, "I get to register for classes as soon as the new catalogue comes in from school. I think I'm going to go ahead and get my Biology requirement out of the way."

"You have to have that no matter what you're studying there. And, I heard about this Fantasy Fiction class that I just have to take."

Elizabeth finally wants to learn. While in the Netherlands, Elizabeth applied to the Academy of Design for her next semester at State.

"Elizabeth," Melena says straightening herself up a bit, "we have to talk about school."

Melena's been holding off saying this, trying to go to court and find another way, but Ernest makes it impossible for her. Besides, she could use the help and the company.

"All right," Elizabeth says, "what do you want to know, my grandiose plan for taking over the world?"

"No, it's not that." She turns toward her. "This is more serious, Elizabeth. You know, you've had quite a year, young lady. I've spent money on sending you to Europe, my medical bills and lawyer's fees. Well, there's nothing left. Even the money from Momma's house is gone. I just don't have any more to send you back to State," she says. "You can't go back to school."

"What?" Elizabeth drops the remote.

The credit card accounts Melena opened have been charged to their limits. She figured some money would have come through from the divorce before now, but it hasn't. All her extra money from The Green Gallery goes toward her very critical pursuits, life and justice, or revenge, depending on how one sees it.

Elizabeth's new plan for the future, to take over the world with large sculptures made out of metal and mechanized parts, deteriorates like torn up pieces of paper falling into the wind, scattering.

"You're going to have to stay here in Larnee with me," Melena says decidedly.

The fact that she can't get away from the home that housed her old life disturbs her. She knows Ernest uses it as a tool against her, their home, his home, a structure built for their long lost dream.

Sometimes being in the house becomes so unbearable for Melena that she screams all alone so no one can hear her. She wants her daughter to help her somehow.

"Maybe you can go to the community college or something," Melena says. "Your father hasn't settled with me yet, and since I don't have the money, that leaves nothing for school. I'm sorry, Elizabeth, but it's just not possible."

*Stay here,* Elizabeth screams in her mind. *Stay here, fade into nothing and rot because I'm trapped.*

"Well." Elizabeth says quietly. The room feels as if it is spinning.

She ignores Melena's presence, nor does she hear the television mounted high on the wall in the corner. Something starts to surface in her mind, fighting off a wave of panic. As the idea comes to her, she says the words slowly.

"I'll find a way."

"Elizabeth, you ..."

Elizabeth shakes her head throwing off any notion the idea might not be true.

"I have to finish college," she says, interrupting her. "I have a life there. Cooper has a room waiting for me and everything."

"I can't help you, Elizabeth," Melena says. "I'm in debt already. I'm really sorry, honey, but I just don't think it's going to work out."

"Oh?" Elizabeth snarls defiantly. Her brain runs on high speed as she ignores her mother.

"It'll work out," she says. "I'll make it work out. I can't stay here. I won't."

"What are you going to do, Elizabeth?" Melena asks angrily. She's offended by this strong opposition.

"Where are you going to come up with that kind of money? Your father certainly isn't going to pay for your education. He doesn't have to now that you're over eighteen. I already tried that in court."

"I know there's a way," Elizabeth says. "There's a financial aid program at school. Lots of people do it. They get loans and then they pay them back when they graduate. I can do that. It's easy."

She's never looked into this kind of thing before. All the financial statements have always gone to someone else as if she were too young to see them or maybe just too ignorant to find them on her own.

"I just don't know if there's enough time," Elizabeth says. "Oh, my God. I have to get back to school."

"Why would it be so bad if you stayed here with me?" Melena asks. This last year was so lonely and hard on her.

"I just can't, Mom," Elizabeth frowns. She becomes visibly angry and tries not to direct her anger toward her mother.

"If I stay in this house, I will lose my mind. You shouldn't be here either. It makes me crazy, and how long have I been home? I have a life at school and I'm smart. I need to be there."

Elizabeth hops off the bed.

"Where are you going?" Melena asks.

"I'll be right back," Elizabeth says. She sounds positive though slightly afraid.

"I'll get the phone book. I've got to call and find out how to do this."

--→--●--◯--●--←--

At her desk in the law offices of McNair and Riley, Sandra McNair examines a billing file filled with copies of the documents Melena has paid her to draft over the last year. Their court and consulting time is listed in the file, too.

Her short, clipped fingernail taps the side of the manila folder, and a smug smile crosses her face.

"Forty-eight thousand."

287

---◆◇◆---

After three hurried weeks of tedious paperwork, filling out applications and forwarding documents to financial aid institutions, Elizabeth accomplished the task that Melena and others thought she could not.

One week before the start of the fall semester, she obtained a school loan, and with it, three part-time jobs to help pay her way. She refused to ask anyone for help.

After securing her immediate future, Elizabeth moved into a large, run down house directly across from campus on Unicorn Lane. The street has a notorious reputation for school block parties, random violence and the crowd that loiters at the blood bank on the corner.

The Starling brothers have not spoken since the failed meditation of their parent's divorce and Blackwell's plans to move from Larnee have solidified. In Hollow Town, the house being built for his family will take some time, so they're vacating and moving to a rental home.

On the weekends, Luke races cars, karts and modifieds, while Blackwell builds his business speaking to thousands and mesmerizing them like a guru. Good looks help both get by as they press forward, growing further and further apart everyday.

Katherine packs their household and Blackwell prepares the transfer from his office in Larnee. Her parents are thrilled to have them moving so near to their own home in the suburbs of Hollow Town.

Melena has taken charge of her newly created roles in life, grandmother and accomplished pursuer of a satisfactory divorce. She has a band of earthly angels who support her, friends and acquaintances familiar with Larnee gossip, always ready to lend a hand.

They all adore her. Many of the well-to-do wish to set her up on dates with debonair, well-mannered and wealthy men, but she refuses. She fears it could hurt her case, and her mistrust of the opposite sex will not diminish.

Yet, Ernest dates freely whomever he wants to and whenever he wants to. But, between the divorce and work, he hardly has the time. Younger women, and women his age, gravitate toward him, but he's not committing.

For more than a year, the entire family has waited in vain for the final divorce hearing, and they're destined to do so for many years.

Neither Melena nor Ernest can get an answer from those who control their lives. Their divorce sits in the hands of their lawyers, pending for how long no one knows.

Following Melena's lead, Elizabeth has joined her, Blackwell, Katherine, Isabelle and Joshua at Katherine's parent's house for Thanksgiving.

The full house contains Katherine's extended family, plenty of food and quaint holiday cheer, but Luke Starling is not there. Outside, the sun shines and it hardly seems like fall.

If they were in Larnee, the weather would be much cooler by now.

"Honey," white-haired Timothy Blake says to his wife of many years, "will you please go sit down for a second with Aunt Betty. She's a little confused about why she's here and I thought an explanation would be best coming from you."

Timothy's red sweater covers his slightly protruding stomach. His face looks jolly, and it's obvious he's had a life of eating well.

Holding a large wooden spoon in one hand, Susan Blake looks at her daughter Katherine and then back at Timothy. Timothy's going with Susan to Africa in six months. Susan is a sturdy, adventurous woman and they've been planning the trip for years.

"Well, Katherine," she says, "keep stirring. I'll be back in just a few minutes."

"Can I do anything for you, Suz?" Timothy asks patting her on the back.

"Yes," Susan says pointing as she talks, "you can walk around the house and make sure everybody's got something to drink and that all the grandchildren are safe and accounted for."

"All right then," Timothy says and sets out into the foyer.

Katherine continues to stir the chunky, yellow conglomeration her mother charged her with and Isabelle runs in from the den banging an empty sipping cup against anything that will reverberate with noise. Melena follows her apprehensively with Joshua in her arms.

"Isabelle," Melena calls after her, "oh, Isabelle." Melena makes a slight lunge for her and misses.

"Angel," she says as Isabelle laughs, "we don't bang things in Grandmommy's kitchen."

Mrs. Blake is Grandmommy and Mrs. Starling is Nanna.

"Elizabeth," Melena calls as the toddler dashes to the right.

"Yes," Elizabeth answers from inside the foyer. She's been trying to get some time alone.

"Come here, please. Isabelle and I need you."

Elizabeth sighs and looks down at her cell phone and the number on the screen. Her thumb rests on the dial button, but she slides it away and erases the display on the LCD. She puts the phone in her purse just in time to catch Isabelle as she runs in from the kitchen.

"I got you," Elizabeth says. She picks her up and swings her upside down in the air.

Melena comes in from the hallway. "Oh, Elizabeth, she just had a snack. Put her upright before she gets sick."

"Again," Isabelle says, "do it again."

"See, Mom," Elizabeth smiles, "she likes it."

"Would you please just stop," Melena says rocking Joshua in her arms. She's still angry that Elizabeth left her though she won't admit it, and she's grown suspicious of her daughter's allegiance.

"I've got an idea," Elizabeth tosses Isabelle up in the air again. "How about I put Joshua in one arm and Isabelle in the other, then sling them around the room to see if they can hold on?"

"Elizabeth," Melena scowls losing her patience.

"They're Starlings," Elizabeth says. "They're going to like things like that."

Melena dares her with her tone. "No, they won't." She knows exactly what Elizabeth means and refuses to acknowledge it.

"Now, you bring her in the kitchen with me right this minute," Melena says, "and let's see how helpful we can be."

They fought this summer at The Green Gallery one day after the store closed. Melena had enough of everyone pushing her. Elizabeth said things that made her so mad sometimes she wanted to react and release her feelings. Melena took hold of a picture she was putting on the floor and smashed it on the ground. Elizabeth asked her if it made her feel better.

"All right," Elizabeth says. "Sorry, Isabelle, but your granny here doesn't want me to swing you anymore."

"Nanna," Melena says over her shoulder.

Elizabeth rolls her eyes. "Whatever."

"Swing me," Isabelle shouts, "swing me."

Quickly, Elizabeth scoops her up and swirls her in the air before taking her into the kitchen. The air is redolent with the aromas of turkey, collard greens and pumpkin pie.

Elizabeth sits down at the table beside Melena and places Isabelle in her lap. Isabelle reaches for a pile of blank paper and Elizabeth slides it to her along with her crayons.

"That's right, Isabelle." Elizabeth pats her on the head and says, "Draw me a picture of a house."

Susan comes in from the living room shaking her head.

"Poor thing," she says to Katherine and Melena. "She didn't remember why we were all here, but I think I got it in her head now. Let's just hope she doesn't go outside again."

"I caught her down here at eleven thirty last night washing dishes," Katherine says. "I hope I'm that helpful at her age."

Elizabeth thinks that she herself usually isn't much help at all and Melena laughs out loud.

"Sometimes I think I don't know where I am," Melena says.

"What's that, Mom?" Blackwell asks coming in from the living room.

"Oh, nothing," Melena says. "I'm just talking about this good boy right here in my arms. Yes, I am."

"Right," Blackwell says and walks over to the counter where he sneaks a bit of pie off the cooling wrack.

Susan smacks his hand.

"You stop that, mister. Here," she says, "I'll put you to work. Katherine, you give me that bowl and, Blackwell, you hold the pan while I pour the cornbread in it."

Katherine lets go of the pan and walks over to Melena.

"I'll take Joshua for a few minutes," she says. "He needs to spend some quality time with his cousins."

Melena smiles as she passes the baby to her daughter-in-law.

"Janee's kids are so well behaved," she says about Katherine's brother's wife. "I saw the girls playing with Joshua and they were just so sweet and gentle."

"Hey, Mom," Elizabeth says, "why don't you color with Isabelle for a minute, and I'll be right back?"

Elizabeth wants to finish doing what she tried to do earlier. On holidays, phone calls to exiled family members are one of the more difficult things to accomplish in a divorced family.

"Where are you going?" Melena asks.

"Just out to the car for a minute." Elizabeth stands. "I'll be right back."

Melena glares at her suspiciously. "Why do you need to go to your car?" she asks. She thinks Elizabeth could be going to do one of two things, smoke cigarettes or call Luke.

"Because I have to get something," Elizabeth says. She turns away from her and walks back through the foyer. As she walks through the hall, Elizabeth picks up her purse, but she waits till she is on the street to pull out her cell phone.

Her foot taps on the pavement as it rings.

"Luke," she says, "Happy Thanksgiving!"

"Elizabeth! Happy Thanksgiving to you, too."

It tears her up that they're apart. She's angry that they were separated so much as children.

"What are you doing?" she asks him.

"Oh, just finished watching a bit of the parade."

"Wish you were here," Elizabeth says. "I feel so out of place."

"You're going to be all right, kid. Don't worry."

"Yeah," she sighs, "but it's Thanksgiving and where the hell are we?"

"Well," he props one foot on the end table, "I'll see you in a little while. You're not going to be there all day."

"No," Elizabeth says, "you're right. I'm not. I just wish things could be easier."

"You know that can't happen right now."

"It'll never happen, ever," she mumbles, starting to sniffle. She's tired of being told that things just are the way they are.

Luke Bartleby thinks about these things, too, but he pretends not to and doesn't tell anyone how he feels. It's his way.

"Elizabeth," Luke says, "you've got to calm down, and don't cry. You're just upset. This is your first holiday being in the middle of this crap. I had it last year, but we'll see each other tonight when we see Dad."

"I just hate it," Elizabeth cries out. "Everything in there seems so damn perfect, and everything is not perfect, not anywhere. Everything is screwed up. I can't stand it."

"Well, I don't like it either, honey, but you know we have to deal with it. Now, I want you to take a few deep breaths and try to relax."

Elizabeth huffs a single breath out.

"Mom snapped at me just because I came outside. She suspects me of everything."

"She's just going through a tough time right now, kid. You have to let her be. I want you to walk around a little bit. You've got to calm down before you go back in there and you can't stay outside too long."

This family game of keeping secrets is something they both know well. Elizabeth walks back and forth beside the long row of cars parked in front of the Blakes'.

"I'm calm," she says after awhile.

"All right," Luke says, "what time are you leaving there?"

"Right after we have lunch," Elizabeth says staring at the Blake's home perched on top of the hill at the top of the drive. "I have my car packed already and everything."

"Look, take your time after lunch and visit with everyone before you leave," he says. "You don't want them to think that you didn't have a good time."

"I'm not having a bad time," she replies. "Everything just sucks, that's all."

"I know." Luke reaches for his coffee. "You go on now and call me if you need me. Let me know when you leave there so that I'll be sure not to be home when you get here."

"*Ugh*," Elizabeth says, "you're so funny."

"Okay," he says, "hug yourself."

"You hug yourself."

"Talk to you later," he says.

"Okay, bye."

Elizabeth glances again at the Blakes' house to make sure no one watches her from the windows, which appear to be free of prying eyes. She opens her phone again, but this time, she dials a different number.

"Hey, Dad," Elizabeth turns away from the house.

"Penelope Pit Stop," Ernest says.

"Happy Thanksgiving."

294

"Well, Happy Thanksgiving to you, too."

"I just wanted to call and say hi," she says. "Luke and I are still coming over later to eat."

"Sounds good," Ernest says. "I didn't cook any of the food, but I ordered us a really good meal. I'm telling you I got it all, corn bread, mashed potatoes, pecan pie, apple pie ...."

He's trying to be so positive when all he can think about is those grandchildren and how she must be wherever they are.

"That's perfect dad," Elizabeth taps her foot against the ground. "Who needs to cook anyway? Listen, I have to go now, but *gobble*, *gobble, gobble.* Have a Happy Turkey Day. Luke and I'll see you soon."

"All right then," he says. "You drive safe. Don't speed with the holiday traffic."

"Hey, Dad," Elizabeth says, "maybe you, Luke and I can go see a movie or something after we eat."

"That'll be fine."

"Okay, Dad, 'bye."

They both hang up and Elizabeth turns back to the house. She turns off her phone and tosses it in her purse as she marches back up the drive.

⊶—◆—⊷

Her children's separation drives pangs down into Melena's heart.

Will Elizabeth go off wild forsaking the power of her sculptures?

Will Blackwell snap from the corporate pressures around him and turn into his father?

Will Luke Bartleby be lost to the void, somehow, somewhere, where he cannot be retrieved again?

Will Ernest run himself into the ground with work, women and sorrow?

Will Melena run over Ernest in the white store van or let her body eat itself up in sickness?

Joined in their efforts, Elizabeth and Melena seek a peace between the two brothers.

Luke and Blackwell speak briefly just before the Christmas holidays, and Elizabeth, previously penciled in for Christmas at Blackwell's, contrives a way to get Luke there on Christmas Eve.

The entire family shows genuine joy to see him, and everyone buries their complicated feelings for another time. Melena, though, has to try harder.

"Uncle Luke!" Isabelle, lithe like a fairy, runs into the kitchen of her temporary home in Hollow Town.

Luke bends down to pick Isabelle up and tosses her high in the air. Isabelle laughs and Melena, cutting potatoes into cubes, looks up from the sink and cries.

"Oh, Luke," she says, "you'll drop her. Put that child down."

Smiling at Isabelle, Luke stands her on the ground and sits down at the table beside Elizabeth. The table's white painted top is set for a meal. Luke takes a handful of carrots.

Blackwell looks at his brother proudly wishing he could pull him away from the dark side.

"Can I get you a beer?" he asks. "How about a glass of wine?"

"Beer will be fine."

Katherine smiles. "How have you been, Luke?"

"Not too bad, just staying around home working on my house."

"Houses," Blackwell says shrugging his shoulders at the one surrounding him. "I know I've been on the phone with the contractor for our new house at least eight times this week."

"Luke," Melena says, "have you decided what you're going to do about a bed for your new house?"

Melena wonders where the down payment for Luke's house came from, but tries to bury that thought and help him with his house the way she helps Blackwell and Katherine.

"No," he says, "I don't know what I'm going to do about a bed. I guess it looks bad to be my age and not have a headboard."

"I've got a catalogue that might have something just perfect for you." Melena washes her hands. "I could get it at cost."

Luke nods his head. "That sounds good."

"I have homemade eggnog," Blackwell says. "Who wants the first sip?" He paces the kitchen with a pitcher and punchbowl glasses.

"Eggnog?" Melena asks. "Does it have alcohol in it?"

"Oh," he chuckles, "there's just a little bit in there."

"I've never had eggnog before," Elizabeth says. "What's it taste like?"

Blackwell hands her a glass. "Why don't you try it?"

"Okay," she says looking at the dainty glass of liquor and cream. Holding it to her mouth, Elizabeth throws her head back to down it.

"*Ugh*," she breathes.

"Elizabeth," Melena says, "you aren't supposed to drink it all at once."

"How do you know?" Elizabeth asks.

"Because ladies don't do things like that."

"Well, it smelled like a shot to me."

Blackwell laughs. "Did you like it?"

"I don't know," Elizabeth says. "It went down too quick. Give me another."

Blackwell refills her glass and hands it back to her. This time Elizabeth takes a tiny sip extending her pinky out from the cup in a delicate manner to mimic Melena.

"*Blach*," she says and sets the cup down.

Blackwell frowns. "You don't like it."

"I don't know," she says. "I'm not sure."

A series of whimpers comes from the baby monitor on the counter. Katherine spins around from the stove and looks at Isabelle.

"Someone's awake," she says. "Come with Mommy, Isabelle, and we'll go get Joshua."

"Okay, Mommy." Isabelle hops up and claps her hands. She

follows Katherine out of the room.

"Hey," Blackwell says to his siblings, "what say we go up in the attic later and make reindeer noises?"

"Yeah," Elizabeth's eyes get big.

"You would know, wouldn't you?" Luke asks.

"Why?"

"We used to have you in bed by seven-thirty every Christmas Eve. You were convinced Santa wouldn't come if you weren't asleep. One time, you cried because we kept you up 'til eight o'clock. You were so gullible."

Blackwell passes around a tray with sugar cookies shaped like Christmas trees and Santas.

"I got some movies for later," he says.

"I hope they're funny ones." Melena puts the potatoes on the stove. "We all need a good laugh."

The room quiets with her statement, so many things going unsaid, and Katherine walks in holding Joshua in her arms. He's dressed in green and red.

"Look at the elf." Elizabeth points.

"Where is my precious?" Melena claps her hands toward Joshua.

"Luke," Katherine asks, "do you want to hold Joshua?"

"Sure," he says and stands to take the baby.

"Luke looks good with a baby," Melena says.

"Yeah," Katherine asks. "When are you going to have one?"

"You have to find the right woman first," Luke replies.

"Yeah," Blackwell says, "that's pretty important."

Melena turns back to her pre-potato kitchen duties. She picks up a bowl filled with chocolate icing and takes out a spatula to spread it over the chocolate cake.

"Who wants to lick the spoon?" Melena asks.

"I do," Elizabeth shouts, but Luke leans forward and takes them from Melena's hands before Elizabeth can get there.

"Hey, I said I wanted it."

"You can have the bowl when I'm done," Melena says. "Don't stick your fingers in it, Elizabeth. Here's another spoon. Now, you two share those."

This childish behavior feels right on a holiday shared by all. To act adult would be too close to bringing things out in the open. These motions make them feel like they're a family again, though one stuck in time.

"His has more icing than mine," she says.

"That's because I'm better than you." Luke grins.

"Right," she rolls her eyes.

Melena's heart gladdens with the presence of her children and they all take temporary comfort in their shared space. Tomorrow is Christmas Day, but in reality, just another day, a day when holiday truces make for a short peace.

⇢�⊙⊜⟨⇠

Around 11:30 the next morning, Elizabeth and Luke drive an hour and a half to Larnee where they will soon arrive at their father's house on a quiet Christmas morning.

On the empty streets they pass, the facades of closed shops are framed in darkened windows, frosted with imaginary snow while a breeze blows from the mountains to the west. Large, metallic red and green Christmas bells fly away from the light poles in flittering gusts.

Elizabeth and Luke watch this scene glide away beside them preferring not to talk. Though they do not speak much, both are relieved to be heading to their second holiday destination.

The stereo in the BMW blasts with Luke's new-found musical discovery. The music makes it easier for them not to talk, and Elizabeth intently studies the town she refuses to ever live in again.

At Ernest's house, they walk around to the back of the car to unload the Christmas packages designated for this half of the holiday.

Elizabeth smiles at the ornate ribbons she twisted on top of the presents convinced that little things like well-curled bows mean something. The two approach the door with their arms full of presents to spread their cheer on a gray Christmas day.

"Hey, Dad," Elizabeth says as Ernest opens the door. "Merry Christmas!"

"Merry Christmas, Dad," Luke says.

"Merry Christmas to the both of you," Ernest says. "Y'all come in."

Elizabeth gives Ernest a hug while Luke follows behind her. "Here, Elizabeth, I'll take some of those," Ernest says. "Y'all didn't have to get me anything. I'm just glad you're here."

Elizabeth thinks of her years of rage, wondering at her tranquility, "Yeah, me, too," she says.

Picking up the remote, Luke flips through the channels and stops on *A Christmas Story*. It plays all day long. Stacking her things on the coffee table, Elizabeth settles into the sofa and laughs at Ralphie on the screen.

"I love this movie," she says.

"What is it?" Ernest asks sitting down in his recliner.

"*A Christmas Story*." Luke sets the remote down. "You should watch it, Dad."

Ernest leans forward away from his wide-backed, tan leather chair. "Have you two eaten anything yet?"

"We had something small," Elizabeth says, "but we figured we'd eat with you."

"Well," Ernest says, "I didn't cook 'cause I figured you'd eat with your mom, but I did order from that same place as Thanksgiving."

"Sounds great, Dad." Elizabeth props her feet up. Hey, Dad, why don't you open some of your presents?"

"You and your brother should open yours first," he says taking some packages from a pile against the wall. He hands two large ones to Luke and several small ones to Elizabeth. Ernest watches his children as they turn the packages over in their hands.

"I didn't really know what you needed or what kind of things you like anymore, Elizabeth, so I took a stab at it. I hope you like them."

"I'm sure I'll love it, Dad, whatever it is." She rips the paper off the first package. "A new Game Boy," she says. "These things are really good for long trips. Thanks, Dad."

Ernest enjoys buying them gadget-type presents.

"Go on and open the rest," he says. "You too, Luke, open up one of those big ones."

Luke tears the paper away from the bigger of the two packages.

"Nice games," Elizabeth says. "I've heard about them."

"What do you think, Luke?" Ernest asks as Luke holds a brand new leather jacket up before him.

"Yeah, boy," Luke says and turns it around in his hands.

Wanting him to get more into the act, Elizabeth nudges him. "Try it on," she says.

He slips on the jacket testing the arms for length in the sleeves.

"That looks really good, Luke," she says.

"Yeah, Dad," Luke sits back down. "This is really nice. Thanks." He watches the TV again.

"Here, Dad," Elizabeth says trying to create excitement. "Why don't you open one of yours?"

"*Na*, you two go on and finish up first."

"Not until you open at least one," Elizabeth hands him a package dripping with silver ribbon. "Here, try this one."

Ernest takes the package out of her hands and opens the paper slitting it down the sides with a Swiss Army knife. He opens the square box, pulls back the tissue and laughs at the contents inside.

"Oh, Penelope Pit Stop," he says. "Thank you."

"I didn't have a lot of money right now," she says. "So, I figured I would just make you a goody box."

Ernest pulls out the items and examines them one at a time. "Shaving cream, shampoo and Snickers' bars," he says. "My goodness, now you two finish opening up your presents."

Elizabeth rips into the rest of her pile, finding a Mag-Lite, a handheld organizer and a tool set for traveling in the car. She turns the flashlight on and off then smacks the handle against the palm of her hand.

"Now, take care of those tools," Ernest says. "They're nice, and they should last you a long, long time. You never know when your car's going to break down and you might need them. You know if you were ever attacked, you could hit someone with the Mag-Lite and knock them out cold. You should keep it where you can get to it easy."

"I'll keep it under my seat," Elizabeth says hefting it in her hands. "What else did you get, Luke?"

"These are nice leather gloves, Dad," Luke says holding up the pair in his hands. He sets them down and looks back at the television. Elizabeth frowns.

"Luke, there's one more for you." Ernest stands. "Hang on one minute." It's been a while since Ernest felt a genuine bond with his son. Since Luke came to Mancon, he's become surlier with Ernest.

Ernest steps into his garage and returns a few seconds later holding a large square box in his hands. He sets it on the floor in front of Luke and sits back down in his leather chair. Presents are the only way he knows to show them that he cares.

"Go on, open it."

Luke takes the knife and slices the box open. He pulls back the edges of the tissue paper then peers inside. He raises his eyebrows.

"A new helmet," he says with real appreciation in his eyes.

"I figured you needed a new one," Ernest says and sits back satisfied with the presents he bought for his children.

Wrapping paper gathered around their feet, Luke and Elizabeth set down their new belongings and relax. Elizabeth pulls an afghan off the back of the couch, lays it across her lap and adjusts the cushion behind her head.

They do not speak much to each other, but sit together and watch TV. Sometime after one o'clock, Ernest wakes out of a brief nap and looks over at his children.

"You two about ready to eat?" he asks.

"Sure," Elizabeth says. "I'm starving."

"Well good," Ernest says. "I'll go warm everything up, and then we can have lunch."

Elizabeth follows him. "I'll help, Dad."

In the kitchen, they unload an assortment of plastic trays filled with southern food. Some trays Ernest empties into other bowls and some of them he leaves in the plastic container.

Elizabeth sets the bowls down on the table, grasping them with a heat mitten as they come out of the microwave.

"Dad, this looks pretty good." She feels sorry for him, knowing that he must be lonely.

"It's not much," he says, "nothing like what your mother used to cook, but I think it'll be fine."

Elizabeth looks at the floor as she thinks of holidays gone by and knows that their separation is for the better.

Ernest says, "I sure am glad you came. You know, for a while there, I didn't think you would ever speak to me again. Your momma has everyone so mad at me. My own brothers and sisters don't even talk to me anymore, but we won't talk about that."

"Okay," Elizabeth swirls a fork through the dish of mashed potatoes.

"You know, Elizabeth," Ernest says as he shuts the microwave door, "I'm proud of you. You used to seem not really all together. I knew about all that drinking and carrying on in your apartment before you left for your trip. You must have learned something over there."

"Yes," she says. "I know what I want to do now."

The microwave buzzes behind him in a continuous drone.

"I'm sure glad you're home though," he says.

"Well, I'm happy to be here," she frowns, thinking about how her mother would feel about her being at Ernest's house.

They finish heating the food and Luke walks into the kitchen to join them as they pile their paper plates full. Taking their lunch into the living room, they finish watching the movie while they have their Christmas meal. Elizabeth yawns, "I think I'll just sit here a while."

Luke's eyes flutter at the sound of her voice and Ernest's head falls forward as he nods off. Elizabeth pulls the blanket over her arms, and Luke stuffs a small pillow behind his head. The three of them nap in the silent warmth of Ernest's home.

--->=◎===<--

Spring comes and brings an abundant growth of hard feelings.

The lawyers send letters and subpoena endless documents. They will pore over contracts and tax records very, very slowly while being paid an immense sum for their services.

Dating now, Ernest tries to find solace in the hope of a new life, but that solace escapes him. Melena, quite lonely save for her friends who invent new and exciting ways to catch their ex-husbands, strategically plots to win what she knows is rightfully hers.

Cozy in the temporary home in Hollow Town, Blackwell contemplates his next step. In his mind, the four-story edifice being built for him is the castle he knew he would one day have. He's told the masses, especially in Asia, about being the best you can be everyday.

But one day, a thick document addressed to him comes by certified mail, and he sighs heavily. Ernest has written Blackwell a letter that he has also sent to Luke and Elizabeth.

The correspondence details the financial and business history of a father and his first-born.

"Dad wants the money back," Blackwell says to Katherine.

"Money from the first house," she says.

It's the lost first version of their dream home, but now he has another.

"Yes."

Blackwell hates losing. Not being number one isn't an option in his mind.

"You know, I had to do what I did for Mom."

Ernest didn't send the letter for the money. He sent it because he's never seen his grandson. Blackwell saw the tape and chose not to call his father when his son was born. "You don't have to explain it to me, honey." Katherine puts her arm around Blackwell.

"Your mother lives for her grandchildren."

They have another cup of coffee and talk. Katherine is proud of the values she and her husband stand for.

Joshua starts to cry and Katherine goes to pick him up.

"Isabelle," Blackwell says.

Isabelle looks up from her toys and comes to sit with him.

At the Mancon office, an hour or so later, Luke sits at his desk looking over records on the computer. Priscilla walks in with a letter in her hand and places it in front of him.

After the first page, he gets up from his desk and walks straight to his father's office. Ernest is busy on the phone, but Luke sits down in a chair across from him.

Ernest gesticulates to emphasize the key points of his conversation. Ten minutes later, he puts the phone down.

"What is this?" Luke says holding up the letter.

"It's exactly what it looks like," Ernest says.

"But you sent it to Elizabeth and me, too."

"Did you read it?"

"I don't have to," Luke says.

"I have a right to defend myself," Ernest snaps suddenly. "My own brothers and sisters won't even talk to me. Your mother told them a bunch of lies. Hell, Ernest points at him, "your brother didn't have the courtesy to inform me his son was born. I gave him everything he wanted. Where is he now? And who am I to him? You and your sister needed to understand that."

"No, we didn't. It's not going to solve anything."

"I don't give a damn if it does." Ernest grips his chair. "Just forget it."

He was hoping for a *Yes Dad, you're right.*

"Everyone can keep using me forever, and when I die, the whole family will finally get what they want."

"Dad ..."

"I'm sorry," Ernest says. "We shouldn't talk about this anymore. Throw the letter away. Forget about it."

That afternoon, Elizabeth walks into her apartment house with her mail in hand. She ascends the stairs.

"What is this?" she asks mystified, squinting at the fine print. Elizabeth frowns and stops.

"I'm not reading this shit," she says. She wipes a tear from her eye, throws the letter in the trash and goes downstairs.

Pausing in front of the answering machine, she fast-forwards through the messages, but stops when she hears Luke's voice on the tape. She knows why he called.

--•==◦==•--

Two days before final exams start, Elizabeth sits in her bedroom studying like mad. Not a single air conditioner cools the seven-bedroom house and the box fan she has positioned in front of her fails to keep her cool.

Pink highlighter in hand, she sweeps across the paragraphs of her biology book, marking the important things she needs to remember.

Elizabeth's eyes flutter, tired from reading the small print, and briefly close for a few moments.

A phone in the house startles her, and she jumps off her bed. Looking around her room, Elizabeth darts to her desk to pick up the cordless.

"Hello," she says still thinking of chimpanzees.

"Elizabeth."

The word comes across the line in a slow, cold steel voice. Elizabeth can hear a thousand remonstrances in that sound.

"Hey, Mom," Elizabeth rubs her eyes, "how are you?"

"Fine," Melena says and a very uncomfortable silence ensues.

"I want to talk to you about something."

"*Uh*, okay," Elizabeth sits down at her desk. Her fears are confirmed by Melena's tone, "Elizabeth, when were you planning on telling me that you have been in contact with your father and have accepted money from him?

In court this morning, she heard Ernest's lawyer say these very words.

"*Ugh*," Elizabeth says in one long, slow breath that emanates from deep in her gut. Threatened by the cool tone of her mother's voice, her mind scrambles in fear.

Melena doesn't wait. "You have been lying to me this whole time, haven't you?"

"Mom ..."

"Don't you *mom* me," Melena says. "I put myself in debt to send you off around the world. I'm the one that looks after you and you lied to me; me, the one person who sees to your well-being."

Melena feels utterly betrayed. Not to mention the lies she's been told, but the very fact that her daughter she raised could seek out the father Melena knows is wicked. She thinks, *You're like him.*

"I don't deserve this, Elizabeth," she says. "You are a traitor won over by money, young lady. I don't know how you can bring yourself to even talk to that man."

"M-mom," tears well in Elizabeth's eyes, "I didn't tell you because I knew you would be mad."

"You've just been playing both of us for money all along, haven't you?"

"What?" Elizabeth asks, angry and afraid at the same time.

"And here I've been thinking how hard you've had it down there with just the grocery money I've been giving you, but no, not you. No, ma'am, you've had your father giving you money all along."

*You'll be just like your brother now*, Melena thinks. *You'll probably work for the devil, too.*

"Mother, I clean the ice cream shop three nights a week, I work at Detour and I tutor those loser jocks. I'm the one that got myself back in school this year. Not him and not you."

"How am I supposed to believe you about anything?" Melena asks. "You're a liar. You lie just like your father lies, and now I know who you really are. How long has he been giving you money? How much has he given you? When did it all begin, Elizabeth? And this time, you had better be honest because I already know the truth."

Elizabeth whispers, defeated, "Why does it matter?"

"I have to know for court, Elizabeth," Melena nearly shouts. She grits her teeth thinking she could wring her daughter's neck.

"I have been asking for money for you thinking that he wasn't giving you any, and now I'm going to look like a fool in court."

"I'm sorry, Mom." Elizabeth shouts, "I was afraid to tell you. I couldn't!"

For moments nothing passes in the dead air between them, and the silence makes Elizabeth want to explode.

"I knew you'd be mad at me," Elizabeth says. She's hysterical knowing the threshold between Melena and her is now crossed.

"*Huh*," Melena says.

"I am very disappointed in you," Melena says. "You associate with that man when you know the things he's done, done to me, done to this family? You're not the person I thought you were, Elizabeth. I suppose you really are more his daughter than you are mine."

"He sent some money with Luke when he came to see me in Europe," Elizabeth blurts out.

"Is that all?" Melena asks.

"No," a tear rolls down Elizabeth's cheek. "He gave me some more earlier in the fall, and then some for my birthday."

"My, my, my, you sure have been living pretty, haven't you? I'm sure you go out to fancy dinners all the time, just like your father and your brother."

"No," she struggles not to shout. "Even with the money he gave me and what you give me, I'm still broke. I've got books to buy, rent, electricity, gas bills ...."

"You know what? I don't think I can believe anything you ever say again."

Melena tightly twists the phone cord in her hand thinking of the punishments she received from Bell as a child.

She sees herself maliciously pruning her mother's flowers in revenge for her bruised behind. The yellow cord snaps violently out of her hand as she speaks.

"No daughter of mine would ever lie to me like that. I certainly would never have betrayed my mother the way that you have betrayed me. And after all those years of me arguing for everything for you, college, dance lessons, clothes."

"Mom!" Elizabeth snaps and screams into the phone.

"This conversation is over," Melena says. "I can't talk to someone like you, and I'll never trust you again."

The other end of the line clicks dead.

Slowly, Elizabeth pulls the receiver away from her ear and looks at it as if it were a poisonous snake that just bit her.

She screams at the phone with an insane howl that no one hears. Turning around in her room, she looks for something to stabilize her, and finding nothing, she throws the phone against the posters on her wall.

The cordless phone breaks into pieces and Elizabeth watches it, thinking it mirrors her insides. Flinging her body on her bed, she cries into her blankets, blinded by emotion.

A few hours later, Elizabeth lies fast asleep. She's been dreaming of another reality filled with the same chaos and pain though it takes several most unnatural forms. The phone rings inside of the large house and groggily she ignores it. It stops, and a few seconds later someone beats loudly on her door.

"Elizabeth," Cooper, one of her roommates, shouts. "Elizabeth! I know you're in there. I saw your car outside."

"What?" she yells back at him.

"The phone," Cooper says. "It's for you."

"Hold on," Elizabeth says. She struggles to the door and unlocks the dead bolt.

"Hey," she says.

"*Ugh*," Cooper curls his lip. "What's wrong with you? You look awful."

"Nothing. Can I use your phone?"

"What's wrong with yours?"

"I broke it." Elizabeth sighs. "Give me your phone and I'll talk to you in a minute."

"Broke it," he says and laughs, "I don't know." She glares at him. "Okay, okay," he says, "but don't break this one."

She snatches it out of his hand and shuts the door behind her. "Hello."

"Hey," Luke says, "what's wrong with you?"

She frowns, "Our family."

"What happened?"

"Mom called me. She found out that I've been talking to Dad. She was so upset. Now, I am a liar, not to be trusted and not her child either."

Feeling lost, cut off and out of everything, Elizabeth starts to sniffle again.

"Hey," he says, "don't cry, kid. It had to happen at some point."

Elizabeth sits on her bed. "You know, even if I had told her before now, the same thing would have happened. She hates me because I talk to him. It would've been the same exact thing no matter what. I guess I just prolonged it."

"Yeah."

"It's not fair," Elizabeth says. "I have a right to have a father even if he's not what everyone wants him to be. I need you, Mom, Blackwell and him. Why can't we just be a family or at least one that isn't so insane?"

"Calm down," Luke says. "You've got to calm down. Getting upset isn't going to do you any good."

"It sucks," Elizabeth shouts. "It sucks and I hate it. I hate everything."

"Elizabeth, honey, I know that's not true. You don't hate everything. You like me and you like movies and Japanese food."

"Yeah," she says her voice retreating.

"Look," he says, "this divorce, the whole damn thing, we both knew it was going to be hard. You've got to buck up because it ain't gonna end anytime soon."

"It's been this way forever, Luke. It will never, ever change. We're cursed. I know it. It's going to be this way forever and we're all going to die miserable, unhappy souls that hate each other, but I'm never going to hate you."

"*Shh,*" Luke says, "I would never hate you either."

A giggle of relief escapes her.

"See," he says, "you're tough. You're going to handle this. Mom's going to be mad at you, but that's inevitable. Hell, she doesn't like me either, but there's nothing we can do about it. She does what she does because she feels she needs to. Do you regret talking to Dad?"

"No," Elizabeth says confidently.

"Well, then you've got nothing to worry about. You're just going to have to let her be angry if that's what she wants to do. But you can't keep getting this upset. I heard you tell Cooper that you broke your phone. What happened?"

"I threw it against the wall and smashed it into a thousand pieces," she says looking at the plastic showered over her floor.

"Did it make you feel any better?"

"Yes, it did."

"Is it still making you feel better?"

"No."

"So, don't go around breaking anything else," he says. "You have to learn to separate all this. If you don't, it'll destroy you."

"I know. I just can't handle it when she gets mad at me. I don't know why. It's like there's this weird switch inside that makes me crazy and depressed when she is."

"Don't let it."

"Yeah, I won't."

Luke asks, "Do you feel better now, kid?"

All they really have from here on is each other.

"Kind of," Elizabeth says and leans back against her headboard.

"Good," he says, "go outside and do something productive. I have to go, but I'll call you tomorrow."

"All right," she looks out the window at the steamy day. "Hey, Luke, don't worry about me. I'll be fine."

"I know you'll be fine."

They hang up and Elizabeth steps out of her bedroom and into the hall on the second floor of the house. She stares at her gigantic Jane's Addiction Triple X poster hanging on the wall opposite her door.

She thinks about that song where the brother keeps slapping the younger sibling trying to convey some lesson about the world. Elizabeth knows now how to survive.

Stepping to Cooper's room, she knocks on the door and looks in the mirror next to it. She frowns at her swollen face and smoothes down her hair.

"Who is it?" Cooper asks.

"The fairy godmother, who do you think it is?" she asks. "Let me in. I've got your phone."

Cooper opens the door. "What the heck happened to yours?"

"Sit down and I'll tell you all about it."

# ACT V

# The Reckoning of the Void

A YEAR GOES BY ABSENT OF any relief. Though Melena held onto the hope that Elizabeth would be a doctor, the inventive sculptress is well into her new curriculum, edging closer to her degree.

While she spends her free time creating gargantuan, mobile creatures made of metal and wood, Elizabeth studies every classical representation she comes across. She wishes to construct an angular model of Rubens' Venus creating the galaxy.

Melena's days come and go, drawn out at a pace that drives her to the point of angry madness. The house her family called a home crumbles and decays.

The pace she must sustain to run the store and her divorce tears her body apart. She weakens beneath the chronic mystery, and her doctors continue to provide her with an arsenal of medications.

Alienated by their choices, Luke and Elizabeth cling together for support. Brother and sister trust only in each other in a family where conversations are clandestinely taped, private words are passed around, and the empty spaces are examined for hidden meaning.

Sometime late in 1998, Melena finally won the right to sell the house. After months, a hopeful young couple with two children made an offer.

Melena, ready to be rid of the albatross, sold them the home for far less than its value. Though he would not see a dime from the sale, Ernest still steams with resentment for the loss of his investment.

One weekend in the middle of fall, the Shades leave Holiday and drive into Larnee to help Melena haul away loads of the remnants of the family's belongings. Melena has been the caretaker of the family's possessions too long.

317

Pearl won't make the two-hour drive to Larnee by herself, and Walker, faithful companion known to the sisters since they were kids, is more than happy to come with her.

"God, dawgit, Melena," Pearl says looking angrily at her sister. Hand on her hip, she wags one finger.

"I told you not to lift nothin' by yourself. You know the doctor told you you weren't supposed to use that shoulder."

"Pearl," Melena says. She stands in the middle of the cluttered basement. "What was I supposed to do?"

"I've got to have everything out of this house in two and a half weeks. There are years and years of stuff here, in the closets, under the beds, in the attic and in this basement there are another four rooms full of it."

"If I sit here and wait for someone to come help me, I'll never be done when the time comes for the new owners to move in," replies Melena.

"Well," Pearl says surveying the piles that Melena has made, "you need to make your children come help you."

"Oh, no honey," Melena picks up a plastic bag filled with trash. "I wouldn't ask them to come help me if my life depended on it."

*Blackwell's so busy now*, Melena thinks, *and the poor thing does what he can. The only way I'd call Luke and Elizabeth is for them to come get their own stuff.*

"I'm not going to be a trouble to anyone," she says.

"Walker," Pearl shouts, "can you come here?"

The two sisters are aging gracefully together.

"Yes, darling," Walker says with a smile, "you called?"

"Don't you think we can get at least four trips to the dump in before we have to turn around and go home?" Pearl asks.

"I do," he says, "and I think we should take the yard sale stuff home with us today. That way we can get rid of it before we come back for the stuff y'all are going to keep."

"Good idea, Walker," Melena says. "I just don't know what I'd

do without you. You know there are a lot of things in this basement that might be of use to you. All sorts of gas cans, cleaning
products, shovels, you know you can have anything you want."

It makes her happy to give Ernest's belongings away.

Pearl walks over to the piles and the three begin carrying hand-
fuls and baskets of broken toys, moth-eaten clothes and other aban-
doned belongings to the Shades' old blue pickup.

"Well, I'll be damned," Pearl exclaims. "Would you look at this
thing? I remember this raft." She taps her sister gently on the arm
with the inflatable tube. "Don't you remember when we were all
down at Beaufort and we took Elizabeth out in this thing? She was
such a precious angel!"

Pearl giggles with the same happy laughter she had as a kid.

"There we were swimming like fools in the middle of the ocean,
all six of us around her in case something happened. You had her
in that little green bonnet and sunglasses."

Walker nudges Pearl in the kind way he always has, "Honey, if
we're going to meet our goal, we've got a lot of work to do, so less
talking and more walking."

"*Aye, aye*, sir," Pearl says and looks back at Melena. "But she sure
was something."

"I always dressed her in the prettiest clothes," Melena remembers.

"You know, mothers just don't do that anymore. Not the way
we did, or the way our mothers dressed us. Don't you remember,
Momma would never let us leave the house without our gloves?"

"Do I ever," Pearl says. "Where's that little velvet coat and dress
set Momma bought for Elizabeth?"

"It's upstairs right now," Melena says, "with the little bonnet and
rabbit fur muff. Momma said she looked just like a little Kennedy."

"And, Luke," Pearl says, "with his little John-John suits, god,
dawgit, those kids were something."

"*Ahhem*," Walker says, "ladies, we are never going to make it to the dump at all if you two don't focus on the task at hand."

"Walker's right," Melena sighs, "no sense wasting time."

"I can manage with this stuff down here," Pearl says. "Why don't you two go on upstairs and get started on the heavy stuff."

"How about it, Walker?" Melena asks. "You up for bringing some of that down?"

"Yes, he is," Pearl nods, "that way Melena won't try to bring it down by herself when we aren't here."

"That's what I'm here for," Walker says. "I am at your beck and call."

Melena moves up the stairs. "Follow me."

Walker and Melena ascend the long staircase, Melena grasping her knee for extra support. They emerge upstairs where another heap of memories lies in wait separated in piles to be taken to the dump.

Downstairs, Pearl moves slowly from the truck to the basement making sure not to carry anything too heavy for her middle-aged frame. She stops, holding various objects up in her hands and turning them over.

She feels like Melena shouldn't be the one with the burden of letting go of these memories. Lamenting the darkened cloud that has cast its shadow over her sister's family, she gently fills their pickup with the forgotten belongings of this household.

⤗⊙⊙⤖

Inside Sandra McNair's sumptuous office, Melena sits across from her lawyer in a mahogany chair waiting for her to get off of the phone.

Sandra's nails, manicured just yesterday in New York, tap the top of her desk absentmindedly while Mr. Thornsby's speech winds down.

"*Mmm, hmm,*" Sandra says stepping in on cue, "yes, Roger. Well, my client simply will not settle for that. It's insulting."

Melena's eyebrows furrow. She hasn't heard any figures, but she trusts that Sandra would only refuse an unworthy offer.

Sandra continues to stare out the window over downtown Larnee. Watching her anxiously, Melena tries to calm herself and breathe.

She focuses on the pastels in the Monet print just above Sandra's head, but the forty-five minute wait in the lobby did little to ease her anxiety.

"Yes, Roger," Sandra says, "I understand you perfectly, I do. But, we must have further documentation on the value of the rental properties. Our experts want to file their own reports upon their determination."

Melena's eyes widen then narrow into slits of ire. Today marks the fourth time in their years-long divorce that this value has been drawn into question.

More experts and another evaluation mean more money out of Melena's pocket and more time without the divorce settled.

Sandra's jet-setting lifestyle and complete lack of efficiency in the case suggest a grave breech of ethics that unnerves Melena no end.

"*Uh, huh,*" Sandra says turning slightly in her chair. She faces Melena, whose face has hardened into a temporary scowl that seems to hang around all the time these days.

Sandra's index finger uncurls like a miniature flagpole signaling one more minute on the phone. Melena nods curtly. Every minute with this woman costs her money.

"Well, Roger," she says, "we're not going to back down. My client deserves much more than that. She was a devoted, caring wife, and she kept the house and the children for over twenty years. So, I suppose we'll be seeing you in court to decide the matter."

Melena falls back against her chair overwhelmed. Court again and still no decision about this one thing. But Sandra will receive her two hundred fifty dollars an hour.

"All right then, Roger," Sandra says, "I'll have my legal assistant call yours to make arrangements." She hangs up the phone and leans toward Melena.

"Melena," she says with a slight shake of her head.

"Those men are impossible. To think that they still won't provide proper documentation on these properties is unbelievable."

Sandra waves her hands in the air for emphasis. She's such a good player, but will the trick work this time?

"It infuriates me," Sandra says, "to see them treat the case this way. You deserve so much more, and he has no right not to give it to you."

"So, what exactly does this mean?" Melena asks. "Besides the fact that we have to go to court again just to get evidence that you seem to be unable to obtain."

Sandra puts her hands down on the polished desk in front of her. "What it means, Melena, is that you are going to get every dime you deserve no matter how hard and how long we have to fight for it."

"*Uh, huh,*" Melena says clasping her hands together in front of her. "You know, Sandra," she says, "I think this means that you and your good friend Roger there will be squeezing another couple of thousand dollars out of us. That way you can continue to fly off on a whim whenever you please. I think that you and Roger, who you seem to be so close to, have been playing a nice little game with me."

Melena shakes her head to fight off the feeling of hysteria she has from what she sees as the lack of control over her own life.

"Yes, that's right," she says, "a nice little game."

Sandra gasps and drops her pencil on the floor. Melena raises her right hand in a stop sign.

"You know what, Sandra, you're fired. I'm tired of being screwed over by you and Roger Thornsby. I'm going to find someone who is willing to get this thing taken care of so I can move on and have a life." Melena slides her purse strap over her shoulder and stands up.

"I'll have my new lawyer contact you immediately," she says.

"You have a wonderful day."

Sandra watches silently as Melena walks out the door.

It closes with a heavy sound and Sandra sits stunned for a second, contemplating Melena's dismissal.

She stares in front of her and scoffs, amused at this turn of events. She buzzes her assistant.

"Danielle, get Roger Thornsby on the phone again immediately. Please tell him it is extremely urgent."

"Yes, Mrs. McNair," Danielle says and picks up her phone.

---

For months, requests for the file on Melena and Ernest's divorce travel between Melena's new and old lawyers.

This isn't the first time one of the lawyers has been fired. Delayed and infuriated with the lack of progress, Ernest let Roger go once, but was forced to rehire him.

The lost time in finding another lawyer like Roger, who understands Ernest's complicated business matters, then briefing them on the case, seemed impossible to Ernest. Behind Thornsby's eyes, Ernest thinks he sees his life draining away.

Mr. Thornsby was rehired in hopes of reaching the case's conclusion, but the conclusion is the very thing that is so elusive.

Why does no one in the system force the embattled pair to a final decision? Ernest and Melena's wasted time and effort must provide money for the different people running the machine.

Now, four years after Ernest walked down those stairs, a preliminary hearing gets under way.

Who will testify and who will not?

Across town at the country club, a rich divorcée twists her straw in her martini. She bats her eyes and says, "Yes, it's true. His oldest son, Blackwell, and the daughter, too, they're both going to testify against him."

At Mancon, Ernest manages like a weathered general,

strategizing how to survive his legal expenses and maintain the reputation of the company he created. Conducting meetings with investors, banks and government agencies, he slaves the hours away.

Several doors down the hall from Ernest's office, Luke Bartleby sits at his desk facing the wall. Locked inside his barless cage, an odd mix of guilt from mother and father, along with his own aspirations, have put him in this cell.

He glances at his racing portfolio sitting on the shelf and then back out the window. The brothers have begun to talk more cordially than before, and Blackwell holds onto the hope of drawing Luke away from their father's influence.

Introducing Luke to his seven-figure preventive healthcare business, Blackwell beckons his brother toward network marketing success. Yet, the lines that divide remain, and nothing can erase the labels that each family member has been given by one another.

A messenger comes to the front door of the Mancon office and rings the bell. Maureen, the bookkeeper, goes to meet him.

"Yes sir, Sheriff," she says looking at the badge and the brown hat, "is there something I can help you with?"

"Yes, ma'am," the young constable says. "I'm looking for Priscilla Rasor.

"Why yes, sir," Maureen says, "just one moment and I'll call her."

Maureen walks over to the front desk and presses down on the intercom key. Everyone in the office will end up knowing about it anyway.

"Priscilla," she says, "you have a guest up front."

"Okay," Priscilla says curiously. She turns away from the proposal she's studying and walks toward the front of the building.

Maureen flashes a flirtatious smile at the constable. "She'll be right with you."

She turns and walks back down the hall toward her own office to let things unfold in her absence. Maureen suspects it could be one of two things. Seconds later Priscilla emerges from the opposite hall.

"Yes, sir," she says, "I'm Priscilla Rasor. What can I help you with?"

"Ma'am," he says shifting his weight to his back foot, "I have an official subpoena for you to appear in court."

The deputy hands her an envelope. "Oh," Priscilla says, "certainly."

She thought this might happen. All this legal business makes her so anxious.

Priscilla walks back down the hall opening the envelope as she goes.

Stopping at the corner on the development side of the office, she reads the document in its entirety. Priscilla sighs and pulls a lock of hair behind her ear, a nervous habit since her youth. She steps into Ernest's office as he's getting off the phone.

"Yes, sir, Mr. Williams," he says. "We certainly will, and you call me if this comes up again." He looks at Priscilla's ashen face and down to the manila envelope in her hand.

"Okay then," Ernest says, "you have a good day, too, bye-bye."

"Ernest," Priscilla blurts out. "I've been subpoenaed."

Leaning back in his chair, Ernest releases a slow breath of exhaustion. "Well," he says, "I thought this was coming. I'm so sorry that you have been involved in this, Priscilla, but with your knowledge of the company, I guess you would have to be the one they would call."

"What if I say something wrong, Ernest?"

"You just say what you know," Ernest says. "You just say the truth."

"I just hate this for you, Ernest."

She thinks a lot of Ernest and the family, but she knows so much has gone wrong between them all. Priscilla leans against the doorframe.

"It's just such a shame, such a damn shame," she says. She still feels bad for being the one to tell Ernest about his only grandson.

"Do you know this case has been going on for four years? The lawyers don't do a damn thing to get it resolved. Then we fire them for prolonging the damn thing."

"Was that Tom Williams on the phone?" she asks.

"Seems they're having another problem with drainage down in Ayden again. I have so much work to do," he says, "and yet, I spend the majority of my time dealing with this divorce."

"Maybe with this hearing, it'll finally be over?"

"Maybe," he says any optimism dampened by doubt.

"You better get ready for that meeting with the town council," Priscilla says. "You and Luke have to leave here in thirty minutes or you're going to be late."

"Right, right," Ernest says. He starts to get out of his chair.

"Okay, Priscilla. Thank you."

"No problem," she says and returns to her desk.

Across Larnee more than two-dozen subpoenas go out for both sides of the hearing. Melena and Ernest have their own separate reasons for calling on various business associates, bankers, tax advisors and persons involved in unexplained liaisons.

The matter reaches all the way to Hollow Town.

Upon receipt of his subpoena, Blackwell's face lengthens, cast downward in shame.

⭒

Weeks and weeks go by with expensive time spent in lawyer's offices preparing documents and testimonies.

In a brief flurry, a possible deal comes down the line with the option of an out of court settlement, but the endeavor fails.

These expensive preparations continue until the whole circus of bankers, accountants, Mancon past and present employees, family and friends parade to court for the preliminary hearing.

Now in the closed courtroom, the family walks divided into the walkway that leads to the front of the courtroom. Melena and Ernest sit at two square tables positioned in front of the judge on either side of the room.

The judge, a stalwart man, peers at the people in court with an unforgiving look. He knows they're all waiting for him, and he loves to watch the room squirm.

A rotating fan moves with a click and drone on the far side of the room to blow stale air back across the court.

"Yes, sir, Mr. Walson," Judge Baxter finally says and raises his large bushy eyebrows.

"I understand, sir, and I, too, see the need to speed these proceedings on, but I don't think you have had adequate time to process the information presented here on these properties."

Melena's new lawyer, Mr. Walson, long gray with age, matches the judge's patriarchal, southern tones, enunciated deliberately for dramatic affect.

"The data we have presented should be more than enough to prove the value of said properties." Mr. Walson coughs and clears his throat.

"Well, I am sorry, Mr. Walson," Judge Baxter says, "it appears we are at an impasse because I do disagree. I will continue this case for another six months."

Melena's jaw drops to the floor and inside her breast an angry spirit does a devil's dance around her inflamed heart. *Another six months in hell*, she thinks.

"Order, order," Judge Baxter whacks his gavel upon his desk several times stifling the shocked clamor of the crowd.

"Order, I say. This court will reconvene on this matter in January of nineteen ninety-nine. All parties will be fully prepared regarding this valuation matter at that time."

He collects his notes and sweeps his robe to the right as he exits to his chambers.

Judge Baxter's re-election campaign has already begun.

Ernest's face turns red, enraged and dumbfounded at the judge's lack of decision. Melena stands up, furious, and storms out of the room.

She flees to the ladies' room. There in this sanctuary, she turns the sink on full blast listening to the rush of water. Melena stares at it wanting to manipulate the stream in her hands and wash away everything that she sees as wrong. Her hands dive underneath the spout, relieved at the chill it puts into her skin.

Diana, her ever-present good friend and confidant, appears in the mirror to her left as the restroom door shuts behind her.

"I cannot believe this, Diana," Melena says and shakes her hands. She rips a paper towel from the dispenser.

"Another damned six months of paying the lawyers and preparing documents, and my life being controlled by him."

Melena wants to leave Larnee. Her heart longs to travel and meet new people, discovering the world outside her marriage, but she will not give up.

"It's a plot," she says. "I tell you it's his sick plot to drive me crazy and have control of my life. They think they'll win. Oh, they think if they drag this godforsaken case out forever, I'll quit, but I will never quit."

"Hell," Melena says, "I may be dead by the end of it, and he may be, too, but I'll be damned if he will ever win!"

Diana shakes her head from side to side in disbelief loosening her thick dark curls. She got a big settlement in her divorce.

"I just can't believe that it's being delayed again," she says. "Here, give me that paper towel and let's get out of here.." She steps toward the mirror and touches her hair.

"We'll go get some dinner or something and just make another plan."

"Diana," Melena says as she barely grasps the fresh new reality, "you are a true friend, but I think I need to be alone right now. I'm just so damn mad."

"I would be, too." Diana adjusts her designer bag on her shoulder. "But I think you're right. They probably think you'll give up the longer it takes and accept a deal that's less than what you deserve. Don't you worry though, I'm going to stay with you the whole time, and make sure you get what's lawfully yours."

"Where would I be without a friend like you?"

"You'd probably be right here standing up for yourself the way you are now." She smiles, "Melena, you are the strongest person I know."

"Come on," Melena says, "I have to get out of here."

Diana motions out the door, "Lead the way."

⊷≡◉≡⊷

Early in ninety-nine, under a hovering storm of turmoil and lies, Blackwell and Luke grow moderately more communicative.

Since he began participating in business with his famed brother, Luke never goes to Mancon, and Ernest's eye and pocket willingly allow his absence.

He hangs near the network marketing heights that Blackwell has attained by speaking to thousands in foreign countries. The possibilities for Luke glitter with fool's gold. He sees money, money enough to have his own racing team.

Elizabeth will graduate in a few short months, but she busies herself writing a controversial thesis on Reubens and the modern female form. She knows that one day her sculptures will change the world through their visual truth.

Plagued with persistent back pain, and a hyperactive hearbeat, all of which make him lie down scared in the dark, Ernest waits in his doctor's office for the results of the last round of tests his old friend Dr. Robert Callar recently performed on him.

Inside the examination room, Ernest sits in a simple chair tucked into the corner. His tall frame and sturdy build fold neatly in it without the appearance of distress.

He makes quick notes on a tiny white pad, then sticks the pen and paper in his shirt pocket. His cell phone doesn't work in this room freeing him from the never-ending procession of business calls he receives. So for the time being, Ernest sits, inaccessible to the world that demands his constant involvement. Gradually, his heavy eyelids shift downward and close briefly.

In moments, he sits with his head leaned backward against the wall, mouth agape, loud snores emanating from his nose.

There is a soft knock, then the door opens with Dr. Callar's voice waking him.

"All right, Ernest," Robert says.

Startled, Ernest's head snaps forward and he blinks his eyes as he looks around.

"Pardon me, Robert," he mumbles and wipes his hand across his eyes. "I was just catching a few."

"Not a problem," Robert says. "From the looks of things, you probably needed it."

"You're right." Ernest sits up. *I want it straight, and I want it now.*

"So, what have you got?" he asks.

Robert leans against the wall. They're close to the same age, but the facts stare Robert in the face. Ernest's body has grown older much faster.

"We've known each other for a long time," Robert says. "I can safely say, that if you hadn't been exercising all your life, then you and I wouldn't be sitting here together today. Seems you have the heart of an eighty year old man, and you aren't even sixty."

"Now, this type of exceeded wear and tear on your heart comes as a direct product of the stress in your life, and you've eaten too much sugar over the years. I've always told you that, but for the most part, you've eaten right and exercised. Problem is, though, you work like a damn dog."

"No choice to that," Ernest says.

Robert sits down in the chair across from his old friend. "It's not only that. You and I both know your divorce equals the stress you have at work. With that, the effect on the body is astonishing when you account for twelve-hour work days as well."

"What I am trying to tell you, Ernest, is that if you don't stop right now with one or the other, you're not going to live much longer."

Ernest doesn't move. A termination to his divorce or his business is not possible, especially for the latter, without anyone eager to take the reins.

He thinks fathers must pass their legacy on or what has the creation been worth?

Robert watches him and says, "Now, I could start you on medication. It'll help control your hyperactive heart, but once you start it, then you have to take it for the rest of your life. If you didn't, the progress would reverse and the results could be fatal."

"There's also a surgical option," Robert says. "We'd shut your heart down completely when we perform it and then restart with a different pulse. I think though, we have some time before we go that route. As your doctor and your friend, I seriously want to see you make some major life changes. If you don't, ..."

"Ernest, settle your divorce. That's the number one thing for you to do, but if that can't happen, you have to back off the business. Now, I'm serious about this."

Ernest's unmoving face shows nothing.

"I know that you have at least five different phones, and everyone calls you all day. If you don't stop most of it, your heart will."

"I see," Ernest says and absorbs it all as if it were some construction problem to be broken down and dealt with in design, parts and labor.

"About your back," Robert takes off his glasses and wipes them with a tissue out of the box on the adjacent counter.

"Your back, though an entirely different matter, is just as important if not more so in the short term. You have a case of disc erosion occurring in your lower spine. Four consecutive vertebrae are being consumed by degenerative arthritis.

Robert draws a diagram for Ernest on a blank sheet of paper

while Ernest follows the lines he makes.

"Gradually," he says, "the arthritis causes the tissue to swell pinching the nerves here, running in your spinal column down to your legs. That's why your left leg keeps going numb."

Ernest steps on his foot to shake it awake without thinking. It has become a habit to him.

"Basically, this condition will cripple you from the waist down permanently in four to six years. A very tricky surgery exists that can be performed to try and stop the damage, but I have to be honest, Ernest, only three hospitals in the country are doing it right now. It involves operating directly on your spine, and there's a high risk of failure."

Ernest stares at him.

"You could be paralyzed from the surgery if it were to fail."

They pause and sit silent for a moment.

"Not a whole lot of good," Ernest says. "If I'd known you were going to hit me with this, Robert, I would have stayed at the office."

"Like I said," Robert says, "there are two choices. Cut the work out or down, and the relief of that stress will help your heart and your back immensely, but it won't solve what's going on in your spine."

"Remove Mancon from your life," he says knowing Ernest will never do such a thing, "and go see a specialist who will help you find a resolution for the degeneration in your back."

"If you do not do these things, your heart will go in three to six years, but if you remedy your heart and do not do something about your back then you'll be paralyzed from the waist down in a period a little longer than that."

"I see," Ernest says breathing deeply. "Not very much hope here, *huh*? I ... you know I can't slow the office down. I can't afford to hire someone else. I can't bring my divorce to an end without killing myself with work until I die. So, I guess I'll end up dead or in a wheelchair or I suppose both."

Robert asks, "Do you have any questions about all of this? There's a lot to understand and maybe if you learn more, you'll see the urgency of the situation."

"No," Ernest replies, "no questions." He's embarrassed by the tears trying to flood his eyes.

"I'm a little upset right now. I can't articulate questions from the thousands of things running through my mind."

He stands up.

"I need to leave," he says. "I feel like I'm suffocating and I need to leave so I can calm down and think this through. I have to be across town at city hall in an hour anyway."

Ernest gathers his coat and shakes his friend's hand.

"You call me anytime and I'll help you with doctors and information as much as I can," Robert tells him. "Don't just go out and drown yourself in work to forget it. Cool off and get back to me on the plan you're going to implement to save yourself. If you don't call me in a few days, I'm going to call you."

"Okay, then," Ernest says needing to escape, wanting to run, "Thank you."

Dr. Callar manages a concerned smile as he watches his friend walk down the hall toward the reception desk

*Maybe he'll get control and take care of himself*, Robert thinks. He tugs at the stethoscope lying against his chest and heads back to the nurse's station to pick up the next patient's file.

--⋗═◎═◎═⋖--

Late in spring, with less than a year invested with the network business venture, a certain Starling pocket empties. Blackwell's bright-colored rainbow has proven ill suited for pursuit by this one.

Sitting in his office at home in Larnee, Luke looks around him at the boxes of unused product filling the tiny room in stacked piles.

The green and blue boxes mix with his racing trophies and memorabilia.

This network business venture fell far from his expectations: a doorway to seven figures and a racecar. Investment met with disappointment. This sport of marketing is not for him. In his disappointment, Luke thinks, *Blackwell could have helped me more.*

Picking up the telephone, Luke dials the preventive healthcare company's distributor service line and listens for the menu cue that will forward his disgruntled call.

Luke waits, swiveling in his office chair from left to right, very slowly. Finally, a human voice comes to the phone.

"Hi, this is Candice speaking. Welcome to Live Well. How may I be of service to you?"

"Hi, Candice," Luke says, "I became a distributor for the company within the last nine months and have since terminated my distributorship."

He sits back and says, having thought it out several times, "I have a good bit of unopened product merchandise in my home that I am unable to sell at this time. I'd like to return the bulk of this product and obtain a refund if possible."

"I'm sorry, sir," Candice says, "but what did you say your name is?"

"It's Luke Bartleby Starling and my identification code is 288 41 3333."

"Thank you, sir. I'm just pulling up your account."

Luke taps his fingers against the armrest. He's already gone back to Mancon, but he still needs the money. His house needs a lot of work.

"Yes, here we go," Candice says in a chipper voice. "You ordered your basic distributor package over eight months ago. Is that correct?"

"Yes, it is."

"Well, I am sorry Mr. Starling," Candice slows down, "but we only accept distributor merchandise within three months of the initial ship date."

"Three months," Luke repeats, previously unaware of this deadline.

"Yes, sir," Candice says. "Are you sure that you cannot sell the merchandise?"

"Candice," his voice remains calm, "my distributor status was canceled two months ago and I've been trying to sell this stuff since then."

Luke opens a box of product and knocks it off his desk onto the floor. He bites his lip wanting to yell into the phone, *give me my damn money back you bitch*. He sighs.

"Well, Candice, I suppose there's nothing you can do for me. Thank you for your time."

"Yes, Mr. Starling," she says, "I'm sorry I couldn't be more of a help to you. Thank you for calling and have a nice day."

"Right," he says and hangs up the phone.

He stares hard at the phone. Luke thinks about calling Blackwell and asking his brother to relieve him of the thousands of dollars of merchandise now littering his home. He's stopped by the echo of a conversation they had two months ago.

"Come on," Blackwell had said with his best pep-talk tone. "You could have that DC market eating out of your hands."

Blackwell really believed he could. After all, Luke's six foot five stature and winning smile sure could take him far.

"I don't think so," Luke said. "It's already covered by five other people. How am I supposed to create a new market in a city I don't even live in that's covered by so many people?"

Blackwell, gifted with Pratt's ability to sell anything, pushed him.

"You have to go out there and network, Luke. You've got that charm. You just have to use it."

"Network," Luke said and thought, *I don't have time for this shit. This isn't getting me any closer to a car.*

"Look, I've already canceled my distributorship. The problem is that I have a lot of money tied up in merchandise taking up half of my office at home. What am I supposed to do with all that?"

"Sell it," Blackwell said. "Find the market in your area and get out there and sell it."

Sell it. Luke let the words suspend in the air. "Don't you need any product? I mean, you're the one making tons of money off this stuff."

"No," Blackwell said, "I don't keep that much product here at home anymore. You really should follow through on your commitment."

Blackwell feels he is imparting some thus far unlearned wisdom and Luke isn't impressed.

"Yeah," Luke said. "Well, thanks a lot for your help then."

"Keep working at it," Blackwell told him, "and you'll be able to move that stuff in no time."

Now, two months later, sitting in his office decorated with the dozens of unopened boxes, Luke stares at the phone.

"I sure ate this one," he grumbles.

He stands to walk into the living room of his house. Two of his roommates sprawl across the L-shaped couch with bits of chips scattered on their shirts. Neither looks up from the game they watch on television as Luke walks into the kitchen, silent in his temporary defeat.

—⊷═◉═⊶—

On the cusp of summer, Elizabeth's graduation presents a new problem, one the children will always have to deal with. In this divorced family, how do you arrange weddings, birthdays or graduations that both sides must attend at the same time?

In the small church where the Academy of Design holds the graduation ceremony, every Starling will be within open, unprotected sight of one another. Ernest will come alone and the only souls brave enough to sit with him will be Luke and one of Elizabeth's friends.

The other attendants, Melena, Walker, Pearl, Blackwell, Katherine and, of course, Isabelle and Joshua will form their own cluster in the chapel. Specifically chosen by Elizabeth, the precise spot they occupy will lessen the chances of the two opposing, highly hostile groups looking at each other.

Elizabeth has planned for the larger party to come in first. She hopes this will prevent any confrontations, since they promised her an exact arrival time thirty minutes prior to Ernest's.

In a nervous panic, Elizabeth rushes to the back of the building as she sees Melena and the rest of the family arriving fifteen minutes behind schedule. She sweats underneath her robes.

"Hi everyone," Elizabeth says and moves down the line hugging each one as she goes. At the end, she picks Joshua up and carries him away toward the front of the church.

"Oh, Elizabeth," Pearl says, "you just look fabulous, darling, absolutely gorgeous in your cap and gown."

"Thanks," Elizabeth says motioning for them to follow her. "I didn't know how to fix my hair with this silly hat. Y'all come on and follow me. I've saved an entire row up here toward the front."

In a line, they follow her down the aisle while she bounces Joshua who wiggles in her arms.

"Aunt Elizabeth," he laughs.

She turns to Melena behind her. "Hey, Mom," she says, "you look beautiful."

These days, mother and daughter maintain a distant relationship calculated in steps and measured in action by Melena. This part of the family sits down and Elizabeth passes Joshua to Katherine.

"So, we're going out afterward, right?" Elizabeth asks.

She knows she needs to be on the lookout for Ernest, and she worries that the benches behind her mother won't fill up with people fast enough to hide Joshua and Isabelle.

"We sure are," Blackwell says looking proud at another family graduation from his alma mater. "I figured we'd do a pub-crawl downtown and wind up at the restaurant around five-thirty or six."

Blackwell is the family's acting man of the house.

"You made the reservations?" Elizabeth asks.

"I sure did," Blackwell says, glad to assume the responsibiity.

"Good" Elizabeth smiles. "Pearl, I thought Bobby and Macy were coming?"

"Oh, honey, they're out parking the car. You know how Bobby is. He just had to find the right spot."

"Oh, well, we have enough room here don't we?"

"We sure do," Melena says. She thinks, *Wonder when the son of a bitch is coming?*

"Okay, then I'll be right back," Elizabeth says and tips her cap. "I'll keep a lookout and send Bobby your way as soon as I see them."

Elizabeth darts to the back of the church and out the door at the corner of the building. Melena watches her. Outside, Elizabeth smiles as Bobby and Macy walk up in the bright May sun.

"Hey, y'all," Elizabeth says and hugs each of them. "Thanks so much for coming. Mom and everybody have a place up toward the front part of the church on the right. They have a seat saved for you two."

"You excited, squirt?" Bobby asks.

"Yeah, I'm excited."

Elizabeth rocks back on her heels and looks at the bright, sunny day all around her against a sky of intense Carolina blue.

She nudges Bobby's arm. "I hope you're ready to drink some beer when this is all over."

"Watch out for Pearl," Macy says, eyes growing large. "You get more than one beer in that woman and God only knows what'll happen."

"You're right," Elizabeth laughs. "Well, y'all go on in. I need to wait out here for Luke and Dad."

"Oh," Bobby says archly. He always liked Ernest.

"Okay, squirt, we'll see you inside. Don't trip."

"I won't," Elizabeth calls back to them as she heads down the sidewalk searching for her exiled father and brother.

A few seconds later, they both come up the sidewalk from down the street. Quickly, she walks over to them.

"Hey, guys," she hugs both. "Angie saved you two a seat in the back left-hand corner. Thanks for ironing my gown this morning, Dad. There was so much traffic on campus today having to pick up the hat, I just didn't have time."

"Not a problem," Ernest says holding a large camera. "Elizabeth, I still don't think I have enough pictures. Let me get one more with you and your brother, and then a couple maybe over by the church."

"Okay, Dad," Elizabeth says. She throws her arm around Luke, who throws his around her, slapping her first in the back of the head. They smile, and Elizabeth starts to laugh as Ernest quickly snaps off two or three more pictures.

Luke turns to her while Ernest adjusts his camera. "I'm going to run on inside for a minute," he says in a low voice.

"Front, right-hand side," she cuts her eyes toward the church. "But don't be long. Dad and I'll be there in just a few minutes."

"Okay," Luke replies and turns toward his father. "Well, y'all stay out here and take some more pictures."

"All right," Ernest says knowingly. He's no fool. Recognizing the stall, he plays along.

"Dad," Luke says, "I'm going to run in there and use the bathroom. I'll see you at our seats."

"Okay." Ernest holds the camera up once again. "Now, Elizabeth, stand over there by that tree and look smart."

"If you insist," she says.

Other families mill about outside the church. They take photos and give gifts in little envelopes. Meanwhile, Luke runs inside and maneuvers through the pews to where his mother sits.

"Hey, everybody," Luke smiles and leans over to hug Pearl and Melena. They all smile and say hello.

"You going to sit here with us?" Melena asks, fishing.

"No," he says shaking Joshua gently by the shoulders until he laughs. "Elizabeth has a seat saved for me with one of her little friends. But we're headed out for beers together afterwards, right?"

"We sure are," Blackwell says. He leans back, arms crossed comfortably. "Good," Luke says. "I'll see you guys afterward."

He turns down the aisle to head for the back corner of the church. By this time, the chapel has filled up considerably. Standing up in her seat, Angie waves him down as he passes by and Luke slides down the pew to take one of the two seats beside her.

Minutes later, Ernest and Elizabeth enter the church together. She's proud to walk in with her father, but she still hopes Melena doesn't see them.

With the ceremony beginning in ten minutes, the chapel bustles with people going to and from their seats. Camouflaged, Ernest slips into the crowd unseen.

Elizabeth's plan seems to be working since Ernest blends into the large group the way that Melena and her crowd has blended in at the front of the church.

Trying to be as cheerful as possible, Elizabeth fights off the nervous tension lingering around Ernest as his eyes dart around the room. His anxiety grows.

He wonders where they are, the son that left him, and the grandson he's never seen. Their absence pains him as if the sprouts of his genetic tree were suddenly severed and taken from him. His dark, weathered eyes look at each child's face searching for resembhlance to his own.

"Come on, Dad," Elizabeth says and leads Ernest down the far left-hand aisle. "There's Luke right there."

She waves at Angie and Ernest hurries down the pew to sit with them. He sits down and pats his hair as if it had been tousled in getting through the pew.

"Okay then," Elizabeth says to herself. She motions to the three of them and calls from the end of the pew. "I'll see you guys once

I'm an official graduate."

"Good luck," Angie says. She has one more semester to go.

Elizabeth takes her seat in the pews at the very front of the church with the other graduates. She sits and glances at a few scattered and familiar faces, wishing she had something to read.

Nothing to entertain herself with, she stares at her hands and waits for the production to begin. *This doesn't feel the way I thought it would feel,* she thinks, settling back as the first speaker takes the podium.

I thought it would feel like something. Something big and I thought I would throw my hat, but I don't think that'll happen, not here. I thought someone would have champagne too. Didn't they have champagne at Blackwell's graduation?

An hour and a half later, Elizabeth files down the aisle with the rest of the graduates, both sides of the family watching her every move. She waves to the members in the front as she passes and stage whispers that she'll meet them downstairs.

As Elizabeth passes at the back of the church, she waves to Ernest who looks somewhat troubled. Meet me outside, she points to Luke and him.

Some of the crowd filters out of the church and some downstairs. Elizabeth waves and walks over to Ernest, Luke and Angie as they come out into the now glaring May sunshine.

Ernest's eyes are red and his face contorts as if he were trying to hold something in.

"Hey, Angie," Elizabeth says, "*um,* why don't you meet me downstairs, *huh?*"

Angie nods and turns to Luke and Ernest. "It was very nice to meet you, Mr. Starling."

"Nice to meet you, too," Ernest manages to say. As she walks to the door, Luke turns to Ernest and hugs him.

"You going to be okay, boy?" he asks using his most endearing name for his father. Luke pulls back and looks at him.

"Yeah, I'm fine," Ernest says. "You go on." Luke turns and nods at Elizabeth.

Luke grabs him by the arm, "I'll call you later, Dad. Drive safely," he says and turns to head toward the basement of the church.

Elizabeth steps toward Ernest and frowns very hard as she sees a tear escape and roll down his cheek. She throws her arm around his shoulder.

"I saw them sitting up there," Ernest says. "That must have been the little boy with them."

"Yeah," she says quietly.

Ernest blows out a loud gust of air from his large chest. "I'll be fine," he says. "It just breaks my heart that those children will never know me. I'll probably die and they'll never know who I was."

"Don't say that, Dad," she says. "Somehow, some way, I'm not going to let that happen."

"Oh, it's not yours to trouble with," he says trying to shake her off, a bit ashamed of revealing his deepest feelings. "Look, you go on and do what you have to do. I'm going to head home now."

Ernest stands up a little taller and his voice grows firm though it still has a brittle quality.

Elizabeth worries. "Dad, are you going to be all right?"

"Don't worry about me. I'll be fine. You just go on and enjoy yourself. You deserve it."

"Thanks." She hugs him again.

"I'll see you later," he says choking.

"Bye, Dad. Be careful. I love you."

"I love you, too." Ernest quickly turns and walks away, overcome by his emotions.

Elizabeth watches him from behind as he moves off toward the car. She allows herself a moment of vexation before dismissing it for the sake of the day.

*Everything is so stupid*, she thinks. *Why does everything have to be so utterly stupid?*

She shrugs her shoulders as she turns back toward the church to look for the stairs down to the basement. Elizabeth puts on her best smile as she goes to greet the rest of her family.

--⊶⊙⊜⊷--

Cicadas, thriving in the summer heat, screech loudly outside Melena's window.

Melena looks down at her watch. Two months have passed since her last hospital visit and she's been strong enough to work, the work she knows has to change her life. Her legs ache from sitting on the floor of her new apartment with boxes, files and documents strewn about her in untidy piles.

This tired court debris decorates her new apartment home and continues to drive her life as the law demands. Melena looks up and shakes her head, irritation etched into her face.

One of the three children in the apartment above her roller-skates loudly back and forth across her ceiling.

Melena thinks, *That little girl must really slam her foot down.*

The noise makes her worry about her life's accomplishments; like maybe she was never supposed to hear such things as upstairs neighbors. She never did before, and now she must, in her fifties.

Since five a.m. this morning, Melena's been sifting, organizing and reorganizing the information to find what the lawyer needs.

Melena's mind works like a sieve. She collects only the most essential monetary or adulterous happenings. How does one sift through her own painful history, without reliving it?

The past must be turned into a patchwork quilt of understanding, but Melena can't figure out how to sew hers just yet. Tears start coming to her eyes.

*If I had money like him,* she thinks, *I wouldn't be sitting here doing this. But I don't, do I? Nope, and you want to know why I don't have the kind of money he does?*

Because he said, "No, honey, you don't need to go to school and get an education. You need to stay home and take care of our children. I'll worry about the money." Where has that left me?

A multitude of papers clutched in her hand, Melena leans back against her bed and looks down at her watch again.

"Ten thirty," she says. "I have to make a decision."

Melena's former lawyer still holds documents pertinent to the case, and Mr. Thornsby's office appears to have joined Sandra in making it impossible to obtain copies of the information.

Every time the Starlings go to court, the judge says the same thing: "Case continued." It's like the sound of a lock closing on a prison cell.

*Ernest is the devil*, she thinks, *and they're all in league with him, all the lawyers and the judges, everyone.*

Melena's side begins to hurt. She holds on to it tightly with her left hand. Every time she steps forward, something happens that pushes her back.

Either her strange illness plagues her with sleepless nights and the inability to digest her food, or the legal system prevents her from resolving her divorce to get everything she knows she deserves.

Reaching for her purse across the piles of paper, Melena lets the bag fall down in her lap. She opens the top and searches through the lipsticks, address books and Sweet'N Low packs for a pink, plastic pill case.

Finding it, she pops open the top that contains her necessary pain pills. She breaks a particular blue pill into two and takes a sip of water before she swallows one half down.

The cordless phone sits on its stand across the room on her makeshift desk. The desk, an old card table, served as the kids' dining table on holidays in her former home.

Melena pulls herself upward, holding onto the bed, and picks up the phone to take it into the living room. She slumps down on the couch, address book in hand and looks up a phone number.

The buttons beep as she pushes them.

A gruff, old voice picks up on the other line and begrudgingly she says, "Yes, hi, Lou. It's Melena. How are you doing today?"

"Well, I'm doing fine," Lou says. "It's a bit too hot out for me, but besides that, things are going well. Were you able to obtain those tax documents from either office?"

"No," Melena's teeth clench between her words. "I wasn't able to get a damn thing, pardon my language."

"Oh," Lou sits down behind the desk he's had for a lifetime. This case has been one of his most difficult.

"I suspect if I was in your situation, I would curse, too, Melena. I suppose our next step is for me to go back and file with the judge."

Melena stares at a giant brass and wood carved clock on the table across from her. It was her father's.

"Listen, Lou," she says, "I hate doing this. But the way this thing has dragged on, and the difficulty in getting these documents transferred, not to mention the costs of hiring new experts to study them, I think I'm going to have to do something I really don't want to do."

Melena bites her lip.

"Lou," she says, "heaven knows you're a saint, but I have to go back to Mrs. McNair as my attorney. She's holding years of evidence that I can't pay to process again."

Melena sighs. "I'm up against the wall here, Lou."

"Melena," Lou says kindly, "I completely understand. Don't you fret one moment about it. I just wish I could help you get this thing resolved."

"Yeah, me, too," Melena says thinking about her next phone call. "I've got to go now. I've got to get things moving again."

"You know, you don't sound very good, Melena. Are you feeling all right?"

"No. I'm not feeling all right. I don't know if I'll ever feel all

345

right again. My life seems like it has never been right or maybe it was and I don't remember."

Lou looks at the picture of his own wife on his desk. He wonders why men have lost their sense of duty.

"You know you can call me for advice anytime, day or night, if you need."

"Yes," she says, "thank you, Lou. I'll speak to you soon."

"Okay, bye now."

Melena presses the off button, hating herself for having to dial Sandra's number. She waits for Danielle, Sandra's secretary, to pick up on the other line.

"Good morning, Mrs. McNair's office," Danielle says. "How can I help you?"

"Hello, this is Melena Starling. Is Mrs. McNair available?"

"No ma'am, she isn't here at the moment. Can I take a message for you?"

"Yes, could you please have Mrs. McNair call me as soon as possible, and please tell her it's extremely urgent."

"No problem, Mrs. Starling," Danielle says eagerly. She loved hearing Melena storm out of Sandra's office the day she fired her.

"She should be back from court late in the afternoon."

"Thank you," Melena says and hangs up the phone.

*I'll just take a little nap*, she thinks holding her side. *That'll give the pill time to kick in before I have to do some more work again.*

Melena, dejected, stands and walks back into her bedroom. She shuts off the light and the bedroom goes dark except for the summer sun filtering through filmy shades.

The plush blankets on Melena's bed make a soft, rustling sound as she pulls them back. Crawling under them, she lies down stiffly, trying to mentally transcend the pain.

# The Passing of Two Years

TWO YEARS MORE HAVE GONE by, bringing the total to seven. Seven shameful years of bitter battle filled with reports from private investigators who spied with their cameras and audio devices on Luke, Elizabeth, Ernest and Melena.

No need to spy on Blackwell anymore though someone probably did at some time, or maybe he was recorded on telephone calls at the house.

One private dick per side, they tried to track every financial movement made with receipts and visual confirmation of things like motorcycles, young women, expensive gifts or trips.

With everyone convinced of their own convictions in this matter, not one of them can or will stop it. They just smile for the pictures.

--➤➣●◖--➤

In November of 2001, Luke, Melena and Elizabeth plan to spend the approaching Thanksgiving holiday with Blackwell, Katherine and the kids.

These last few years, Luke and Elizabeth have made an effort to alternate spending each holiday with one side of the divided family. Their attempts haven't always worked.

In wait for the pending January divorce trial, Melena and the kids seem to get along. They sometimes share their lives over the phone during lunches stolen away from the office. These communications go smoothly until Melena becomes sick again.

Now, she lies in a room on the fourth floor of the Larnee Community Hospital on a Saturday afternoon. When she came in this time, it had been six months since her last overnight visit to a medical facility.

Blackwell, in Europe on business, cannot look in on her, and Luke is out of town until tomorrow. As soon as Elizabeth gets word of her mother's whereabouts and condition, she leaves Hollow Town.

Elizabeth travels with her current boyfriend and heads immediately for the hospital. When she arrives, she has a number of things she knows she has to determine. Does Mom have clothes? Does Mom have a toothbrush? What about the other stuff?

Past mistakes of neglect have been drilled into her psyche and, for some reason, Elizabeth didn't think of these nurturing type questions on her own. Except for Barbies, she never was the doll type. Maybe she's selfish, but Melena always wanted her to go play and have her own fun.

Slowly, she pushes open the heavy door leading to Melena's room. Inside, it looks cold and shaded though the sun shines outside the thickly curtained window.

Elizabeth walks straight in and smiles at her mother who appears to have just awakened.

"Hey, Mom," Elizabeth says, trailed by a tall guy with long black hair who moves across the floor like a quiet ghost.

"Curtis and I drove up as soon as Katherine called."

"Hey," Melena says smoothing down her tangled hair.

"Curtis, y'all don't look at me. My hair's a mess."

Elizabeth goes to the bed and hugs Melena around her neck to avoid disturbing her IV's.

"Hey, Mrs. Starling," Curtis says. He sits out silently in the corner where Elizabeth can watch his mysterious, gothic demeanor.

"How they treating you, Mom?" she asks. "No solid foods?"

"No," she shakes her head, "but I had some green Jello earlier, and I've been drinking ginger ale."

Still held at an emotional distance by her mother, Elizabeth observes her fondly. She hopes her face looks as youthful as her mother's when she is fifty.

"You know, Mom, you don't look bad at all," Elizabeth says. "When did the pain start coming on this time?"

"Dr. Bowden ran some more tests on my pancreas last week because I was in agony day and night. Sure enough, it was enlarged again."

Elizabeth asks, "And no reason why?"

"Right," Melena presses the button on the hand monitor to raise herself up in the bed.

"Finally, I got so weak because I couldn't eat that they put me in here to regain my strength."

"Did they find anything new?"

"No, no," Melena says looking toward the door, "but something strange happened here yesterday morning." She tugs on the pillow behind her head, yawns and continues.

"When I got here, they took me down to the basement level for a CT scan and a few other tests that I think they've probably run on me a thousand times."

"You know what kind of trouble I have with my veins and people drawing blood from me." She says, "They're just so thin and tiny, Curtis, that most nurses have a hard time with it."

He nods and Elizabeth sits down in a chair beside her.

"So," Melena says, "this nurse was running my tests and he brought me down in the wheelchair where he and I were the only ones. I mean, I didn't see any one at all in the hallway or hear anyone in the other rooms."

Elizabeth knows her mother's suspicions intensify like an alarm system in such vulnerable situations.

"He came over to the chair," Melena says, "grabbed my arm without saying a word and shoved that needle into what he thought was a vein. I looked at him and thought, oh, boy. It hurt and after a few seconds he realized he didn't get one."

"You know how I am. I talk to everyone. So I said, 'Oh, you know usually they have to call someone from Pediatrics to take my blood because my veins are so small.'"

Melena pauses and Elizabeth nods expectantly at her.

"And?"

"And, he got in my face, looked me in the eye, backed up and said, 'Ma'am, would you please let me do my job?'"

Melena and Elizabeth's eyes get bigger. Melena thinks most men are bad.

"So, I thought, *whoa*, because he was too aggressive like he might snap so I kept quiet to see what would happen. Then he went back at my arm again and kept stabbing me and stabbing me with that needle. He couldn't find one vein and, oh, gosh, was I hurting."

"Who is he?" Elizabeth interrupts. "Where is he? I want to know who this asshole is right now."

This moment is Elizabeth's big chance to stick up for her mother and show her just how much she cares.

"Oh, honey," Melena says, "just listen. So, I said to him again real nice and calm, maybe you should call someone from Pediatrics, I really think it would be better."

Melena looks at Curtis.

"You understand now, here I am sitting in the damn X-ray room next to a cold slab. We're in the very basement of the hospital, down some lonely corridor and I'm alone with this strange man in this room."

"When I said that, he backed away from me again and threw his arms down and said, 'Ma'am, I am trying to do my job. Are you going to keep me from doing my job or are you going to sit there and be quiet and let me do it?'"

Elizabeth's jaw drops and her hand flies to her mouth.

"I looked at him," Melena says, "and I said if you come near me one more time I will scream louder than you ever heard anyone scream. I told him to go get someone else right that second because he was not going to touch me again. Look at my arm."

Melena pulls the sheet back from across her chest.

Elizabeth leans over to look at the oval shaped, purple and black bruise now exposed on six to seven inches of Melena's right arm.

"Holy shit," Elizabeth says eyeing the diameter and intensity.

Elizabeth asks, "Well, what the hell happened then?" Curtis watches their exchange.

"He stood there looking at me for a few minutes," Melena says, "and I kept thinking, he's going to kill me. He could just kill me with a needle and poison and no one would ever know what happened. I bet that's what your father tried to do for years."

Elizabeth ignores her. "He stared at me," Melena says, "for what seemed forever, then went outside for a while and came back to bring me upstairs."

Elizabeth stands and starts to head out the door.

"Elizabeth," Melena asks, "where are you going?"

"I'm going to the nurses' station to find out where the hell this man is. He can't push you around that way, and look what he's done to your arm!"

"Elizabeth don't," Melena says, "I've already talked to the hospital administrator. She's been by twice to see me already."

"And? What is the jerk's name?"

"They don't know yet," Melena replies. She calmly tries to keep Elizabeth from causing a scene the way her father would. "But she's trying to find out."

"You mean to tell me," Elizabeth shouts, "they don't know who's working where in their own damn hospital? How do they plan on keeping you from running into this guy again?"

"She's working on it," Melena says. "The lady promised me she'd make sure I did not see this man again the whole time I'm here."

Elizabeth turns to walk out the door. Melena calls after her, "Elizabeth Starling, you get back here."

"Mom, it will be fine. I just want to go get a few answers. I am not going to yell or be bitchy about it."

Elizabeth doesn't wait for her mother's response but instead goes down the hall. Curtis looks at Melena and shrugs his shoulders while Melena leans back shaking her head.

"You know, Curtis," Melena says, "her hair is getting so long again."

He mumbles back, "Yes, it is."

After a ten-minute conversation with the nurses, Elizabeth feels little more informed, though the station head swears to her Melena will not see any more male staff.

With this news, Elizabeth returns to Melena's room where her mother and Curtis watch television. They talk about the "Discovery Channel" while trying to find topics to divert Melena's mind and make her feel more at ease.

"Do you have plenty of underwear, Mom?"

"Yes," she says, "Diana and I thought of that this time."

"How about clean socks and a toothbrush?"

"Yes," Melena says thinking about the time she spent days in the hospital without a toothbrush or fresh underwear.

"We made sure I had everything. You know, that Diana is so sweet bringing me to the hospital and looking after me. I really have some great friends."

Seeing Elizabeth fret over her now, Melena is reminded that her daughter cares about her. For today, she doesn't think about the choices Elizabeth has made, those choices that feel to Melena like ultimate betrayal, each one another dagger in her heart.

Hours later Elizabeth and Curtis prepare to leave, but not before Elizabeth comes back into the room with her arms full of several confiscated items.

"Your heater's not working right," Elizabeth says. "I got you some extra blankets and I just told the nurse to have someone come check it."

"I think you're right," Melena says, "and you know I hate to be cold."

"That's why I got these." Elizabeth lays the blankets on top of her mother. Wrapping Melena's feet tightly into a cocoon, Elizabeth laughs and tucks the extra fabric under Melena's legs.

"You won't get cold now," she smiles, "and there's plenty of ginger ale and fresh ice right here on the table if you want it."

Curtis says, "I hope you feel better."

"Thank you, Curtis, and thank you, angel, for stopping in. You all better get a move on if you're going to make it back home before it's too late."

Melena, comforted by the extra attention, maintains her excitement about Thanksgiving. The thought of her kids together makes her very happy.

"Oh, Mom, don't worry about us." Elizabeth leans over and hugs Melena.

"We'll be fine," she says. "I love you, Mom."

"I love you, too." Melena pats her back, "Be sweet."

Elizabeth pulls the heavy door closed behind her and walks down the hall with Curtis.

"I wish she didn't have to be in there," she tells him.

Curtis says, "It's better than her being home alone." They talk about loneliness and finding some dinner as they walk to the car.

On his way back to town around noon the next day, Luke drives to the hospital. When he arrives at Melena's door, he finds her asleep, and so he quietly sits down in the chair next to her and allows his eyes to close.

A little later Melena wakes up slightly, startled to see him sitting there.

"Luke," she says and he jerks in the chair.

"Hey, Mom," Luke says sitting more upright.

"I didn't know you were here," she says. "How long have you been sitting there?"

Luke looks at his watch. "I guess I got here about an hour or so ago. You were asleep so I thought I'd wait for you to wake up."

Melena's holiday-inspired beneficence extends to all three of her children.

She wipes the sleep from her eyes and presses the button on the bed remote to raise herself up. "I bet I look awful. Do I look awful?"

"No, you don't look awful," he says always proud of his mother's beauty. "Besides, you're supposed to be resting and not worrying how you look."

"Luke, hand me that ginger ale from over there, and the little ice bucket, too."

Luke stands up and hands her the can from off the shelf. It's his turn now to be dutiful to Melena and he needs the experience as much as she needs the little things he does to help her. He looks in the plastic container.

"There's no ice. It all melted," he says. "I'll be right back."

He turns from her room and goes to the ice machine across from the nurse's station. The brunette at the desk smiles at him and a few minutes later he walks back in with ice and a few Styrofoam cups.

"I thought you might need extras," he says.

"You want some of my ginger ale?"

"No, thanks," Luke sits back down. "I'm fine."

A nurse raps on the door and smiles as she enters the room. "Hi there, Mrs. Starling, I just came to check on the IV. It's doing a lot better now, right?"

"Oh, yes," Melena says, "much better, but you know this bruise over here still looks pretty bad."

"I sure hate that," the nurse says. "Sometimes messing with tiny veins can be so tricky even if you've been drawing blood for years."

Melena motions at Luke.

"This is one of my handsome sons," she says.

"Well, hi there, handsome son. We sure like your mom."

"Thank you," Luke says, "I sure like her, too."

"He's a good boy, Mrs. Starling. I can tell. Well, I'll be back to check on you in a couple of hours. If you need me, you know what to do."

"Okay," Melena says, "thank you."

Melena waits as she watches the heavy-set nurse walk out the door. She whispers and leans toward Luke.

"That's the nice one," Melena says. "I'm so glad she's back working again. One of them is so mean that I wouldn't dare ask her for anything."

"Which one?" Luke asks.

"Oh, it's nothing. I don't even think she'll be back on duty again for a while." Melena's pain medicine elevates her mood considerably. It allows her to forget about the things that really bother her.

"So, how was your trip?" she asks.

"It was good," Luke says. He thinks about the test car he drove yesterday and how Melena would freak out if she knew.

He had that car burning up the track so fast the owner made him drive it twice with a brand new set of tires on it the second time.

"Elizabeth came with Curtis yesterday." She smoothes the blanket down over her. "He sure is a quiet boy."

"Yeah," Luke says, "wonder how long he'll last."

"I know," Melena shakes her head.

"She does break up with them pretty quickly, but I think she does it because she realizes they aren't the one, so she doesn't see a reason to hold on. At least, that's what I hope."

"I think you're right," Luke says reaching for the television control. "How about a little TV?"

"You have to be the navigator," Melena says.

Luke slides his chair closer to her bed and turns it so that he is adjacent to her facing the television on the wall.

She says, "You'll have to turn the volume up so we can both hear it."

They watch TV together for countless hours, sometimes chatting, while other times Melena dozes off lulled to sleep by her medications.

Luke falls asleep in his chair, too, waking up with stiffness in his neck. After a while, Luke goes home to take a shower and take care of a few things before he returns to the hospital around dinnertime.

It has been a long time since Melena and he have gotten along so well. Even if the affection she shows him stems only from her holiday plans, Luke doesn't care.

He needs it. He's already grown distant and cold in his relationships.

For the next couple of days, Luke spends all his free time at the hospital with Melena, before and after work, gladly picking up the slack for his two siblings.

Elizabeth, stuck at her office on the other side of Hollow Town, manages two affordable housing communities part-time and creates metal sculpture in the off hours.

Melena hates her daughter's choice of employment with Mancon, but that fact is another she's not dwelling on now. Elizabeth calls twice daily to speak with her, and with Luke, when he happens to be there.

The Thanksgiving holiday approaches and everything has such a happy, loving air of family to it. This emotion is so rare a thing for the Starlings, and it's a wonder how much better it makes their lives seem.

They all think they're doing fine behind their walls.

Around five-thirty p.m. on Wednesday, Luke steps off the elevator and walks down the hall toward Melena's room. He thinks about the files on his desk at work and how he desperately wants to throw them all in the trash.

Running his hand through his full head of dark brown hair, he stops as he approaches the door. Something is wrong.

Melena's voice trails through the cracked door in an all too familiar tone. She sounds angry, possibly crying, and she talks to a man who responds to her in a soft, consoling voice. Luke taps the door and pushes it open gently.

"Hey, Mom," he says stepping in.

His hands fall flat to his sides as he recognizes the furious state of emotion written across her face. Glaring at him with fire in her eyes, she barely nods and the stranger interrupts the uncomfortable silence between them.

"Hi, there," the man says standing. "My name is John. I'm the hospital chaplain."

Luke holds out a rigid hand, "Nice to meet you." He looks around wondering what to do.

Melena continues to stare at her son.

"Can you come back in a half hour or so?" she asks. "We're in the middle of something right now."

"*Uh*, sure," Luke says stunned and turns to go out the door. He pulls it close behind him and shakes his head as he walks back down the hall.

*What the hell is this about,* he thinks, *a chaplain?* Wrestling with his confusion, Luke takes the elevator down to the hospital gift shop for a few magazines and some coffee.

In the tiny store, he flips through several publications glancing at pictures of movie stars and cars while he tries to occupy his time.

The older lady behind the counter watches him fondly, thinking him a new father. She smiles at him as he comes around with one *Car and Driver* magazine and one *Better Homes and Gardens*.

"You must have a pretty young wife upstairs somewhere having a baby?" she asks Luke.

"No, ma'am," he says hating to be reminded of his own loneliness. Luke hasn't cared about anyone since Emily. He pulls out his wallet.

"I'm here visiting my mom."

"Oh, well I could've sworn you were a father-to-be," she says. "You've got that nervous look about you as if you were expecting."

As Luke takes his change from the lady, he forces a polite smile, but it disappears into irritation as he turns to go out the door. The coffee shop sits across from the gift shop and Luke picks up his usual espresso drink, comforted by the aroma of the strong brew.

Back in the elevator, he checks his watch and figures he can wait outside Melena's door for the next few minutes.

Standing by her room, he listens for any audible clue as to the presence of the chaplain inside Melena's room.

All he hears is the trailing murmurs of their discussion. A bit later, John emerges from the room and straightens his shirt as he steps into the hallway.

He nods to Luke.

"Have a good evening," he says quickly walking away.

Luke enters Melena's room and sets the *Better Homes and Garden* magazine down on the table beside her bed.

"How you doing, Mom?" He sits in the chair across from her.

"Not too good, Luke." Her hands cross in front of her and stay there, hard as stone.

"Why did you have the chaplain here, Mom?"

"Because Luke, I needed to talk to someone. I needed to talk to someone who has morals and a good Christian sense of right and wrong."

"Oh, okay," he says.

Now that Melena has come off her main pain medicine, her renderings of Luke's life as a despot have grown to gargantuan proportions. For today and the foreseeable future, he's amongst the fallen.

"Tell me this, Luke," she says eyeballing him, "how in the hell do you work for your father when you know what kind of man he is?"

Luke's eyes fall to his feet and his shoulders slump low. He keeps his voice quiet and controlled.

This ability to compartmentalize emotionally came to him when he was very young whenever his parents would fight or she would leave. Box everything inside and put it on ice. His method is the only thing that keeps him from snapping at her accusations. Sometimes, he just wants to yell back the words that have stayed in his mind for one reason or another.

But will he ever speak?

"*Huh?*" he asks knowing but wishing she would stop.

"You've never wanted to believe anything I said about your father," she says, "but I know you know the sort of man he is."

It breaks her heart that all her children just don't stand up for her the way she would stand up for them.

"You know he had affairs. I even have the damn proof, but you won't look at that tape because all you care about is money."

Desperate, Luke holds his pose for another few seconds and looks up at her.

*I can't look at that tape*, he thinks. *I don't need to. Seeing him outside of a hotel with a woman won't change anything in my life. Whatever happened is over.*

"What do you want me to do, Mom?" he asks slowly. "Do you want me to quit my job? Do you want me to sell my house and my car? Would that make you feel better? Because if that's what you want me to do, I will."

Melena's muscles tighten and a wave of heat rushes through her, inflaming her further. If she could, she would throw something through the window.

She says, "You're just like him, damn it." Her eyes flash wildly.

"You've been corrupted by him because you've worked for him for so long. You know he is Satan. Your father is that evil, and you work for him. How does that feel to work for Satan, Luke?"

The facts of Melena's life, her bills and lack of money overwhelm her with fear.

"He's a lying, cheating, corrupted abomination of sin and evil and you work for him and take his damned money. You don't care about anyone but Luke and getting what Luke wants."

She screams shrilly, "Now, your sister's working for him, too. Neither of you ever cared a damn about what happened to me. All you care about is yourselves."

Melena got excited about Thanksgiving with her children, then she got sick and in her path back out of the hospital, she stumbled upon the anger she had buried.

"Here." Her hands pat the bed. "Here, I have suffered, miserable and imprisoned by this divorce for seven years. What have you done to help me? Nothing. You two go on and live your happy lives.

"You aren't my children," she says. "You know I never would've treated my mother the way you two have treated me. I would have fought for my mother."

"Just because Blackwell chose to cut Dad out of his life, does not mean we have to," Luke snaps back. "For you, his choices mandate certain behavior for the rest of us, and that's not fair."

He doesn't care how mad Melena gets.

"Blackwell's choice belongs to him and our choice is ours," Luke says. "My father is still my father, no matter what he's done, and I'm proud of the relationship I have with him. I'm not going to feel guilty about it."

Melena grabs her side in pain and flings her head back against the pillow.

"Oh," she says, "you certainly are something special, aren't you?"

"Don't you dare bring your brother into this. Blackwell loves me and he has done everything he can for me. At least he knows right from wrong."

Luke shakes his head and stares at the lines in the marble floor. He keeps his head down as Melena's words rush over him in waves. Following the lines to his feet, his eyes stop at the tip of his shoe and he stands.

"Mom, I'm going to go now," he says.

"I really wish this hadn't happened."

"Yeah, me, too," she snaps. "I wish life never would've happened."

Luke walks to the door as Melena stares out the window. The door shuts behind him and she turns toward the phone. Holding her blankets tight in her hands, Melena counts to ten in slow, deep breaths trying to calm down.

A tear rolls from her eye and she dials Katherine.

In the hallway, toward the elevator, Luke nods absently as one of the ladies at the nurse's station calls out to him to have a good night. He pushes the down arrow on the wall and the button lights up as he waits for the elevator.

*What just happened?* he asks himself. *I just came up here to see her, and now ... god.*

--≻≕≕☯≓≔≺--

Thanksgiving Day, nine-thirty in the morning, Elizabeth smiles as Fancy, her best friend, knocks at her front door. After Melena and Luke's exchange during his hospital visit, her other holiday plans vanished immediately.

Elizabeth sets down a batter-covered stirring spoon and rushes over to throw the glass-paned door open wide. Each pane sports a Power Puff Girl from a Valentine window decal set.

"Happy Turkey Day," Elizabeth says hugging Fancy as she comes through the door in a sweatshirt and toboggan, her hair poking out in two pigtails.

"Happy Turkey Day to you, too." Fancy looks at the television over Elizabeth's shoulder. "I see you got the parade going on the old TV set so I must be in the right place."

"Yes," Elizabeth smiles and shuts the front door behind them, "these are the pre-festivities festivities. I'm relaxing and fixing a few things before I head to Curtis' house. His roommate's making all the food, but since I'm not going to get to eat Mom's cornbread, I figured screw it, I'll make it my damn self."

"As well you should," Fancy unwinds her thick green scarf from her neck.

"I think my day is going to consist of some cakes and trifles I picked up at the store and three Jet Li movies." Fancy smiles big with her bright, green eyes. "I'm so excited," she says. "I'm going to sit on my couch all day and eat."

"No, you're not," Elizabeth replies pulling her into the kitchen. "Fancy, you just have to come to their house. It's so old and cool. Plus, there's going to be so much food."

"I don't know." Fancy sets a brown paper bag down on the table. "I really think I just want to stay home."

"Well, we'll just have to fight because I won't allow it," Elizabeth takes a rectangular pan from the cabinet below.

"You are not staying home by yourself on Thanksgiving. You are coming with me and you're going to like it. I refuse to take no for an answer." Elizabeth looks at the bag on the table.

"So, Fancy, what's in the bag?"

"Oh, you know," she sits down. "Just a little Seven."

"You read my mind," Elizabeth opens the cabinet above her sink. She pulls out two glasses. "Here, can you believe it? I even have ice in the freezer."

Elizabeth looks back at the bowl of cornbread batter, hands the glasses to Fancy and shakes her head.

"Fucking holidays!"

Elizabeth pours the batter into the greased pan.

"Luke's coming," she says. "He said he's going to get there about one, but he's always late and I think he probably feels weird coming."

The batter oozes down. "You got to make your own good time though, right? I mean, at least he and I get to hang out."

The ice clinks into the glasses. Fancy has her own reasons for coveting solitude on the holidays. She pours the liquor.

"You're still upset about everything, *huh*?" she asks.

"Oh, no," Elizabeth says, "I'm not upset about anything."

"A month ago we had a nice little Thanksgiving planned. It's Mom's year for the holidays and we were going to get together me, her and Luke, that's if Blackwell and Katherine went to her parent's house, but not now."

"How much Seven Up do you want?"

"I don't care. You fix it." Elizabeth puts the pan in the oven.

"You know this is some kind of shit," she says. "We're at war, we could all die tomorrow from a bomb or a plane out of the sky, and a family can't get together for one measly holiday."

She thinks, *So little time, why spend it angry?*

"We can't even find enough damn decency and kindness," she says, "for one stupid holiday. All those people died and they never got to have another holiday with their families." Elizabeth wipes her hands.

Fancy holds a glass out to her. "You still haven't talked to your mom, *huh*?"

"No," Elizabeth says and takes the drink out of her hand. She touches Fancy's glass.

"Happy Thanksgiving," they say and smile. Elizabeth takes a big swallow, draining half of it in the first gulp.

"Blackwell emailed me two days ago," Elizabeth says. "He asked me what I was doing for Thanksgiving. You know, I called them twice last week, never heard back and then I get an email. Well, I left him a message and said I had plans already. I couldn't keep waiting to hear from them."

"What about your dad?" Fancy asks.

"Hold this," Elizabeth says. Fancy holds a Corning Ware dish while Elizabeth fills it with the ingredients for a green bean casserole.

"This year wasn't supposed to be his year so he made plans with his new girlfriend. I think we're going to see him tomorrow."

"What's this one like?"

Fancy's heard all about Ernest's previous girlfriends.

"Oh, I don't know." Elizabeth doesn't really care; none of them have ever lasted.

"At least, she's his age. You know all I want is for us to pretend like we're a family once in a while," she says.

"Is that so impossible? I wish we could get through one holiday together, but who am I kidding? That'll never happen. We'll never be a family."

"You can't expect so much now," Fancy says. She knows she has the answers.

"You guys are still wrapped up in the whole divorce thing, and until it's over, everyone will keep acting crazy."

Elizabeth wonders, *Is that the future of the Starlings, to be crazy until it's all over?*

Fancy sets the dish down on the counter.

"That looks good," she says and takes another sip of her drink. "My mom always used to make that. So, can you take a break now? Can we watch the parade?"

Elizabeth puts the dish in the oven on the rack underneath the cornbread and they step into Elizabeth's tiny living room and plop down on the couch.

"I'm getting a dog," Elizabeth says and takes another sip of her Seven and Seven. She almost finishes it.

"That'll be good." Fancy props her feet up on the coffee table. "I love the cats. Hey look, there's Pickachu."

"I love Pickachu," Elizabeth says. She stares at the enormous yellow balloon as it's pulled down the New York City street.

"What about you?" Elizabeth asks. "Why didn't you go to your mom's?"

"I'll see her this weekend," Fancy says, "and I have work tomorrow. Who all's going to be at Curtis's?"

Fancy tries to act like she doesn't care about a whole lot, especially being alone on the holiday, and her charade comes off pretty convincing.

"Curtis, Trip, I think Jeff, then Luke, me and you." Elizabeth nudges her in the side.

"I've got two bottles of wine so we can get intoxicated. How's that sound?"

"I can't get too f'd up," Fancy says. "I'll have to drive back and they live in the boonies."

"You could spend the night over there and leave early," Elizabeth says. "I have to leave early to go to Larnee tomorrow anyway."

She thinks about driving there for the second half of the holiday, which to her always seems contrived and pathetic.

Fancy says, "All right there, Skipper. You talked me into to it, but I'm going just like this."

"As well you should," Elizabeth says. "You're beautiful as ever. I just have to wait for that stuff to come out of the oven, then we are out of here."

"Cool."

"Hey," Elizabeth says, "let's have another drink, now. That way we'll be all right to drive before we head out."

Fancy drains her glass. "You fixing this one?"

"Of course, I am," Elizabeth says, "with sugar on top."

⋅⊷⩵◉⩵⊷⋅

The familial mishap of Thanksgiving passes and the kids move on blaming themselves for counting on anything other than turmoil. Luke and Elizabeth secure a Christmas Eve date with Ernest, and with it, rolled up into the package, Ernest's new girlfriend and her adult son.

This holiday night with its conjoined participants has become a grandiose event. Following dinner, the cheery group will make a late appearance at a Christmas party in one of Larnee's most famous homes. There by the hearth, Elizabeth, newly single since she told Curtis good-bye, will show a small sculpture commissioned by the wealthy hostess.

Outside their first stop, the wind chills the air as Elizabeth steps from Luke's car. Gathering her black pea coat around her, she tucks her nose under her scarf.

Ernest opens the front door of Vivian Banderly's house and says, "Merry Christmas, you two."

Dressed in a conservative gray sweater that Vivian picked out, Ernest helps Elizabeth with the holiday packages.

"Merry Christmas, Dad," they say and alternately embrace him. "Take those," Elizabeth says, "and I'll be in with the rest."

Luke and Ernest walk toward Vivian's house one after the other.

Elegant decorations glitter in the foyer of Vivian's home, and a huge fir rises toward the vaulted ceiling in the living room. Luke and Ernest place the presents at the base of the tree.

Vivian calls out to them, "Merry Christmas, Luke." Her voice is husky, sexy. "My hands are in the middle of something so you'll have to come see me in the kitchen."

"Be right there," Luke says.

Elizabeth walks in as Luke passes in front of her on his way to the kitchen. She stops to stare at an odd-looking elf standing four and a half feet tall. Its mechanical body moves robotically. She thinks it looks scary.

"Who are all these presents for?" Ernest asks.

Elizabeth joins him by the tree. "Well, they're our presents, silly. It's Christmas Eve and we have to open them, don't we?"

"You sure you want to do that here?"

Ernest never knows how to handle these things and he doesn't want to impose on Vivian and her son. Elizabeth wants to insert the three of them into Vivian's picturesque evening just so she can have a positive memory.

Ernest watches her place her packages, then rearrange the ones he and Luke set down.

"Yeah," Elizabeth says, "where else are we going to do it?" She fluffs the loops of the present's decorative ribbon and stands. "You don't have a tree and we're going to be here till late, so why not?"

"All right," Ernest says.

"Where's Vivian?" Elizabeth takes off her coat and unwraps her scarf. She's decided to like this woman and Vivian makes it easy.

"She's in the kitchen and Tate's upstairs. We've got tons of food and wine. I think she bought the whole grocery store." Ernest takes Elizabeth's coat from her and sets it down on a bench in the foyer.

"Merry Christmas, Vivian," Elizabeth says as she walks into the kitchen.

Vivian wheels around from the counter with a knife in her hand. Her bobbed, straight blond hair falls quickly into place.

"Merry Christmas, Elizabeth!" Vivian exclaims. "Don't you look pretty? Did you have a nice drive?"

"I did." Elizabeth looks around at the various hors d'oeuvres laid out on the counter top. "Who made all of this?"

"Well, I sure didn't," Vivian giggles. "I'm whipping up vegetables out of the bag. The turkey's nearly done and what do you want to drink, honey? We've got cases of wine or some beer if you'd like?"

Vivian and Ernest love to drink wine.

"Wine would be good, thanks."

"Ernest? Oh, there you are." Vivian smiles at Ernest as he walks in the kitchen. "Ernest, please fix Elizabeth and Luke something to drink."

"I'll just have a beer," Luke says grabbing a handful of pistachios.

Vivian turns from the stove. "Tate's girlfriend, Ashton, was here earlier. Too bad you kids didn't get to meet her. She's such a delightful girl, pretty and smart."

"That's right," Ernest hands Elizabeth a glass of wine. "She was valedictorian at State this year."

"I'll be damned," Elizabeth pops a piece of chocolate into her mouth. She has a brief moment of jealousy over this girl Ashton who she assumes has led a charmed life.

*Maybe if my family wasn't so dysfunctional,* Elizabeth thinks, *I could have been valedictorian, too. I'm so glad I didn't have to meet Ms. Ashton.*

"You know," Luke leans on his elbows, "they asked me to be valedictorian, but I was too busy to make any speeches."

"Oh, yeah," Elizabeth says.

Vivian hands Luke a carving knife. "Luke, honey, how about carving the bird for us? I'm ready to bring him out."

"Are you sure you want him to do that?" Elizabeth asks. "He might eat it all."

Elizabeth's really trying to fit into this charming scene that Ernest and Luke seem to naturally belong in. She still carries her own baggage that makes her feel an outsider to this perfect circle.

"Not if I can help it," Tate says striding into the kitchen. He matches Luke's and Ernest's six-foot-five height and looks like the boy in a Banana Republic ad.

"Merry Christmas," Luke and Elizabeth say.

"Merry Christmas to you, too. Good to see you guys. Luke, I believe you'll do a wonderful job carving that turkey, and I'll stand by to sample."

"Oh, Tate," Vivian laughs. "He's just saying that because he doesn't want to get stuck doing it."

Tate stretches toward the ceiling. "No, no. Honestly, Luke is your man."

No one really knows how Tate feels either since he and Vivian have suffered their own private tragedy, which they never talk about. Like Luke though, he's buried all his complicated feelings and sealed them in a well.

"So, Tate," Elizabeth takes her wine glass in hand. "I heard your girlfriend was valedictorian."

"Yeah," he pats his belly, "she gets it all from me."

They all laugh.

"Actually," Tate says, "she's really, really smart, and I'm, well, I'm not stupid. Let's just put it that way."

Luke asks, "How's it feel having a genius for a girlfriend?"

"It was daunting at first, but I just tease her whenever I can and that makes up for it. Hey, Ernest, how about handing me a beer out of the refrigerator?"

"Sure thing," he says.

"All we're waiting on now are the beans and the slicing of the turkey," Vivian says.

"Can I put anything on the table?" Elizabeth asks. She wants Vivian to like her, too, and she tries to be helpful.

"Let me see." Vivian looks around the room again. "You can take the rolls, the butter and, oh, here, let me get a dish for it. Ernest you go ahead and fill the carafes for the table."

*Carafes,* Elizabeth thinks. *Where are we, the fucking White House?*

Elizabeth walks into the dining room with the rolls and butter dish in her hands. Her jaw slackens at the sight of the sparkling table and the mirrored wall behind it, reflecting candlelight from the table.

Below the candles, Vivian's burgundy covered dining table is set elaborately for five people, seven courses.

*Who the hell set this table?* Elizabeth wonders.

Each setting has crystal water glasses and ornate, tinted crystal wine glasses. The wine glasses shine in the candlelight and have been placed on the table adjacent to name cards, which designate the seating.

*Red for me,* Elizabeth thinks, *she got that right.*

A huge spray in the center of the table draws Elizabeth's attention. Natural sprigs of foliage emerge from a swan-shaped holiday piece dusted with fake snow.

Elizabeth wonders what Melena would think of all this glamour and walks back into the kitchen.

"Who set the table?" she asks.

"I did mostly," Vivian takes a sip of her own wine, "but your father helped me. Poor thing, he didn't even know which side the fork and the spoon go on."

Vivian laughs, Elizabeth winces and Ernest rolls his eyes. Vivian thinks Ernest will make a nice man-project for her to mold and shape into a partner befitting of herself.

Elizabeth has never heard anyone call her father a "poor thing," especially in a cooing voice. It makes her nauseous, and she knows her father doesn't like it.

With an oven mitt, Vivian takes the pot of vegetables off the stove and drains the water out to pour the contents into a crystal dish.

"I think we're ready," Vivian smiles. "Now you kids go in there and get your plates. Ernest and I will go last."

One by one they load up with holiday delicacies. Then, they file into the dining room to wait patiently in their high-backed chairs until all are settled, poised to gorge themselves.

Vivian holds up her glass. "We have to toast. Oh, Ernest, fill up Elizabeth's glass." She uses that same cooing voice. "It's empty and she needs some wine for the toast."

Elizabeth thinks, *Dad's never done this stuff before. We've never had this kind of "frou frou" holiday. If Vivian wants a refined, society-type, she's got the wrong guy.*

"Thanks, Dad," Elizabeth says as Ernest sets the crystal carafe back down.

"Now, we're ready." Vivian clears her throat.

"May we all have a Merry Christmas and a safe and Happy New Year!" The crystal glasses clink as they touch.

"Dig in," Vivian says and they do.

Pleasant though awkward, this kind of piecemeal holiday will always be there for them since they can't go back to the family they've lost.

---

It's April, and the weather is changing. Some days it storms with a cold rain and some days it storms with sunny showers that wash the past winter away in a glittering gold.

This rain will bring new blossoms.

Late in the month, three days before Elizabeth's birthday, Ernest's and Melena's hearing begins.

Communications between mother, father, son, brother and sister have trickled to a dying stream. Erroneous rumors and threats float between lawyers, clients and the divided socialite scene.

They tell Ernest that Blackwell will testify against him, and they tell Melena that Luke and Elizabeth will testify against her.

From both law offices, last minute items fly back and forth to be copied and further investigated, earning both lawyers more money, money, money.

Nervous scores of friends, family, associates, doctors, experts, bankers and employees wait. Some come and enjoy the dramatic display, but others sit uncomfortably.

In her lawyer's office, Melena listens to Sandra check off a list of details.

Pacing the room in a crisp suit that makes her look harsh and unforgiving, Sandra crosses in front of the windows. She taps each written detail with her pen several times as she reviews it.

In a low chair in front of the desk, Melena stares at a bottle of Perrier. She reflects on how much Perrier Sandra drinks, and stops. Melena's ears perk up as Sandra finishes her last sentence. The words are Sandra's shark teeth with which she chews at the family. It's been just her and Roger circling and baiting the family for years.

They don't offer the courtesy of finishing their prey.

Melena's stomach flip-flops and her fingernails dig into the wooden armrest of her chair.

"What did you just say?" Melena says through clenched teeth.

"Let's see," Sandra clears her throat.

"I said that Ernest claims that the money from the sale of the automobile in question went directly to your son Luke as a lump-sum gift."

*Luke's house*, Melena thinks, *that's how he got the money for the damn down payment.*

"A total of $50,000, I believe. Also, Mr. Thornsby informed me that your son will come to court to attest to that fact."

"Excuse me?"

Sandra reads the memo from Roger.

"Luke Starling will testify to the dispensation of said money." She looks up. "What this means, Melena, is that because of his testimony, you cannot obtain your half of those funds."

Swallowing the lump in her throat, Melena lifts her purse from the chair beside her and stands up.

"Where are you going?" Sandra demands.

"I'm leaving."

Melena walks to the door.

Sandra says, "Melena, you cannot leave. The hearing is in two days and we have a number of things to go over. We must review our strategy."

"Do not tell me what to do, Sandra. I am leaving right now. I know all about our damn strategy backwards and forwards. Don't forget, I am the one who has been living with this damn divorce over my head for seven years, and I, not you, am the one who has done the leg work."

Melena shakes her head. "You sit here and sip your damned bottled water," she says. "You know where to reach me, if you really need to. Otherwise, I'll see you in two days."

Melena opens the door, walks out of Sandra's office and past Danielle without a word. Quickly, Sandra buzzes Danielle to get Roger on the phone.

Outside the building, a gray overcast sky looms. Melena presses the unlock button on her key chain, opens the door and sits inside her Jeep.

Retrieving her cell phone from her purse, Melena unfolds it and dials Luke at Mancon. Her hand grips the bottom of the steering wheel as she waits for him to answer.

Luke, flipping through a stack of files he was supposed to look at yesterday, answers the phone unaware.

"Luke."

He's never needed more than one word to pick up on her mood.

"Hey, Mom," he says. "How are you?"

"Not so good. Listen, Luke," she says. "I'm going to ask you something, and this time, I want you to come out and tell me the truth. Are you coming to court to testify against me?"

He drops his head to rest against the desk.

"What?"

"They claim money from the sale of that damn Corvette went to you as a gift from your father. That's a hell of a lot of money, Luke."

Ernest's nepotism has served as a weapon.

"The lawyer said you were coming to court to prove it," Melena says. "That would keep me from seeing any of it. Twenty-five thousand dollars, Luke, how can you stand to do that to your own mother?"

Her tears are scorching.

"No, Mom."

"No," Luke insists, "I would never testify against you."

He can't stand it anymore and wonders why she will never understand or believe him.

*All the times she left,* he thinks, *she left both of us.*

Melena doesn't hear him and during this storm, she won't. After all, she's always been able to blame him for so much.

"No," Melena says. "Not you Luke, but you sure will take some money, won't you?"

Cornered, she fights back and, now, Luke's body collapses to slide down to the floor beside his desk. He tries to speak, but Melena won't let him.

His office door stands shut, and if it didn't, everyone would know how helpless Melena makes him feel.

"Just you and your dad, *huh*?" she says. "You've spent too much time with him your whole life and now you're just like him."

Her speech pains both of them.

Luke listens and tries to remember how to stay neutral while a long-fostered resentment for Ernest wells.

Harsh phrases, not unlike Melena's previous dialogues on the topic, are spoken again as she calls God, the devil and everything else under the universe to the ring.

Meanwhile, Luke looks at the fibers of carpet and thinks, *she hates me. She really hates me.*

Holding the phone to his ear with one hand, his heart breaks inside of him, but his mother's heart broke a very long time ago.

Melena continues to paste hers back together, like Blackwell and Elizabeth, who have found themselves in recurring meltdowns similar to this one. Their tortured souls fall apart, and when Melena hangs up on him, Luke stays there for a while making his emotions disappear.

--->=◉◉=:<--

Two days later, the divorce unfolds on Larnee.

With the trial begun, the family at the center waits, in character, for the roles their own defenses have created.

Silent in their secrecy, no one talks to anyone else, save Luke and Elizabeth.

On Monday, the show begins, and every day the lawyers regale the court with the various, sordid details of Ernest and Melena's life together.

The tales retold run until the following Wednesday.

In Hollow Town, away from these familial tribulations, but not yet free of them, Elizabeth sits at her desk looking at a pile of leases up for recertification.

Every first Friday of the month, amongst the downtown bars and hipster restaurants, the art galleries stay open late for their new shows. There, Elizabeth's midsize and smaller sculptures sell well to the wealthy.

These profits would sustain her, but Elizabeth's continuous projects demand more money than the galleries can pay her now. Her installation series, *The Terror of Rilke*, consumes her scraps of metal and shapes them into thousands of interconnected, razor-like feathers.

For these inventions, Elizabeth took her job with Mancon and so she affords the space to create.

She forces herself daily to ignore her parent's hearing at all costs. Her second semester grad exams are due in a week and she can't allow the emotional distraction of family to get in her way, especially with another show coming, too.

The futility of non-aesthetic work threatens to drown Elizabeth, but school and sculpture keep her breathing. She stays up late at night fashioning metal with a hammer.

The phone beside her desk rings. Startled, Elizabeth picks it up.

"Barkwood and Deer Trail apartments," she says brightly.

"Yo."

It's Luke. He sounds young.

"Hey," Elizabeth says, "what are you doing?"

"It's over."

"Over, what do you mean? What's over?"

"I mean, it," he says with the emphasis of a hated idea. "The hearing, all of it, it's over. It's over for good."

She puts down her pen.

"The judge told them to end it today."

Elizabeth asks, "The judge really made them end it?"

This dormant judge, awakened from his seven-year slumber, puts an end to one matter, but leaves open another. The law, and the judge who pretends to uphold it, will allow Melena and Ernest to fight each other forever.

They both seem to escape full release from or retribution by the other, but they live in ruin.

Elizabeth stares out the window above her desk, past the hallway and out the front door, glad no one's standing around to watch her.

"But," she says, "I thought you said it was supposed to be two weeks or something."

"I did," Luke says, "but he made them pick a settlement amount right there. He said he wouldn't hear anymore of their conflicting arguments."

Elizabeth turns around in her chair. "Damn," she says. She doesn't know quite how to feel or what to think.

"Neither of them is happy," Luke says. He feels a joyous insanity that the law finally put his parents in their place and his joy is what Elizabeth hears in his voice.

"Apparently," he says, "it's a shitty deal for both of them. They said Dad was pissed off and Mom left crying."

"Oh, god," Elizabeth sits back.

She wonders, *Will Mom get to leave Larnee? Will this life end and will we be friends?* She thinks of Blackwell and Luke.

"But maybe," Elizabeth says, "it really is over and this will be the end of everything we've ever known."

Has summer finally come?

"I don't know," Luke says, hiding the fact that he knows better.

"They're both mad. Everyone said so, and I think it's going to take a long, long time before anything can change."

"*Wow*," she says.

"You know what really sucks though?"

"What?"

"At least a hundred sixty thousand dollars of Mom's settlement goes to lawyers' fees." He shakes his head.

"All that money," he says, "and where's it going? To the damn lawyers."

Is there a winner? Who can find the winner? Melena and Ernest will pay for the legal attention their lives demand though the cost is high and neither gets a prize.

"Mom could have a house," Luke says. "They could've done anything. Seven years amount to crap, a big pile of crap. Nothing came from this time, but crap and no one wins."

Elizabeth never imagined an end like this since she never thought one was possible. She always knew Melena and Ernest would end in a violent tangle. A part of her still believes it cannot be over, not this way.

"You think," she says but a knock sounds on her office door. "Just a minute," she calls.

"Luke, someone's at my door. I have to go."

"I'm done with you anyway," he says. "Call me later, kid."

"I'll call you when I leave work and you call me if you hear anything different," Elizabeth tells him.

"I will," he says. "Hug yourself."

"You hug yourself."

He hangs up the phone and Elizabeth clicks hers off and gets up from her chair a little wobbly. She opens her office door, caring less and less about the work that surrounds her.

---

Communication within the family resumes with Elizabeth and Melena. The shredded existence of their family has always come back together here first. The women are fated to reconstruct the family bonds, but fighting and separation will be their future.

Ernest and Melena will always do battle since no one wants to put an end to their warring.

Who's responsible for the allowance: the judge, the shark lawyers the father, the mother, the sister or the brothers?

Who cares?

Why doesn't anyone fix it?

Why don't those in power do it when it's their job?

Who cares?

No one cares.

When they come together under their fragile bonds, the Starlings strive to avoid anything controversial. Elizabeth and Melena have brief, light conversations over lunches or short phone calls.

Their voices sometimes rise against one another. Elizabeth flares at Melena fueled by years of memory, but there are times when they fly at each other like wild fire across the forest.

Mother and daughter alike, they move their separate ways. Valcor, Elizabeth's dog, is the safest topic they discuss with one another, followed by Elizabeth's new apartment.

Staring at her phone, Elizabeth contemplates how to bring her fractured siblings and her mother back together. She imagines herself the only capable glue.

It's five-fifteen and she still has her work clothes on. Propping one boldly-hued shoe on her coffee table she dials Melena.

"Hello," Melena says. She's at home lounging in a Liz Claiborne tracksuit.

"Hi, Mom," Elizabeth says, "you busy?"

Melena throws a damp paper towel in the trash. "No, not right now. I was fixing to make myself a grilled cheese sandwich."

"That sounds good."

Elizabeth sits back. She's ready, and she has to skip every subtlety or her courage will dissipate.

"I have to talk to you about something," Elizabeth says, "and I want you to know I'm not telling you this to make you mad. I have to say it because I can't stand to see it go on anymore."

Talking is the only way.

She takes a deep breath. "Have you spoken to Luke lately?"

"No," Melena says huffily. She thinks he should have called her long ago to apologize for his behavior at the hospital. "I haven't talked to him since before the hearing."

"Are you gonna talk to him again?"

"Elizabeth, he can call me if he wants to."

"Why would he do that, Mom? He probably thinks you hate him and would just yell at him if he called you."

Luke put his walls up long ago specifically for these situations, and those walls won't come down.

"Elizabeth."

"Mom," Elizabeth says, "Luke was never going to go to court, ever. He never would talk to anybody about anything. He's never been on one side."

Melena doesn't say anything and Elizabeth wonders if she's going to yell at her, but she can't stop now.

"Luke loves you Mom," Elizabeth says. "He wouldn't do anything against you or hurt you. You should call him. I wish you would. He doesn't say it, but I know his insides are torn up. It kills him."

Elizabeth is all wound up. "You know, we can't go on like this."

She looks at a picture of her and Luke dressed up for Easter when they were kids. They look so innocent and hopeful.

"The divorce cannot continue to destroy us. Now isn't the time, but sometime we have to come together. We could die any day, then think about the time we'd have wasted."

Elizabeth thinks she must be listening, but she still fears she'll be stopped.

"You should do whatever you feel like you need to, but calling you was what I thought I needed to do. Now, I've called you, and even if nothing comes of it, well, I know that I tried."

"Elizabeth," Melena interrupts her. "I just can't think about this right now." I still have a lot of issues and resentment at some of things you and your brother have done. I recognize it, but it will take me time."

Her voice strains, "I can't talk about this anymore right now."

Melena bites her lip. For a second, she wants to yell and say, *How dare you, stick up for them.* She sees Elizabeth pleading for her brother as a maneuver for the dark side, but somewhere in her mind she knows that can't be right.

"I'm gonna have to speak with you later."

"*Uh*, okay, then," Elizabeth says. "Bye."

She sighs and sets the phone down, feeling some relief. When she goes to bed later that night, she knows part of an unspoken responsibility has been taken care of.

The next morning, Elizabeth sits at her desk drawing out a new scheme. She wants to demonstrate image reflectivity within the structure of body language in familial relationships.

The telephone rings and she drops her pencil.

"Barkwood and Deer Trail."

"Elizabeth." It's Melena and she sounds amiable to the point of being calm. "It's Mom."

"Hi, Mom."

"I hope I didn't catch you at a bad time, but I wanted to call you and tell you that I phoned Luke."

Elizabeth smiles and draws a curved line.

"He didn't answer," Melena says, "but I left him a message on both of his phones. I told him that I loved him and for him to call me when he gets a chance."

"You did?"

"Yes," Melena says. "I do love him. I love you, too. I love all three of my children, Elizabeth."

"None of us are perfect," Melena says, "and while there are things that will continue to bother me, I will never stop loving any of you. You were right yesterday with what you said. We just can't talk about the divorce. It's the only way we can move on."

"Exactly."

"I won't keep you. I'm where I was heading, but I just wanted to call you and tell you that so you won't worry about your brother anymore."

"Okay, Mom," Elizabeth says. "I love you."

"I love you, too, Elizabeth," Melena says. "Good-bye."

A hard, horrible thing has taken a brief respite, but do not be fooled. This thing is not over. Whatever it was, it left scars and will come back before the wounds can close.

From this conversation a day will come when they will begin to meet for lunch again or go see a movie. Attempting to live on good terms, their relationship will continue to ebb and tide trying to grow past their boundaries with each cycle.

The system that allowed the Starling's divorce to run on for years escapes public attention and spins the family's world. The people, the ones who elect the officials, believe those who should monitor the courts, are judging in behalf of the people's welfare. No one in the system watches, though, and the big, big mess keeps on spinning.

# The Epilogue

MORE THAN A YEAR LATER, in a fancy neighborhood on the outskirts of Hollow Town, Katherine, Blackwell, Isabelle and Joshua sit around their brand new copper and glass patio table. The view from their upper deck is framed by tall oak and maple trees that stand against the background of a mauve evening sky.

Theirs is a good life.

Still wearing their red and white soccer uniforms, Isabelle and Joshua talk excitedly about their community league games from earlier in the day.

Katherine smiles at them, her beaded, silver bracelets coming to rest on the table. She is content with her children and the joy she feels from her personal pursuits.

In his hands, Blackwell holds two large pieces of watermelon, and he is the figure he thinks Ernest should've been. His position on the VP advisory board for Live Well has made him a sought-after speaker amongst the company groups.

He passes one piece of watermelon to Isabelle and one piece to Joshua, both slices equal in size. In this deliberate manner, Blackwell will dole out his advice helping to fashion his children with his rules and suggestions. His international success will grow and the lessons he learns with each venture will help him foster the moral character of his family.

Ernest will not see the children save for the phantom visions in his mind. There they dwell and do not grow.

Life treats them well, though, and Blackwell shares a certain strength with his wife that they, in turn, share with their children. This fortified structure of theirs makes them capable of being able builders.

Somewhere away on reprieve from her former life, down on the Atlantic coast of Florida, Melena sits high atop her friend Willomena's balcony. She looks over the great rolling ocean below and at the moonlight lying on top of the water.

Her Chanel No.5 scents the breeze that sweeps her hair from her face. A tall glass of iced tea sits on a table beside her.

She looks beautiful for her years. Melena feels now as if her life has been half-reckoned for, while the other half, her future, lies in wait. The world could belong to her now.

From inside the condo, a gentle hand taps on the glass door behind her. Melena turns to see her lovely friend beckoning her to come inside as their guests have arrived. Melena was destined to do well at parties.

Waving at them with a smile, she rises from her chair, and takes her glass to join the friendly throng. Of course, all her dear friends try to introduce her to men, who try to pursue her, but still she refuses their advances.

Outside his garage in Larnee, Ernest stands in front of his Harley V Rod. Leaning over painfully, he holds his knee with one hand and wipes away a smudge from the chrome piece behind his seat.

Pulling the rag away, he surveys the bike for other blemishes. Ernest likes to keep his machines, bikes and tools with the utmost of care, obsessing over their state while he neglects his body and the wishes of his doctors.

Tossing the rag into the garage, Ernest closes the door and straddles the bike. Its wide rear tire sits low to the ground and he doesn't think about anything more than the sound of the engine when riding.

Ernest turns the key and wipes a speck off the gas tank. He revs the modified engine loudly as the handle cranks beneath his hand. Dogs in the yards of the surrounding houses bark.

Easing backward out of the drive, Ernest straightens the bike and looks up at the long stretch of road, empty and vast in front of him.

No woman will own him and nothing will defeat him as long as his body runs because he is a machine. Ernest works, believes in working and doing what he wants and cherishes his self-preservation.

He has the money and refuses to accept defeat.

The engine gurgles with a *chug a chug chug* and the thick rear tires spin and burn on the asphalt. A cloud of charcoal gray smoke ascends behind him.

Ernest rockets away from the haze in seconds. He and the bike catapult as one to the end of the long street where he pauses at the stop sign. A long tire burn marks the pavement from in front of his house to halfway down the road, then diminishes.

North in Virginia, off on a speedway track, Luke, unbeknownst to the rest of the family, sits strapped into a racecar. The speed jostles him at 230 miles per hour as he holds the wheel.

Zipped up in his new blue flame-resistant racing suit, Luke's lucky helmet protects his head. His blue and white racecar runs with half a lap lead, and no one can catch him.

Moving low into turn four, the roar of the cars, deafens him. Luke thinks of nothing because he doesn't have to.

He feels the car's tires eating the endless length of space in front of him and his world becomes quiet.

In Hollow Town, a rowdy festival has arrived and hardcore and heavy metal music blare at the local outdoor pavilion. Thousands of beautiful, freaky people, pierced, tattooed and plain, frolic in front of the main stage and the side stage where the hard rock bands play.

Booths manned by politicians try to sway the views of those in attendance, while the metal music and the deafening thunder of hard rock drive those listening into a frenzy.

Deep in the chaotic pit in front of stage, people move in a serious and violent dance. Some fight Kung Fu while others run in stomping circles.

Elizabeth, covered head to toe in mud, whirls like a horizontal pinwheel locked in and cutting her way through the happy horde.

Around her, a hundred or more mud-covered bodies move in a giant circle. She darts among, and through them, spinning and laughing.

They swing their fists at one another and stomp their feet on the ground. In the eye of the storm, others throw their kicks and display their moves in a soulful, furious art.

Elizabeth's face emerges from the mass of people at the edge of the pit. She smiles and swerves into the raging ring, and the battle at its center. A random fist comes from the left to catch her in the jaw. She spins, fist flying in an arc. It lands, while she laughs and spins again.

# About the Author

AMANDA STONE HOLDS A DEGREE from North Carolina State University in Literature and Language with a focus on modern/postmodern and gothic novels. This fresh, prolific writer studies languages and has produced fiction in multiple genres for the past ten years.

She studied in Europe researching art history and architecture for her upcoming epic novel, *Via Lactea*. During graduate school, Ms. Stone co-created and starred in performance art pieces with the group The Center for Transgressive Behavior.

Extremely active and involved, Amanda teaches American Kickboxing at the Raleigh Institute of Martial Arts while studying Muay Thai kickboxing, Thai Chi and Kung Fu. Stone's *Raging Silence* solidifies her reputation as a dramatic writer, while her upcoming fiction *Via Lactea* brings a storm to speculative fantasy with this epic novel.